THE ASHES & THE STAR-CURSED KING

A CROWNS OF NYAXIA NOVEL

THE NIGHTBORN DUET BOOK TWO

CARISSA BROADBENT

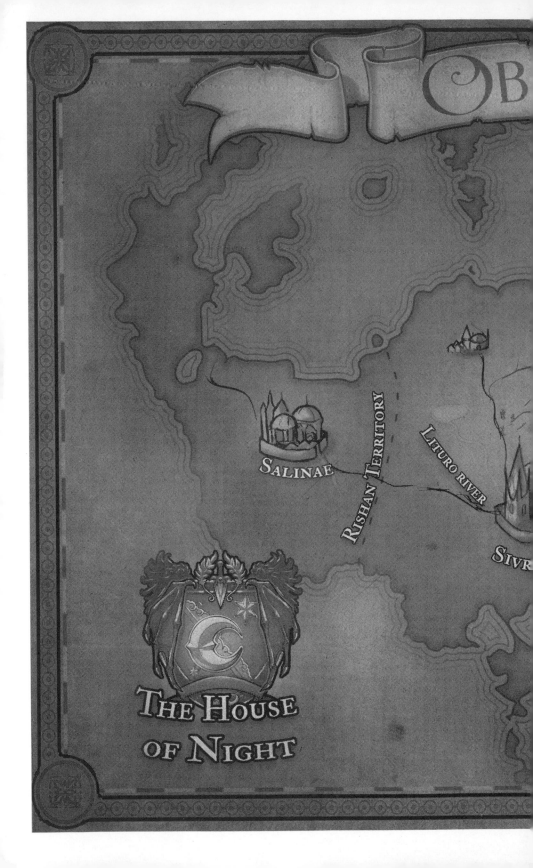

RAES

THE BONE SEAS

THE HOUSE
OF BLOOD

THE HUMAN NATIONS

THE IVORY SEAS

THE HOUSE
OF SHADOW

NYAXIA'S
HOOK

PROLOGUE

The king knew, in this moment, that his greatest love would also be his ruination, and that both would come in the unlikely form of a young human woman.

He'd been putting off this realization for a long time. Longer, maybe, than he wanted to admit to himself. Clarity, strangely enough, came in a moment of utter chaos—in the raging screams of the audience, in the blood-soaked colosseum sands, in the flurry of bodies and sweat and gore as the young woman barely managed to stave off the brutal onslaught from her aggressor.

The king wasn't doing much thinking then. He was only reacting. Trying to get the Bloodborn's attention away from the human. Trying to get between them. Failing every time.

The Bloodborn contestant had one goal and one goal alone: to go after the human.

One strike, and another, and another, and the young woman was on the ground, the Bloodborn towering over her, and the king couldn't feel anything but his heart in his throat as the sword rose.

And then the king looked up into the stands, and his eyes so easily fell to the Bloodborn prince, standing there with his arms crossed and a cigarillo at his lips, smirking.

He understood exactly what that smirk said: *I know what you want. You know what I want.*

It was here, in this moment, that the realization hit him.

You have fucking destroyed me, he had told the young woman the night before.

She would destroy him.

And it would be worth it.

Because the king didn't even think, didn't even hesitate, as he met the prince's eyes—and he nodded.

One little movement, and he sold away his kingdom.

One little movement, and he knew exactly what he had to do.

The next seconds blurred together. The prince's smirk becoming a satisfied smile. His signal to his Bloodborn contestant. The contestant's hesitation, so perfectly calculated, and the human woman's sword through her chest.

And then it was just him and her, and a prize that only one could live to claim.

Only one choice was left then, of course. He didn't question it. He had just made a deal to save her life—a deal that would destroy his kingdom, and that he had only one way out of.

Three hundred years was a long time to live. More time, he'd often thought, than any creature deserved.

The two of them stared at each other for several long, silent breaths, unmoving. He could read her face so easily. It was endearing that someone so prickly was also so transparent. Right now, her conflict—her pain—shone through the cracks in her walls.

She wouldn't move first, he knew.

So he did.

He knew her so well by now. He knew exactly how to push her to unleash all that ruthless, deadly, devastatingly-fucking-beautiful power. He was a good actor. He played his role well— even if beneath it, he flinched with every wound his blade opened on her flesh.

Many years later, the historians would whisper, *Why? Why did he do this?*

If they could have asked him that night, he might have said, *Is it really so hard to understand?*

Her eyes were the last thing he saw when he died.

They were beautiful eyes. Unusual. Bright silver, like the moon, though usually darkened by clouds. He found many things about the human woman beautiful, but he thought her eyes were the most stunning of all. He'd never told her so. The moment her blade came to his chest, Nightfire surrounding them both, he wondered if he should have.

Those eyes always revealed more than she ever thought they did. He saw the exact moment she caught him in his act—realized he had tricked her.

He almost laughed. Because of course she noticed. She, and those eyes, had always seen right through him.

It was too late, though. His hand gripped her wrist as he felt her balk.

His last words were not, *You have beautiful eyes.*

His last words were, "End it."

She was shaking her head, the cold fire in her face fading to dismay.

But he knew he was doing the right thing, and those eyes reassured him. Because they were strong and determined and unique, neither human nor vampire, fierce and thoughtful.

Better than his. More deserving of what would come next.

"*End it,*" he said, and pulled her wrist.

And he did not look away from those eyes as he died, by the hand of the only person who deserved to kill him.

Maybe the king always knew that his greatest love would be his ruination. Maybe he knew it the moment he met her.

He'd know it the second time he died, too.

PART ONE

NIGHT

1

ORAYA

My father lived in the hazy moments before I opened my eyes every day, caught between waking and dreaming.

I treasured those moments, when my nightmares had faded but they'd yet to be replaced with the grim shadow of reality. I would roll over in silk sheets and draw in a deep inhale of that familiar scent—rose and incense and stone and dust. I was in the bed I had slept in every day for fifteen years, in the room that had always been mine, in the castle I had been raised in, and my father, Vincent, the King of the Nightborn, was alive.

And then I would open my eyes, and the inevitable cruel clarity of consciousness would roll over me, and my father would die all over again.

Those seconds between sleep and waking were the best of the day.

The moment when the memory returned to me was the worst.

Still, it was worth it. I slept whenever I could, just to claw those precious seconds back. But you can't stop time. Can't stop death.

I tried not to notice that those seconds grew fewer each time I woke.

This morning, I opened my eyes, and my father was still dead.

BANG BANG BANG.

Whoever was knocking on the door did so with the impatience of someone who had been at it for longer than they'd like.

Whoever was knocking.

I knew who was fucking knocking.

I didn't move.

I *couldn't* move, actually, because the grief had seized every one of my muscles. I clenched my jaw, tighter, *tighter*, until it hurt, until I hoped my teeth cracked. My fists were white-knuckled around the sheets. I could smell the smoke—Nightfire, my magic, eating away at them.

I had been robbed of something precious. Those hazy moments where everything was as it had been.

I slipped from sleep with the image of Vincent's decimated body still seared into my mind, just as dead and just as mutilated in my sleeping moments as it was in my waking ones.

"Wake up, princess!" The voice was so loud that even with the door closed, it boomed through the room. "I know those catlike senses of yours. You think I don't know you're awake? I'd rather you let me in, but I'll barge in if I have to."

I hated that voice.

I hated that voice.

I needed ten more seconds before I could look at him. Five more—

BANG.

BA—

I threw back the covers, leapt from my bed, crossed the room in a few long strides, and threw open the door.

"Knock on that door," I breathed, *"one more fucking time."*

My husband smiled at me, lowering his raised fist, which had indeed been ready to knock one more fucking time. "There she is."

I hated that face.

I hated those words.

And I hated most of all that when he said them now, I could hear the hidden undercurrent of concern—could see the way his smirk stilled as he took me in, feet to eyes, in quick but thorough evaluation. His gaze paused at my hands, drawn into fists at my sides, and I realized I was clutching a scalded scrap of silk in one.

I wanted to use it to threaten him, remind him that the silk could be him if he wasn't careful. But something about the flicker of concern over his face, and all the things it made me feel, killed that fire in my stomach.

I liked anger. It was tangible, and strong, and it made me feel powerful.

But I felt anything but powerful when I was forced to recognize that Raihn—the man who had lied to me, imprisoned me, overthrown my kingdom, and murdered my father—genuinely cared for me.

I couldn't even look at Raihn's face without seeing it spattered with my father's blood.

Without seeing how he'd once looked at me, like I was the most precious thing in the world, the night we had spent in bed together.

Too many emotions. I stomped them down viciously, even though it physically hurt, as if swallowing razor blades. Easier to feel nothing.

"What?" I asked. It was a deflated question, not the verbal strike I wanted it to be.

I wished I didn't notice the slight disappointment on Raihn's face. Worry, even.

"I've come to tell you to get ready," he said. "We have guests."

Guests?

My stomach churned at the thought—the thought of standing in front of strangers, feeling them stare at me like a caged animal, while struggling to keep myself together.

You know how to control your emotions, little serpent, Vincent whispered in my ear. *I taught you that.*

I flinched.

Raihn's head cocked, a wrinkle deepening between his brow. "What?"

Fuck, I hated that. Every time, he saw it.

"Nothing."

I knew Raihn didn't believe me. He knew I knew it. I hated that he knew I knew it.

I stomped that down, too, until that emotion was just another numb buzz in the background, coated over with another layer of ice. It took constant effort, keeping them that way, and I was grateful I could focus on that.

Raihn stared expectantly at me, but I said nothing.

"What?" he said. "No questions?"

I shook my head.

"No insults? No refusal? No argument?"

Do you want *me to argue?* I almost asked. But then I'd have to see that little concerned twitch on his face, and I'd have to recognize that he *did* want me to argue, and then I'd have to feel that complicated emotion, too.

So I just shook my head again.

He cleared his throat. "Alright. Well. Here. This is for you." He'd been carrying a silk bag, which he now handed to me.

I didn't ask.

"It's a dress," he said.

"Alright."

"For the meeting."

Meeting. That sounded important.

You don't care, I reminded myself.

He waited for me to ask, but I didn't.

"It's the only one I've got, so don't bother arguing with me about it if you don't like it."

So pathetically transparent. He was practically poking me with a stick to see when I'd react.

I opened the bag and glanced down to see a pile of black silk.

My chest tightened. Silk, not leather. After everything, the idea of walking through this castle in anything other than armor...

But I said, "It's fine."

I just wanted him to go.

But Raihn now never left a conversation without a long, lingering stare, as if he had a lot to say and it all threatened to bubble up before he left my room. Every single fucking time.

"What?" I asked, impatient.

Mother, I felt like my stitches were popping open, one by one.

"Get dressed," he said at last, to my relief. "I'll be back in an hour."

When he was gone, I closed the door and sagged against it, releasing a ragged exhale. Keeping myself together for those last few minutes was agonizing. I didn't know how I was going to do it in front of a bunch of Raihn's cronies. For longer. For fucking *hours*.

I couldn't do it.

You will, Vincent whispered in my ear. *Show them how strong you are.*

I squeezed my eyes shut. I wanted to lean into that voice.

But it faded, as it always did, and my father was dead once more.

I put on the stupid dress.

RAIHN WAS NERVOUS.

I wished I didn't recognize this so easily. No one else seemed to. Why would they? His act was meticulous. He embodied the role of conqueror king just as easily as he had embodied the role of human in the pub, and the role of bloodthirsty contestant, and the role of my lover, and the role of my kidnapper.

But I saw it, anyway. The single muscle tightening at the angle of his jaw. The slightly glazed-over, too-hard focus to his stare. The way he kept touching the cuff of his sleeve, like he was uncomfortable in the costume he wore.

When he returned to my room, I'd stared at him, caught off guard despite myself.

He wore a stiff, fine black jacket with blue trim and a matching sash over his shoulder, striking against the silver buttons and subtle metallic brocade. It was achingly similar to another outfit I'd seen him wear once: the outfit he had worn at the Halfmoon ball, the one that the Moon Palace had provided for him. Even then, though, he'd left his hair unkempt, his chin stubbled, as if the entire thing had been reluctant. Now, he was clean-shaven. His hair was neat and tied up to reveal the top of his Heir Mark over the back of his neck, peeking over the neck of his jacket. His wings were out, revealing the streaks of bright red at their edges and tips. And...

And...

At this, my throat grew so thick I couldn't swallow — couldn't breathe.

The sight of the crown on Raihn's head drove a spike between my ribs. The silver spires sat nestled in Raihn's red-black waves, the contrast of the two jarring when I had only ever seen that metal against my father's sleek fair hair.

The last time I had seen that crown, it had been soaked in blood, ground into the sands of the colosseum as my father died in my arms.

Had someone had to pick through what remained of Vincent's body to get that crown? Had some poor servant had to clean his blood and skin and hair from all those intricate little whorls of silver?

Raihn looked me up and down.

"You look nice," he said.

The last time he had said that word to me, at that ball, it had sent a shiver up my spine — four letters full of hidden promise.

Now, it sounded like a lie.

My dress was fine. Just fine. Plain. Flattering. It was light, finely-made silk that clung to my body—it must have been made for me, to fit that well, though I had no idea how they had known my measurements. It left my arms bare, though it had a high collar with asymmetrical buttons that wrapped around my side.

I was secretly grateful that it covered my Heir Mark.

I avoided looking in the mirror when I changed, these days. Partly because I looked like shit. But also because I hated—*hated*—to see that Mark. Vincent's Mark. Every lie, seared into my skin in red ink. Every question I could never answer.

Covering the Mark was, of course, intentional. If I was going to be paraded in front of some kind of important Rishan people, I'd be expected to seem as nonthreatening as possible.

Fine.

A strange look flickered over Raihn's face.

"It's not closed."

He gestured to his throat, and I realized that he meant the dress—in addition to the clasps in the front, there were buttons in the back, too, and I'd only managed to make it halfway up.

"Do you want me to—"

"No."

I blurted it out fast, but in the seconds of silence that followed, I realized that I had no choice.

"Fine," I said, after a moment.

I turned around, showing my greatest enemy my bare back. I thought to myself, wryly, that Vincent would be ashamed that I was doing such a thing.

But Mother, I would take a dagger over Raihn's hands—would rather feel a blade than his fingertips brushing my skin, far too gently.

And what kind of a daughter did it make me, that despite everything, some part of me craved an affectionate touch?

I drew in a breath and didn't let it out until he fastened the last button. I waited for his hands to move away, but they didn't. Like he was thinking about saying something more.

"We're late."

I jumped at the sound of Cairis's voice. Raihn pulled away. Cairis leaned against the doorframe, eyes slightly narrowed, smiling. Cairis was always smiling, but he was also always watching me very, very closely. He wanted me dead. That was fine. Sometimes I wanted me dead, too.

"Right." Raihn cleared his throat. Touched the cuff of his sleeve.

Nervous. So nervous.

A previous version of myself, the one buried beneath the dozens of layers of ice I put between my emotions and the surface of my skin, would have been curious.

Raihn glanced over his shoulder at me, mouth twisting into a smirk, shoving his emotions down the same way I did.

"Let's go, princess. We'll give them a show."

THE THRONE ROOM had been cleaned up since the last time I was here—artwork and decor replaced, floors cleared of the broken pieces of Hiaj artifacts. The curtains were open, revealing the silver-shrouded silhouette of Sivrinaj. It was calmer than it had been a few weeks ago, but little sparks of light occasionally burst through the night in the distance. Raihn's men had gotten most of the inner city under control, but I could see clashes throughout the outskirts of Sivrinaj from my bedroom window. The Hiaj were not going down without a fight—not even against the House of Blood.

A twinge of something far beneath that ice—pride, maybe. Worry. I wasn't sure. It was so hard to tell.

My father's throne—Raihn's throne—sat upon the center of the dais. Cairis and Ketura took up their places behind it, against the wall, dressed in their best fineries. Ever the dutiful guards. I assumed I would be there, too, in the single chair perched there.

But Raihn took one look at it, cocked his head, and then dragged it up to place it beside the throne.

Cairis looked at him like he'd just lost his mind.

"You sure about that?" he said, quietly enough that I knew I wasn't intended to hear.

"Sure am," Raihn replied, turned to me, then motioned to the chair while taking his own, not giving Cairis the chance to disagree. Still, the advisor's pursed lips said more than enough. As did Ketura's ever-present dagger glare.

If I was supposed to be moved by this show of... of generosity, or kindness, or whatever the fuck this was supposed to be, I wasn't. I sat and didn't look at Raihn.

A servant poked her head in through the double doors, bowing as she addressed Raihn. "They're here, Highness."

Raihn glanced at Cairis. "Where the fuck is he?"

As if on cue, the scent of cigarillo smoke drifted through the air. Septimus strode in through the hall, ascending the dais in two long, graceful strides. He was followed by his two favorite Bloodborn guards, Desdemona and Ilia, two tall, willowy women who looked so similar I was certain they must be sisters. I'd never heard either of them speak.

"Apologies," he said breezily.

"Put that out," Raihn grumbled.

Septimus chuckled. "I hope you intend to be more polite to your own nobles than that."

But he obeyed—putting out the cigarillo on his own palm. The smell of smoke was replaced by that of burning flesh. Cairis wrinkled his nose.

"That's nice," he said drily.

"The Nightborn King asked me to put it out. It would be rude not to."

Cairis rolled his eyes and looked like he was trying very hard not to say anything else.

Raihn, on the other hand, just stared across the room at those closed double doors, as if burning straight through them to what lay beyond. His face was neutral. Cocky, even.

I knew better.

"Vale?" he asked Cairis, voice low.

"He should've been here. Boat must be late."

"Mm."

That sound might as well have been a curse.

Yes, Raihn was very, very nervous.

But his voice was calm and breezy as he said, "Then I guess we're ready, aren't we? Open the doors. Let them in."

2

RAIHN

The last time I had stood in this room with these people,
I'd been a slave.

Sometimes, I wondered if they remembered me. I
was nothing to them back then, of course. Another faceless body,
something more akin to a tool or a pet than a sentient being.

These people, of course, knew who I was now. Knew what
my past held. But I couldn't help but wonder, as they filed into
the vast, beautiful throne room, whether they actually remembered *me*. They certainly didn't remember all those little
mundane cruelties, to them just another part of another night. I
remembered, though. Every humiliation, every violation, every
strike, every casual agony.

I remembered it all.

And now here I was, standing before the Rishan nobility,
with a Goddess-damned crown on my head.

My, how things had changed.

Not as much as I wished, though. Because secretly, even after
all this time, I was still terrified of them.

I hid the truth with a performance that was so carefully
curated—a fucking impeccable mimicry of my former master. I

stood on the dais, my hands behind my back, my wings out, my crown perfect, my eyes cold and cruel. That last part wasn't difficult. The hatred, after all, was real.

The nobles had been called from every corner of Rishan territory. They were old power. Most of them had been in power when Neculai was king. They were as finely dressed as I remembered, swaddled in silk garments so intricate that it was obvious some poor slave had spent weeks toiling over every stitch of embroidery. Their faces held the same haughtiness, the same elegant ruthlessness that, I knew by now, was shared by all vampire nobility.

That was the same.

But a lot was different, too. Two hundred years had passed. And maybe those two hundred years hadn't marked their bodies, but they were hard years, and those hard years had certainly marked their souls. These were the handful of powerful Rishan who had survived a violent coup and then two centuries of Hiaj rule. They'd lorded over the ruins that Vincent had allowed them to keep.

And now they were here, standing before a king they already hated, ready to fight like hell for their pile of bones.

The worst of privilege. The worst of oppression.

I lifted my chin, smirk at my lips.

"What a somber bunch," I said. "I'd think you'd all be happier to be here, considering the circumstances of the last two centuries."

I'd intended to make my voice sound like his. A perpetual threat. Only thing these people understood.

Still, it was a little shocking to hear it coming out of my mouth.

I loosened my grip on my magic, letting wisps of night unfurl around my wings—highlighting, I knew, the streaks of red feathers. Reminding them who I was, and why I was here.

"Nyaxia has finally seen fit to restore us to rule," I said, pacing along the dais with slow, lazy steps. "And with the power she has granted me, I will lead the House of Night into a stronger era than ever before. I have reclaimed this kingdom from the Hiaj. From the man who murdered our king, raped our queen, decimated our people, and took our crown for two hundred years."

I was so deeply aware of Oraya's stare, digging into my back as I listed Vincent's misdeeds. I was constantly conscious of Oraya, actually, through this entire act—knowing she could see right through it.

But I couldn't show distraction. Instead, I let my lip curl in disgust.

"Now, I will make the House of Night once again something to fear. I will restore it to what it used to be."

Every *I* was carefully chosen, reminding them with every sentence of my role.

I'd watched Neculai give some version of this speech countless times, and I'd watched these people lap it up like kittens at milk.

But no matter how good my acting was, I was not Neculai.

They just stared at me, the silence heavy not with reverence but with skepticism—and just a little bit of disgust.

Despite the Mark, the crown, the wings, they still saw a Turned slave.

Fuck them.

I paced the dais, staring them down. I stopped short when I saw a familiar face—a man with ash-brown hair speckled with gray at his temples, and sharp dark eyes. I recognized him immediately—faster than I'd like—because the memories came in an unwelcome, violent slash. That face, and hundreds of nights of suffering.

He resembled Neculai, in some ways. The same hard-angled features, and the same cruelty in them. That made sense. They were cousins, after all.

He'd been bad. Not the worst. That prize went to his brother, Simon, who, I noticed with a quick scan of the room, was not here today.

I paused before him, head cocked, smirk at my lips. I just couldn't help myself.

"Martas," I said pleasantly. "It's a surprise to see you here. I could have *sworn* my invitation was addressed to your brother."

"He couldn't make the journey," Martas said blandly. Downright dismissively. And there was no mistaking the way his eyes flicked up my body, the twitch of disgust at his lip.

The room was utterly silent. Harmless words on the surface. But everyone here knew what an insult they were.

Simon was one of the most powerful Rishan nobles that still remained alive—hell, *the* most powerful. But he was still just a noble. When a king summons, you fucking come.

"Really?" I said. "That's a shame. What was so important?"

Martas—that snake—actually looked me straight in the eye, and said, "He's a very busy man."

A dark, bloodthirsty pleasure seeped through my careful composure.

"I suppose you'll have to swear fealty on his behalf, then." I lifted my chin, staring down my nose at him, smiling broadly enough to reveal my fangs. "Bow."

I knew exactly what was about to happen.

Simon and Martas had believed that they had a clear path to the throne. They were the king's only remaining relatives—surely, they must have thought, Simon would find an Heir Mark on his skin when Neculai died, as Neculai's oldest next-of-kin.

But unfortunately for them—unfortunately for me—Nyaxia wasn't so predictable.

The pricks had probably spent the last two hundred years assuming that no one had the Mark at all. Must have been an unpleasant shock a few weeks ago, when I revealed mine and then summoned them to Sivrinaj to kneel before the Turned slave they'd abused for seventy years.

They had no intention of doing so, and I knew that.

Martas did not move.

"I cannot," he said.

One might have expected a gasp through the room, a ripple

of murmurs. No. The crowd was silent. No one was surprised.

"My brother only swears his fealty to the rightful king of the House of Night, and I bow only to that man," Martas went on. "You are no king." The sneer at his lip twitched again. "I've seen the way you've defiled yourself. I can't bow to someone who has done such things. Nor to someone who stands on a dais beside a Bloodborn prince."

Defiled myself.

What a way to phrase it. It was almost fucking elegant, the way he made this about some non-existent moral code—as if I'd chosen anything that had happened all those years ago, and as if he hadn't been one of the ones holding me down.

I nodded slowly, considering them. I smiled at him. It was now entirely genuine. I couldn't have suppressed it even if I'd wanted to.

Bloodlust hammered through my body with every heartbeat, taking over.

And then Martas said, words growing faster, hand thrust to the dais, "You say you've freed us from the Hiaj, but I see Vincent's whore sitting right next to your throne."

His eyes flicked over my shoulder. Landing, I knew, on Oraya.

I knew that look. Hatred and hunger and desire and disgust, all rolled together. "Fine if you want to fuck her," he snarled. "But look at her. So untouched. Not a scratch on her. All you need is a mouth and a cunt. Why did you bother keeping the rest?"

My smile disappeared.

I no longer found it fun to toy with him.

I had been keeping everything about this meeting calculated, deliberate. But now I moved on nothing but impulse.

"I appreciate your honesty," I said calmly. "And I appreciate Simon's."

I stepped down the stairs in two long strides and placed my hands gently on either side of Martas's face. He really did look so damned similar to how he had centuries ago.

Maybe people never changed.

I had *felt* different ever since Nyaxia restored the power of the Rishan heir line. I'd felt something change in me from the moment Neculai died, but I'd been able to stifle that power, subdue it into something easier to control and less likely to draw attention. But ever since that night, my magic had surged back with an uncontrollable force, like Nyaxia's gift had ripped open a new vein of it.

It was actually something of a relief to use it at full force again.

I let it go.

Asteris was both exhausting and exhilarating to use. It felt like the raw power of the stars bursting through my skin, tearing through my body.

It tore through Martas's, too.

The room went white, then black, then snapped back into an unpleasant sharpness.

Warmth spattered over me. A dull *THUMP* cut through the silence, as a broken, crushed body fell to the floor in a pile of silk.

The light faded, revealing a sea of shocked, silent faces. I held Martas's head, the features twisted into satisfying confusion. Now, *that* was a new expression for him.

A few people near the front of the crowd took several quick steps back to avoid the pool of black blood spreading over the marble. There was no screaming, no hysterics. Vampires, even vampire nobles, were well accustomed to bloodshed. They weren't horrified, no, but they were surprised.

Maybe it was unwise to murder the brother of my most powerful noble.

In this moment, I didn't care. I felt nothing but satisfaction. I wasn't built for this bullshit—the preening, the parties, the politics. But this? The killing?

I was good at that. Felt good to give it to someone who deserved it.

I glanced over my shoulder. I wasn't sure why—I did it

without thinking.

The look on Oraya's face struck me.

Satisfaction. Bloodthirsty satisfaction.

The first time in weeks I'd seen something that looked like fight in her eyes. Goddess, I could've fucking wept for it.

There she is, I thought.

And something about the way she stared at me, right in the eyes, speared through my costume and my performance. I could practically hear her saying it, too: *There he is.*

I turned back to the crowd, stepping backwards up the dais steps.

"I am the Nightborn King," I said, voice low and deadly. "Do you think I'm going to beg for your respect? I don't need your respect. Your fear will do. *Bow.*"

And I let the head fall with a sickening wet *thump,* rolling down the stairs right into his former body. Fittingly, the position it had fallen into did indeed resemble a bow of prostration.

The nobles stared. The world held its breath.

I held my breath, and tried desperately not to show it.

I was walking a very thin line here. Vampires respected brutality, but only from the right people. I wasn't one of the right people. Maybe I never would be.

If one or two refused to bow, I could handle that. But Heir Mark or no, I needed some loyalty from my nobles, especially if I ever wanted to get out from beneath Bloodborn control. If *all* of them refused—

The door burst open, the slam against the walls splitting the silence like a sword through flesh.

Vale stood in the doorway.

I never thought I would be relieved to see that man. But Ix's tits, I had to physically stop myself from letting out a sigh of relief.

He took in the scene—me, the crowd, the advisors, Martas's bloody body—and immediately strung together what he'd just walked into.

He strode purposefully into the room, so fast his long dark

waves flew out behind him. The crowd parted for him. A woman followed him, then lingered at the back of the crowd, looking around the throne room with wide, curious eyes, curly chestnut hair piled atop her head.

"My king," Vale said, as he approached the dais. "I apologize for my tardiness."

Before me, he immediately dropped into a smooth kneel— right at the center of the crowd, right into the pool of Martas's seeping blood.

"Highness." His voice boomed through the throne room. He knew exactly what he was doing—knew to make himself as visible as possible. "You have my sword, my blood, my life. I swear to you my loyalty and my service. It is my greatest honor to serve as your Head of War."

A strange echo of the past in those words. The last time I'd heard Vale say them, it was to Neculai. Inwardly, I cringed at hearing them directed at me.

Outwardly, I accepted them as if they were nothing but what was expected.

I lifted my gaze to the others, waiting.

Vale was a noble. He was respected. He'd just tipped some precarious scale.

Slowly at first, and then in a wave, the other nobles lowered into bows.

This was exactly what I'd wanted. Needed. And yet, the sight made me so viscerally uncomfortable. I was all at once very conscious of the crown on my head, worn by centuries of kings before me, kings who were cursed to rules of cruelty and paranoia. Kings I had killed, directly or indirectly, just like they had killed the ones who came before them.

I couldn't help myself. I glanced over my shoulder again— just for a split second, barely long enough for anyone to notice.

Oraya's eyes skewered me. Like she was seeing that little shard of dark honesty, stripped bare.

I looked away quickly, but that stare stayed with me, anyway.

3

ORAYA

The look on Raihn's face lingered with me longer than I wish it did. Why would he give me that? Something so honest.

I hated that I knew it was honest.

I was ushered out of the throne room quickly after that, Raihn striding away without giving his nobles a second glance, casual in a way that I knew was calculated. Ketura's guards flanked me, and Raihn walked several steps ahead, though I could see the whitened knuckles at his side. He didn't even say a word to me as Cairis, Ketura, and the noble—his new Head of War?—flocked around him, the group of them disappearing down a side hallway while the guards ushered me to the staircase that led back to my rooms.

Septimus joined me several steps up. I smelled him before I heard him. He walked silently, but that damned cigarillo smoke gave him away.

"Well that," he said, "was interesting, wasn't it?"

He eyed the guards, who had visibly stiffened in his presence. "Oh, pardon my rudeness. Am I interrupting?"

The guards said nothing. As always.

Septimus smirked, satisfied with this non-answer.

"I knew your husband's past was a subject of... we'll call it controversy, among the Rishan nobles," he went on, to me. "But I have to say, that exceeded my expectations. Suppose I'll probably have to call in more troops from the House of Blood." He flicked ash to the marble staircase, grinding it under his heel. "Looks like the Rishan won't be much help, if that's the best they have to offer."

We turned up another flight of stairs.

I had nothing to say. Septimus's words floated through me like background noise.

"You," he said at last, "have gotten much quieter."

"I don't just talk for the sake of hearing my own voice."

"That's a shame. You always had such interesting things to say."

He was playing with me, and I hated it. If I'd had the energy, maybe I would've granted his wish and snapped at him.

I didn't have the energy, so I said nothing.

We made it to the top floor. Just as we rounded the corner, my bedchamber door ahead, quick steps approached from behind. Desdemona, one of Septimus's guards, fell into stride beside him.

"Pardon, Highness. We have an issue."

Septimus and Desdemona fell back, while I kept walking. Still... my ears perked.

"It's about the attack on Misrada," Desdemona was saying, voice low. "We'll need to pull troops from the armory if we want to get enough men in two weeks—"

My door swung open, jerking my attention back. The familiar haven—prison—of my bedchamber opened before me.

"Well, then do it," Septimus was saying, sounding impatient. "I don't care about—"

I walked inside.

The door shut behind me, closing me in once again. I loosened the buttons on my dress and immediately flopped onto the bed, waiting for the all-too-familiar sound of my door. Four clicks. Four locks.

Click.

Click.

I waited. Seconds passed. Footsteps faded.

My brow furrowed. Curiosity piqued for the first time in weeks.

I sat up.

Had I imagined it? My mind had been blurry lately. Maybe I'd missed the other two.

I went to the door and squinted into the crack. Two shadows interrupted the sliver of light from the hall. The upper two locks —simple sliding bars—were closed.

And the bottom two had been left open.

Fuck.

My first day here, I'd managed to get three of the locks open. It was the bottom one, the big deadbolt, that had evaded me. But now...

I stepped away from the door, sizing it up the way I'd size up an opponent in the ring. A glimmer of a foreign, unpracticed sensation—hope—stirred in my chest.

I could get those locks open. I could *get out.*

It was nighttime still, albeit nearing dawn. I should wait until the sun rose and the vampires had mostly gone to their respective rooms. Then I winced—thinking of the room right next to mine, and the man within who'd be back any minute. Vampire hearing was impeccable. If I tried to get out while he was there, he'd know it.

But... I'd paid attention to Raihn's movements, too. He spent very little time in his room. Oftentimes, he didn't return until well after sunrise.

So, I'd have to gamble. Wait until tomorrow—wait long enough that most vampires had gone to sleep, but not long enough that Raihn had.

And then what?

You know this castle better than anyone here, little serpent, Vincent

27

whispered to me, and I flinched, as I always did when I heard his voice.

He was right, though. Not only had I lived in this castle my entire life, I'd learned how to sneak around it with no one noticing—not even the last King of the Nightborn.

I just needed to bide my time.

4

RAIHN

"That," Cairis muttered, "was a shit show."

"I don't think it went that badly."

Ketura closed the door behind us. The room was simultaneously too empty and so messy you couldn't think in it. It had been a library before—a room devoted to displaying items that were very beautiful, very old, or very expensive, and usually all three. Ketura had commanded most of the castle be stripped —for information, for traps—and some poor servant had gotten halfway through pulling the books off the shelves before she decided that this particular room was the only acceptable base of operations.

Now, it was a haphazard disaster—the shelves on one side bare, piles of books shoved into a corner. The long table at the center of the room was covered with notes and maps and books and a few discarded glass goblets from the night before, congealing red crusted at their bottoms.

Vincent had been in power for two-hundred years. There was a lot of clutter to strip away.

I was secretly grateful for it.

The night the Kejari ended, I had flown here with a pit of

dread in my stomach. I'd had more than enough distractions—Oraya's unconscious body in my arms, Vincent's blood all over my hands, an Heir Mark burning on my back, and an entire fucking kingdom on my shoulders. And yet, I'd still paused at the doors of this castle, the memory of the past chasing me.

Maybe that made me a coward.

But two hundred years was a long time. The place looked very different under Vincent's rule. It was enough to disguise the worst of the memories, night-to-night. Still, I couldn't bring myself to visit some wings at all.

I dragged a seat out and sat down heavily, propping my heels up on the corner of the table. The chair groaned slightly under my weight. I let my head fall back and stared at the ceiling—silver tiles, etched with Hiaj wings. Ugh.

"What were you going to do if Vale didn't show up when he did?" Cairis asked. "Slaughter them all?"

"Doesn't sound like a bad idea," I said. "It's what the great Neculai Vasarus would have done."

"You aren't him."

Something about his tone made my head snap up.

He said that like it was a bad thing.

That thought sickened me. For some reason, my mind drifted back to the night of the wedding, and the promise I had made Oraya when I'd practically begged her to work with me.

We'll rip apart the worlds that subjugated both of us, and from the ashes we'll build something new.

I'd meant every word of it.

But Oraya had just looked at me with hatred and disgust, and hell if I could blame her for that. And now here I was picking blood out from under my fingernails, deciding how to best make myself just like the man who had destroyed me.

She could always see right through the bullshit.

A knock rang out, thankfully interrupting that line of conversation. Ketura opened the door, and Vale stepped in. He paused and bowed his head to me as he closed the door behind him.

"Highness."

Sometimes, it's the little things that make the reality of a situation hit you.

Vale's over-the-top declaration of fealty hadn't done it. But this, this casual little half bow, the exact same one he used to give Neculai—it made me feel as if I was two centuries in the past, my former master standing right behind me.

Ketura had wanted Vale as my Head of War. She was good at execution, but we needed someone strategic. And Cairis had insisted that it be someone with noble blood—someone respected by all the people who wouldn't respect me. "To legitimize you," he'd said.

Legitimize. I had a blessing from a goddess and an ugly magical tattoo I couldn't get rid of. Yet it was *Vale* who was going to give me "legitimacy."

It was hard for me to forget. No, Vale had never participated in the depravity quite like the others did. Maybe he thought consensual lovers were more enthusiastic. Maybe he inflicted enough bloodshed at work that it wasn't what he wanted to do for fun.

Didn't make him a saint. And it didn't mean that he didn't still look at me as a slave.

"I apologize for my lateness today," he said. "Storms over the seas."

"You can't control the wind. And I'm sure your wife probably needed time to recover."

A blink.

"From the Turning," I clarified. Then smiled. "Congratulations, by the way."

Vale's eyes hardened, gleaming like those of a guard dog barely tethered.

Did he think I was threatening her? It's what Neculai would have done.

But no. I just didn't like that Vale had Turned some human woman and dragged her over here. I didn't like it at all.

"It went as well as it could have," he said. "She's resting. A bit seasick on the journey. I wanted to get her settled."

His expression softened, and that... that, I wasn't quite expecting. It looked oddly close to actual affection.

I wasn't sure if that made me feel any better. Neculai had loved Nessanyn, his wife. Hadn't saved her from anything.

"Well. I'm glad you made it." I gestured to the table and the maps strewn across it. "Plenty to catch you up on, as you can see."

THE CONSENSUS, after hours of talking, was that we were in deep shit.

Vale thought it was stupid that I had taken Septimus's deal.

He thought it was very stupid that I had done so without negotiating his terms.

And he thought it was *monumentally* stupid that I had kept Oraya alive.

I dismissed these criticisms as casually as I could manage. I couldn't justify why I had made those decisions without revealing more than I wanted to about my true motivations—motivations that held none of the vicious cruelty they wanted to see from me.

Still, the reality of our situation was bleak. The Hiaj were not backing down. They held on to several key cities. Two hundred years of power had made their forces strong. Vincent, even at the height of his power, hadn't rested. He'd continued building his strength and whittling down the Rishan until we had almost nothing left.

That meant our brute strength relied almost completely on the Bloodborn. And yes, the bastards were efficient at what they did. They had bodies, and they were willing to throw them at anything. With the Bloodborn's help, we'd managed to beat back many of the biggest Hiaj strongholds.

But it also meant that if Septimus decided to withdraw, we

would be fucked. The Rishan forces just weren't capable of holding up against the Hiaj alone.

Vale did not hide his frustration with this situation. A couple of centuries away from polite society had made him even more blunt than he used to be, which was saying something. Still, I had to admit that he was good at what he did. He ended the meeting with a list of recommendations to strengthen our position, and when we disbanded, he was already following Ketura out the door with a list of questions about our armies.

Cairis, though, lingered after Vale and Ketura were gone. I hated that—the hovering. He used to do it back then, too, when he was going to try to whisper something in someone's ear and make it seem like it had all been their idea.

I sighed. "I don't need to be handled. Just say it."

"Fine. I'll be straightforward. That went badly. We already knew the nobles hated you. Now—"

"Nothing was going to stop them from hating me. Actually, maybe we should've thought of that as a test. Which noble would bow willingly?"

"If it was a test," Cairis said drily, "then no one passed."

"Exactly. So let's just execute them all."

He gave me a long, steady stare, like he was trying to decide if this was a joke.

It was not. I raised my eyebrows, a silent, *Well?*

"Do you have people to install in their places?" he said.

"I could find someone."

He leaned across the table, weaving his fingers together. "Who? Do tell."

I hated when Cairis was right about things. He was just so damned smug about it.

"I'm just saying that you need to be careful." His voice lowered, as if to evade prying ears. "We already rely far too heavily on the Bloodborn."

Understatement. Septimus practically had me bent over his desk.

"The last thing we need," he went on, "is to destroy the

loyalty of the scant forces we do have. Appearances are everything. Which brings me to…" He cleared his throat. "Her."

I rose, my hands stuffed in my pockets, and paced the room. "What about her?"

A beat of silence that said, *You know what.*

Cairis seemed to be choosing his words with uncharacteristic care. "She is a danger to you."

"She can't act against me."

"She won the Kejari, Raihn."

My hand found its way to my chest—right where her dagger had pierced it. There was no scar, no mark. There wouldn't be—with Oraya's wish, the act had been undone. I could've sworn I felt it sometimes, though. Right now, it pulsed with a vicious throb.

But I hid all that as I turned to him with a smug smirk. "You can't say it doesn't look good, to have Vincent's daughter leashed at my side."

I'd always been a good mimic. I slipped a little of Neculai's cruelty into my voice, just like I had that day in the ring, when I justified letting Oraya live with a litany of atrocities.

Cairis's face was stone, unconvinced.

"After what he did to Nessanyn," I added, "don't you think we deserve that satisfaction?"

He flinched at the mention of Nessanyn. Just like I knew he would. Just like I often did, when old memories caught me off guard.

"Maybe," he admitted, after a long moment. "But it doesn't do anything to help her now."

I swallowed and turned to the wall of books, pretending to admire the trinkets on the shelves.

I didn't like to think about Nessanyn. But I'd been doing it a lot these last few weeks. She was everywhere in this castle. All of it was everywhere here.

I couldn't help Nessanyn when she was alive. I couldn't help her when she was dead. And here I was, just using her memory to manipulate the people around me.

She had been used her entire life. Now she was being used in death, too.

Cairis wanted me to be just like Neculai. He didn't even know how close he was to getting that wish.

I withdrew my hands from my pockets. Some of Martas's blood still remained under my fingernails.

"Don't you hate them?" I said.

I'd meant for the question to sound more lilting, more casual, than it really did.

Because Cairis had been there for all of it, too. Just another one of Neculai's pets.

And yet now he could sit here and advocate for an alliance with the people who had inflicted unimaginable degradation upon us. It genuinely amazed me.

"Of course I hate them," he said. "But we need them. For now. Who wins if you kill them all and we lose the House of Night to Septimus? Not us. She used to say that, too, remember?" I turned to see a soft, distant smile on his face—a rare expression from him. "'Remember who wins.'"

He said it fondly, but my teeth ground.

Yes, I remembered. Couldn't even count how many times I got right up to the edge, just about to strike back. And whenever it happened, Nessanyn would stop me. *Don't let them win*, she would beg, her big brown eyes deep and damp. *Who wins if he kills you?*

"I remember," I said.

Cairis shook his head, a sad smile at his lips. "We were all a little in love with her, right?"

Yes, we were all a little in love with Nessanyn. I had been the one sleeping with her, but all of us loved her. How could you not, when she was the only kindness you knew? The only one who treated you like a person instead of a collection of body parts?

"So think about that," he said. "That's what I do. Whenever I feel it, I ask myself, *Who wins?*"

He said it like it was some great proverb, some enlightening wisdom.

35

"Hm," I said, thoroughly unconvinced.

I DIDN'T REALLY SLEEP MUCH these days.

The castle had an entire wing that was intended to be the king's residence. I'd visited it nearly a full week after the takeover, putting it off for as long as I could. The decorations were different, and yet so much was the same.

I'd walked through all the rooms in silence.

I paused at a doorway, at a dent carved into the dark wood— a dent I remembered being made with Ketura's head, centuries ago, then barely even visible beneath the blood. I could still feel the marks where her teeth had dug into the trim.

I'd paused, too, at Vincent's bureau. It had all been pulled apart, his clothes strewn across the room. The top was adorned with little trinkets that were probably worth more than most estates. But mixed in among those treasures were little aged pieces of paper with handwriting that I recognized as Oraya's— though in the clumsy curls of a child. All were studies, it looked like. Notes on fighting stances.

The corners of my mouth had tightened. Of course, even as a little girl, Oraya would have taken her studies seriously. Endearing. So fucking endearing.

And then, just as quickly, the smile faded. Because apparently, I wasn't the only one who thought so, if Vincent had held onto these tattered papers for all these years.

No, I didn't stay in the king's wing.

My suite was right next to Oraya's. Both had multiple rooms, but our bedchambers shared a wall. It was a bad habit, but every time I returned to the room, I hesitated at that wall. Tonight was no exception.

When Oraya cried, it was this horrific, violent sound. Silent at first, and then the silence would shatter into the jagged inhale of a sob, like she was suffocating herself and her body rebelled for air. It sounded like a wound tearing open.

The first time I'd heard it, I made an excuse to go over there —pounded on the door and pulled some bullshit request out of my ass when she opened it. I couldn't even remember what had come out of my mouth.

Come on, fight with me. Let me distract you.

But Oraya had just looked so empty. Like it was physically painful to be in my presence in that moment. Like she was begging for mercy.

Now, I placed my hand against our shared wall and listened, against my better judgment.

Silence.

And there it was.

I swallowed thickly. My fingers curled into a fist against the brocade wallpaper.

One wall. Thin enough that I could hear through it. Might as well be iron.

Don't you dare stop fighting, princess, I'd told her, the night before the final trial. *It would break my damned heart.*

And I had been so fucking smug when I'd wrung that fight out of her in that last battle.

Well, she wasn't fighting now.

I didn't go to her room anymore. I'd make sure that headache tea was sent to her the next evening. I'd make sure she had what she needed. But what she needed, right now, certainly wasn't me.

I got into bed, but didn't sleep. Nessanyn's words floated through my mind, this time with a cynical tinge that was distinctly mine.

Who wins?

Well, Nessanyn sure as fuck didn't.

And Oraya didn't, either.

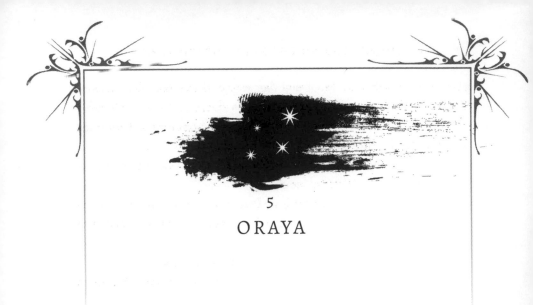

5

ORAYA

I waited until the sun was high over Sivrinaj to make my
move. I'd spent the night praying that no one would come
bother me, replacing those precious locks behind them. I
was fortunate.

Raihn had left overnight and hadn't returned yet. I was
acutely aware of that, both because my escape relied upon his
absence and because I knew he could show up at any moment.

I had twisted a silver hoop earring I found in the dresser into
a clumsy hook. The top lock, a sliding bolt, slipped easily. But
the second... the second gave me trouble. I had very little space
to work with between the various locks, and the metal was stiff.
Several times, I stopped just short of snapping my makeshift pick
in half.

"Fuck," I hissed.

You have more power than this silly little hook, Vincent whispered
in my ear.

My gaze fell from the broken silver to my fingertips
holding it.

All the doors and windows and locks in this place were, of
course, fortified against magic. But even if that hadn't been the

case, my magic had felt very far away these last few weeks. Calling upon it required me to dig too deep, right into all these tender wounds I couldn't even think about opening—I worried that I'd bleed to death before I could close them again.

But... Nightfire, maybe, could melt that one little bar of metal that held this door closed.

I dreaded so much as trying. But if I had a chance at freedom, I wasn't about to relinquish it because I was too scared of myself to try.

The first call to my magic was met with nothing.

I gritted my teeth. Dug deeper. It hit on things I'd been trying to bury these last few weeks.

I taught you better than this, Vincent whispered.

I thought of his voice. His face, framed against the sands of the colosseum, bloody and raw and—

The burst of Nightfire was too hot, too bright. It engulfed my hand. I clamped down hard on the wave of grief, anger, sadness.

Control, little serpent, Vincent snapped. *Control!*

I can't focus with you lecturing me, I thought, then swallowed shame at the sudden silence of his voice.

I took a deep breath, two, until my heartbeat slowed. The flame dimmed a little.

Control.

I whittled the Nightfire down until it was a small orb, then dipped my broken twisted silver into it. The Nightfire hovered at its end like a flame to a match.

There was no way this was going to work, I thought, then jammed the twisted metal through the gap between the door and the frame—pressing metal to metal. I poured my magic into my connection to that little Nightflame—

—And *pushed*.

The door flew open. I went rolling across the tile floor, stopping myself just short of sliding into the opposite wall.

I looked down. A twist of partially melted, scorched metal lay on the tile. I slipped it into my pocket, then turned around to see my bedchamber door.

Wide open. The hallway was empty.

I was out. For now.

Goddess fucking help me.

I quickly—silently—closed my door, rubbing away scorch marks best I could. The second lock was broken, but hopefully no casual passerby would notice that.

It was wartime. I'd seen firsthand what that looked like in this castle. Daylight or no, most hallways would be occupied or heavily guarded. Certainly the weapon stores. And definitely exits.

But I could get around that.

My lips twisted with a smirk of satisfaction. The movement felt uncomfortable, like the muscles were out of practice.

Good thing I knew this castle better than anyone.

VINCENT HAD BEEN A VERY cautious man. He'd renovated this castle to add passageways and tunnels and confusing hallways that led nowhere—infinitely aware of the possibility that, one day, his fortress could be turned against him.

He'd showed me some of these hallways when I was young, making me memorize the paths to his wing. Even when I was only a child, he never sugarcoated why it was so important that I knew this. "This is a dangerous world, little serpent," he'd said. "I'll teach you how to fight, but I'll also teach you how to flee."

He never showed me all the passageways, of course—he didn't want to give me *too* much freedom. But I'd explored the other ones, too, in secret.

Today, though, I followed the path my father had left for me. It was downright stupid to run straight for the outdoors. Yes, it was daylight, and that might help me—but guards would be watching everywhere. I needed to know what I was getting into. I needed a weapon—

My step faltered as I remembered what I had done the last time I'd held a blade. The last heart I'd pierced.

I shook away the memory of Raihn's dead face, narrowly escaped the image of Vincent's, and continued down the hall.

I could hear distant voices near the stairwell. One of the entrances to Vincent's web of hallways was nearby. No one had discovered it yet, it seemed. It was well hidden, the seams of the door covered by strategically placed tapestries. Sometimes these passageways were locked, but today, I was lucky. The door opened easily to my touch.

The tunnels were narrow, lit by forever-fueled Nightfire torches. They had been constructed around the existing layout of the castle, so they were convoluted and awkward to navigate. Many of the doors inside were locked, leaving me little option but to push forward and down several sets of stairs. Most of the other exits here would lead into hidden passages within various bedchambers—the last thing I wanted was to end up in some Rishan general's room. Instead, I traveled down several sets of tight, winding stairs. Farther still, until I reached the ground floor—until I passed it.

I had rarely been allowed to come here as a child, but I still remembered exactly where it was. Vincent treasured his privacy, and he got very little of it. So, near the beginning of his reign, he'd had a new basement dug out beneath the easternmost tower of the castle—an underground wing that was specifically for him.

It had two access points. One led right up to the ground floor —I could escape through there. But more importantly, Vincent had often kept weapons and supplies in his rooms. I could arm myself before I left.

The wing's entrance was closed—a set of oak double doors, stained black, that seemed to melt right into the shadows save for their silver handles. I held my breath as I eased them open, very slowly, very silently. I didn't know for sure that the Rishan hadn't discovered this place. Vincent's wing was private, but not a secret.

But my luck, it seemed, held out a little longer. Not a soul.

An empty hallway stood before me. This one, unlike the dark, poorly maintained paths I'd come from, looked like it belonged in this castle. Indigo blue tile floors. Black doors. Silver knobs. Hiaj art framed in gilded presentations on the walls. Eight doors lay ahead of me, four on each side, and then a stairwell that led up, cradled by swooping silver rails.

I hadn't been here in so long. I didn't know or remember what all these rooms contained. I tried the first two doors to find them locked. The third. The fourth. *Fuck.* Maybe they were all locked, and I wasted my precious freedom to come down here for—

The fifth door opened.

I froze. Stopped breathing. Stopped moving.

I stood in the open doorway, my hand still on the knob.

Oh, Goddess.

Vincent's study.

It smelled like him. For a moment, it felt agonizingly like my father hadn't died. Like he was in this room somewhere, a book cradled in his hands, a serious line between his brows.

The past barreled over me like splintered steel, just as sharp and just as painful.

It was a small room, smaller than Vincent's other offices. A large wooden desk sat at its center, and two velvet armchairs in the corner near the fireplace. Bookcases lined the walls, boasting hundreds of black and burgundy and silver and blue spines of old but well-kept books. The desk was covered with clutter— open tomes, papers, notes, and what looked like a pile of broken glass at its center.

When I could make myself move again, I went to the desk.

It was far more cluttered than Vincent usually left things. Then again... at the end, he'd been...

Well. I avoided thinking about the way he'd been in those last few months.

My eyes fell to a wine glass sitting among the notes, dried red caked at its bottom. If I looked closely, I could see little smudges near its stem—fingerprints. I reached out to touch it, then pulled away just short, not wanting to mar those remnants of him.

Even losing Ilana hadn't prepared me for this. The sheer degree of fucking obsession that grief forces upon you. It took everything I had to force my mind to think about something other than him — it had exhausted me so completely.

But now that I was here, surrounded by him, I never wanted to leave. I wanted to curl up in this chair. I wanted to cocoon myself in the coat left casually slung over one of the armchairs. I wanted to wrap this wine glass in silk and preserve his fingerprints forever.

I picked through the papers on the table. He'd been working hard. Inventories. Maps. Reports about the attack on the Moon Palace. I rifled through the stack of letters, and paused, my hand shaking, at a piece of parchment.

Debrief, the top read. *Salinae.*

It was written in very matter of fact, straightforward language. A simple accounting of resources and outcome.

The city of Salinae and its surrounding districts have been eliminated.

One sentence, and I was once again standing in the dead remnants of Salinae. The dust. The toxic mist. The fucking *smell.*

The way Raihn's voice had wavered when he held that street sign. *This is Salinae.*

And now here on my father's desk was this brief, one-page report, outlining so drily how he had destroyed my homeland. Murdered any family I'd had left.

Lied to me about it.

You weren't going to tell me, I'd spat at him.

You are not like them, he'd snarled at me.

The parchment quivered in my hands. I put it down quickly, pushing it to the back of the pile.

As I did, I glimpsed a faint silver glint. I pushed aside an open tome. Buried beneath it was a tiny, crudely made dagger.

A lump rose in my throat.

I had made this not long after I'd come into Vincent's care. It was the first time I'd felt comfortable enough to ask for a project to work on and safe enough to actually do it. I'd liked chipping away at stone—I didn't even remember why, now. But I did remember making this little dagger, and the pit of nervousness in my stomach when I'd presented it to him. I had held my breath when he surveyed it, face stoic.

"Good," he had said, after a long moment, and he'd tucked it into his pocket, and that had been that. The first of countless times I'd found myself reaching for Vincent's approval and wondering desperately whether I'd gotten it.

And now here it was, lying with the death warrants of thousands.

Two versions of him that I couldn't reconcile in life, and now was even further from understanding in his death.

Vincent the king, who would kill my whole family in the name of power, who would slaughter an entire race, who would lie to me for nearly twenty years about my blood to protect his crown.

And Vincent the father, who kept this little makeshift trinket I'd made him, right there with all his most precious possessions. Who had told me he loved me with his final breaths.

How convenient it would be, if I found a letter tucked away in one of his drawers. *My little serpent,* it would read. *If you're reading this, then I am gone. It would be unfair for me to leave you with no answers...*

But Vincent was not the kind of man who wrote down his secrets. Maybe I'd told myself I was coming here for supplies, but really, I was coming here for answers.

A fucking dream.

Because instead, this was a room that made as little sense as he did. I found nothing here but discarded pieces of him, just as disparate in death as they were in life.

My eyes burned. My chest ached. A sob bubbled up inside of me with such violence that I had to press my hand over my mouth to stifle it.

I never used to cry. Now, it seemed like the more I tried to stop myself, the more viciously it clawed its way out of me.

I choked it down with an ugly sound that I was grateful no one could hear.

No fucking time for this, Oraya, I told myself. *This isn't what you're here for.*

My gaze fell to the center of the desk—the pile of broken glass. That was peculiar. It was mirrored, the shards neatly stacked on top of each other, as if someone had assembled them into a perfectly aligned pile. The metal reminded me of the full moon, silver bright and gleaming with hammered indents that shivered beneath the cold light. Elegant swirls adorned its smooth edge, driving to the center before being interrupted by the jagged edge. I squinted and could make out a faint cast in those carved lines—red-black. Blood...?

Why would he keep this broken trinket here? Right in the middle of his work?

I touched the edge of the top shard—

A gasp ripped through me.

The edge was razor sharp. It sliced open my fingertip, leaving a streak of red rolling to the edge—but I barely noticed either the cut or the pain.

Because the shards began to *move.*

In the span of a blink, the shards of glass spread out, locking into place with each other—forming a shallow, mirrored bowl, the drops of my blood rolling down to be cradled in its center.

And yet, as shocking as this was, what left me staggering was the sudden, overwhelming, disorienting sense of *Vincent*— Vincent as he'd been in this room, standing where I stood, blood spilling into the same bowl. A sudden, intense anxiety rose in my throat, all in broken pieces—fragmented thoughts of cities, generals, Sivrinaj, Salinae, hundreds of feathered wings staked throughout the city walls. Anger and possession and determination, but beneath it all, a powerful *fear.*

I yanked my hand away, gasping. I felt nauseous, dizzy.

"Vincent?"

I thought I'd imagined the voice at first.

"Vincent? Highness? I—how can—"

The voice was faint and distorted, as if coming from some-where very, very far away, and through heavy winds.

But even so, I recognized it.

"Jesmine?" I whispered.

I peered into the bowl again. My blood pooled there, spreading out more than such a small quantity of liquid should have, coating the silver.

I squinted and leaned closer. The flickering reflection of the Nightflame made it hard to see, but was something moving—?

"Oraya?"

The voice—confused—was definitely Jesmine's. I could barely hear her.

I was now bent over the desk, my forearms braced, my awareness pulled in so many directions—to the faint presence of Jesmine, somewhere many miles away, to the presence of Vincent in the past.

This was a communication tool of some kind. A spell, a—

Voices.

Not Jesmine's. No, these were here, in the hallway outside.

One was Raihn's.

Fuck.

I yanked my hand away from the device, and the silver collapsed back into countless shards, falling again into a neat pile. I winced at the metallic sound they made crashing against the wood.

I swept them up and shoved them into my pocket, my eyes glued to the door.

The two voices grew closer. The other, I realized a few seconds later, was Cairis's.

"—long to find it," Cairis was saying.

Footsteps. Down the other staircase. My escape route.

"Has the guard gone through all this yet?" Raihn asked.

"Not yet."

"He made a lot of changes to the place."

There was a strange note to his voice at that—one that seemed obvious to me, but that Cairis breezed right by.

"They'll start in on these rooms as soon as they're done with the upstairs studies," Cairis said.

"Anything useful?"

"Nothing new. We already know who we need to kill. The hard part is getting to them. But getting rid of Misrada will help with that. Septimus seems confident."

"Well, as long as *Septimus* is confident." Raihn's voice dripped with sarcasm. "At least that will get some of them out of our way."

The footsteps grew louder. I shrank back as I watched the sliver of light beneath the door—watched shadows flicker across it.

I stopped breathing. I shrank back against the wall, trying to put as much space between me and them as I could.

But they just kept walking. "This place was kept out of the way," Cairis said. "Maybe he kept the good shit down—what?"

My short-lived breath of relief stilled.

One set of footsteps—Raihn's—had stopped.

"What is it?" Cairis said, again.

"Nothing. Just curiosity."

Raihn was a good actor. He always sold his lies well.

"You go ahead," he said to Cairis. "I'd like to look around in here instead first."

Fuck. *Fuck.*

"You want me to call someone to help you?"

"Honestly, I'm dying for a little privacy. Want to hear myself think for once."

Cairis chuckled, and I glanced frantically around the office. The only hiding place was under the desk. A comically terrible choice. Still, it was better than nothing.

As I ducked down beneath the desk, I caught one final glimpse of all my father's work—papers and diagrams that showed exactly how much he loved his kingdom, and how much of his blood and sweat he poured into building and protecting his empire.

His empire. *My* empire.

And here I was cowering under a fucking desk.

A sudden, agonizing wave of shame swallowed me as I slid beneath the wood.

Just as one set of footsteps faded away, and the other drew closer.

Just as the door swung open and a familiar voice said, "Did you really think I wouldn't smell you, princess?"

6

ORAYA

Fuck.

I looked around for something, anything, I could use as a weapon. That would be too easy, apparently.

"Are you going to come out from under that," Raihn asked, "or are you going to make me get you?"

My jaw clenched so hard it shook.

Suddenly I felt just like I had in the Moon Palace, when he had taunted me in the greenhouse. I was cornered then, and I was cornered now.

I rose and turned to face him. My hands curled at my sides. I wished I didn't see the flicker of disappointment in Raihn's eyes at my concession.

He leaned against the doorframe, surveying me, that brief reveal disappearing beneath the smirk at his mouth, his performance reassumed.

I said nothing.

"I know you're very good at sneaking around places you aren't supposed to be," he went on. "Should I feel lucky you don't have your blades on you this time?"

He touched his thigh, calling back the first time we had met

—when he'd grabbed me in an attempt to save my life, and I'd thanked him for it by driving my dagger into his leg.

What did he think he was doing here? Playing with me like nothing had changed between us. Like we were still just two contestants in the Kejari, reluctant allies.

My voice was hard and sharp. "Somewhere I'm not supposed to be? This is my home."

I was never very good at seeming cold and collected when my emotions were thrashing under the surface of my skin. Vincent had reminded me of it often.

Raihn saw the truth.

His smirk disappeared.

"I know that," he said. No hint of teasing this time.

"No, you don't," I shot back. "You don't understand that because you're keeping me a prisoner here."

"You're not a prisoner. You're—"

You're my queen, he always said.

Bullshit. I couldn't stand it anymore.

"Stop," I snapped. "Just—just *STOP*. Stop with the lies. Stop with the willful ignorance. You lock me in my room every night. You sleep in the next apartment so you can guard me—"

Raihn moved abruptly—two steps forward so he was up against the other side of the desk, leaning close to me.

"I am trying to keep you alive, Oraya," he said, voice low. "And it's hard fucking work, alright? I know none of it is ideal. But I'm trying."

I wanted to say, *So what? Let it happen, if it's so hard to stop it. Let them kill me.*

You're better than that, little serpent, Vincent whispered in my ear.

"How benevolent of you," I shot back. "How *selfless*."

Raihn's palms now pressed to the table, and he looked directly into my eyes.

"Do you think I *want* any of this?" he spat. "Do you think I *want* to listen to you sob every night?"

The blood drained from my face.

At my expression, his mouth thinned. I could practically hear him silently scolding himself for saying it.

I knew there was a possibility that he heard me. I knew that Raihn had always seen everything I didn't want him to. But fuck, to hear it acknowledged—it violated some unspoken contract. My cheeks warmed.

I took a step back, suddenly desperate to put more space between us, and Raihn matched it forward. His gaze was steady and unblinking—as inescapable as if he'd grabbed me and pinned me to the wall.

"I made you an offer," he murmured. "The night we—"

A stutter to his voice. I heard what he didn't say: *The night we were married.*

Neither of us ever acknowledged that. Our marriage.

"I made you an offer that night. And it still stands. It always will."

Another step back. Another step closer.

"I hate this place." He exhaled the words, ragged, like he'd torn them from deep in his chest. "I hate these people. I hate this castle. I hate this fucking crown. But I don't hate you, Oraya. Not even a little." His face softened, and I so wanted to tear my eyes away and didn't. "I failed you. I know that. I'm probably still—" He shook his head a little, as if to shut himself up. "But you and I are the same. There is no one I would rather have help me build a new version of this kingdom. And honestly, I... I don't know if I can do it without you."

I finally allowed my gaze to fall from Raihn's face. Allowed it to drift down, to the desk between us, scattered with Vincent's notes and plans. Raihn now leaned over that desk, his palms pressed down on those papers. All evidence of my father's kingdom and how much he had loved it.

My father's kingdom. *My* kingdom.

The faint pulse of my Heir Mark over my throat and chest burned stronger now. Itched, like an acid bite.

At least that will get some of them out of our way, Raihn had said, so fucking casually, when talking about the people who now relied on me.

"You don't want a Hiaj's help," I spat. "You're too busy killing all of us."

"Us?" Raihn's scoff was immediate, vicious, like he couldn't even stop himself. "When the hell did it become 'us?' They never treated you like you were one of them. They treated people like you like fucking livestock. They disrespected you, they—"

"You killed my father!"

The words burst out of me. The accusation, the ugly truth, had been pressing up beneath the underside of my skin for weeks. Every time I looked at Raihn, they screamed in my ears. All those accusations: *You killed my father, you lied to me, you used me.*

YOU.

KILLED.

MY.

FATHER.

They drowned out every word he said to me.

They silenced him immediately, and then hung there between us, palpable and cutting as razor blades.

"*You. Killed. My. Father.*"

I didn't even realize I was speaking aloud this time, the words scraping from between my clenched teeth.

With each word, I relived it—Raihn's magic flaring as he pinned Vincent to the wall. Vincent's body falling, nothing more than a pile of broken flesh.

Silvery smoke unfurled around my clenched fists. My shoulders rose and fell heavily. My chest hurt—Goddess, my chest *hurt* so, so much. I'd let out too much and now I struggled to wrangle it all back under control.

For a long, horrible, silent moment I was so sure I was going to fall apart. Raihn at last moved around that desk, approaching me slowly, watching me so steadily I could feel it even when I squeezed my eyes shut.

Like he was waiting. Like he was ready.

"I am so sorry, Oraya," he murmured. "I'm just—I'm so sorry that it all happened this way. I'm so sorry."

The worst part was, I couldn't even doubt that he meant it.

Sorry. I remembered the first time Raihn had apologized to me, plainly, like it had been a simple truth, and how it had meant so much to me that it rearranged my entire world a little to hear it spoken that way. I'd felt like I'd been given a gift I had been waiting so long for—for someone to validate my feelings that way, to concede to me even at the expense of their own pride.

I'd been so desperate to hear those words from my father.

I'd finally gotten them in his final breaths. *I love you. I'm sorry.*

And did they change anything? Did they *mean* anything, in the end? What fucking good did a few words do?

I opened my eyes and met Raihn's. His face was so starkly honest, so raw, that it startled me. I could see that he was opening a door for me, coaxing me through. Ready to take my hand and guide me there.

"But you'd do it again," I said.

I slammed that door shut.

He flinched.

"I am trying to save so many lives," he said.

Helplessly. Like he didn't know what else to tell me.

Well, what else was he going to tell me but the truth?

I fucking hated that I understood that, in some dark corner of myself. Raihn had made a bargain he had died trying to avoid fulfilling. Raihn had thousands of people relying on him. Raihn had his obligations tattooed onto his flesh.

But I'd been denying for too long that I had my own obligations seared into my skin, too. And I'd just listened to Raihn talk about killing the people who now relied on me. Talk of a new kingdom was one thing. But it was talk. Because I'd just watched him put on a performance to gain the favor of the very same people who abused him.

Fucking hypocrite.

We wanted to talk about hard decisions?

Raihn took another step closer. "Oraya, listen…"

But I jerked backwards. "I want to go back to my room."

It was impossible to miss the disappointment in his eyes.

"Take me back or let me walk there myself," I spat.

To his credit, he knew when there was no arguing with me. He didn't say another word as he opened the door and walked silently a step behind me, all the way back to my room.

7

ORAYA

I wasn't sure when I decided what I was going to do, only
that by the time I made it back to my room, it was no
longer a question. I waited until long after Raihn's footsteps had faded down the hallway. I didn't want to take any
risks, especially not when Raihn had made it so clear just how
embarrassingly well he could hear what went on inside my
chambers.

And then, finally, I reached into my pocket and withdrew
that little clump of glass, placing it on my bed. It looked just as
unremarkable in here as it had on Vincent's desk—like stacked
shards, now stained with my blood.

I still didn't understand what this was, or how it worked. But
I mimicked what I'd done in the study, sliding the still-bleeding
pad of my thumb over the smooth edge.

Just as it had before, the shards immediately scattered into a
pile of broken glass. I touched them again, and it reassembled
into the mirrored, shallow bowl.

Now that I was watching more closely, I noticed that the
pieces, when assembled, still trembled a bit—in some areas, they
didn't seem to line up quite right. I sliced my thumb on the edge

again and watched my blood swirl down the decorative whorls, pooling at the bottom of the basin.

I was prepared, this time, for the wave of—of *Vincent* that would follow. But it wasn't any less painful to feel it, nor any less difficult to keep myself from shutting it out. I didn't hear the sound of his voice or see his face, but I unmistakably felt his presence, like at any moment I'd turn around and he would be standing behind me. Deeper, more visceral certainty than any single sense could conjure.

The blood at the center sputtered and widened, shivering at the edges with the trembling shards of glass. The image in the blood seemed like a reflection from another location, distant and faint. Maybe it would have been easier to see in a pool of black blood. Or perhaps it was so faint because this device—whatever it was—was never intended to work for me. I was only half vampire, after all.

I squinted into the half-formed image. I could make out the faintest suggestion of a person's face, as if leaning over the mirror from the opposite side.

"Jesmine?" I whispered.

"Highness?"

It was unmistakably Jesmine's voice, just like I'd thought before, albeit very distant and fuzzy. I leaned closer, straining my ears.

"It is you—" she said. "Thought—from the—where are—"

"Slow down," I said. "I can't hear you."

Just as I always told you, little serpent, Vincent whispered to me. *You must learn how to be more patient. Wait, and feel it.*

I drew in a sharp breath.

Goddess, his voice felt so close, I could practically feel his breath on my ear. The sudden wave of grief struck me before I could steel myself against it.

Jesmine's image solidified, her voice growing stronger, even though I still had to strain to hear her.

"—you can use it," she was saying. I could make out her expression now—confused, intrigued. Dirt—or blood—appeared to smear one of her cheeks, her hair pulled back in a frizzy knot, a bandage wrapped around one of her arms. A stark difference from the polished seductress I was so used to seeing slink around Vincent's parties.

"Use it?" I asked.

"His mirror. You can use it."

His.

I didn't need to know the details of what this thing was, exactly, to know that it was powerful, old magic—just from the way it felt, so inextricably linked to Vincent's soul. And if this was his, and it ran on his blood…

"We don't have time," I muttered, mostly to myself.

No, I didn't have time to question any of this. Not when we had work to do.

Jesmine nodded seriously, her face shifting from that of a curious subject to a general. "Are you safe, Highness?"

Safe. What a word. But I answered, "I am. And your status?"

"We are in—"

"I don't want to know." I was relatively certain that if we'd made it this far, no one was listening to our conversation—but I couldn't be sure.

Understanding fell over Jesmine's face. "Yes, Highness. Do you—how much do you know of the state of the war?"

I cleared my throat.

It was embarrassing to admit just how little I knew. Now, with this connection to Vincent burning bright and painful in my chest, it seemed even more shameful.

I had been handed incredible responsibility, and how I felt about it made no difference—so far, I'd squandered it.

Jesmine's image flickered, and I pulled the bowl closer to me, as if to drag her back by force.

"I want your assessment, not the Rishan's," I said. A convenient way of brushing off my own ignorance.

"We've lost… many of our remaining strongholds. We're still fighting to defend those that remain, Highness. Fighting with all we've got. But—" A wrinkle of hatred flitted over her nose. "The

Bloodborn are numerous and vicious. The Rishan we could handle. The Bloodborn are... challenging."

That aligned with what I'd been seeing here. Raihn could wax philosophical about his dreams all he wanted. The ugly truth was that he had invited dogs into his kingdom and let them hide behind his crown while they murdered his own people. He was heavily reliant upon their forces.

Raihn had told me, once, that dreams counted for little. What counted was action.

Well, his actions were not enough. And mine had been severely lacking, too.

Jesmine's face blurred again, her next words fractured. "Do you — orders?"

In a desperate attempt to save my connection to her, I pressed my thumb to the edge of the bowl and let more blood flow into it, but that just made her image ripple and made the headache at the back of my skull pound ferociously.

The sound of distant footsteps made me still. I peered over my shoulder at the door to my chambers — closed. The footsteps didn't approach, then faded to an echo at the opposite end of the hall.

I turned back to the mirror. "I don't have much time," I whispered.

"Do you have orders?" she asked urgently.

Orders. Like *I* had any authority to be telling Jesmine what she should be doing.

"They're coming after you at Misrada in two weeks," I said, quickly and quietly. "It will be a big move. They're stretching themselves thin — even the Bloodborn. They'll be leaving the Sivrinaj armory unmanned in order to get enough forces there."

Jesmine's brow furrowed in thought.

"I don't know if we could defend against that kind of manpower."

"I don't know if you could, either. But maybe you don't have to."

I hesitated here—standing on the precipice of a decision I couldn't take back. The decision to *fight*.

I could feel Vincent's presence like a hand resting on my shoulder.

This is your kingdom, he whispered to me. *I taught you how to fight for a significant existence. I gave you teeth. Now use them.*

"Evacuate Misrada," I said. "Go after the armory while it's unguarded. Raid it, or capture it, or destroy it—whatever is possible with what you have. Do you have the resources?"

Even through the foggy reflection, the steel in Jesmine's stare was clear.

"It will be tight. But we have enough to try."

I didn't let myself waver, didn't let my command falter, as I said, "Then do it. Enough running. Enough defending. We don't have time for half measures."

It was time to fucking fight.

Part Two
New Moon

INTERLUDE

There is nothing more dangerous than a bargain. No greater horrors than those you choose. No worse fate than one you beg for.

The man does not understand this yet.

There was little, actually, the man understands, though he doesn't know that yet, either. He came from a small life in a small town, and spent most of his time trying to run from it. Of his limited options, he chose the one that gave him the most freedom. He loves freedom, the feeling of the sea wind through his hair. He loves it tonight, as his ship travels through the treacherous waters near Obitraes. They call it Nyaxia's Hook—that little curved strip of land, given its name because it so often snagged unwitting human sailors like helpless fish on a line. The night is dark. The water is rough. The sky is stormy.

The sailors do not have a chance.

Most of them are killed immediately, when the ship—too small for such a perilous journey—smashes upon the unforgiving rocks of Nyaxia's beckoning hand. They drown in the salty seas, bodies broken over the rocks or impaled on the remains of their own ship.

But this man, despite his unremarkable upbringing, knows one thing above all:

He knows how to fight.

He is thirty-two years old. He is not ready to die. His body has been mercilessly shattered in the violent impact of the ship. Still, he swims to shore, muscles straining against the churn of the surf. He drags himself onto the beach.

When, barely conscious, he forces his head up to look at the sight ahead of him—the silhouette of a city the likes of which he had never seen before, all ivory curves and moon-cold light—he thinks he has never witnessed anything so beautiful.

The man is so close to death that night.

The gods love to take credit for fate. Is it fate that saves him? Or is it the fickle hand of luck, rolling dice that land in just the right way? If it is the gods' hands at work, then they are laughing to themselves tonight.

He crawls as far as he can, one inch after another, the sand beneath his hands turning to rock, then soil. He can feel death following him, can feel it bubbling in his every bloody breath. The man once thought himself brave. But no mortal is brave in the face of an untimely death.

Death would have taken him if fate, or luck, had not saved him—or damned him.

The king happens across him at just the right moment.

This king was in the habit of collecting souls, and the young man's soul is exactly the kind he enjoys. He flips over the half-conscious man, assessing his beaten but well-formed face. Then he kneels beside him and asks him a question that the man will spend the rest of an endless life replaying:

Do you want to live?

The man thinks, What a stupid question.

Of course, he wants to live. He is young. He has a family waiting for him back home. He has decades ahead of him.

No mortal is brave in the face of an untimely death.

The man's answer is a plea:

Yes. Please. Yes. Help me.

Later, he will hate himself for this—for begging so pathetically for his own damnation.

The king smiles, and lowers his mouth to the dying man's throat.

8

RAIHN

From the first moment I had seen Septimus, I'd hated him.

I'd known exactly who he was, and even if I didn't know him by reputation, his appearance—which screamed *Untrustworthy Bloodborn Royalty* in every way—would have given it away quickly.

When he'd sidled up to me during the Kejari, I'd wanted nothing to do with him. But he was like a virus, or an unpleasant odor. The fucker just kept coming back.

It was casual enough, at first. He would linger too long wherever Mische and I happened to be, in the days immediately preceding the Kejari. In the beginning, I'd thought he was doing what most Bloodborn nobles did during the tournament: taking advantage of the fact that they were actually allowed to interact with the other Houses, and figuring out where they could exert their influence.

Easy enough to dismiss.

But then, maybe the third or fourth time he cornered me, I began to get suspicious. And I'd already decided I didn't like him by the time he had pulled me aside and told me, *I know who you are.*

That was enough to spook me. I'd ripped apart my own inner circle trying to figure out how he knew—still, to this day, I didn't know how he had found out. But that was when the pressure began.

You can't do this by yourself. The Rishan aren't strong enough. Doesn't matter if you win.

You'll need help.

Let me help you. Let us help each other.

I told him to go fuck himself. I never considered taking the deal. I'd learned a long, long time ago the danger of someone offering you everything you've ever wanted.

But then he noticed Oraya.

And I still remembered the exact moment I knew he understood he could use her against me: that moment at the Halfmoon ball, when he'd called her by Nessanyn's name.

I denied him right up until the end. Right up until he was dangling Oraya's life in front of me. And then I broke.

When you've lived through certain things, you know how to recognize someone who's desperate. Septimus, I knew, was desperate—in a dangerous kind of way, the kind he was very good at keeping far away from the surface. He'd do absolutely anything to get what he wanted, and what scared me was, I still wasn't entirely sure what that was.

Desperation made for a terrible deal.

This thought was at the forefront of my mind as I sat in my office with him and Vale, listening to Septimus tell us, oh-so-casually, about how he couldn't send Bloodborn troops to Misrada, after all.

Vale was not happy. He wasn't bothering to hide exactly how not happy he was.

"That's unacceptable," he said.

Septimus's stupid fucking face arranged into that stupid fucking smirk.

"I understand why you feel that way," he said, "but the nature of the matter is what it is. I can't bend time and space, sadly. Desdemona confirmed it multiple times. We just can't get the forces there in time. We'll have to make the move later."

"So let me make sure I understand." Vale leaned across the desk. "We now have to reschedule an operation that we've had planned for weeks on account of *your* shit generals' poor foresight? With a *day's* notice?"

Septimus's smirk faltered. I'd noticed that he was perfectly happy to accept whatever insults you wanted to lob his way, but he didn't like it much when you disrespected those who worked under him.

He let out a puff of smoke through his nostrils. "My *shit generals* are doing most of the work putting down this little rebellion of yours. Maybe if your own forces were willing to fight for you, it would have been handled faster."

Vale looked like he was close to blows. Against my better instincts, I shot him a warning glance. Vale held that stare for a moment—fought it, because even after these last weeks, he still wasn't really ready to accept me as his superior—before shaking his head and leaning back in his chair.

"This is what I did not miss about this job," he muttered, as if he couldn't help himself. "Working with incompetence."

Septimus chuckled. Then his gaze slid to me.

"You're terribly quiet, Highness."

I had indeed been quiet. I'd been watching Septimus, thinking about this suspiciously neat little last-minute rescheduling of his. There was more to it than he was saying. I had no doubts there, even if I didn't know how or why.

I'd been so busy thinking that I'd neglected my role. I wanted Septimus to keep on dismissing me as the brutish, Turned king. Let him keep thinking I was someone he could take advantage of.

My returning smile was more of a baring of teeth. "What would you like me to say?"

Septimus shrugged, as if to say, *You tell me.*

"Do you want me to bitch at you for your poor planning and your carelessness?"

Again, he shrugged. "If you wish."

"Why would I waste my breath? I already wasted enough of it planning this offensive with you. Maybe I don't feel like giving you any more of my time."

He cocked his head, staring me down a little too thoughtfully for my comfort.

I sat up straighter. "I don't see what else there is to talk about." I waved my hand at him dismissively. "I have actual work to do, if you're done."

A brief, cold smile, as Septimus rose. "Quite done."

It was now baffling to me that the first time I'd laid eyes on Sivrinaj's skyline, I'd thought it was the most beautiful thing I'd ever seen. I'd thought it looked like nothing less than salvation.

What a fucking joke.

That view had looked a lot like this one, from the roof of the armory on the outskirts of the city. It had been night then, too, the city drenched in moonlight. I supposed there was a certain architectural appeal to it, all those domes and towers and spires, marble and ivory and silver. The kind of thing you could only admire until you'd seen firsthand the blood that had been spilled to build it, and the rot that festered underneath.

"You shouldn't be out here, Highness," Vale said, for the fourth time in the last fifteen minutes. The words didn't change, but his tone did, growing increasingly frustrated.

"I heard you the first time."

He let out a grunt of wordless disapproval.

I turned around, taking in the rest of the landscape. The armory was located right where the city limits gave way to the desert—smooth rolling dunes to the north, rocky inclines down to the sea to the south. It was a foggy, overcast night, which I didn't like. Poor visibility to the ocean. Poor visibility above.

I glanced over the rail to the city streets below. To the west were the human districts, blocky patches of tan and gray. Just beyond them, the slums of the vampire territories of the city. A few haphazard barriers, clumsy constructions of wood and stone, still remained in some of the streets. The remnants of the Hiaj's attempts, in the days after the coup, to claw back some sections of the city. Failed attempts. But they'd put up a fight.

And I never forgot that they were still fighting.

It was a quiet night, now. But these kinds of things always happened on quiet nights.

It had been a quiet night when the Moon Palace was attacked.

It had been a quiet night before Neculai's kingdom fell.

And it was especially quiet here now, given that Septimus had pulled away his Bloodborn forces, leaving the Rishan here to guard the armory, scattered and disorganized due to a last-minute change in orders.

Nothing was supposed to happen tonight, thanks to Septimus's decision.

But I just thought about Septimus, and that little fucking smirk, and his very casual change of plans.

People, especially Nightborn and Shadowborn nobles, were far too quick to dismiss the Bloodborn as mindless beasts. They were bloodthirsty bastards, but they were smarter than anyone gave them credit for. If they weren't hobbled by the curse, which cut down their numbers and their lifespans, I had no doubts they could've taken over Obitraes. Hell, maybe the world.

It was upper-class arrogance to underestimate them, and I didn't have the luxury of that.

"I want more guards here," I told Vale.

A lesser general would have told me I was being overly cautious. But Vale, to his credit, didn't question me.

"What do you suspect?" he asked quietly.

"I..."

I don't know.

Damn my pride, but I wasn't about to say those words aloud, especially not to Vale.

It was the truth, though. I didn't have a concrete theory. I didn't think Septimus would openly turn against us—at least, not yet. He'd locked himself into this alliance, too. He'd have to work harder at getting out of it than this.

But sometimes, there's just something in the air.

I sniffed and shot Vale a wry smirk. "You smell that?"

"What?"

"Blood."

I leaned back against the stone wall, my hands in my pockets. "I'll stay here tonight."

"But—"

"Pull whoever we can spare from their posts throughout the rest of the city. Put them here."

A pause. I could tell that he wanted to call me stupid for staying here personally, even if—*especially* if—I suspected something might happen.

But he just said, "As you wish, Highness."

And without another argument, he spread his silver wings and launched into the sky with a *whoosh*. I lifted my chin and stared after him as he disappeared into the soupy mists.

I settled at the stone lip of the wall and unsheathed my sword. It had been a while, but there was a comforting familiarity to the way my muscles had to move to wield it. I lay the blade over my lap, taking in the dark steel, the faint red smoke rolling from the blade. I knew it by heart. Like an old friend.

I almost wanted something to go wrong tonight. Give me something to kill. I missed it. It was simple, easy, straightforward. The opposite of these last few weeks.

At least, it used to be.

The memory of Vincent's face in his final moments flitted across my mind, unwelcome. Nothing simple about that.

I pushed that thought away, leaning back and watching the thick clouds drift across the sky. Waiting for something. Even if I didn't know what.

Let them come.

I was looking forward to it.

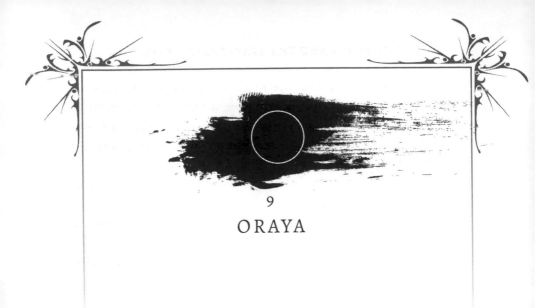

9

ORAYA

I knew something was wrong before the explosion hit.

I was no stranger to gazing longingly out this bedchamber window. An entire life locked in this room had that effect. But these last couple of weeks, I'd been doing more than gazing. I'd been waiting.

Waiting for a mass exodus of Bloodborn and Rishan soldiers.

Waiting for a mass exodus that didn't come.

The Bloodborn left a few days ago, and though it wasn't quite the scale of movement that I'd been expecting by the way I'd heard them talking, it was enough to keep me hopeful. I'd thought the Rishan would be following tonight.

But hours passed, and the Rishan didn't move. A knot of unease tightened in my stomach as I watched and waited, growing with every passing minute. I tried to use the mirror again, this time to warn Jesmine, but was met with nothing but misty clouds in my pool of blood. Apparently, she'd already moved. The attack was already underway.

Soon, I was pacing the length of the windows, eyes glued to the armory in the distance, mind racing.

Jesmine was a strong, competent general, I told myself. She

wouldn't have moved unless she had verified that she had a path to success. And the conditions of the night were ideal. Cloudy, to hide Hiaj flying in the skies. Many of the Bloodborn had left. That was something. It just wasn't the skeleton force that I'd been expecting. Unless I'd missed something.

But Vincent whispered in my ear, *You know better, little serpent, than to be willfully ignorant.*

No. He was right. I stopped at the window, fingertips pressed to the glass. Something had changed. The Bloodborn that had pulled out certainly wouldn't be enough to take a city like Misrada.

And—

The explosion wiped away all my thoughts.

It was loud—so powerful I felt it in the pads of my fingers against the glass, even from across the city. A burst of shimmery smoke erupted from the distant armory in a plume of white and blue.

I watched, breathless, as the flare of light burst, then dimmed. I hadn't seen anything quite like it since…

Since the attack on the Moon Palace, many months ago.

Jesmine. Fucking brilliant. Petty. But brilliant. She'd used magic wielders to recreate the destruction of the Moon Palace, creating a violent distraction. I didn't blink as distant silhouettes plummeted through the clouds and smoke—countless Hiaj, diving down into the wreckage.

The sight chilled me down to my bones.

I needed to get down there.

I needed to get down there *right now.*

The explosion had triggered an eruption of activity in the halls beyond my chamber. I ran to my door and leaned against it, listening to the frantic sound of distant running footsteps and shouting voices. Then I pounded at the oak, so hard my fist began to ache.

Whoever was on the other side took a long time to open it, like they weren't sure whether it was a good idea.

A young Rishan man with wavy blond hair and a look of

general bewilderment on his face stood there, looking as if he was immediately regretting his decision.

I blinked. "You aren't Ketura."

When I had a guard, it was most often her.

"No," he said. "I'm Killan."

If Ketura wasn't here, that meant that she had been pulled away somewhere else. Perhaps she was already at the armory.

Shit.

"Let me through," I said, already moving, but Killan clumsily blocked my path. I craned my head to see several more soldiers, donning armor, rushing down the hall.

"I am your queen," I snarled. "Let me pass."

Let's see if all Raihn's *you-aren't-a-prisoner-you're-a-queen* bull-shit actually meant anything.

"I can't do that, Highness," Killan said. "I've been instructed to guard you. It's dangerous out there."

I've been instructed to guard you, the boy said, like I didn't see his nostrils flaring when I got too close. He wasn't equipped to guard anything. He didn't even know how to resist the smell of human blood.

If *this* was all that was left in this castle, that meant they were really desperate.

I took a step backwards. Two.

Killan loosened a visible exhale of relief.

Remember who you are, Vincent whispered.

What the hell was I doing, asking this boy for *permission* to leave? Letting him think he could *guard* me?

I'd won the Goddess-damned Kejari. I'd won battles against vampire warriors twice my size and ten times my age. I was the daughter of Vincent of the Nightborn, the greatest king to rule the House of Night, and I was his rightful Heir, and I was *better than this.*

Mother, I had missed anger. I embraced it now like welcoming an old lover back into my arms.

Nightfire roared to my fingertips and tore up my forearms.

It wasn't hard to deal with Killan. The boy had probably

never even hit another living thing with that sword, and he certainly wasn't prepared for me to be the first. The touch of Nightfire had him gasping in pain, bloodless wounds opening over his arms where I grabbed him and flung him against the wall. He tried to fight back, weakly, but I knocked his sword from his grasp, sending it clanging to the marble floor.

It felt so good to fight again. So good I wanted him to push back harder. I wanted more of a challenge.

I wanted to *hurt* a little.

But Killan didn't offer much of a fight. No, he just panted, his heart beating fast—Mother, how could I hear that heartbeat so clearly?—as I pressed my forearm to his throat, Nightfire nibbling at his skin.

My foot reached to the left and dragged his sword back. I reached down to grab it, and Killan tried to slip my grasp.

Useless. Seconds and I had him back against the wall, this time with his own sword poised at his chest.

He looked so afraid.

That used to bring me a lot of satisfaction. To see them afraid. A few brief moments where they felt the kind of powerlessness I had felt my entire life.

For a moment, I felt satisfaction in it now, too.

If it feels this good to have one person look at you this way, little serpent, Vincent murmured, *imagine how good it feels to see a kingdom look at you like this.*

A shiver ran up my spine. A person could lose themselves in that kind of power. And I wanted to, as long as it made me feel something other than weak.

But the uncomfortable truth was that Killan was not one of my targets in the human slums. Killan was barely more than a child, tasked with a job he wasn't ready for.

Kill him, Vincent insisted. *He will tell the others you're gone.*

Voices down the hall. Distant footsteps. Fuck. No time.

I lifted my sword arm.

"Please," Killan begged. "I—"

SMACK.

I slammed his head against the wall.

His body went limp. He was bigger than me, and physically stronger, but he hadn't been expecting that. It was difficult to knock out a vampire. He wouldn't be unconscious for long. I dragged him into my bedroom and locked it behind me—all three clicks.

The footsteps were growing closer. The castle seemed to have come alive with anxiety. Distant shouts rang out, harsh with command.

I only had a few minutes. If that.

I grabbed Killan's sword and his hooded military cloak, and I ran.

I'D HAVE GIVEN anything in this moment for wings. Even if I did have the stamina to sprint across Sivrinaj—a ridiculous thought —it still would have taken far too long to make it to the armory on foot.

I needed a horse.

Horseback travel wasn't especially common in the House of Night, given that wings were often much more efficient. They were typically only used by humans—or by the Nightborn Guard.

Which meant I had to sneak my way down to the stables. Killan's cloak was a shit disguise when anyone could smell my human blood, but it was better than nothing. It was only thanks to the utter chaos in the castle that I'd managed to make it to the ground floor undetected. Uniformed figures ranging in rank from Nightborn Guard members to common foot soldiers, barely more than servants, flooded the halls.

It was easy enough to lose myself in this, slipping all the way down to the stables. A number of horses had been tacked and lined up, and I grabbed the first one I saw, a little chestnut mare.

I briefly considered the possibility of trying to blend in, but I didn't have the luxury of time. The minute anyone saw my face or got close enough to smell me, they'd know exactly who I was. Worse, as I hoisted myself onto the horse and leaned down to adjust my cloak, I glimpsed my chest and cursed.

My Mark.

I was wearing a camisole, not my usual leathers, which left my upper chest exposed. The cloak covered some of the red ink, but not all of it.

Fine. Speed it was.

My horse was uncomfortable, as if sensing that it was being separated from its herd for unsavory purposes. Horses in Obitraes tended to be especially flighty creatures. This one danced anxiously as I urged it from the stable doors, ducking my head to hide beneath my hood. The heat of the night, arid and thick, startled me. It took me a moment to realize that it was probably because I hadn't even been outside in weeks.

Raihn's words from one of our first meetings now rang through my head:

Vincent's little princess, locked up in her glass castle, where everyone can look but never touch.

What a fucking hypocrite.

"Hey! You, boy! Where are you supposed to be?"

A gruff voice startled me. I urged my horse into a trot onto the city streets, tugging my hood higher.

"Boy!" the voice called again, but I kicked my horse into a canter, leaving his shouts behind me.

The human districts. I knew those streets better than any vampires did. I could cut through and make it to the other end of the city faster through roads that weren't congested with soldiers and checkpoints.

I dug my heels in, the canter becoming a gallop as we swung down a quiet, dark side street. But just around the corner the beast abruptly spooked, rearing back and nearly sending me tumbling to the cobblestones. I barely managed to right myself, rubbing the mare's neck and uttering hushed comforts.

It was so dark that at first my feeble human eyesight couldn't make out the figure in front of me. But then—

They stepped closer, hands raised. A ray of moonlight fell across the swoop of his hair—silver—and the curve of a nonchalant smile.

"Didn't mean to spook you," he said. "My evening stroll got a bit chaotic."

Septimus.

Fuck.

I inclined my head, hiding it farther beneath the shadow of my hood. Would it matter, though, to vampire eyesight? To vampire smell?

"Apologies," he said. "You have important things to do, don't you? I think it's that way, though. All kinds of barricades down this road."

I nodded, still struggling to keep my face hidden.

Septimus tucked one hand into his pocket and brushed past me, patting my horse's shoulder as he did.

"Good luck out there. Looks like some nasty business."

I released an exhale as he passed, unwilling to question my luck even if I had the time to. Maybe he'd dismissed me. Or maybe he'd recognized me. Even if he had, I couldn't let myself stop to think too hard about what that meant.

I had a task, and a clear road ahead of me. I kicked my horse back into a canter.

I took the left path.

THE ATTACK WAS a near-perfect mimicry of the attack on the Moon Palace. I had to admire Jesmine's commitment to her pettiness. As far as she knew, Raihn had been responsible for the Moon Palace attack. To her, this would be justice. And Mother, she was damned good at her job. It was amazing what she'd managed to execute. It felt like I was galloping into the underworld itself.

Nightfire smoke had a very particular smell—one that seemed to burn your nostrils from the inside out. The stench of it was overpowering by the time I crossed the second bridge from the human districts back into the vampire territories of Sivrinaj. I was at the outskirts of the city at this point, and as soon as I turned the corner to the first main road leading to the base, I cursed to myself.

The scene before me was one of pure carnage. The searing white of Nightfire stung my eyes. It consumed most of the armory.

It seemed that Jesmine had decided—probably wisely—that retaking and holding the base was impossible so close to the heart of Sivrinaj. So destroying it would have to do.

But they were far from unopposed. Rishan soldiers surrounded me, casters fighting back the flames, warriors charging into the bloodshed. On the roof, barely visible through the Nightfire light, warriors tangled. I jerked my horse backwards as a bloody, mangled Hiaj body landed at its feet with a sickening wet *thump*.

I stared down at him. He blinked at me. His face was covered in blood, shapeless in a way that implied most of his bones had been broken. A brief flicker of recognition sparked in his eyes, and his mouth opened, but no sound came out.

For a horrible moment, I was looking at my father's body, mangled just like this one, trying to speak to me in his final moments and failing.

My head snapped up as a distant scream rang out—the kind that set the hairs upright on the back of my neck.

I recognized that sound immediately. It was the same sound that had pierced the air during the Moon Palace attack.

Demons. Jesmine had gotten her hands on a summoner.

My horse had heard that scream too, and it was extremely uninterested in going anywhere near it. It reared up in a violent, sudden lurch, then bucked, and I had to throw myself off its back as it bolted back into the darkened streets of the city.

I let out a barrage of grunts as I rolled against the cobblestones. I cursed and pushed myself up to my feet, groping around until I found Killan's sword again. It was a clumsy, unremarkable weapon. I didn't like fighting with traditional swords — they were big and awkward and didn't move as fast as I did — but something pointy was something pointy.

I staggered to my feet and set my sights on the burning armory. The doors had been blown open. An entire quarter of the building was simply missing.

Jesmine would be inside. *My soldiers* would be inside.

I was running into the flames before I gave myself time to think about it.

10

RAIHN

I fucking knew it.

If there wasn't so much death all around me, I might've reveled in that a bit more. As it was, it was hard to appreciate my sense of superiority.

I was lucky I made it through the explosion alive. Many Rishan warriors hadn't. Someone had managed to breach the armory walls and plant sigils, apparently, because the explosion came before the Hiaj or the demons did. I was walking through the halls when it happened, and I felt it a second before the Nightfire split the air.

You smell that? Blood.

Well, I certainly smelled it now. It was the first sense that came back to me as I regained consciousness after the explosion. Then I pushed myself up, and staggered into hell.

Nightfire everywhere, silhouettes of Hiaj and Rishan soldiers alike running through the blaze. Nightborn demons—four-legged, hairless beasts—darted through the flames at impossible speeds. A distant wail rang out as they clamped their teeth around some unlucky soldier, halls away. They were identical to the ones that had been planted at the Moon Palace all those months ago.

An intentional choice, I was sure. All of it. The Nightfire. The demons. A deliberate, downright artful imitation of that night. Jesmine's little *fuck you* for the attack I'd refused to confess to.

Was it terrible that I was a little relieved?

I wasn't the best king. Not even an especially good general, like Vale, with his affinity for strategy and politics.

But I was a fucking incredible warrior. Really, really good at killing things. It was comforting to sink back into something familiar as I cut my way through the carnage.

Ever since Neculai's death, I'd felt his power—the power of the Rishan Heir line—pulsing deep beneath my skin. I'd always been relatively strong since I'd Turned, but when he died… if the Mark wasn't enough to tell me what I was, I would have been able to *feel* it, like a new spring of power inching to the surface.

For a couple of centuries, I'd done my best to ignore it. I didn't want to accept what I was. Neculai's fingerprints were already all over me. He'd made me everything that I was. I didn't want my power to become his, too.

But ever since Nyaxia's gift—ever since she restored the full power of the Rishan Heir line—there was no more ignoring it. I'd felt it from that first night, after I carried an unconscious Oraya back to the castle and returned to help retake the city. I'd felt it when I'd ripped Martas's head off his body. And I felt it now, with every Asteris-laced swing of my blade, power spilling from my pores with such magnitude that I couldn't have hidden it even if I still wanted to.

I hated how much I loved it.

I turned a corner and cut through another demon. Easy enough, but wherever I killed one, more were ready to charge from the smoke. Above, I could hear voices and footsteps—Hiaj warriors, who had dived down from the cloudy sky, taking advantage of the poor visibility. Closer, Vale's voice rang out through the halls, commanding our soldiers to push them back before they could make it to the ground floors.

It was almost funny, just how many stars aligned to make this night a perfect deadlock.

If we'd pulled our forces like we'd originally planned, the Hiaj would have taken over easily. If the Rishan nobles had sent support like they were supposed to, we would have outnumbered our attackers. If the Bloodborn were still stationed here, then we would have crushed the Hiaj before their assault could even begin.

But as it stood, we were matched one-to-one. Our soldiers were healthier, but the Hiaj were more skilled, and they had the benefit of surprise and the demons on their side. I passed several corpses on my way downstairs, people who were so evenly matched in their respective battles that they'd killed each other instead of finding a victor.

I hit the bottom floor. I needed to get to the back—close the gates.

I turned a corner and stopped short.

I recognized her immediately, even through the smoke. The Nightfire seemed to bow to her—warping around her body as if conscious of every curve and angle. Tendrils of long black hair flew out behind her. She was fighting with a sword, a shitty one, which she was clearly uncomfortable with—and I knew that right away, because I knew her and how she moved and how she fought, knew her so well that all it took was one split second to know when she was off-balance.

She was fighting a wayward demon, which let out a keening wail as she impaled it, releasing a putrid spray of black blood. With a strangled roar, she pushed its limp body away from her. Then turned around and lifted her head.

Those fucking eyes. Silver as steel. Just as sharp. Just as deadly. Every time, I felt that little pulse in my chest, the urge to rub the scar that didn't exist.

Her face went hard and cold, and for a split second, I was so relieved to see that look. Fight.

There she is.

That one moment of relief drowned out all the other reasonable thoughts, the thoughts I was supposed to be having, and those hit me in an avalanche soon after.

She got out.

She came here.

She knew to come here.

She was trying to escape. Or…

Or she was responsible for this.

She leapt away as soon as she saw me, taking a few strides backwards. The Nightflame around her surged and danced, clinging to her form. I wondered if she knew that it did that. Was it conscious, or just a new part of her, like my magic was?

"Let me pass," she said. A command, not a request.

I smiled a little. "Or what? You'll stab me again? For what, the third time now?"

The Nightflame flared again, curling around her body.

I should have hated that Oraya had gotten a burst of power of her own from her ascension to Heir. But damn if I didn't love to see it. Just like I loved to see the strength in her stare as she gritted her teeth and stepped closer.

"I'm not fucking around, Raihn. Let me go."

"I can't do that, Oraya."

"Why?"

It was shockingly earnest—a wrinkle between her brows and everything. She took another small step, gaze never leaving mine. It was a throwing knife of a word, already drenched in her blood. "*Why?*"

It struck me harder than it should have.

It was a bigger question, I knew—we both knew—than the single word. Bigger than two people in this hallway. It was a *why did you betray me?* question, spoken with the same devastating tone as when she'd hurled the reality at me in Vincent's wing: *You killed my father.*

I could practically see the accusation in her eyes. No, more than that—an observation. Because like always, she saw right through me.

Why?

Because if I let you go, I'm committing treason against my own throne.

Because if I let you go, I'll have no choice but to fight against you out there.

Because if I let you go, you become my enemy in earnest.

And I can't kill you, princess. I've tried. I can't.

Too many damned words. Too much honesty.

I settled for, "You know why, Oraya. I'm not done with you."

A sliver of the truth, mixed in with the goad: *Come on. Fight me.*

I wanted her to fight. I'd missed seeing that in her. I'd been begging her for this for weeks.

I raised my sword. She did the same. The Nightfire danced with her every breath, rising with the hatred in her face.

Then her gaze rose. Eyes widened.

I glanced over my shoulder just in time to see a lithe female form with outstretched featherless wings rushing towards me, sword drawn.

Jesmine. You don't forget the face of someone who spent hours torturing you.

I barely dodged her attack, countering, our weapons clashing together. She'd drawn blood, her blade slicing open my left shoulder, where I'd been a little too slow to dodge. A stupid mistake.

She moved like a dancer, well-trained, elegant, unemotional. Her expression was focused, calm as the surface of a winter pond beneath the marks of battle—dirt, blood, scorched burns.

She glanced at Oraya, and I made the mistake of doing so, too—a stupid distraction at a critical moment. Jesmine's next strike was to kill.

"*Stop!*" Oraya's voice cut through the steel and chaos. "Stand down."

Jesmine's face contorted in confusion.

Oraya stepped closer, a sneer at her lip. "He's mine, Jesmine. Stand down. Get to the others."

I wouldn't hurt Oraya, but I had none of the same affection

for Jesmine. When she hesitated, baffled by her queen's order, I seized the opportunity.

I could barely even regulate the new depths of my power now—I didn't even have to call the Asteris before it danced at the edge of my blade. Jesmine was good, good enough to dodge despite her distraction, good enough to barely redirect the swing of my blade with hers—but the force of it sent her flying across the hall, her body crumpling in the ruined stone.

She'd barely fallen before Oraya was on me.

I felt her coming because of the Nightfire—that telltale buzz in the air a split second before she ran at me.

I could've killed her. Could've turned just enough to levy a blast of Asteris strong enough to pull her flesh from her bones. Instead, I had to take that extra precious moment just to make sure I'd reeled it in, holding myself back before I blocked her.

It put us on equal footing, and Oraya seized on that opening.

It had been weeks now since she'd fought, but if that break in practice hurt her, she didn't show it. If anything, the pent-up energy seemed to fuel her every strike.

Still... so much was the same.

We fell into our steps like a well-practiced dance, the intensity of every move turned up double, triple what it was months ago. Our magic, her Nightfire and my Asteris, surrounded us like thickening clouds, light and darkness, heat and cold. Every strike I blocked reverberated through my entire body, despite Oraya's small size—she threw that much force into each one. And she was quick, forcing me to strain to keep up with her.

She was so good. I honestly couldn't help but admire it.

And yet, neither of us drew blood. The Nightfire collecting around her sword did its work on me, yes, but each of her lunges were half-measures, making shallow cuts if they got past my blocks.

Still, she was fast. Too fast. Faster with each blow, like she was letting go, losing control.

The Nightfire grew brighter and brighter.

Three strikes, the last one so fast I couldn't dodge it, pain snaking across my chest—a line from my shoulder to my hip.

If she thought I didn't see the little flinch across her face when she saw the blood, like it jerked her out of her haze, she was wrong.

I used that hesitation against her, countering before she could move, reversing our positions. She was against the wall, her sword barely holding mine back, my body pinning her against the stone.

The Nightfire was so bright now, I couldn't see anything but her face.

It was all her. Deadly and stunning. Even her hatred was fucking beautiful.

We remained there, locked together, both panting. Just like it had been in the Kejari. Like fighting a mirror.

"You're holding back," she said.

A throb in my chest, in the ghost of a wound that didn't exist.

I smiled. "So are you," I said, completing our script. I leaned closer, close enough that my lips almost touched her ear—and for a moment the urge to skim my teeth along her earlobe, to press my mouth against her throat, was overwhelming. The scent of her, stronger than ever now, made it hard to focus.

"You're dying to kill me," I murmured. "So what the fuck are you waiting for?"

I didn't move, but I felt the cold press of her blade to my chest—stinging where the tip threatened to break skin. I pulled back just enough to look at her, our foreheads touching. Her eyes, big and round as the moon, stared into mine.

Sometimes, I felt like I knew Oraya better than anyone I had ever met. Sometimes, she was the most confounding mystery. Now, she was both—her hidden pain so obvious, and yet her trembling grip around her blade a question that I didn't know how to answer.

A trickle of blood ran down the center of my abdomen.

Oraya's breath, shaky and quick, mingled with mine.

"Well?" I rasped. "Are you going to kill me, princess?"

I really wanted to know. Maybe tonight would finally be the night.

Oraya didn't speak. Her teeth gritted, mouth snarling. The flames encircled us like a lover's embrace.

Another drip of blood down my chest.

But she didn't move.

She wouldn't do it.

She wouldn't do it.

This truth hit me with sudden certainty. A confirmation of something that honestly confused me.

Because Oraya did have every reason to kill me.

For the briefest moment, her rage gave way to something else, something she closed her eyes and looked away to avoid showing me, but I grabbed her chin and tilted her head back to me.

My mouth opened.

— And then blood spattered over my face, as Oraya jolted, an arrow now lodged in her flesh.

11

ORAYA

I was stupid. I was distracted. I didn't see the arrow coming until it was too late.

I felt the blood before the pain—thick wet warmth spreading over my side beneath my arm, which had been lifted to hold my blade.

The sword clattered to the floor.

The world dimmed, as the white heat of Nightfire ebbed.

Suddenly I was moving, no longer against the wall but to the side of it, sliding to the ground without my permission.

Raihn grabbed me and pulled me behind him. His form, massive and silhouetted by the flames, loomed before me.

"—the *fuck* do you think you're doing?" he roared.

My eyes fell to the other end of the hall, struggling to see through the smoke and my blurring vision. A young Bloodborn soldier cowered under Raihn's vicious glare, eyes widening as they fell to me, and he realized who I was.

"She—she was attacking you—" he stuttered.

A torrent of curses flew from Raihn's mouth, falling into mush in my head. Through the fire, I could make out more silhouettes pouring through the hallway—more Bloodborn? Reinforcements. *Fuck*.

My hand pressed to my wound. It bled heavily. Half vampire or no, blood was always my weakness. It always seemed ready to pour out of me at any opportunity.

Then my head turned, and I made out a figure through the smoke, crouched in the corner. Jesmine. I recognized her even as little more than a hazy silhouette. She stared at me through the smoke, creeping forward as Raihn berated his soldier.

She took half a step closer, but I shook my head.

She hesitated, eyes narrowing, questioning it. But I shook my head again, harder this time, a wordless command: *Go. Now.*

Maybe we could take the Rishan, but if Bloodborn were here now, Jesmine and her people—my people—were about to be decimated.

She crept closer again, the smoke clearing enough for me to see the protest in her eyes—the unspoken, *What about you?*

I tried to wave her away. The motion was too much. My vision blurred. Darkened.

I didn't remember losing consciousness. But suddenly, I was flat on the ground, staring into Raihn's face as he leaned over me. He was saying something I couldn't make out. It didn't matter, because I was slipping away before the words left his lips.

I didn't want his eyes to follow me into unconsciousness.

But they did, anyway.

12

ORAYA

For the first time in weeks, I did not dream of Vincent.

Instead, I dreamed of Raihn, and the way his face looked as he died, and the way my blade felt sliding into his chest.

I dreamed it over, and over, and over again.

I OPENED my eyes to a familiar cerulean glass ceiling. Raihn's dead face faded away into scattered silver-painted stars.

I tried to move but my body didn't cooperate, rewarding me with a sharp pain in my side.

"Not yet."

My chest ached. It hurt to hear Raihn's voice. It took me a minute to muster up the courage to turn my head—I half expected to see him the way I saw him in my nightmares. Dead, my blade in his chest.

But no, Raihn was very much alive. He was beside my bed,

leaning over me. I realized that the sharp pain in my side was because he was dressing my wound, and—

Goddess.

I shifted uncomfortably as I realized that I was topless, save for the bandages wrapped around my chest.

Raihn chuckled. "You were at your most seductive."

I wished I had a barbed retort for that, but my brain felt like my thoughts were moving through sludge.

"You've been given some drugs," he said. "Give it a minute."

Mother, my head hurt.

I remembered the attack. Running to the armory. My blade pressed to Raihn's chest, for the second time.

You want to do it, so do it.

And I didn't. Couldn't. Even with his heart right there for the taking.

I could have ended all of this. Could have taken back my father's throne. Could have avenged his death.

I swallowed, or tried to. As if sensing it, Raihn finished securing the bandage to my side and then handed me a glass.

"Water," he said.

I stared at it, and he scoffed.

"What? You think this is when I'd poison you?"

Honestly? Yes. I'd escaped. I'd fought him. I could only assume that they didn't know my part in what had happened, or else I'd be chained up in a dungeon right now.

Raihn laughed softly—a sound so oddly warm I felt it run up my spine.

"That face," he said, shaking his head. "Just drink, alright?"

I was very, very thirsty. So I did.

"Amazing what a close call some foot soldier's arrow can be," he muttered.

Raihn was bandaged up, too. He winced a little as he stood— I took a little pride in that, at least. He'd been healed, and well, but the remnants of Nightfire burns remained on his cheeks, and stains of dark blood bloomed through the fabric around his torso from the gash I'd opened.

I swallowed and finally felt like I could speak.

"You don't have more important things to do than play nursemaid?"

"As always, you have such a strange way of saying 'Thank you.'"

"I'm just…"

Surprised.

He raised an eyebrow. "What if I told you all the nurses are afraid of you? The Nightfire queen who just tried to take down the Rishan army."

"I'd say that's smart of them."

Stupid of me to play along with this. This pretend version of what we'd been in the Kejari.

My head was killing me. I sat up, hissing an inhale at the pain that shot up my side. Raihn was right. That one soldier got a hell of a shot in.

"It was enhanced with blood magic," Raihn said, as if he could read my mind.

Fucking Bloodborn.

That final piece of what had happened—the Bloodborn reinforcements arriving—fell over me like a blanket of cold dread. Jesmine's men were well matched against the Rishan—an equal fight we might have won. But the Bloodborn tipped the scales. They were efficient and brutal.

Raihn stood at my bedchamber window, looking out over the nighttime cityscape of Sivrinaj. I wondered if perhaps he was staring at the Hiaj bodies now no doubt staked through the city walls.

He said nothing, so I said nothing. I wouldn't give him the satisfaction of asking.

He turned around after a long moment, staring at me, his hands in his pockets. He looked tired. None of his kingly finery. He looked just like he had when we'd shared an apartment in the Moon Palace. Familiar. The version of him I had thought I knew.

His face was hard, tired.

"I know you want to ask, so I'll tell you. We didn't capture any Hiaj. We cleared out a few dozen dead bodies. Just as many Rishan as Hiaj, which should be satisfying to you. Just as it should be satisfying to know that the armory was destroyed. We lost enough valuable weaponry that it'll take us the better part of a year to replenish the stores."

I tried not to have any reaction.

It wasn't satisfying. I'd sacrificed bodies we didn't have for this. It was something, but it was closer to a draw than the victory I'd craved.

And here I still was. Captive.

Captive… but, oddly, alive.

I frowned down at myself. At the bandages around me, then at the bottles of medicine on the bedside table.

"It would've been convenient for you to let me die," I said.

Raihn crossed his arms over his chest. His brow twitched. "Would've been convenient for you to kill me in that armory," he said simply. "Why didn't you? You had your shot."

Good question, little serpent, Vincent whispered. *Why? You had the perfect opening.*

The truth was, I didn't know what had stopped my hand. Or at least, I told myself I didn't know, because that was easier than acknowledging the uncomfortable possibilities.

I didn't answer.

Raihn's face shifted, sliding into seriousness. He looked out the window, as if lost in thought. It was an odd expression, like there was something he wanted to say, but couldn't—like a darker thought had just crossed his mind.

"There are some things we need to talk about," he said.

I didn't like the sound of that.

"Things like what?"

"Later." His eyes fell to me for a moment longer, then he broke our stare and went to the door.

"Rest. I'll be back in a bit to come get you."

"Get me?" I asked. "And bring me where?"

But he just replied, "Like I said. We have some important things to discuss."

And he was gone without giving me another glance.

RAIHN DID, as promised, come back a few hours later. I was sore and my head hurt fiercely, but I'd managed to get myself up and dressed. I wore my leathers, even though the stiff fabric against my still-tender wound made me wince.

Even when this castle had been Vincent's, I'd worn my leathers every day. I never allowed myself to forget that I was surrounded by predators, even in my own home. But lately, I'd been lax. Lazy. The beasts that circled me now were more bloodthirsty than ever, but I'd been so foolishly consumed with my own grief that I'd let myself flop around in silk and cotton, practically offering myself up to them.

No more.

When Raihn came to get me, he looked me up and down with a raised brow.

"Hm," he said.

"What?"

"Nothing. You just look ready for battle."

I gave him a flat glare as we started down the hall.

"Where are we going?" I asked.

"Just somewhere private to talk."

"My room isn't private?"

I couldn't quite figure out the strange look he gave me at that. "I'm not bringing Septimus to your room."

My brows leapt. I almost stopped walking.

"We're meeting with Septimus."

"Unfortunately."

I snuck a glance at his profile. He was staring straight ahead, face tense.

Unease stirred in my stomach. Something wasn't right here. Raihn wasn't going to execute me. If he was going to, he already

95

would have. He wouldn't have wasted the medicine or the time to heal me. Torture, though... torture was not out of the question. Maybe Raihn himself wouldn't do it. But Ketura certainly would, or any of his other generals, if they knew of my role in the armory attack. It was what any king would do—would *have* to do —if faced with a traitor inside their own house.

On instinct, my hands went to my hips. Of course, I had no blades.

Raihn didn't say another word as he led me down the hall, then down a set of stairs and into the next wing, where he opened a door at the end of the corridor.

It was a small space, maybe once a study or sitting room. It was hard to tell, because like most of the rooms in this castle, it had been stripped bare, the bookshelves now empty and not yet repopulated. A single round table sat at its center.

Septimus was there already, not bothering to rise when we entered. Vale stood nearby, his arms crossed, watching me the way a falcon eyed prey, and Cairis rose from his chair when the door opened.

Cairis smiled at me and pulled out one of the empty chairs across from Septimus. "Sit."

Septimus gave me a small smile that didn't reach his eyes as I obeyed.

Vale sat beside Cairis, but Raihn remained standing—behind me, and only a couple of feet from my chair, so I could feel his presence but not see him. It made me wildly uncomfortable.

Everyone was staring at me. I was used to being stared at, but not like this—like I was an object of curiosity.

Septimus placed something at the center of the table. A little cluster of shards of glass, stacked on top of each other, silver sigils etched into its surface.

Shit.

The device I'd found in Vincent's study.

"This probably looks familiar to you," Septimus said.

I tried very hard not to react.

I didn't speak, teeth gritted against the sudden certainty that

I was about to be tortured. This was why Raihn had kept me alive.

Behind me, his voice shivered down my spine.

"I don't think we need to ask stupid questions that we all know the answers to, right?" His voice was low, rough. Teasing, with a dark edge. "Oraya doesn't like games."

Septimus gave a weak shrug. "Fair. It's not a question, then, Highness. You *do* recognize this device. You recognize it because you used it."

Give them nothing, Vincent said.

I kept a careful grip on my nerves, my heartbeat. I was locked in a room with monsters. *Fear is a collection of physical responses.*

I could practically feel Raihn breathing behind me. I wished he would stand somewhere else.

"You don't even know what this is, do you?" Septimus said. "This mirror, my Queen, was created specifically for King Vincent. Your father."

I wondered if hearing those words—even hearing Vincent's name—would ever stop aching.

"It's a communication device, and a very useful one, as it can be used to look in on certain individuals no matter where they are in Obitraes—perhaps even anywhere in the world, even if you don't know their location. An excellent way to keep discreet communication in times of war. Very powerful. Rare. Some poor sorcerer toiled over this for a long time." Amber-threaded, silver eyes crinkled with that perpetual charming smirk. "Vincent likely gave his blood to make this thing."

"And?" I said, coldly.

"And," Septimus said, "*you* were able to use it."

"I don't know what you mean," I said.

His laugh was lower now, colder.

"We don't need to pretend."

And there was just something about the way he said it…

Something about the snide little tone to his voice that made me think of the two open locks to my room.

Vincent's study, the only open door in the entire wing.

And this device, sitting right there, ready to be found.

Would Vincent ever have left such a valuable object out on his desk? Even in the throes of warfare? *Especially* in the throes of warfare?

Watch that face of yours, Vincent whispered to me, but it was too late. The sparkle of satisfaction in Septimus's eyes said he saw my realization.

"Every bet I've placed on you has been a winning one, dove," he said. "Over and over again."

Raihn abruptly stepped out from behind me, crossing the table to stand across from me. His hands clasped behind his back, his face hard despite the smile at his lips—a strangely joyless expression.

"You're lucky, princess," he said. "It turns out, you're not just a traitor. You're also useful."

I'd been manipulated. Was Raihn a part of that, then? Using my grief and my captivity against me? Of course he was. After everything, that shouldn't have been surprising. It certainly shouldn't have hurt.

"Most offspring aren't able to use blooded instruments of their parents, or vice versa," Septimus said. He ran his fingertip back and forth along the glass shard, spreading black blood along its edge. Unlike when I had done the same, the device didn't react at all.

I watched it with my jaw set, far too transfixed. I wanted to take his hand off for rubbing his tainted Bloodborn blood on my father's property.

"The fact that you were able to actually use this, and communicate information to your general... that's unusual and impressive," he went on. "Perhaps it's because of your Heir Mark. Who can truly understand the magic of the gods?"

I didn't know why it made me so uncomfortable to hear this. To think about all the connections I still had to Vincent—the connections that he had told me my entire life didn't exist. Part of me wanted to cling to whatever I had left of him, wear it as a badge of pride.

Another part of me hated him for it.

I shut those complicated thoughts away. "So you plan to what, cut me open and start dripping my blood all over Vincent's possessions? As if I haven't had vampires lusting after my blood my entire life. Creative."

Septimus chuckled, the way one would laugh at the antics of a small child.

"Not *all* of Vincent's possessions. Just some of them."

"Your father had a lot of secrets," Raihn said quietly, in a tone that meant so much more than the words alone.

My biting response died on my tongue, because even I couldn't argue with the ugly truth of that. Too many secrets.

Then Septimus said something that I truly—down to my bones—was not expecting.

"You're familiar, I assume, with the story of Alarus and Nyaxia?"

I—what?

"Of course I'm familiar," I said. "Is there a soul in Obitraes who isn't?"

What the fuck could that possibly have to do with anything?

"I don't like to judge," Septimus said, lifting one shoulder. "So you must know, then, that Alarus is the only major god ever to have been killed."

"Get to the point, Septimus," Raihn grumbled. But even as he scolded Septimus, he was watching me.

Septimus raised his hands, in a lazy *fair enough.*

"We're vampires. We know death better than any other. And we all know that any being that dies leaves something behind. Bones. Blood. Magic. *Offspring.*" Septimus gave me a knowing half smile. "And that goes for gods, too. As what we leave behind holds some of our power, so, too, do a god's remains."

Despite myself, my curiosity was getting the better of me, just because what he was saying was so... bizarre. "You're talking about finding Alarus's... corpse?"

"I think Alarus is much more than a corpse by now. I think his remains, whatever they are, have spread throughout Obitraes."

"What makes you think so?"

He smiled. "I found some. In the House of Blood."

I didn't even have words. My lips parted and nothing came out.

"Teeth," he added, answering the question I was too shocked to ask. "Just a few."

Teeth?

I choked out, "And what the fuck does one do with the teeth of the God of Death?"

"Not much, perhaps. But we could do a lot with his blood."

"His blood."

This was ridiculous.

"Yes," Septimus said simply. "I suspect that some of it remains in the House of Night, and that it could be very, very useful if found. And I suspect your dear old father knew that, too." He leaned across the table, long fingers intertwined, smirk slowly spreading into a grin. "I think he knew it, and he harnessed it, and he hid it. And now *you* get to find it for us."

I stared at him for a long moment. It was so ludicrous I couldn't even find words—this idea that Vincent, ever practical, ever logical, might have once searched for fucking *god blood*.

"Do you actually want me to justify this with an answer?" I said.

"The Nightborn King once had a bit of a reputation. An affinity for *seers*." Septimus placed a long emphasis on the word *seers*. The meaning of it wasn't lost on me.

Nyaxia's magic offered little in the way of seering, though it was said some Shadowborn sorcerers could do something close. So when vampires were interested in magic beyond Nyaxia's capabilities, they had to work with humans who followed other gods—usually Acaeja, the Goddess of the Unknown, and the only god of the White Pantheon to have a somewhat civil relationship with Nyaxia.

Some Obitraen kings through the years kept pet seers, whether of Acaeja or some other god. There were many useful things a king could do with such magic. But I couldn't imagine Vincent being one of those rulers—a vampire so desperate for power that he'd throw coins at some gray magic wielder. He wasn't especially religious, but he was also nothing if not loyal to Nyaxia and the power that she gave him.

"I still don't understand what you're asking me to—"

"We aren't asking anything," Septimus said. Downright politely, which made me even angrier. "If Vincent found this god blood, he no doubt would have safeguards in place to make sure that only he could use it. Which means that we need you."

This was all fucking outlandish. I didn't know why they bothered asking me.

I crossed my arms, lifting my chin. "I refuse."

"Step back and look at this situation, Oraya," Raihn said. His voice was cold, calm—unlike him. He leaned closer, his palms pressed to the table. I couldn't look away from his eyes, rust-red.

"You betrayed the King of the House of Night," he said. "You told the Hiaj general to attack the armory that night. You acted against your own kingdom. That's not a small thing."

Acted against my own kingdom.

Those words, and the haughty tone in which he said them, pissed me off.

I rose, slowly, and leaned across the table to match his movements, looking straight into his eyes.

"Is it *treason*," I spat, lip curling, "to act against a usurper? Or is that just an Heir defending her crown?"

Raihn's mouth twitched, just a little. "Good question, princess," he said. "Depends on who wins."

There he is, I thought.

This was real.

Then his smirk disappeared, that mask of rage back. The mask of the Nightborn King.

"Make no mistake, you're lucky to be alive," he said. "And

the only reason we have to keep you that way is that blood of yours. So think long and hard about turning down this offer."

"I don't need to. You want me to open my wrists for you and give you my father's blood so you can go find a weapon to wipe out my people?"

The thought sickened me. Actually sickened me.

"You don't have a choice," Raihn said, and this time, I almost laughed in his face.

Because with that little slip of his mask moments ago, now I knew—*this* was the act, and I wasn't afraid of what Raihn pretended to be.

"No," I said. "I will not do it. If you want to kill me and take my blood that way, then fine."

Silence for several long seconds, as we stared each other down.

Finally, Septimus chuckled.

"It's been a few weeks of high emotions," he said. "Give her some time to think it over, Highness. It's always so much less fun to force."

13

ORAYA

Raihn knocked at my door just a few hours before dawn.

I knew it was him right away. I'd spent the rest of the night after that conversation with Septimus waiting for him to show up. That wasn't the end of the fight. Any minute, I told myself, and he'd be at my door, trying to force me into this.

I was ready for it.

I didn't get up, of course, when he knocked. Prisoner or not, I didn't feel like rising to meet my own punishment.

Click, click, click, click, as the locks released. The door swung open. Raihn stood there wearing a dark cloak, a pile of fabric over one arm.

He tossed it on the bed—a matching cape. "Put it on," he said.

I didn't. "Why?"

"Because I said so."

"That's a shit reason."

"Ix's tits, princess. Put on the damned cloak."

I narrowed my eyes at him, confused and trying not to show it. A few hours ago, he'd been all but threatening to torture me.

"I'm not sure why I'd go anywhere with you or do anything

you ask me to," I said curtly. "When you've already made it so clear you'll just force me to do whatever you want."

He sighed. "We can't have this conversation here. Just put on the cloak and come on," he said, raised his hood, and left the room.

I sat there for a few long seconds, then cursed to myself under my breath. Mother damn that human curiosity.

I put on the cloak and followed Raihn. He'd gone next door, to his chamber. He held the door open for me, then closed it behind us.

I had never been in this room. The apartment had been empty when I lived here as a child—Vincent would never let anyone but himself so close to me, considering the fragility of my human skin and the draw of my human blood. There were only two chambers in this wing, so keeping this one unoccupied left me isolated—safe.

It was a mirror image of my own—a small sitting room, a washroom, a bedchamber. I eyed the open door to Raihn's bedchamber—much messier than I would have expected, the sheets and blankets a pile on the bed—and tried not to think about the fact that our rooms shared a wall.

Raihn strode to the other end of the sitting room, where two large windows stretched to the ceiling. He unlatched one of them, letting it fly open. A rush of dry desert air rustled his hair around his face as he climbed up on the sill, turned to me, and offered his hand. With a puff of smoke, his wings unfurled.

I didn't move.

"Come on," he said.

"Absolutely not."

"We both know you're going to agree. So let's skip the part where we go back and forth about it. We don't have a lot of time."

"Are you asking me or are you commanding me?"

His mouth tightened. "Can I really command you to do anything? If you really want to go back to your room and sit there by yourself, you can do that too. Your choice."

He pulled his hood up a bit more, the shadow over the top half of his face highlighting the smirk on his mouth, the strength of his jaw, the light pooling in the lines of the scar on his left cheek.

Mother damn him, I wished he wasn't right, but he was.

I approached warily. He reached for me, then hesitated.

"May I?" he asked, his voice a little rough.

I nodded, trying very hard to look nonchalant.

It wasn't the first time Raihn had flown with me. But it was the first time since... the end of the Kejari. The thought of being that close to him, the thought of allowing him to hold me... it...

Fear is a collection of physical responses, I told myself, trying desperately to slow my rapid heartbeat before he could sense it.

Even though this was a whole different kind of fear than the adrenaline rush of bodily danger. Harder to numb.

I stepped onto the sill, and he pulled me into his arms, one tight across my back, the other under my thighs. I wrapped my arms around his neck in a way that felt far more natural than it should have.

He smelled the same. Like the desert and the rush of the sky. The warmth of his body felt the same, too—firm and stable.

For a brief, terrible moment, we paused just like that. His muscles tightened, as if struggling with the instinct to pull me closer, to make this a real embrace. Such a subtle movement, but I still felt it, because my awareness of him was so agonizingly acute.

My attempts to slow my heart had failed, and Raihn undoubtedly heard it. My eyes fell to his throat—right at the angle of his jaw, where muscles flexed as he swallowed and turned his head slightly to look at me.

I didn't want to meet his eyes, because that would have put our faces far too close together.

His thumb rubbed that single circle on my upper back.

"You're safe," he murmured. "Alright?"

He sounded a little sad.

And then he hurled us into the night sky.

He brought us, to my surprise, to the human districts. He kept us out of sight during the flight and landed in the yard of an abandoned building. As soon as he set me down, I took two steps away from him, eager to put space between us.

Our hoods had fallen back in the wind. Raihn casually replaced his and started walking to the main streets. "This way."

"Where are we?"

I didn't recognize this part of town. I'd been all over the districts, but this was near the outskirts of Sivrinaj's borders—far even for us, during our nighttime training sessions.

"I want to show you something." He glanced over his shoulder, the hood obscuring all but his profile. "Oh. And I brought these for you. In case you want to have some fun while you're here."

He held out two sheathed weapons—blades.

Shock stole my steps for a moment, then I had to half-run to catch up to him. I snatched the weapons from his hands in case he thought better of it.

I unsheathed them. Watched the light play over the carvings on the black steel—Nightborn steel. The good shit.

Not just any blades. *My* blades.

I'd thought it would feel right to have these in my hands again, like being reunited with an old friend. Instead, I had to brace against the sudden, visceral memory of what I had done with these very weapons the last time I'd held them.

"Why would you give me these?"

"I figured you'll need them. No poison in them, though. I haven't had time to track any down, but maybe we should call it a precaution."

Raihn was walking fast. I didn't have much time to admire them, stumbling along as I affixed the sheaths to my belt while keeping up with him.

Leathers. Weapons. Human districts. It was all eerily familiar, and yet, so wildly different.

We emerged onto a denser street, little clay buildings packed together like crooked teeth. "Keep that hood up," Raihn muttered, though there was no one around, and crossed the street to a rickety building with four stories that all seemed to be a little misaligned, like a stack of unsteady bricks. A single lantern swung in the breeze at the door, the suggestion of light seeping between curtained window panes. Raihn opened the door without knocking, and I followed.

It led us into a small, dim lobby, with a single desk and a narrow staircase. A rotund, middle-aged human man dozed at the desk, an empty glass of very pungent-smelling alcohol drawing amber circles on scattered papers.

Raihn ignored him, and I followed his lead as he went up the stairs. At the top floor, he reached into his pocket and produced a key. Apparently, the lock didn't work very well anymore, so he grumbled through three attempts before the door finally swung open.

He gave me a sly smile beneath the hood. "After you, princess."

Tentatively, I stepped into the room.

It was an apartment. A stark contrast to the one we had just left in the castle—the entirety of the place was smaller than the bedroom alone there, the only furniture a single small bed, a dresser, and one tiny desk that I suspected Raihn probably couldn't even fit at. It was clearly occupied, though—the desk held books and papers, one half-open dresser drawer revealed a glimpse of crumpled fabric, and the washroom lantern was still lit. The bed was a little messy, like someone had slept in it recently and made it very hurriedly.

I walked around the room slowly, brow furrowed.

"Who lives here?"

Raihn closed the door and latched it behind us.

"I do."

I halted mid-stride. My brows lurched.

He chucked softly. "It's still satisfying to shock you. Fine. Maybe 'living here' is a bit of an exaggeration." He unhooked his cloak, tossed it onto the bed, and then fell backwards onto it with a grunt of satisfaction. "It's... somewhere private to go."

I thought of all those days that I never heard Raihn's footsteps return to his rooms.

"You sleep here?"

"Sometimes." A pause, then, "Sometimes I can't... sometimes I just want to get away from that place."

I watched him practically deflate onto the bed. He did immediately seem more at ease here. Like the remnants of whatever mask he wore within the walls of the castle had finally fallen free.

I didn't want to see this version of Raihn—the version that reminded me far too much of the man I'd...

I cleared my throat, stuffed my hands into my pockets, and wandered the perimeter.

"No one knows about it," Raihn said.

"No one but me," I corrected.

I could hear the smile in his voice. "No one but you."

"Stupid of you."

"Maybe."

"Since I'm a traitor and all."

"Mmm." The bed creaked as Raihn sat back up. I turned around to see him giving me a stare that made me jolt. All seriousness.

"We need to talk," he said, "and we needed to do it somewhere I knew no one else would hear us."

"I thought you said everything you needed to say. Or Septimus did, at least."

My words were pointed, the accusation clear.

"I say what I need to say, in front of them."

"You manipulated me," I snapped. "You've been playing games with me since the beginning."

Raihn's face hardened.

"You committed an act of war, Oraya."

I let out a choked laugh. "*I* committed an act of war? *Me?*"

This was a mistake. I shouldn't even be here. I was armed now. I could—

He winced, then raised his hands. "I—let's not. This isn't what I'm here for."

"Then what?"

He stood, went to the dresser, and pulled something out of the middle drawer—something long, wrapped in fabric. He lay the object over the desk beside me and unwrapped it.

My heart caught in my throat.

The Taker of Hearts. Vincent's sword.

It was an incredible weapon—he'd had it for centuries, and never refuted or confirmed the legends surrounding it. That it was god-forged. That it was cursed. That it was blessed. That he'd carved out a little chunk of his own heart to have it made. He'd told me these legends when I was a child, sometimes—always with a completely serious face but a glint of amusement in his eye.

Legends aside, the reality was impressive enough. The weapon was incredibly powerful, enhancing Vincent's already-significant magical strength. It was his and his alone, rejecting all other wielders. I used to joke that the sword was Vincent's true greatest love. For most of my life, I think I believed it.

Now, the image of Vincent's bloodied face, straining to look at me in his final breaths, cut through my mind.

I loved you from the first moment.

My chest was very, very tight.

Raihn stepped back, leaning against the wall, as if to give me space alone with it. "You can pick it up," he said—oddly gently. "Just be careful. Hurts like a bitch if you touch the hilt too long."

I unsheathed the sword and lay it over the desk. It was light, a slender and elegant rapier. The blade was bright red, swirls and sigils carved into its length that matched those on my own. The hilt was made of Nightsteel, forming delicate spirals around the handguard, which resembled the bones of Hiaj wings.

I stared at it for a long time, not trusting myself to speak. A slow-rising tide of grief and anger swelled inside me.

Raihn had been keeping this sword. My father's most prized possession, now owned by the man who had killed him.

"Why are you showing me this?"

Surely he couldn't think it was some kind of sentimental peace offering.

"Could you wield it?"

I blinked in surprise and turned to Raihn. I briefly questioned if I'd heard him right.

"No," I said. "No one can wield it but him."

"But no one could use the mirror but him, either. And you used that."

"That's different. This is…"

His.

Vincent had warned me many times against even touching the weapon. For all the obvious reasons one would warn a child against such a thing, in the beginning, but later because he made it very clear it would be dangerous for me to even hold it. The weapon could only be wielded by him, and what was painful to vampires could very well be deadly to me.

"Why?" I asked pointedly. "Is this another thing you want me to do for Septimus?"

The shadow of anger that passed over Raihn's face was fleeting, but powerful. "No."

"Then why would you hand me a weapon like this and want me to use it?"

After I'd acted against him. After he had made it so clear the role I was intended to play.

Handing me this weapon—hell, even letting me know that it still existed—was a downright stupid move.

He said simply, "Because you're right."

I'd told myself so many times that I'd never let Raihn surprise me again. And yet, here we were.

"Because the things you said in Vincent's office that night— they're true," he said. "There is no excuse for what I have allowed the Bloodborn to do to this kingdom. Septimus is preying on both of us. I allowed myself to be manipulated into an alliance that I didn't want, into a deal I can't get out of, and now here we fucking are."

He paced closer, step by step, and I didn't move away. I glanced to the floor, uncomfortable, when he spoke of being forced into his alliance, but I still saw his face, anyway—that moment when Angelika had been ready to kill me, and I'd watched Raihn look up into the stands and nod.

Another paradox I couldn't reconcile. Raihn had murdered my father and taken my kingdom and imprisoned me, but he had done it all to save my life.

"I know I'm right," I said. "And?"

A faint smile of amusement, gone in seconds. "And I want you to help me do something about it."

"If this is another speech about—"

"No. This is about blood, Oraya." He didn't blink. His eyes didn't leave mine. "This is about getting the Bloodborn out of our fucking kingdom."

"Your allies. The ones you're relying on to keep your throne."

"Allies," he scoffed. And there was something about the way he said it, under his breath, that made a realization crash through me.

Septimus had manipulated me to test his theory, knowing I would never cooperate with him. And until now, I'd assumed that Raihn had been right beside him in that—maybe even that he had instigated it.

Now, I was suddenly certain that I had been wrong.

"You didn't know," I said. "You didn't know about any of this, either. The mirror. The armory attack. The god blood."

The look on Raihn's face confirmed my theory long before he spoke.

Because there had been Rishan forces at the armory, but no Bloodborn. If Raihn had been involved, there should have been many more Rishan troops at the base that night. But they were as unprepared as we were. He ended up losing just as many soldiers as I did.

Only Septimus had come out of it all unscathed—with both

the Rishan and the Hiaj weakened, and his theory confirmed.

"He's a snake," Raihn muttered. "He didn't tell me about any of it until afterwards. I showed him what he wanted to see. Threw my dick around. Shouted. Big, stupid warrior shit. And then I went along with him, after giving him just enough resistance to make it believable."

Raihn and his performances.

"I made a deal I can't get out of," he went on. "I've granted Septimus that much. But... regardless of whether we find what he wants, he may not even be the one who can use it. And there are other things in the House of Night that are just as powerful. But to wield them, I'll need your help."

I scoffed, and he raised his palms.

"Easy, viper. Let me finish," he said, before I could speak. "Help me find the god blood. Help me fulfill Septimus's ridiculous quest. But then, I want you to help me use it to betray him and throw those Bloodborn bastards out of this kingdom once and for all. And after that, you're free to do whatever you want."

I scoffed again. "Whatever I—"

"*Whatever you want.*"

I didn't mean to look surprised. Mother damn my face.

He laughed softly. "You never believed me, but I never intended to keep you captive. I'm asking you—not forcing you—to help me. And after that, you have my word that we're done."

"What is your word worth?"

"Not much. It's seen better days. A little banged-up. But it's all I have to offer, unfortunately."

I stared down at my father's sword. He'd died with it soaking up his blood mere feet from him in the colosseum sands.

The House of Night was my father's kingdom.

It was *my* kingdom.

Raihn had lied to me so many times. And yet...

I found myself considering this.

"Won't Septimus suspect this?" I asked. "He has eyes everywhere."

"No vampire has eyes here." He gestured to the dim, dusty

room—distinctly human. "You're right, though. We'll have to be careful. Make sure he sees only what he expects to see. I'll play the part of the brute king. You play the part of the prisoner wife who hates him."

"That will be easy," I said. "I do hate you."

I'd thought those words to myself countless times—*I hate him, I hate him, I hate him*—and yet, when they slipped over my tongue, they tasted rancid, bitter for all the ways they were true and untrue. Because they should not be anything *but* true, when I was standing before the man who murdered my father.

Raihn's face went still, just for a split second, like he was collecting himself after a blow.

And then he smiled, easy and comfortable.

"Oh, I know," he said. "That's for the better. You aren't much of an actress."

He extended his hand. "But," he added, softly, seriously, "you are one hell of an ally."

Ally.

A lifetime ago, he had offered me an alliance. I knew it was a mistake to take it then, too.

But I was powerless now, just as I was then. A human in a world of vampires. An Heir with no teeth. A daughter with no way to avenge her father.

Raihn was offering me power. More power than I'd ever dreamed of wielding.

And power was the currency of revenge.

I took Raihn's hand. It was warm and rough, and much larger than my own. He folded his fingers around mine, just slightly. Even his touch felt different now—like all the magic that pulsed beneath the surface of our skin called to and repelled each other, as if recognizing its natural enemy.

Raihn was stronger than ever. But so was I. And with the power that Raihn talked about—the power that belonged to me by birthright—I would be unstoppable.

He was offering me everything I needed to destroy him.

"Deal," I said.

14

RAIHN

I do hate you.

I knew Oraya hated me. Who could possibly blame her for that? I didn't know why it bothered me so much to hear it. Bothered me enough that it overshadowed my victory.

"Victory."

I'd gotten her to agree to something she essentially had no choice but to do. And I wasn't stupid—I knew that there was a good chance that the entire time, she'd be waiting for her moment to kill me. I knew that perhaps that's exactly what she told herself as she took my hand and agreed to our deal.

It was a gamble for both of us.

But she'd had her blade right there in that armory, right at my heart, and she hadn't taken the shot.

That was something.

And the truth was, my… complicated personal feelings for Oraya aside, I needed her. Without her, I had no chance of getting out from under Septimus's grasp. Maybe a small, pathetic part of me had also been grateful for that—grateful to have any excuse to have her as an ally again, even a reluctant one.

Oraya didn't say anything as we flew back to my chambers.

It was embarrassing how much carrying her reminded me of what our relationship used to be before I razed it. I could feel how terrified she was the entire time. That heart rate, her breathing, the heat at her skin.

All the comfort we'd built, destroyed.

As soon as I let her down at my window, she backed away from me. I wondered if she knew she had a pattern to the way she did that—three long, quick steps back, like she couldn't wait to put as much distance between us as possible.

I remained on the ledge, relishing the breeze against the backs of my wings for a little longer. I let Oraya back all the way across the room before I stepped inside. She didn't want me any closer, and I'd respect that.

"We'll need to get started right away," I said. "Tomorrow, probably. As soon as I let them all know that you've agreed."

"Them?" she said.

"Vale, Cairis, Ketura. Septimus and his goons."

It was hard to miss the way she stiffened at the mention of all those names.

"They won't bother you," I said. "I'll handle your training."

Her brows lowered. "Training?"

"What, did you think you were going to wield legendary god power and overthrow the most vicious vampire house without getting back into shape?"

Her brows lowered again. "I'm in great shape. Don't know about you, though. That fight was a little too easy."

Ix's tits, it was hard not to laugh at that face.

I raised my palms.

"Fine. I admit it. You keep me on my toes, too. I've never been better than I was when I was with you."

That sentence tasted disgustingly earnest rolling off my tongue.

Oraya heard it, too, shifting uncomfortably.

"One more thing," she said.

"What's that?"

"You're going to stop locking me in my room."

My brows rose. "Oh, I am?"

"Yes. You are."

"And why is that?"

"Because we're supposedly allies again, and allies don't lock each other up every night."

"I have some allies I certainly wish I could lock up," I remarked.

"You can frame it as a concession you had to make to get me to do this willingly. That's reasonable. And true."

My brows rose. "Is it?"

"It is."

Leaving Oraya unguarded was a bad idea for a lot of reasons. The obvious ones, of course—because she was the Hiaj Heir, and had acted against me less than a week ago, and had every reason to sneak around gathering information and finding ways to pass it off to the people who were trying to kill mine.

But none of those reasons bothered me as much as the others —not protecting my crown from Oraya, but protecting Oraya from my crown.

"This castle isn't a safe place, princess," I said. "Not even for me. *Especially* not for me. And that goes double for you. You sure you really want that?"

"You keep telling me that I'm a queen, not a prisoner. So prove it. No one locks queens up in their bedchambers."

Neculai had locked Nessanyn up.

That was a sudden, unwelcome thought.

I pushed it away, deciding that this was a fair point. Besides, everything with Oraya was a risk. Always had been.

"Fine," I said, with a half-shrug. "Done. No more locks."

Her shoulders lowered slightly with relief. I liked seeing that.

"Then I'm going to bed," she said.

"Good. You'll need the rest before we get started."

She went to the door and opened it. And before I could stop myself, the word was coming up my throat.

"Oraya."

She turned back. Even from across the room, her steel gaze cut deep. A pang pulsed in my chest.

I didn't even know what I'd intended to say.

Thank you?

You won't regret this?

The former was patronizing. The second was a promise I couldn't make. I'd lied to Oraya enough. I didn't want to do it again.

Finally, I settled on, "I always meant it. The offer I made you."

There is no one I would rather have ruling this kingdom beside me than you.

I saw in her face that she knew exactly what I was talking about.

"I know," she said, after a long moment, and left.

AFTER ORAYA WAS GONE, I spent a few minutes standing at the window, watching the sun rise over Sivrinaj, the smoky sky turning purple, then pink. The familiar burning at my skin started slow at first, as it always did, and it was almost fully dawn by the time I reluctantly pulled away.

A message had been left for me while I was gone. I picked up the parchment and read it. For a long time, I just stared at it. Then I cursed, shoved it into my pocket, and threw open the door.

I went downstairs, all the way down to the guest wing, staring straight ahead until I reached the one closed door. I pounded on it, not bothering to be polite, continuing even when there was no answer.

"Gods, have a little patience!" a light, cheerful voice came from inside, with a rush of footsteps.

The door swung open.

The moment it did, I said gruffly, "*You* aren't supposed to be—"

But I barely even got those words out before Mische's face split into a grin that I saw for all of half a second before she threw herself at me.

And damn if it wasn't good to see a friendly face.

Mische threw her arms around my neck and hugged me like she'd thought she'd never see me again. And of course, I hugged her back, because what was I, a monster?

Her hair had gotten longer, now near her shoulders. The caramel curls still smelled like sweat and the desert from her travel.

"You aren't supposed to be here," I said. "Told you not to come."

I tried to sound very mean and failed.

"Oh, fuck you," Mische said affectionately, the way someone would say, *I missed you too, idiot.*

15

RAIHN

"It was boring just wandering around by myself. What else was I supposed to do?"

"Stay out of trouble. Stay away from the capital of a civil war. Go find somewhere safe and relaxing to be."

Mische's nose scrunched. *"Safe* and *relaxing?"*

She said this like the thought was ridiculous, and to be fair, anyone who had met Mische even once would know that it was. Mische was the opposite of safe and relaxing. Mische was so impulsive and reckless that sometimes, it genuinely scared me.

Once she finally released me from her chokehold of an embrace, she'd dragged me into her sitting room. She was wearing a dusty white shirt and trousers, still travel-stained. But if she was tired, she didn't show it, curling up in an armchair and drawing her knees up to her chest as she demanded, wide-eyed, that I tell her everything. She'd heard the biggest news, she said, but she wanted to get it all from me.

There was not a single person in the world I was more comfortable with than Mische. She'd seen me at my worst. And yet... telling her the entire story of what had happened in the final trial of the Kejari and beyond... it was hard. I hadn't collected all the events in one place like that before. My eyes fell to a particular spot on the carpet as I told her, as sparsely as I could, what had happened.

By the time I was done, Mische's excitement had turned to such raw, eviscerating sadness that, when I flicked my gaze back to her, it made me choke a laugh.

She looked like she was near tears.

"Ix's tits, Mish. It's not that dramatic."

But Mische just unwound her legs, crossed the room, and gave me one more long hug—this one not the puppy-excited squeeze of a reunion, but the quiet embrace of a supportive friend.

I wriggled away from her grasp.

"I'm alright. And you stink."

"You can't lie to me," she muttered, then sat, cross-legged, on the floor, her chin propped in her hands.

"Seriously, Mische…" I picked at my fingernail. I wasn't sure if the blood still stuck underneath it was someone else's or my own from my incessant picking, but I couldn't bring myself to leave it alone. "Things are rough here. You should go back to the country."

It was the easy thing for me to say, for me to push Mische out of Sivrinaj, and yet a loud part of myself cursed at me for even saying the words—even knowing, of course, that she wouldn't listen.

I'd missed her. No, that was an understatement. She was my only family, blood or no. There were two people alive right now who, I felt, for better or for worse, really knew me. Oraya and Mische. When Oraya looked at me, it was all accusation—*I see what you really are.* But when Mische looked at me, it was affection. And I'd missed that, but it was also uncomfortable. Was always harder to play the roles I needed to play when Mische was around, knowing me too well.

"It was boring as shit out there. Besides, did you really think that I would just leave you here alone?" A wrinkle deepened between her brows. "Or her?"

Her. Oraya.

Despite it all, it warmed my heart a bit to know how fond Mische had grown of Oraya. It was like she'd known, right from the beginning, how important she would become. I'd always wondered if Mische had a bit of mind magic in her. Just a touch of it. Those things weren't in the domain of Atroxus, but her empathy was a bit uncanny.

I felt like I needed Mische, and I hated that. But maybe Oraya needed her even more than I did, right now.

"Mm," I said, vocalizing none of this.

"Things are bad?"

I thought of Oraya's ragged sobs in the middle of the day, when she thought no one could hear her. Thought of the empty nothingness on her face for weeks.

Thought of her voice — *I do hate you.*

"Yes," I said. "Things are bad."

The concession was bitter with regret.

I'd long ago given up on some image of myself as a morally decent person. I'd killed hundreds with my own hands over the years. Thousands indirectly, as a result of my actions in the last Kejari or this one. I'd done what was necessary to survive. I tried not to beat myself up about it.

But I would always regret this. Breaking Oraya. That was a sin that I'd never be able to atone for.

A long silence. Then Mische said, softly, "I'm just... really, really glad that you're not dead, Raihn."

I laughed a little, but she snapped, "Not a joke. I mean it. What were you thinking?"

I wasn't sure *I* was glad I wasn't dead. When Oraya had killed me, I'd felt certain that I was doing the right thing. Giving Oraya the power she needed to seize her potential. Giving the House of Night a clean start. No messy alliances with the Blood-born. No complicated pasts.

That had seemed worth dying for in that moment. The dying, after all, wasn't the hard part. The coming back was where all the mess started.

I just said, too casually, "I wasn't really doing much thinking," even though it was a blatant lie.

Her brow furrowed. "But you worked so hard for this."

I had to clench my jaw to keep from saying the truth.

For this? No.

I'd entered the Kejari because Mische had. Because she'd forced my hand. Because one day, when we were traveling, she'd caught me on a particularly bad night, and I'd told her all of it—the truth of who I was and the scar on my back, the things I'd never uttered aloud to another person.

Every emotion painted over Mische's face, and that night, I'd watched her sadness for me, and then her confusion, and then, the thing that actually hurt: the excitement.

"You," she'd breathed, eyes lighting up, "are the *Heir of the Rishan line* and you aren't doing *anything* about it? Do you have any idea what you could *do?*"

That had fucking killed me. The *hope*.

We'd gotten into a fight that night—one of our worst, even after years of constant companionship. The next night, Mische had disappeared. I'd been beside myself by the time she returned, nearly at daybreak, and she'd showed me her hand: her blood offering scar.

"We're entering the Kejari," she had said, smugly. Like she'd just signed us up for a painting class or a city tour.

I hadn't been so angry in years. I did everything I could trying to find a way to get her out of it. But in the end, I ended up there right beside her, just like she knew I would.

After my initial outburst that first night, I never told her how I felt about that. I held that discomfort in a tight knot in my chest, buried deep.

It was hard to be angry at Mische.

But harder than the anger was the concern.

It was no small act, to enter the Kejari. I thought often—unwillingly—about Mische, and the decision she made, and the way that sheer fucking luck had saved her life.

Only one person could win the Kejari. What had Mische's plan been, if things had unfolded differently?

I didn't like to think about that.

I tore my eyes from Mische's accusatory stare, and they drifted to the hand she had propped over her knee, and the burn scars barely visible under the fabric of her sleeve.

If she saw that look, she ignored it, instead cocking her head and giving me a light, reassuring smile. "Don't look so depressed," she said. "It'll turn out. I know it will. It's just hard right now, but it's good that you're here."

"Mm." If only the truth was as easy as Mische's optimistic platitudes. I gave her a sidelong glance. "And how've you been?"

"Me?" Her face went serious for a minute, before she gave me a carefree shrug. "Oh, you know me. I'm always good."

I knew her, alright. Knew her well enough to know when she was lying. And to know when not to push.

I reached over and rustled her hair, making her wrinkle her nose and jerk away.

"It's too long," she said. "I've got to cut it."

"I like it. Change looks good on you."

She scowled. Then she caught my eye and the expression melted into a grin.

"Caught you," she said. "You're happy I'm here."

"Never," I said.

Fine, she had me. Fucking guilty.

16

ORAYA

aihn was true to his word. After that, the door was no longer locked. I wasn't about to fall all over myself with the benevolence of this gift—I had no doubt that guards were still keeping their eyes on me. Still… I liked freedom. The next night, I walked the castle halls by myself. Guards and soldiers gave me strange looks, but no one bothered me. It felt uncomfortable in a way I couldn't pinpoint.

Maybe it was because the castle already looked so different. It was all a mess, still. Then again, I couldn't help but contrast it to the decay that I'd seen when I had walked these halls during the Kejari—when I'd noticed for the first time the stagnant decay lurking beneath my home.

No one could call this place stagnant now.

I paused at the balcony that overlooked the feast hall. It was one of the few rooms that hadn't been moved much. The tables were still in the same arrangement. The furniture hadn't been changed.

For a moment, I saw the sea of brutality Vincent had shown me during our final argument, his fingernails digging into my arm as he pushed me against this very railing—forcing me to look down upon the humans below, slumped over those tables like drained livestock.

I shuddered and turned away.

Training. That was what I needed.

Raihn was right—I was out of practice. I'd felt that when we fought at the armory, and the way my muscles ached the next day was a lingering reminder.

I turned around and paused, staring down the hallway before me.

All at once, it hit me why it had felt so strange to walk these corridors.

Because I'd never been allowed to before.

Vincent may not have put locks on my door, but his command was more than enough to stop me from leaving—and he made those expectations very clear. Yes, I snuck out, but that was in the middle of the day, creeping around like a little shadow, shrinking from every set of footsteps.

Never before had I ever been able to move about this castle freely. Never.

That was... a strange realization.

"Isn't it nice to see you out and about?"

I tried very hard not to show that I'd startled, and failed. I turned to see Septimus bowing his head in apology. "Sorry. Didn't mean to scare you."

It sure seemed like he did, the way he slunk around like that.

"I'm glad you came around," he said. "I heard you've agreed to help us on our little mission."

"You say that like I had a choice."

He lifted one shoulder in a half shrug. "Still. Better this way. Forcing you would have been difficult for everyone. I expect especially difficult for your husband."

I hated it when people referred to Raihn that way. For the first time in my life, I was grateful for my too-expressive face. The sneer of disgust that flitted over the bridge of my nose before I could stop it.

I had a role to play, after all.

I'm the brute king, and you're the prisoner wife who hates me.

Septimus chuckled. "I wouldn't want to be on the wrong end of *that*," he said. He reached into his pocket and withdrew a cigarillo box. He slid it open, then hesitated, his hand hovering over the row of neat black rolls. A strange look came over his face — rigid stillness, like a wave of ice had fallen across his features.

My brow furrowed, my gaze following his — to his hand over that box, frozen mid-movement, like his muscles had locked without his permission. His ring finger lurched in erratic spurts that shook his entire hand.

For several long seconds, we stared at his hand.

Then, he smoothly switched the box to his other hand, swiftly withdrew a cigarillo, and held it between his teeth as he put the box away again.

It was like the moment had never existed. He winked at me, smile smooth and charming and forever unbothered.

"Have fun training," he said. "I'll leave you to it. We're going to have a busy few months ahead."

And he sauntered off without another word.

FINE. I was out of shape.

It felt good to have my blades back again, but restoring that piece of my routine had only made it more obvious how much had changed. I had gone from a life of moving all day, every day, to lying in my bed staring at the ceiling. It was amazing how much conditioning could decay in a month.

A month. More than that. It hadn't really hit me how long it had been, until I physically felt the way my body had changed in that time.

With every panting breath, every drill, every strike against the stiff fabric of the training dummy, it dug a little deeper.

A month.

More than a full cycle of the moon that my father had been dead.

I tried to outrun this thought. Tried to make my muscles hurt more so my heart hurt less. It didn't work. The thoughts still chased me.

A month.

And I'd just made an alliance with the man who murdered him.

And now I'd cracked open the door to a single innocuous thought, and before I could stop myself, it was becoming something monstrous.

A month.

How many times had I been in this training ring with Vincent? Countless. I could practically hear him now, barking orders at me.

Faster. Harder. Don't be sloppy. You aren't trying hard enough, little serpent. That will not be good enough when it counts.

He'd pushed me so hard. Sometimes I'd end our sessions collapsing in a pool of my own vomit.

I pushed you because I wanted you to be safe, Vincent whispered in my ear.

He pushed me so I could protect myself.

Everything in this world is dangerous to you, he reminded me.

Because I was human.

But I wasn't.

It was a lie. All of it.

My strikes against the dummy grew faster, harder, sloppy. My lungs burned. Chest ached. Nightfire bloomed at the edge of my blade, surrounding me with flecks of white.

But I wasn't.

How many times had I practiced my magic with Vincent in this ring? How many times had he told me that my power would likely never amount to anything?

Had that been a lie, too?

Did you know? I asked him now, driving another blow into the training dummy, the stuffing collapsing under the force.

127

Vincent's voice was silent.

Why didn't you tell me?

Why did you lie to me, Vincent? Why?

Silence. Of course.

The Nightfire flared in a wild surge, surrounding me in a blinding burst. With a ragged roar, I slammed my weapon into the dummy, sending it toppling to the floor. My strike was so clumsy, so vicious, I accidentally sent my blade with it, the metal hitting the ground with a deafening clatter.

I barely heard it over the sound of my panting breaths.

And then I heard a familiar voice behind me.

"Didn't realize just how lucky I am to be alive until I saw that."

Raihn.

I squeezed my eyes shut, quickly swiping away tears. *Fuck.*

"Right," I choked out. It sounded pathetically weak.

"You sound out of breath, though."

Oh, fuck him.

"I'm just out of practice."

"Want a partner?"

"No."

He approached anyway.

I still didn't want to look at him, embarrassed about what I'd allowed him to see. Me crying and punching the air like a child. Nice.

But his silence was too long. Too meaningful.

Finally, I turned to him.

"What?" I snapped.

He opened his mouth, then seemed to think better of it.

"Nothing. You sure you don't want to spar? Better than punching the dummy. Going to have to train with me eventually." He reached for his sword, raising a brow. Only now did it occur to me how strange it was that he always kept it on him, even when he was walking around his own castle. Maybe he felt just as uncomfortable in this place as I did.

He added, with a conspiratorial half-smile, "I'm only offering because I don't see any windows you can throw me out of this time."

I didn't know why I hesitated. I did need to remind myself of how Raihn fought—needed to make sure I would be able to strike him down when I had to.

And yet... it made me uncomfortable.

I shoved that sensation away and bit out, "Fine. If you want to spar, then let's spar."

And I didn't give Raihn time to react before I lunged.

But he was ready. He blocked and countered me easily.

All of it was easy—that was what made it so difficult.

When I had fought Raihn in the armory, I'd so hated to be reminded of how well we knew each other, how seamlessly we fought together. Now, wielding my blades rather than that clumsy sword, the ghosts of our final battle in the Kejari surrounded us. The ache of my muscles faded away. The two of us hurtled across the training ring together as if locked in a dance.

I hated this, and I loved it. It was something solid to grab onto, something mindless and painful in all the physical places I could handle. And yet, every one of Raihn's strikes reminded me of the familiarity we'd once had. Reminded me of what he had used it to do.

A month.

I let out a wordless grunt of exertion as the clangs of metal against metal came faster, faster, faster. I saw his mouth twist, just a little—heard what he didn't say aloud:

There she is.

The Nightfire erupted around me, this time not just clinging to my blades and my hands, but embracing my entire body.

Raihn jerked backwards, his arm flying up to shield his face, and that was enough to yank me from my trance.

Awareness of my body crashed back into me. My panting breath. Burning lungs. Screaming muscles. Just as quickly, the Nightfire withered.

I stumbled to the ground as Raihn raised his sword in a yield.

He was panting, too. He wiped sweat from his forehead with the back of his hand. "That," he said, "is impressive. Seems like it comes to you a lot easier than it did before."

Thank you didn't feel like the right answer. I inspected my blade, polishing it with my sleeve.

"Did you do that on purpose?" he asked.

It was the kind of question that was really a statement, and that annoyed me.

"When I first got my Heir Mark," he said, "everything just... rearranged. I still can't describe how different I felt afterwards. And then, when Nyaxia..." He flinched. Shrugged. "It just changes a lot. It was like I didn't know what my own body was capable of anymore."

His words rang uncomfortably true. But he didn't ask me if I felt that way, too. Maybe because he already knew the answer.

"You're half vampire, Oraya," he said quietly. "Not just half vampire, but an Heir. Have you thought about what that might mean?"

I lifted my gaze to meet Raihn's, steady with that open question, and with that look, I had to acknowledge all the other things it meant.

It meant I no longer knew anything about myself. My magic. My lifespan. My blood. The limits of my own flesh.

It meant that my entire life had been a lie.

I didn't say anything, and Raihn—to my relief—did not push. Instead, he offered me his hand. I didn't take it and pushed myself up on my own.

He huffed a laugh and shook his head as he turned away. "Never change, Oraya. Come on. Let's go."

"I wasn't done."

"You look like you're about to collapse. You can come break yourself again another time." He glanced at me over his shoulder. "Maybe you're due for a trip to the human districts? You look like you need to kill something."

"Oh, I need to kill something," I muttered. But as much as I wanted to argue with him, I was exhausted. So I followed.

"What's so important?" I asked, as we walked down the hall.

"I found your bodyguard."

"Bodyguard?"

Ugh. Just when I'd gotten freedom for the first time in my life?

He chuckled. "Even I have bodyguards, princess. You think I'd let you wander around this pit of beasts alone?"

"You sound like *him*," I grumbled, and tried not to notice how Raihn's smile disappeared at that.

He led me all the way back to our rooms. He opened the door to his chambers and beckoned.

"Meet your bodyguard."

The words weren't even out of his mouth before Mische was pushing past him, the grin on her face bright enough to light up the darkest corners of the castle.

And Goddess damn me if I didn't find myself returning it.

Raihn put his hand—gently—on her shoulder, as if to physically restrain her from throwing herself at me. But she caught herself at the last minute anyway, stopping short of hugging me and instead offering me an enthusiastic, if awkward, wave.

"I missed you!" she blurted out.

Honestly?

I'd missed her, too.

RAIHN WAS, to my genuine relief, mostly exaggerating when he said that Mische would be my "bodyguard." She wouldn't be shadowing my every move, but if I accepted, she'd be given the other bedchamber in my apartment and accompany me on trips.

"I don't need to be watched," I grumbled.

At that, a little wrinkle of concern had formed over Mische's brow.

"If you want me to go somewhere else," she said, "I can."

I glanced at Raihn. "I don't think it's up to me."

He replied simply, "It is up to you. Tell her to find another place, and she will."

Ugh. That seemed so... cruel.

"Why doesn't she stay with you?" I asked.

"I snore."

Mische sighed. "He *does*. He really, really does."

I knew he did, because I'd heard those snores every day for months, myself.

"Besides," Raihn said, "if it's not Mische, then I'll have to find another guard for you. One of Ketura's, if you'd prefer that."

I glared at him, and he half-shrugged, adding, "Act of war, and all that."

Mische stared at me like a stray puppy begging to be let inside.

I sighed and pinched the bridge of my nose.

"*Fine*," I muttered, as Mische grinned and started dumping her clothing into the drawers.

17

ORAYA

"Lahor."

Raihn tapped the map again. "Lahor."

I stared at the city at the tip of his finger — a little ink drawing of broken stone. A single, tiny sigil was inked above it — a taloned claw holding a rose.

The last two weeks had passed in an uneventful blur. Sleeping. Training. Waiting for the next move.

The next move, apparently, turned out to be Lahor. One night, after training, Raihn pulled me into his chambers and dragged an extra chair to his desk, which was covered with maps and papers. He'd pulled out a heavy atlas of the House of Night, and pointed at a city on the far eastern shores.

Now, I stared at it.

"Alright," I said, in a tone that said, *Why the hell are you showing me this?*

"You're familiar with it?"

"Of course."

I'd memorized this map when I was a small child and these ink lines were all I'd had of the outside world. Lahor had always interested me, because its crest matched the one that Vincent bore on some of his clothing.

The thought of Vincent came with the obligatory stab of grief, and then, shortly after, a wave of realization.

"You're asking, I assume," I said, "because it's Vincent's homeland. But he didn't talk about it much."

I'd rarely asked about Vincent's past. I learned quickly that he didn't like to talk about it, and I wasn't in the business of saying things that Vincent did not like.

"It was a very long time ago that I lived there," he had told me. "It's not my banner anymore. All of the House of Night is mine."

I'd accepted that. After all, it had taken me years to see Vincent as a person who had existed beyond the walls of his castle—as a fallible being with a history. Hell, maybe right up until the end, I hadn't seen him that way.

"If Vincent had needed to hide something," Raihn said, "and he needed to put it somewhere where only he could find it, do you think that's where he'd go?"

I didn't answer for a long moment, my chest tight.

At first, I wanted to say no. Vincent hadn't wanted to even acknowledge his past before his reign. But then again, just because Vincent didn't want to acknowledge something didn't make it any less true. The lie of my own blood was more than enough proof of that.

"I don't know," I said at last.

I knew so damned little of my father.

"Septimus wants us to go there," Raihn said. "He thinks that Vincent hid something there. Something to do with the god blood."

"And why does Septimus think this?"

A dark laugh. "I wish I knew how that man knows half the things he does."

I felt that, too. Especially since I had my own secrets to protect.

"I have to admit," Raihn said, "it does seem like the perfect hiding spot. Right there on the eastern tip of the House of Night. No one needs to go there for anything. Inaccessible as fuck. Overrun with hellhounds and demons. And Vincent had kept some odd trinkets from there in his chambers, which seems unlike him. The place, from what I hear, is little more than ruins now. Fallen into some disarray since Vincent left it two hundred years ago."

My brow furrowed in thought. "I think his niece lives there. Or... niece once removed. Twice removed."

Evelaena? Something like that.

"Right. Another reason why this will be complicated. I don't think she'll be very happy to see us."

To see us?

"*We're* going?"

"What did you think we were going to do? Send a couple of servants to go search for us?"

At my flat stare, Raihn laughed. "My, how you've adjusted to royal life, Your Highness."

"Fuck you," I muttered.

But then the truth of his words sunk in. *Complicated.* That was right. No Hiaj would welcome the Rishan king at their gates. Not even accompanied by me. Perhaps *especially* not accompanied by me, because this was Vincent's only living relative—who probably thought *she* would be Heir when Vincent died.

"That was the face I made when I thought about it, too," Raihn said.

"Tell me we're taking an army with us."

"Right, with all those loyal warriors that I have to spare." He raised his brows at me. "What about you? You plan on calling in some loyal and cooperative Hiaj soldiers to escort us? Or are they all too busy trying to kill my people?"

My face answered his question.

"Exactly," he said.

"Wouldn't it be smarter if you stayed here? A king shouldn't leave his castle unguarded."

"A king shouldn't leave his queen unguarded, either, especially not one as prone to getting into trouble as you." He gave me a sly grin. "Besides, if you think I'm going to miss the chance to get out of this damned place and go get my hands dirty, you don't know me at all."

I thought he would say that.

PART THREE
CRESCENT MOON

INTERLUDE

Turning is a fate worse than death. It is death, in a way—death of a version of yourself that you will never see again. Born vampires cannot possibly understand, nor are they usually especially inclined to. To them, the turmoil of the Turned is a sign of weakness. A snake, after all, does not mourn its skin.

What they will never understand is how much that skin takes with it.

The man clings to his humanity through every second of his transformation. It must be ripped away from him, stitch by stitch. Turning is a terrible process. It nearly kills him. He loses weeks, months, to illness, taken in an onslaught of delirium. Dreaming of his home. Dreaming of his mistakes. Dreaming of the family he does not yet know he would never see again.

He barely remembers the aftermath of the shipwreck when he emerges from this haze.

The king is beside him, perched at the edge of his bed, watching him with the kind of detached interest that one affords a new pet.

He offers a goblet, and the man gulps it down frantically, liquid spilling down his chin. He has never tasted anything so wonderful—so sweet, so rich, so—

The king pulls the goblet away.

"That's enough for now," he says, with a thick accent, patting the man's shoulder and setting the cup aside.

The man wipes the mess from his face with the back of his hand and blinks down at the smears of red left behind, confused.

He does not understand yet, you see, what happened to him.

He puts aside his hand and his confusion. His family, he thinks. How long has he been here? Time blurs. The ship seems like a lifetime ago.

"Thank you," he chokes out. "Thank you for your hospitality. But I need to go."

The king smiles and says nothing.

Perhaps he didn't understand him, the man thinks. He is far from home. What country had he ended up in? He knew once, but now —

It doesn't matter. The man doesn't speak any language but the commoner's tongue he'd grown up with.

"I need to leave," he says again, speaking slowly, each word enunciated, pointing to the window — the window that overlooks the sea.

The king still does not answer. His smile broadens slightly, revealing the tips of his pointed teeth.

Those teeth — the sight brings with them the memory of the night of his almost-death —

Do you want to live?

Dread rises. The man ignores it.

"Please," he says.

But the king just strokes the back of his head. "You have no more home," he says, somewhat pityingly, words serrated with the thick tang of his accent. "You exist only here."

Years later, the man will remember little of this conversation. But those four words will remain, even when the specifics of the rest are long lost: You exist only here.

It will become the truth. The king has given the man a new life, but the catch is that this life belongs solely to him.

This is the moment that the man understands how much his life has just changed.

He shakes his head, trying to get up, but the king pushes him back to the bed easily. The man is too tired and dizzy to fight, though he claws through it with every bit of his remaining strength —

But when the king offers him his wrist, the scent dazes him.

"It will not be so bad," the king says, as he guides the man's head to his skin.

18

RAIHN

I practically skipped out of that castle.

Weeks out of that place. Weeks away from those stone walls, and those people, and that musty incense smell that reminded me far too much of two-hundred-odd years ago. It was every gift I'd ever gotten rolled into one. Better than any birthday.

Cairis would stay behind to manage the affairs of the Crown, and Vale, to continue directing the battles across the House of Night. He seemed a little relieved to have an excuse to remain.

Ketura and a few of her most trusted soldiers would come with us. I tried to talk Mische out of it, but this, of course, was futile. She made it about two sentences before she cut me off and said, "Do you want me to let you finish this before I tell you I'm not listening? I'm a *bodyguard*, remember?"

Then again, maybe it was for the better. Better to be out there with us than to be in this place, alone.

Septimus—of course—insisted on coming himself, too, bringing his second and a small force of Bloodborn guards with him.

Lahor was one of the most remote cities in the House of

Night—all the way at the tip of the eastern shores, surrounded by water on three sides. Truly in the middle of nowhere. The journey alone took almost two weeks. We moved quietly, taking advantage of our limited forces to move swiftly, days spent in unassuming inns where no one would ask questions or in makeshift camps on the road. The winged among us flew, while the Bloodborn followed on horseback. I carried Oraya, which was about as awkward as it had been last time. It was impossible to focus on anything with her quick heartbeat throbbing in my eyes and her steel-sweet scent in my nostrils and her body stiff and uncomfortable next to mine—all these distracting reminders of what we'd been to each other before and just how far away that was now.

We traveled over rolling desert sands, smooth swells of pale moonlight-drenched gold. When I'd first come here, after I'd made it through the worst of my Turning sickness, I still remembered so clearly stumbling to the window in my room in Neculai's castle. I'd staggered against the glass, eyes glued to those distant dunes.

I had thought, *This place has no fucking right to be so beautiful.*

I'd never seen the beauty in all the typical trappings of vampire allure. Their physical appearances, their gold and silver, their fashion.

But as much as I wanted to hate those dunes, I couldn't.

For days, we flew over the deserts—sand and sand and sand, interrupted by occasional cities and townships and the rare lake or river surrounded by scattered greenery.

But when we grew closer to Lahor, those smooth waves of gold were shattered by sudden gashes of broken stone. First a couple, then more and more as the hours passed, until the ground below us looked like distant crumpled parchment—all hard angles and sharp edges, cut through only by a single road. No movement below from other travelers, only distant roving packs of hellhounds and demons.

Lahor was that kind of place. The kind of place that the world just moved on without.

No one had much of a reason to come here. Except for us.

WHEN WE LANDED, Oraya made a face of such abject disgust, I wished I could capture it and keep it for the next time I didn't have words to describe how much I hated something.

"Impressed with your ancestral homeland, princess?" I said.

The wrinkle over her nose deepened. "What is that *smell?*"

"Viprus weed. It grows on the cliffs near the water here," I said. "It spreads quick and then rots as soon as it touches air, so whenever the tide goes out—"

"Ugh." Mische made a sound like a cat hacking up a hairball. "Gross."

"Would be even worse if you could see it. Looks like entrails. And then it shrivels up like—"

"Oh, I get it."

"You've been here before?" Oraya said.

I shot her a little smirk. "I've been everywhere."

"Aren't we lucky to have a world traveler as our guide," Septimus said. He was smoking, of course. His horse, a big white beast with pink-rimmed eyes, snorted and shook its head—as if just as offended by the stench as we were.

He looked up at the gates ahead of us. "Looks like a beautiful city."

The words dripped with sarcasm. Earned sarcasm.

Maybe once, a very long time ago, Lahor had been a beautiful place. With a very active imagination, you could maybe see the ghost of what once stood here. Obitraes was an old, old continent—far older than Nyaxia's patronage and far older than vampirism.

Lahor, though, actually looked it. Now it was little more than ruins.

The wall that stood before us was formidable, perhaps the

only well-maintained part of this city. Black onyx, stretching high above us and out to either side. The skyline beyond the wall, though… it was what bones were to bodies. What had once been buildings were now jagged spires of shattered stone, the mere suggestion of architecture — towers cracked and leaning on uneven piles of stone. The only lights upon this skyline were distant, wild flames along the jagged peaks of a few of the tallest, broken spires.

The towering onyx doors before us remained firmly closed.

"How quaint," Septimus said.

"Quaint," Ketura echoed, eyeing the road behind us and the packs of hellhounds yipping and howling not far from us. It was rare that so many of these beasts would come so close to a town. More evidence that Evelaena was not doing much to maintain her homeland.

"So now what?" Oraya said, turning to the door. "We knock?"

"It's your cousin, princess. You tell us."

Evelaena knew we were coming. Oraya and I had penned a letter to her before we left, announcing our visit — a tour of all notable vampire nobles in the House of Night. Cairis had heaped sickening amounts of flattery into it. We'd ensured that she had received it, but we'd gotten no response.

That didn't surprise me. Even my own nobles weren't especially inclined to return my letters.

I jerked my chin towards Septimus's companions. "You think you can take down this wall?"

"I hope you're joking," Ketura muttered. "Stupidest idea."

I was half joking.

Oraya had slowly approached the door, staring up at it. Something about the expression on her face made me pause. I approached her.

"What?" I asked, softly.

"It just feels… strange here."

She lifted her palm, as if to lay it against the door —

And then a deafening grinding rang out as the stone swung

open. The sound was hideous, squealing and cracking, as if the gate protested moving at all after decades or centuries.

The curtains of stone darkness parted, and Lahor spread out before us. It was even worse than it had seemed in silhouette—the road ahead nothing but slabs of broken stone, every building half-open and crumbling, every window nothing but broken shards of glass.

Standing before us was a boy, no older than sixteen at most. He wore a long purple jacket that didn't fit him well, once fine but now several hundred years out of style. Waves of pale blond hair framed a delicate face and wide, empty ice-blue eyes. Those eyes seemed to stare through us, not at us. And then, just as the grinding finally stopped, they went suddenly sharp, taking us in with eviscerating keenness before sliding back to cow-like vacancy.

He bowed low before us.

"Highnesses. My lady Evelaena welcomes you to Lahor. Come. You must be eager to rest after your long journey."

19

RAIHN

The castle was the only building in this place that seemed to be—almost—in one piece. It was the tallest building in the city, which was to say, it was the pile of rubble that towered over all the other piles of rubble. It was cold and damp inside, ocean breezes flowing in through broken windows, strong enough to rustle heavy, velvet curtains that reeked of mold.

We didn't pass a single soul as we were led through the halls, into an expansive room with tall ceilings and towering windows that overlooked the churning sea beyond the cliffs. Some of the panes were tinted red. Maybe that once had been some kind of design decision, but now it looked eerie and disparate, because so much of the glass had been shattered.

Yet, even on such a sad canvas, the view was breathtaking. There were few places anywhere in the House of Night where you could see the water like this—ocean surrounding you on all sides. A gust of wind bellowed through the room, salt so heavy it made my eyes water, the stench of Viprus thick enough to gag on. A dais sat before the windows, bearing a rotting velvet throne with only one armrest and a cracked back.

And upon that throne was Evelaena.

She was only a distant relative of Vincent's, and much younger than him. During his bloody night of ascension to power, he'd killed most of his close family members, carving a carefully mapped path to his inheritance. Yet, she resembled him. She had the fair eyes—not the moon-silver that he'd passed on to Oraya, but the cold ocean blue favored by most of his line. Her cheekbones were high and features severe, as if made of glass. Her blond hair fell over each shoulder, so long that it pooled in her lap in dry waves.

She rose. Her white gown dragged along the floor as she stepped down the dais steps, the hem bloodstained and dirty. It, like the boy's jacket, was an outdated style, like she'd gotten it about a hundred and fifty years ago. Maybe it had been beautiful back then.

Her gaze passed over me, then Septimus, and then landed on Oraya—and stayed there, as a slow grin spread over her face.

I could practically feel Oraya stiffen. Hell, I did, too. I resisted the urge to step in front of her as Evelaena approached.

"Cousin," Evelaena purred. "What a joy to finally meet."

Oraya—ever transparent—blinked in shock at the sound of Evelaena's voice. So, so young. Like it could've belonged to a fourteen-year-old girl.

Evelaena lay her hands on Oraya's shoulders, and I could see every muscle in Oraya's body tightening to avoid pulling away.

"Evelaena," she said—and nothing else.

She clearly didn't know what else to say. My wife was not much of an actress. But I could be good enough for both of us.

My hand slid around Oraya's shoulders, casually displacing Evelaena's.

"Thank you for your hospitality, Lady Evelaena. I have to admit, we weren't sure what we'd find. We never received your response to our letter."

Evelaena smiled, but a familiar, intoxicating scent—just a whiff of it—dragged my attention away. At first, I thought I was imagining it—but then I swept my thumb over her shoulder, right where Evelaena's hand had rested.

Warm. Wet.

Blood.

My fake smile withered. My gaze shot to Evelaena, who folded her claw-tipped hands at her lap, leaving little specs of bright-red blood on her dress.

A wave of the exact same emotion that had fallen over me before I ripped Martas's head off his body stifled me.

Evelaena just kept up that dreamy smile.

"I wasn't sure that you would be interested in coming so far east. Such a journey! You must be starving. Come. I've had a feast prepared." Her eyes brightened. "More than a feast! A ball! One of the grandest Lahor has seen in decades. Come! Come!"

Well, that sounded morbid.

IT WAS MORBID.

When we were brought to the ballroom, I actually stifled a laugh—because honestly, I couldn't help myself.

The room had been grand once, and still held the distant echo of its long-ago magnificence, albeit all covered with a faint layer of dust. Long tables sat over mosaic tile floors on one side of the room, the windows overlooking the sea beyond them. The other side was a dance floor, a roaring bonfire in the hearth and an orchestra before it, magically enhanced, ghostly music echoing against the ceilings. Yes, this had all the trappings of a ball—the entertainment, the tables of food and wine, the finery.

Except, of the dozens of "guests" that turned to regard us with silent curiosity as we arrived, not a single one appeared to be more than fifteen years old.

Most were far younger—ten or twelve, wearing clothes so ill-fitting that they dragged skirts and pant hems over the dusty floor. Almost all of them were blond, with fair eyes.

Surely these couldn't all be her children. Or if they were all members of her family, where were the other parents?

Evelaena took no notice of the sudden, awkward silence. She stretched her arms out. "Come! Sit!"

The children wordlessly turned to the tables and took their seats.

I'd witnessed plenty of disturbing things in my time, but the silent, simultaneous obedience with which dozens of children did this would certainly be among the most unnerving.

The seats at the head of the table, closest to Evelaena, were, apparently, ours. She motioned to them and we, ever the respectful guests, took our chairs.

"You must be famished," she said. Her eyes fell to me and her smile stilled.

Hatred. Easy to see it. I knew how to recognize it by now. That wasn't a surprise. I'd killed Vincent, after all. There was a reason why Oraya's name had come first in our letter.

I glanced at Oraya's shoulder, and the little beads of scabbing red on her shoulders.

Not that that seemed to be going any better.

We couldn't trust this woman. We had to get what we needed and get the fuck out of—

The smell made my head snap up.

Blood. Human blood. Lots of it. Still beating. The truth was, I was hungry after so much travel—the truth was, even after all this time, when I first smell it, it takes me a minute to collect myself. Ketura's eyes brightened. The Bloodborn peered over their shoulder.

Evelaena perked up, too, her smile brightening.

"At last," she crooned, shifting aside so that her child servants could hoist a naked woman onto the table.

20

ORAYA

The woman was still alive. Her throat had been cut, but not enough to make her bleed out fast. Her eyes, big and dark, danced wildly about the room. Landed on me.

A sudden intense wave of nausea made vomit rise in my throat. Images from another feast hall, another table, another human bleeding out on a wooden slab—shown to me by my own father—assaulted me.

I glanced at Raihn. His face was still for a moment—frozen, as if stuck momentarily between masks. Then it softened into a predatory grin.

"What a treat."

I took a drink from my wine glass because I desperately needed something to do with my hands and immediately choked. Whatever flowed over my tongue was thick and savory, punctuated with an iron bite.

Blood.

My stomach lurched.

And yet—yet my body did not reject it. It accepted it. Some dark, primal part of myself purred as I forced myself to let the blood slide down my throat.

Goddess, what was wrong with me? I swallowed hard just to keep myself from throwing up.

The woman before me kept looking at me, her eyes blurring out and then refocusing. Like she knew that I wasn't one of them.

Several other humans had been placed on the tables. Most were listless, alive but not moving. Some still weakly struggled and were secured to the table to keep them from moving—a sickening sight, when it was children doing the securing.

Mische sipped blood from her wine glass, doing a poor job at hiding her fascinated disgust. If the Bloodborn were surprised, they didn't show it, gracefully accepting human wrists and throats, observing the rest of the room with wary interest. Septimus offered a pleasant smile and raised his glass in a wordless toast before setting the goblet down in favor of the woman's limp wrist.

At the other place settings, children climbed over the tables, clustering around the corpses like starving flies, their only sounds the frantic drinking and the stifled moans of pain of their human offerings.

Raihn cast me a glance so quick I thought I might've imagined it. Then he grinned. "You have spoiled us, Evelaena," he said, placed his hands on either side of the woman's head, and turned her face towards him. Her eyes widened, a little whimper of fear escaping her lips—more like a gargle, actually. This woman was already dead, I knew. Nothing could save her now. She'd drown slowly in her blood, conscious while the rest of them drained her.

I watched Raihn, a knot of disgust in my stomach. I'd never seen him drink live prey before—let alone from a human. I shouldn't have been surprised to see him do this. He'd tricked me many times before. He was a vampire, after all.

And yet, a little silent sigh of relief passed over me when I saw the shift in his face when he looked into her eyes. I wondered if I was the only one who saw it—the brief trade of the bloodthirsty hunger for silent compassion, intended only for her.

He tilted her head back, lowered his face, and sank his teeth into her throat.

He bit hard—hard enough that I could hear his teeth slicing the muscle. Little flecks of blood spattered my face, which I promptly wiped away. He drank for several long seconds, his throat bobbing with deep gulps, before lifting his head again, crimson at the corners of his mouth and seeping into the lines of his grin.

"Perfect," he said. "You have fine taste, Evelaena."

But Evelaena frowned down at the woman—whose eyes now stared half-closed, vacant, to the other side of the room, bare chest no longer fighting for breath.

"You killed her," she said, disappointed.

A quick, painless death. A mercy.

Raihn laughed, wiping the blood off his mouth with the back of his hand. "I got a bit overzealous. But she's still plenty warm. Will last the next few hours, at least."

Evelaena looked put out by this. Then a smile rolled over her lips. "You're right. No need to waste. Besides, there are many more where she came from."

His grin stiffened, so tight it looked like it might crack.

A regular occurrence here, then. Then again, wasn't it a regular occurrence everywhere? I'd just let myself be sheltered from it for so long.

The Oraya of the past wouldn't be able to hide her revulsion. She'd let it all show on her face, and trigger a messy argument, and we'd all get kicked out of this city before we even had the chance to start looking for what we came here for.

But then again, the Oraya of the past wouldn't be here at all.

So I decided to try my hand at acting. I lifted my glass and offered Evelaena my best, most bloodthirsty smile. "No such thing as too much for a family reunion," I said. "Drink, cousin. You're too sober for how late it is tonight."

The tension snapped. Evelaena laughed, her childlike delight befitting of a little girl presented with a doll. She clinked her glass against mine, hard enough to send blood wine sloshing over both of our hands.

"The truth, cousin," she said, and drained her glass.

"You're much better at this than I would've thought," Raihn whispered in my ear, several hours later. He snuck up on me— the sensation of his breath against the crest of my ear sent a shiver over my skin, leading me to take a big step away from him.

"It wasn't very hard," I said.

"Still. I give you points for even trying it. Feels like a very different kind of move for you." He nudged my arm with his elbow. "Daresay you're evolving, princess."

"Your approval means so much to me," I deadpanned, and Raihn's laugh sounded like one of genuine delight.

All night, I had been working on getting Evelaena as drunk as possible, and I had been very, very successful. Raihn and I stood in the corner of the ballroom, watching her spin around in circles with one of her child nobles, laughing hysterically while the child's face remained that of porcelain-still calm. The humans, now mostly drained, lay slumped over tables and against the walls, though a few of the children still crawled over them to lap at their throats or thighs. The Bloodborn remained clustered together, watching the scene before them warily, lazily sipping their blood.

"She," Raihn said, "is going to be in a lot of pain tomorrow."

"That's the idea."

There's no one looser with secrets than a drunkard. No one easier to slip around than a vampire who needed to spend the next two days recovering from gorging themselves the night before, on blood or alcohol or, better yet, both.

"I loved the night after parties, when I was growing up," I

said. "They'd all be asleep and I could do whatever I wanted for a few hours. If she's drunk enough, she'll tell us what we need to know, and then she'll be out of the way for the next day or two."

"Sounds perfect."

Perfect, so long as Evelaena was the only one we had to worry about. I still wasn't sure that was the case. Lahor might be a city of ruins, but there had to be *someone* living here other than her.

"Have you seen anyone else?" I asked, voice low.

"You mean, other than the fifty-something golden-haired children in this room? No."

We both paused, watching those children. They crawled over the bodies and grabbed at goblets, ignoring Evelaena's wild flailing until she pulled them in and insisted they dance with her.

Even for vampires, their stares were so... still. Empty. And every one of them fair-eyed blonds.

"They're Turned," Raihn said, voice low.

I glanced at him. "What?"

"They're Turned. The children. They're all Turned."

I looked at the children—lapping at pools of blood like stray cats drinking gutter water—with fresh horror. The suspicion had been there, in the back of my mind, but now that the thought had been yanked to the forefront... the horror of it rose up my throat slowly. With every second I considered it, it became a greater atrocity.

Born vampires aged normally. But children who were Turned would be stuck that way for eternity, both their minds and bodies frozen in eternal, crippling youth. A terrible fate.

"How do you—" I started.

"Have you tried to talk to any of them? Many of them don't even speak Obitraen. Found one that only knew Glaen."

Another wave of disgust. "She brought them here from the human nations?"

"I don't know how they got here. Maybe she pays traffickers. Maybe some were shipwrecked. Maybe she gets some of them from her human districts. Hell, there are enough of them. Probably all those things."

I watched Evelaena spin around the room gleefully, clinging to one of her child servants, who seemed to stare a thousand miles past her.

All the same appearance. All so young. And young forever, now.

My stomach turned. Raihn and I exchanged a glance—I knew we were both asking the same silent questions and both repulsed by every potential answer.

"Your cousin," he said, between his teeth, "is a fucked up piece of work."

I shook away my discomfort. "Let's just get whatever the hell we're here for and get out."

I started walking into the thick of the party, but Raihn grabbed my arm.

"Where are you going?"

I yanked away from his grip. "Getting some information out of her before she passes out."

I tried to pull away from his grip, but he tugged me closer.

"Alone?"

What the hell kind of a question was that? I expected my face to earn the usual chuckle and teasing remark, but he remained serious.

"What about these?"

His fingertips ran over the curve of my shoulder. Goosebumps rose on my skin, a chill trailing his touch. Then a twinge of pain, as he brushed the still-bleeding, half-moon marks Evelaena had left behind.

It was so shockingly soft that my rebuke tangled on my tongue. It took me a moment too long to say, "It's nothing."

"It's not nothing."

"Nothing I can't handle. I'm used to being hated."

"No. You're used to being dismissed. Being hated is infinitely more dangerous."

I pulled my arm away, and this time, he let me go. "I won the Kejari, Raihn. I can handle her."

Raihn gave me a half smile. "Technically, *I* won the Kejari, actually," he said, and didn't move, but he also didn't take his eyes off me.

EVELAENA WAS ALREADY VERY, very drunk. When I approached her, she released the hands of her child companion and held hers out to me, instead.

I genuinely could not bring myself to take her hands, but I let her drape them over my shoulders.

"Cousin, I am *so* happy you have finally come to visit me," she slurred. "It does get so very lonely here."

Not that lonely, if she'd Turned an army of children to keep her company.

She swayed a little closer, and I watched her nostrils flare with the movement. She had been gorging herself all night—there was no way she was hungry, but human blood was human blood.

I stepped away from her grasp, looping her arm through mine and holding it firmly, so that she couldn't get any closer.

"Show me my father's possessions," I said. "I always wanted to see where he grew up."

I wondered if the words sounded as unconvincingly sickly saccharine as they felt coming out of my mouth. If they did, Evelaena was too drunk to notice.

"Of course! Oh, of course, of course! Come, come!" she crooned, and stumbled with me down the hall.

I didn't look back, but I felt Raihn's gaze following me the whole way down the hall.

21

ORAYA

"Not much still exists," Evelaena slurred as she led me down dark, crumbling hallways. There were almost no torches, and my human sight struggled to avoid the uneven tiles and cracks in the floor—coupled with the fact that an extremely drunk Evelaena had attached herself to me, it took a lot of concentration just to keep myself putting one foot in front of the other.

"But I kept it," Evelaena went on, as she dragged me around a corner. "I kept all of it. I thought he might... thought he might come back someday. Here!"

Her face lit up, and she jerked away from my grasp. In the darkness, I tripped over a raised slab of stone and had to catch myself against the wall. Evelaena flung open the door. Golden light bathed her face.

"Here!" she said. "Here it all is."

I followed her into the room. It, unlike all the hallways that we'd come down, was lit with a steady, golden glow—sconce lanterns lined the walls, all lit as if awaiting the imminent return of its occupant. The room was small, but immaculate—the only place in this entire castle that seemed to be, truly, in one piece. A neatly made bed with blankets of violet velvet. A desk, with two golden pens, a closed leather-bound book, a single pair of gold wire-framed glasses. An armoire, one door open, two lone, fine jackets hanging within. On the coffee table, a single spoon, a single saucer. One shoe, neatly placed at the corner of the room.

I stood there staring at it all as Evelaena flung her arms out and spun around.

"Is this it?"

I was grateful that she was too drunk to hear the complicated emotion in my voice.

"All that remains, yes," she said. "He didn't leave much behind, all those years ago. Much of it was lost when..." Her gleeful smile faded. A shadow fell over her. "When it all happened."

She turned to me abruptly, her big blue eyes watery and glistening under the lantern light. "A mistake, surely," she said. "That he would destroy so much when he left. This is why I kept all of this. Some of it took years to find in the dirt and rubble. I kept it. Cleaned it. Put it here, to wait for him."

She picked up the single shoe, her finger dancing along the edge of the laces.

I paused at the desk, and the strange collection of random items atop it. One of them was a little ink drawing of Lahor—at least, what I thought was Lahor, but the perspective was from an angle I didn't recognize, looking down at the city from the east.

"Is there anyone else here who knew him back then?" I asked.

"Here? Living here? In this house?" Evelaena seemed confused by the question.

"Yes. Or... well, anyone. Any of..." I settled on, thinking this would go over well, "any more of our family."

The records didn't speak of anyone else. But hell, Lahor was very, very isolated. Who knows?

She stared blankly at me, then burst into high, manic laughter. "Of course not. There's no one else here. He killed them all."

I didn't know why I wasn't expecting this answer. I stilled, not sure how to respond.

She paused. Turned. Peered over her shoulder at me.

"Everything here changed that day," she said. "The day he left."

Evelaena was much younger than Vincent had been. And yet, I hadn't done the exact math—had assumed she was born after Vincent's ascension. But that was a hasty assumption. It hit me just how hasty it had been when I looked into her eyes now.

"You were there." I meant it as a question. It came out as a statement.

She nodded, a slow smile spreading over her face. "I was," she whispered, conspiratorially, like we were telling ghost stories. "He did it before he left for the Kejari. Set up all the pieces. Even then, everyone knew he would win. Especially him. So he had to set up everything beforehand. Get rid of everyone who stood in his way." She touched the wall, like stroking the arm of an old friend. "Lahor was beautiful a long time ago. Kings lived here. It is a safe place. These walls sheltered kings during the reign of our enemies. Perhaps they will do so again, one day." Her gaze slipped back to me, amused. "All the little kings were here, and one king slaughtered all the rest."

Little kings.

Vincent had always spoke so dismissively about his own rise to power, and all the things he had done to facilitate it. But none of it was simple. None of it was small.

"I hid here," Evelaena said.

"Here?"

"Here." She pointed—to the bed. "Underneath it. I was so small, but I remember." She tapped her temple. "He did the older ones first, then the children. His father, my father, their sisters. He probably thought he needed to do those when his strength was up, because it would be difficult. I think my father gave him a good fight."

She spoke of all of this dreamily, calmly, as if speculating on history rather than the deaths of her family.

"Then he came here. He got Georgia, Marlena, Amith."

"Children?" I asked quietly.

"Oh, yes. So many of us. And then there were none."

"Why did he let you live?" I asked. "Because your birth position couldn't threaten him?"

Evelaena laughed, like I'd just said something very charming and foolish. "Birth position didn't matter. My uncle was a very thorough man."

Then, before I knew what was happening, she reached for the straps of her dress and slid them off her shoulders. The light fabric pooled around her waist, leaving her torso and breasts bare—and revealing a star-shaped scar right between them.

"He didn't let me live," she said. "He dragged me out from under there and put his sword through my chest. I lay right here beside my brother and sister's bodies. I thought my playmates and I would go to the next world together." She smiled serenely. "But the Mother was with me that night. The Mother chose me to live."

Goddess.

I asked, "How old were you?"

"Five summers, perhaps."

My throat thickened.

I knew what Vincent was capable of. It shouldn't have shocked me—disgusted me—to think of him slaughtering children when he slaughtered the rest of his family. And yet, the knowledge that *this* was the truth hiding behind his nonchalant non-answers, behind his matter-of-fact acceptance...

I have never hidden from you, Vincent whispered in my ear, *the fact that power is a bloody, bloody business, my little serpent.*

No. But it had taken me far too long to look closely at what that meant.

"I'm sorry that happened to you," I said quietly.

Evelaena's strange solemnity broke, melting back to her wine-dipped euphoria. A grin spread across her bloodstained mouth. "I'm not. It all went as the Mother wanted it to. And it wasn't so very horrible, considering all that we gained."

It was horrible, though. It was so horrible I had to bite my tongue hard to keep from saying so.

"I know he knew that, too," she said. "That I survived for a reason. To look after Lahor. Someone needed to. But he was so very busy. I never received any answers to my letters."

Her gaze fell back to me, piqued with interest I'd spent my entire life learning how to recognize. "Strange, how no one knew that his blood ran in yours."

She took a step closer, and I took a step backward.

"How strange of him," she murmured. "To let a daughter live, the closest link to his line, when so many had been sentenced to death for much lesser crimes." Her eyelashes fluttered. Another step—she was now so close I could feel her body heat from her bare skin, vampire-delicate.

"Half human, yes?" she whispered. "I can smell it." Her fingers reached for my cheek, my jaw, my throat—

My hand fell to my blade.

"Step back, Evelaena."

Her nose brushed mine, eyes lifting as her full lips curled. "We're family."

If I had to take her down now, I'd have to stab her right in the center of her chest—right over the scar that my father had left on her when she was only a child. What sickening poetic justice.

I didn't want to kill Evelaena—at least, not yet. We hadn't even come close to getting what we came here for, and who knew what chaos killing the lady of the house would unleash.

I said firmly, "Step back."

She didn't move.

"There you are."

I never thought I would ever again be grateful to hear that voice. And yet, here I was.

Raihn leaned against the doorframe, taking in the scene with an expression that told me I was absolutely going to hear more about this when we were alone.

Evelaena turned to Raihn, approaching him. She didn't bother to cover herself. Actually, by the way she was looking at him—with that still-insatiable hunger—it seemed very intentional not to do so.

I found this more irritating than I had any right to.

His gaze flicked over her impassively before returning to me. "Dawn's coming," he said. "Forgive me if I need to steal my wife away, Lady Evelaena."

Evelaena ignored him, her hand going to his chest. I watched the press of her fingers against him and had a hard time looking away.

"Tell me, usurper," she murmured. "How did my uncle's dying breath feel? I have so wondered." Her fingertips rose, dancing over the bridge of his nose, the hollow of his cheekbone. "Was it cold against your face? Or warm?"

But gently, politely, Raihn took Evelaena's wrists and moved them away, instead slipping a wine glass into her grasp.

"I didn't take any pleasure in that death," he said.

And his gaze flicked over her shoulder at the end of that sentence—spoken so solemnly, with far more truth than I expected.

He held his hand out to me. "Come to bed."

Evelaena stepped aside, still staring at Raihn with a blank, indecipherable look on her face. I placed my hand in Raihn's.

And then I jumped as Evelaena burst out into uproarious laughter.

She laughed and laughed and laughed. She laughed as she threw her head back and drained her glass of wine, and she didn't stop as she turned away and staggered back down the hall, not even bothering to put her dress back on.

As her voice faded down the hall, Raihn shot me a silent, wide-eyed, *are-you-hearing-this?* look.

He leaned close and murmured, "I almost wished I didn't interrupt, just to see where that was going to go. Wasn't sure if she was going to seduce you or eat you."

Honestly, I wasn't, either.

"I had it under control," I said.

He squeezed my hand, and it was only then that I realized I was shaking. He pressed his other hand over mine, as if to still the tremors, before letting go.

"I can't wait to get out of here," he muttered.

22

ORAYA

Lahor was, so far, not very helpful.

Evelaena had given us all suites near each other. They were once-grand apartments that were now dusty and rat-infested, with cracked windows that let in flecks of the overnight rain over the tile floor. When Mische pulled back the covers of her bed and several roaches ran out, she simply stared down at it with a look of utter disgust on her face, threw the covers back into place, and said brightly, "This can be Septimus's room."

This, Ketura had found exceedingly amusing. I think it was the only time I'd seen the woman laugh.

Not that we were doing much sleeping, anyway. The keep had gone eerily quiet, even to the vampires and their far superior hearing. That was when we acted. We went through the libraries, the studies, the empty bedchambers. Septimus's companions were excellent at slipping through hallways unnoticed, bringing back anything that looked even remotely as if it could be useful. Soon, our chambers were full of a comically mismatched assortment of objects—books, jewelry, weapons, artwork, sculptures. All of them were seriously damaged, reeking of mold or rust. All were presented to me with a silent raised eyebrow of, *Well?*

After a dozen instances of this, I held the half-rotted atlas between two fingers. A few bugs scurried from between the pages, irritated at having their home disturbed for the first time in what appeared to be centuries.

Clearly, this was it. The answer to all our problems. The key to historically unknown power.

I gave Septimus a deadpan stare that must have said everything my words didn't.

"We came all this way," he said, letting out a puff of cigarillo smoke through his nostrils. "Have a little patience, dove."

"Evelaena said that Vincent never returned here."

"Evelaena doesn't seem like the most reliable person. Not to insult a host."

"No," Raihn said, "but she doesn't seem like she would just forget that the uncle she's obsessed with showed up."

"Unless she's keeping it from us intentionally. He kept plenty of memorabilia from this place. Why else would he do that?"

"Nostalgia?" Mische offered, but even she didn't sound convinced.

Vincent had no love for this place. I'd suspected that before, and now, there was little doubt of that in my mind. He wasn't the type to wax nostalgic about the past, especially not parts of it that he felt little affection for. Lahor certainly fell into that category.

If he'd kept any connection to this place... it would have been for a reason.

I sighed.

"What am I supposed to do?" I muttered. "Just touch everything in this castle and see... what, exactly?"

Septimus shrugged.

"You'll know."

"What if I don't?"

"Then we wasted a trip and will try something else."

More time to search. More time for the Bloodborn to sink

their claws into this kingdom. More time for Raihn to establish his hold on it, too.

I heaved another exasperated sigh and kept wading through objects.

Hours and hours and hours of useless shit.

EVENTUALLY, we gave up. So much of the keep was so badly damaged. Even the artifacts that seemed like they had once been quite valuable were now little more than junk. I doubted that I would just magically "know" when I would come across a possession of Vincent's, but even still, it was obvious to me that these were worth nothing to him.

Eventually, when we'd made it through all the unoccupied, safe rooms of the keep, we allowed ourselves to rest.

My suite had only one bedroom—Raihn, to my relief, took the couch without complaint, leaving Mische to sleep beside me. She was snoring within minutes of crawling into bed, limbs sprawled out in all directions.

I curled up into a little ball and stared at the window at the glimpse of night-drenched Lahor through the opening in the curtains. Dawn was still at least an hour away. Sleep called to me, but I didn't want to know what I'd see in its depths.

Eventually, I couldn't just lie there anymore.

I slipped out of bed and grabbed my blades, going out to the sitting room to see—

"Where are you going?"

Raihn stopped mid-movement. He was half-shrouded by gauzy curtains, leaning out the open window.

He looked me up and down, an eyebrow raised.

"Did you sleep in your armor?"

I glanced down at myself, briefly self-conscious.

"Where are you going?" I asked again, instead of answering.

"Probably the same place you were. Feeling restless, too?"

I didn't want to admit it aloud.

I glanced back at the open bedchamber door, and Mische sleeping beyond it. Reading my face, Raihn said, "Oh, don't worry about her. Nothing wakes her."

Then he outstretched his hand. "Come on. Let's go get into some trouble."

I didn't move. Fine, he was right, I *was* going to sneak out into the city. Admitting that to him was a whole different concession.

He sighed.

"I know you, Oraya. Don't tell me you aren't curious."

I peered over his shoulder, out the open window to the eerie, desolate skyline beyond.

He smiled. "I thought so. Come on. Let's go."

This was a stupid idea.

I took his hand anyway.

LAHOR HAD SEEMED ABANDONED WHEN we first arrived here, and the strangeness of the keep—seemingly occupied only by Evelaena and her stable of Turned children—had only made that sensation stronger. But the city, while dilapidated, was not deserted. People did indeed actually live here, congregating in the few habitable buildings throughout the city.

Or maybe "living" was too generous a term.

Raihn and I wandered through uneven, cracked roads and paths through dilapidated piles of brick. Those within peered at us with hungry, wary eyes, whispers falling to silence as we passed.

"Do you think they recognize us?" I whispered to Raihn.

"No," he said. "No way these people know what a couple of

royals from hundreds of miles away look like. They don't recognize us, but they definitely recognize outsiders."

That wasn't hard. The people who lived here were twisted shadows of vampires or humans—all equally hungry. The eyes that stared at us were shadowed, more akin to those of starving animals than sentient beings. Unlike most cities in Obitraes, the city wasn't divided into vampire and human territory—instead, everyone seemed to scurry for whatever workable shelter they could find.

Life anywhere in the House of Night was always dangerous and bloody. But here? The feral desperation festered like an infected wound. Raihn and I passed several vampires crouched over another, lying open and bleeding in the middle of the street.

A vampire body. Blood that wouldn't even be able to keep them alive on its own, providing only the temporary pleasure of relief. But hunger that intense didn't care.

It was hard not to shiver at the way their heads snapped up when we passed. The way their eyes followed me.

Raihn stepped a little closer to me after that, his hand on my back. We made the silent, mutual decision to drift away from the populated areas, instead wandering out toward the dunes.

Eventually, we came to the edge of a lake. It was an eerie, beautiful scene, the body formed by a crater in the ruins, remains of past destruction now cradling glassy water. Broken remnants of marble slabs jutted from the water's surface, ghostly under the moonlight. Beyond it, several of Lahor's tallest towers, spires of shattered stone, loomed over us.

Goosebumps rose on my arms.

"Must've been something," Raihn murmured. "Long time ago."

Yes. It was as beautiful as it was sad.

Raihn's head turned. "Look."

He nudged my arm and lifted his chin to our left. At the edge of the lake, a woman knelt down, filling a bucket. A human—I recognized that immediately. Her stupidity was mind-boggling to me. Why a human would be out after nightfall—even so close to dawn—in this place was beyond me.

But then again, living in constant danger made one numb to it. I knew that too well.

She didn't see the Hiaj vampire flying overhead, landing on one of the nearby ruins and slowly climbing down, his eyes on her.

But we did.

I stiffened.

"Want to take care of that?" Raihn murmured in my ear. "I get the impression you've been anxious to kill something lately."

I rubbed my fingertips together.

He thought right, as much as I hated to admit it. I craved death like an opiate addict craved their fix. And yet, a part of me was afraid.

Afraid to pierce another chest when the last one I had pierced was Raihn's.

Afraid to hear my father's voice in my ear.

Afraid of whatever I might not feel anymore.

The vampire crept closer.

"If you don't move," Raihn said, "then I will."

But the words weren't even out of his mouth before my decision was made.

I slipped through the ruins to circle around behind my target. I was out of practice. The terrain was unfamiliar. I wasn't as silent as I usually was in my nighttime hunts in Sivrinaj. The vampire had turned to meet me by the time I reached him.

That was fine. I wanted more of a fight.

He came at me with his claws, but my blade was faster.

I nearly took his arm off when he swung at me. Blood dotted my face, iron-sweet when my tongue ran over it.

My target hissed and dove for me. I sidestepped, let him run himself into the wall. He wasn't used to fighting, not really. Even compared to the laziest of Sivrinaj's hunters, he was sluggish and unfocused. Starving. Untrained. Practically an animal.

Wings first, Vincent reminded me, and I tore two slashes through each one. Hiaj wings — so satisfyingly easy to pierce.

His claws opened a cut over my cheek. I didn't even flinch. A strike to his leg, to make him stumble. His right shoulder, to take out his dominant arm. And then finally I had him, pinned.

He didn't know my name or my title. He only smelled my human blood — the blood that made me unworthy of being anything other than food in his mind.

And now there was fear in his eyes.

For a brief moment, there it was. Power. Control.

Push hard to make it through the breastbone, Vincent whispered.

But I didn't need my father's advice anymore. My strike was quick and true, piercing cartilage, sliding right into his heart.

Too late, the memory hit me — of the way that this same blade had felt sliding into Raihn's chest. That rust-red stare, urging me on.

End it, princess.

I snapped my eyes open, forced myself to replace Raihn's face with this one. This person who deserved it. Uncomplicated. Easy.

I yanked my blade free. The vampire started to slide down the rock.

But I couldn't stop myself before I stabbed again. Again. *Again.*

And finally, when the vampire's chest was little more than pulp, I let the body slump to the ground.

I stared down at him, my shoulders heaving. His chest was a mess of broken flesh. For some reason, I thought of Evelaena's scar, and how she might have looked lying on her bedroom floor, blood all over her chest, too.

"She got away."

Raihn's voice startled me. He'd flown up and perched atop the ruins. He nodded toward the lake. The human woman now wandered back down the path, bucket balanced against her hip, seemingly oblivious to how close she had just come to death.

I glanced down at the dead body. Another starving beast

raised to see humans as nothing more than something to use. Another animal who was only a tool to those above him. On, and on, and on.

The futility of it was, all at once, dizzying.

"I feel like you usually take much more joy in this," Raihn said.

"Just needed to be done," I said, sheathing my weapon. "So we did it."

"You did it. I watched."

I glanced at him, and he smiled. "Enjoyed the view."

I turned away and didn't say anything. Out of the corner of my eye, I saw his face fall.

I started to walk back to the path we'd taken, but he lingered behind. He tilted his head back, squinting into the distance. Then he pointed.

"Let's go up there."

I followed his gaze, to the spires of ruined towers that loomed over us.

"Why?" I asked.

"Because look at it. Must be a hell of a view."

I squinted up at it. He was, I had to admit, probably right. He didn't give me a chance to argue with him, anyway, before he extended his hand again.

I really did think about arguing. But curiosity got the better of me.

So, I took his hand, and let him pick me up again.

Immediately, I regretted that decision. This—flying with him —never stopped being awkward. I had to work very hard at not noticing the way his arms folded around me, how close they pulled me, how a tiny primal part of me enjoyed the warmth of his skin. And I had to work *especially* hard at ignoring the reassuring sweep of his thumb over my lower back, and the way it made it so hard not to think of this version of Raihn as the man I had allowed into my bed, and my body, and even, perhaps, my heart.

Our eyes found each other's briefly, the moonlight cold over the warmth in his rust-red irises, before I looked away.

With several powerful pumps of his wings, we launched into the air. My uncomfortable feelings about our closeness dissolved when I looked up to see the stars growing closer above us, as if wrapping us in an embrace.

It was like a drug, that feeling. Made it so easy to let go of all the complicated things I'd left on the ground.

Raihn picked up speed as we rose, and we approached the top of the tower with such incredible swiftness that I had no idea how he was going to make that landing.

A second later, I realized: he wasn't.

He flew straight past the tower. Higher than its tallest rocky peak. Higher than the next, and the next. Moisture clung to my cheeks, the air damp and cold. The moon, a cloud-coated, pregnant gibbous, felt so close I could caress it.

"Look down."

Raihn's breath was warm on my ear.

I did.

The sea spread out before us, an endless expanse of rippling glass. Behind, the landscape of Lahor, tragic and beautiful in its disrepair, the ugly reality we had been walking through invisible from up here. Even Evelaena's castle was so small from this distance, just a little child's collection of bricks. Beyond Lahor, the deserts of the House of Night rolled endlessly on, smatterings of lights glowing in the far distance, consumed by the foggy mist.

My eyes stung—maybe with wind, maybe not.

Peaceful.

I hadn't meant to speak aloud.

Raihn murmured, "It is."

He hovered here, holding me tight. It was cold this high up, but I didn't feel it. Perhaps I should have been afraid that nothing but his grip was keeping me from death. I wasn't.

"Sometimes," he said, "when I'm down there, it seems like nothing about this place can ever be peaceful. But..."

But then, there's this.

I swallowed. Nodded. Because I couldn't even deny that I knew exactly what he meant.

Finally, he dipped. We·soared back down, returning to the earth, and gracefully landed at the top of the stone tower. Half the wall had collapsed, leaving the uppermost room to be little more than a circular stone ledge against a crumbling semi-circle of brick. The place must have been even older than it looked from the ground. Even the suggestion of windows had been worn away by the elements over the years.

Raihn put me down, then turned to take in the view—a vast panorama of the land and the sea, Lahor on one side, the ocean on the other.

"Not as good as up there," he said, "but still good."

"Definitely not as good as up there," I said.

He glanced over his shoulder at me. From this angle, the moonlight silhouetted him, painting a silver line along his face, catching a peculiar look in his eye.

"What?" I said.

"Nothing."

He didn't stop staring at me. It didn't feel like nothing.

Then he said, "It's just that I should have guessed that you were half vampire. Right from the first time we flew together."

"Why?"

"Because you've never looked so happy as you do when you're up there. Should've been obvious that you were made for it."

Something about the way he just said that made my brow furrow. I shot him a quizzical look.

"Well," I said. "I'm not made for it."

"I disagree, princess."

I scoffed and motioned to my back for emphasis—distinctly wingless. "I don't know. I think I lack some important parts."

But Raihn seemed unmoved.

"Wings are conjured," he said simply. "You're half Night-born. You probably have the ability to use them."

I blinked. It took a moment for his words to sink in.

"That's—"

Ridiculous.

But...

The first time Raihn took me flying, I *did* feel like I had found a missing piece of myself in the sky. Like it was as natural to be there as it was to breathe air.

He's wrong, I told myself, clamping down on the hint of hope.

He stepped closer. "You haven't even stopped to think about all the things you might be capable of, Oraya."

I scoffed. "This is ridiculous."

Another step. His eyes sparkled with amusement.

I now had to tip my chin back to meet his stare. His lips curled as he leaned closer. His breath warmed my mouth.

"You want to find out?"

Time slowed, stilled. My heartbeat was fast. I should have moved away. I should have pushed him back. I didn't.

The tip of his nose brushed mine. For a moment, the over-whelming—traitorous—urge to close that small distance between us seized me. A primal, nonsensical desire, low in my stomach. Desperate.

His gaze flicked down to my mouth. Back to my eyes.

"Do you remember," he whispered, "that time you threw me out of the window?"

My brow furrowed. "Wh—"

He gave me a firm, forceful push, and then I was falling.

23

ORAYA

I was going to die.

I was going to die I was going to die I was going to die.

That one reality, a certainty, cycled through my mind with every heartbeat as the world rushed around me, nothing but smears of color and darkness and nothingness. My limbs flailed vainly.

One second. Two. Free fall. Might as well have been a lifetime.

Raihn's voice rose over the rushing air. "You can do this, Oraya!"

He sounded so certain. I wanted to laugh at him.

He shouted, "Look at the *sky!*"

I forced my eyes open. Forced them up—to the starry velvet above. It was jarringly still. So close I felt like I could reach out and touch it.

I realized that the air, even while plummeting, did have a rhythm to it, like a pulse I could align with my own. I stretched out my limbs, drew in a breath—let the violent rush of the sky fill my lungs, even though the force of it burned my chest.

I let myself become a part of it.

And then, time seemed to stretch and slow. The direction of the air shifted. My stomach dropped, leveled out.

Behind me, Raihn let out a wordless whoop—a sound I barely heard over the rush of wind in my ears and my own thrumming heartbeat, a heartbeat that grew faster and stronger as I tilted my face toward the stars.

And then looked down.

The world was no longer rushing closer. Instead, it all spread out beneath me, ruins and sand nothing but abstract shapes in the moonlight.

"*Mother*," I whispered. My voice was shaking.

Maybe I was already dead, and I was hallucinating. I didn't want to move, in case it all shattered.

Raihn swooped down beside me, and I chanced a glance at him. He was grinning with pure, childlike joy. That smile—it made my stomach clench.

"Fucking amazing, right?" he said.

And it was his reaction that made it actually sink in.

I couldn't do anything but grin and nod. Yes. Yes, it was fucking amazing.

I was fucking flying.

The reality of this hit me all at once, immovable and confusing, and suddenly I was thinking too hard about the wings that I swore I must have been hallucinating, and the air beneath them, and these new unfamiliar muscles that I had no idea how to control—

Raihn's eyes went wide. He lurched toward me, hand outstretched.

"Oraya, watch—!"

Everything went black.

Vincent smelled like incense, a scent that was clean and old at once, elegant as preserved rose petals. It reminded me of very expensive things one shouldn't touch, but it also reminded me of safety. My father, in his strange way, was both of those things — distant and comfortable.

Vincent rarely touched me. But now, he grabbed my shoulders and hoisted me up, holding me firmly as I shook away the fuzziness from my senses.

"What in the name of the Mother were you thinking?"

My head hurt. I rubbed my eyes, and opened them again to see Vincent's staring directly into mine, silver ice-cold.

He shook me once, firmly. "Never do that. *Never.* How many times have I told you that?"

He was always calm and reserved, but I knew how to read my father. These rare moments when his fear for me slipped through his constant stoicism shook me down to my bones. I was only eleven years old. Vincent was the beginning and end of what I knew. When he was afraid, I was terrified.

I looked up at the balcony above.

"I was just trying to climb —"

"*Never* do that." He grabbed my wrist and lifted it, as if for emphasis. His fingers were long, wrapping easily around my arm. "Do you know how breakable your bones are? How quickly your skin tears? It would be so easy for this world to take you away forever. Don't give it reason to."

My jaw was tight, my eyes burning. The truth of my father's words sat heavy in my stomach, leaden with my embarrassment.

Of course, he was right.

I had seen Vincent leap from that very balcony and fly off into the night. I'd seen him fall farther and land on his feet without a scratch.

But Vincent was a vampire, and I was human. He was strong, and I was weak.

"I understand," I said.

I'd always been bad at hiding my emotions. Vincent's face softened. He dropped my arm and touched my face.

"You are too precious to be taken away by such a mundane danger, my little serpent," he said gently. "I wish it were different."

I nodded. Even young, I knew a wounded pride was better than a wounded body. Better to be ashamed and alive than over-confident and dead.

"Now get ready for bed," he said, releasing me and rising, turning to his armchair just within the double doors. "You're on chapter fifty-two of the histories, if I remember correctly. We'll do two more tonight before you sleep."

"Yes, Vincent," I said, grateful that he was giving me an opportunity to impress him in my studies after my embarrassing little misstep. I rose and took a few steps into the library.

Then...

Something prickled at the back of my neck. A strange awareness of realities that didn't line up.

The realization that this library wasn't on this floor.

That I read the histories when I was fourteen, not ten.

That Vincent was...

My chest constricted. Breath withered in my lungs.

"We don't have to look at it, little serpent," Vincent's voice said behind me.

So gentle.

So sad.

But the truth was the truth. I did have to look at it.

I turned around slowly. Vincent was in his armchair, a book on his lap, the firelight playing over the familiar planes of his face, a mournful smile at his lips.

I knew that face so well.

Now I grabbed onto the sight of every angle of it, desperately, as if to keep it from slipping away.

"You're dead," I said.

My voice now belonged to my adult self, not the version of myself from thirteen years in the past.

"Yes," he said. "I'm afraid so."

179

My shoulders rose and fell faster. Emotion burned in my chest, swallowing everything in its path.

My grief for him.

My love for him.

My hatred of him.

My anger.

My confusion.

All of it wrenched through me at once, too many wildly conflicting thoughts, too many words that I couldn't form on a tongue that was glued to the roof of my mouth, trapped against a jaw clenched so hard it shook.

He rose, his eyes never leaving mine.

"It's alright, little serpent," he whispered. "Ask me. Ask me what you want to know."

I opened my mouth.

"Wake up, Oraya. Wake up."

Fear. There was fear in that voice. I recognized the fear before I recognized the words.

The intense kind of fear, the kind that was the flip side of deep affection.

My head pounded. My entire body hurt.

I opened my eyes. Raihn leaned over me, framed against the starry sky. He let out a visible exhale of relief.

"Awful lot of concern for someone who threw me off the top of a building," I said.

His exhale became a chuckle.

"I wouldn't let you fall." He gave me a lopsided smile. "But I knew *you* wouldn't let you fall, either."

"How long have I—"

"Just for a couple of minutes. You took a nasty hit though."

I felt like it. I was dizzy enough that I actually took Raihn's

hand when he offered it to me, and pulled myself upright. I felt...
strange, like my entire body was off balance. I glimpsed something out of the corner of my eye and turned, and he let out a
grunt as he jerked to the side, dodging.

"Careful with those things."

I craned my neck to look behind me — at them.

My wings.

I could only glimpse them, and though I felt their presence on
my back, I struggled to isolate the muscles to move them around.

But even at a glimpse...

I stared at them in shock. In silence.

They were Vincent's wings. Featherless, of course, as all Hiaj
wings were. The skin was darker than night, so black light
curled up and died within them. The talons were silvery white,
like drops of moonlight. And...

And I had the accents of red. Marks of the Hiaj Heir.

Bright, bloody red, running down the wing in delicate
streaks, collecting at the edges and along their outline.

I tried to move them and did so, jerkily, in a way that I'm
sure looked ridiculous.

Wings.

My wings.

I turned in a circle as I tried to get a better look at them —
watching the way the moonlight fell over them with narrowed
eyes, like any angle might reveal a flaw that would betray my
hallucination.

No. They were real.

I was making myself dizzy.

"Take it easy," Raihn said quietly. "It'll take a minute to
adjust to them."

He spoke so gently, with so much knowing calm. He too, I
realized, would've been an adult the first time he conjured his
own wings.

My wings.

My wings.

It seemed like a ridiculous joke. Like a fucking miracle. How many times had I dreamed of having them? How many times had I looked at the sky and wished I could reach out to those stars like the vampires did?

My cheeks hurt because I was smiling so hard. I laughed a little, a sound I didn't mean to make.

And then suddenly—

Suddenly—

My chest tightened, bracing against a wave of something much more complicated, something that swallowed my joy in a single gulp.

I drew in another breath and instead of a laugh, this time a strangled sob came out, bubbling up before I could stop it. When I inhaled, it scraped through me like a serrated knife, ugly and gasping, red-hot with the overwhelming, searing intensity of my anger.

I was on the ground again.

I barely heard Raihn gasp my name. Barely felt his hands on my shoulders when he was immediately at my side, crouched next to me.

"What's wrong, Oraya? What's wrong?"

He spoke with such raw, vulnerable concern, voice low, comforting. That concern twisted a knife in my stomach.

I swallowed my next sob and only half-succeeded.

"How did you know?"

I wouldn't lift my head, wouldn't look at Raihn or allow him to look at me. The words were so disfigured I didn't know how he even understood them.

"What?" he asked, softly.

"How did you know I could do that?"

"I just... knew. You're half vampire, and a powerful one. You're made for flying. And I've seen over and over again what you're capable of. It was just..."

Obvious.

He didn't need to finish. I understood him.

Raihn, someone who had known me for less than a year, had seen that potential in me. And it was him—my enemy, someone who had every reason to cage me—who opened the door for me to seize that power.

The truth I didn't want to look at now stared me in the face, impossible to ignore, no matter how tightly I squeezed my eyes shut.

In the darkness, I saw Vincent the night of the Halfmoon ball, when we had danced together. He'd been so uncharacteristically sentimental that night. So affectionate.

I had asked him why he never took me flying.

And I remembered now, as clearly as if he was standing in front of me all over again, what he had said:

The last thing I wanted was for you to think you *could and start throwing yourself off of balconies.*

I choked out, "He knew."

He knew. He always knew.

It wasn't about protecting me. He didn't want me to jump because he didn't want me to find out I could catch myself.

That night, he had been so sentimental because he knew he was about to order the slaughter of Salinae. He knew he was about to kill any hope I had of finding any family I had left.

He knew, and he knew he was about to lie to me, and he knew he was going to lose me for it.

He knew all of it.

"*He knew.*" The words ripped from my throat, shaking with tears and jagged sobs. "He knew, and he never—he never told me, he never—*why?*"

Raihn murmured, "No one can answer that question."

In a fit of rage, my head snapped up, my anger strong enough to drown out my self-consciousness. I probably looked like a wild animal, face ruddy and tear-streaked, mouth twisted into a snarl.

"Don't fucking pity me," I hissed. "Give me one honest thing, Raihn Ashraj. I want to hear someone say it."

I was tired of performances and lies. Tired of dancing around the fucking truth. I craved honesty the way a flower craved sunlight. I even craved the pain of it, driven deep into my heart.

Raihn's face shifted.

For all his faults, he didn't pity me. He didn't hide the truth.

"I think Vincent was very afraid of you, Oraya."

"Afraid?" I let out a choked laugh. "He's—he was the Night-born King. And I'm just—"

"You aren't '*just*' anything. You were his Heir. You were the most dangerous person in the world to him. And I think he was terrified of you because of it."

It sounded unbelievable. *Absurd*.

"*Look* at this."

I leapt to my feet, thrusting my hand out to the view of Lahor below us—this dead, pathetic, broken city, a mere ghost of what it once was.

Just like me.

Raihn had taken half a step back, and I realized, dimly, that Nightfire now engulfed my hands, blazing up my arms. I noticed this very distantly, as if I was standing far outside my body.

"*Look* at what he did to this place," I ground out. "He killed dozens of people the day he left. He killed children he partially raised. Children that didn't even truly pose a threat to him. Just because he was that fucking *thorough*."

It is important to be thorough and cautious, little serpent.

How many times had he said that to me?

I was talking so fast I could barely breathe, my words rough-hewn by anger. "So why would he let me live, if I was so danger-ous? Why didn't he kill me the day he found me? Instead of—instead of taking me home and lying to me for almost twenty years. Why wouldn't he just kill me instead of caging me, instead of *breaking* me—"

Suddenly, Raihn was right in front of me, so close the Night-fire surely had to burn. If it hurt, he didn't show it. His hands gripped my shoulders, tight.

"You are not broken." I'd never heard him sound so furious, though his voice didn't rise at all. "*You are not broken.* Oraya. Do you understand me?"

No. I didn't. Because I *was* broken. Just like Lahor was

broken. I was just as broken as this city and its ruins and ghosts. Just as broken as Evelaena and her two-hundred-year-old scar and her twisted obsession with the man who gave it to her. What fucking right did I have to judge her for that when I was no different?

Vincent had ruined me. He had saved me. He had loved me. He had stifled me. He had manipulated me. He had made me everything that I was. Everything that I could be.

Even the greatest parts of my power, the parts he never wanted me to find, were his.

And now here I was, poring over every wound he gave me. And no matter how much they hurt, I never wanted them to heal, because they were his.

And I missed him too much to hate him the way I wanted to.

And I hated him most of all for that.

All at once, exhaustion fell over me. My flames shriveled away. Raihn still held my shoulders. He was so close that our faces were only inches apart. It would be so easy to lean forward and fall against his chest. If this was the version of him I had known in the Kejari, maybe I would have done that. Let him support me for a little while.

But it wasn't.

"Look at me, Oraya."

I didn't want to. I shouldn't. I'd see too much. He'd see too much. I should pull away from him.

Instead, I lifted my head, and Raihn's stare, red as dried blood, nailed me to the wall.

"I spent seventy years trapped by the worst of vampire power," he said. "And I spent so much of that time trying to make them make sense. But they don't. Rishan. Hiaj. Nightborn. Shadowborn. Bloodborn. Hell, fucking gods. It doesn't matter. Neculai Vasarus was—" His throat bobbed. "Evil doesn't even cover it. And for a long time, I thought he didn't love anything. I was wrong. He did love his wife. He loved her, and he hated that he loved her. He loved her so much he choked the life out of her."

Raihn's eyes had drifted far away—drifted somewhere in the past that I knew, just from the look on his face, hurt him to stare at directly.

"There's nothing they're more afraid of than love," he murmured. "They've been taught their entire lives that every true connection is nothing but a danger to them."

"That's ridiculous."

"Why?"

Because I was still stuck on this—on this idea that Vincent had been afraid of me. This idea that went against everything I had ever known.

His mouth twisted into a wry smirk. "Love is fucking terrifying," he murmured. "I think that's true no matter who you are."

I stilled.

There was something about the way he said that—the closeness of him, the steadiness of his stare—that jolted me back to my senses.

What was I doing?

Why was I showing him this? Raihn was my kidnapper. He had lied to me. He had used me.

Raihn had murdered my father.

And now he was lecturing me about the sanctity of love?

He was right. Love was terrifying. To be so vulnerable to another person. And I'd—

I stopped that thought.

No. Whatever I had felt for Raihn was not love.

But it had been vulnerable. More vulnerable than I ever should have let myself become.

And look at how I'd paid for it.

Look at how *my father* had paid for it.

My anger, my grief, drained away. In its place was the thick burn of shame.

I yanked away from Raihn's touch and tried not to notice the flicker of disappointment on his face.

"I'd like to be alone," I said.

My voice was harsh. A finality.

Silence. Then he said, "It's dangerous out here."

"I can handle it."

He paused. Unconvinced, I knew.

I wouldn't look at him, but I knew if I did, he'd have that look on his face—that fucking *look*, like he wanted to say something that would be too earnest, too real.

"Just go," I said. It sounded more like a plea than I wanted it to. But maybe that was what made him listen.

"Alright," he said softly, and the sound of his wings faded off into the night.

24

ORAYA

I sat on top of those towering ruins for a long time, trying and failing to feel nothing.

The sky slowly warmed, cold moonlight replaced by the gold touch of dawn, revealing all the ugliest truths of this city.

He had been so eager to forget this place. But this place never forgot him. Never recovered from the nonchalant cruelty of his departure.

I hated how familiar that felt.

All of it was like the room that Evelaena now kept as a twisted shrine to him. Nothing but discarded trash, and she projected such meaning onto it. A shoe. A hairbrush. A stupid scribble of ink —

I blinked.

A scribble of ink.

Recognition nagged at the back of my mind. Somewhere I had seen this view before —

I stood, then took several steps back, watching the way the landscape shifted with my perspective. The sea a bit to the right, the tower slightly overlapping it...

No. Not quite. But close.

I closed my eyes and pictured it: the ink drawing on Vincent's desk, perfectly preserved for centuries.

Then I opened my eyes and peered around the edge. Another tower stood just slightly to the south of this one—it somehow managed to look even older. But by my estimation, the viewpoint would line up. If I was right… the sketch of Lahor that Vincent had made might've been drawn from those ruins.

I hesitated, taking a moment to flex my back muscles. They were fiercely sore, and every movement felt clumsy with the wings attached to them. I didn't *regret* sending Raihn away, exactly—no, I told myself, I definitely didn't regret it—but it might've been wise to get some more wing instruction before I had.

I wasn't going to let you fall. But more importantly, I knew you weren't going to let you fall.

The words floated through my mind unprompted.

Mother, I hoped he was right.

I kept my eye on my target, and I jumped.

Whatever I did to get from one tower to the other was probably better described as "controlled falling" than "flying."

But I made it.

Barely.

I let out an ugly *oof* as my side jammed against a pile of ancient brick. Pain tore through my left wing as it scraped a stray shard of rock—it was amazing how disorienting it was for the boundaries of your own body to suddenly be twice as wide in both directions. The impact threw me, sending me rolling across the brick floor with a collection of ragged grunts.

I pushed myself to my hands and knees, collecting myself. I was more shaken than I'd like to admit. Wings were sensitive, apparently, because the cut hurt fiercely. I craned my neck to try to see the injury with little success.

I lifted my head, and suddenly my wound didn't matter anymore.

"Fuck," I whispered.

Wings spread out over the wall before me.

Hiaj wings, slate gray with tinges of purple. They were life-size, or maybe bigger, pressed against the crumbling remains of the stone wall. Growths that at first looked like bulging veins spread along their length, clinging to the formation of the bones and reaching across the expanses of skin, tinted red, forming a knot at the center that pulsed bright crimson.

A heart. It looked almost exactly like a heart.

But as I pushed myself up and dragged myself closer, I realized the growths weren't veins at all. They were some kind of… fungus, maybe, though one that looked sickeningly life-like. The heart at the center of the wings, though… that looked so *real*. Was it flesh, petrified like the wings? Or something else?

I didn't remember getting to my feet, nor crossing the room, but the next thing I knew, I was standing right before it.

The veins and the heart pulsed in small, rhythmic movements, slowly quickening. I realized, after a moment, that they mirrored my breathing. The hairs stood upright on the back of my neck. I'd never been so repelled by something and simultaneously so drawn to it. It was disgusting. It was the most beautiful thing I'd ever seen.

One part of me thought, *I need to get far, far away from whatever this is.*

The other part thought, *Septimus was right. I do just* know.

Simple, uncomplicated fact. This was what we had been looking for. It was beyond questioning.

And I'd just found it alone.

My hand was outstretched before I even told my body to move.

My fingertips brushed the heart-like growth. It was so cold I almost jolted away. But before I could react, several veins slid along the surface of it, reached for me, and —

I let out a hiss of pain. Drops of my blood, bright human red, smeared against the fungus as the veinlike cords slithered back around the heart. It momentarily seemed as if the wings were flexing, stretching — an illusion of shifting muscles.

Then the fibers pulled away, retreating along the walls of the ruins, and the thing that had so resembled a heart opened.

Warmth suffused the air. The red glow drenched the shadows. I stared into it, blinking, forcing my eyes to adjust.

The heart had shifted, now mimicking open, cupped hands. At its center was a crescent moon of polished, gleaming silver, painfully white against the fading red surrounding it. It was perhaps the size of my palm, the two tips sharp as blades—so sharp that at first, I thought that maybe it was intended to be a weapon, until I noticed the delicate silver chain attached to one end.

A pendant.

Once the light faded, it was unremarkable, if very pretty.

I reached for it—

My father's blood is hot and slick on my hands. The wings are still warm. I need to keep wiping the blood on my shirt. I look like what I am — a monster, just like the ones that crawl through the ruins of Lahor every night.

I do not have regrets.

This is not what the historians will write one day about me.

No one will remember the names or faces of the children that I killed tonight. A Nightborn tradition of power, killing children. My father killed my younger brother minutes after he drew his first breath. I was sixteen years old when I watched him throw that little bloody wad of fabric over the railing, feeding it to the demons circling below. He always made it clear that I was to function as his heir, but never as a threat.

I hid so carefully, all these years. Tramped down every scrap of my power. Endured every abuse. I did it all with a placid stare on my face, never letting him see the hatred beneath.

It was not useful to hate my father. It was useful to learn from him.

So I learned.

It was so satisfying to see it on his face when he realized his mistake. That he had underestimated me my entire life.

Whenever I think of the faces of the children, my nieces and nephews and cousins, I replace them with that of my father. The realization of his hubris, his miscalculation.

It made every year in this shithole worth it.

I think only of my father as I nail his wings to the wall, muttering spells beneath my breath.

I think only of my father.

I think of the Kejari.

I think of a crown on my head.

I do not have regrets.

I do not have regrets.

I COULDN'T BREATHE. My stomach churned. I couldn't see anything, couldn't feel.

My hand hurt—Mother, my hand hurt so fucking much. It was that pain that rooted me back to the world, and I clung to it. I forced my eyes open. My vision was blurry, as if I'd just been staring directly into the sun, though this tower was still dim with only the warm beginnings of sunrise slipping through the shattered stone.

I looked down.

My hand was covered in blood. I flipped it over to see that I'd been clutching the pendant, so tightly that the sharp edges had carved a perfect imprint of the crescent moon into my palm.

What the hell had just—

"Do you know," a light, childlike voice came from behind me, "how long I have been trying to access that?"

A chill fell over me.

I forced myself to my feet and was rewarded with a wave of dizziness so strong I staggered against the wall. I righted myself and turned to see Evelaena standing silhouetted against the sunlight, one of her child companions, a stoic-faced little boy, beside her.

Fuck.

It was past dawn. How could they be here?

The beginnings of sunburns—a dark, purplish cast—had started on Evelaena's cheeks, though she wore a heavy cloak with the hood pulled low over her face. Her wings were creamy, fleshy pink, and the burns on them were worse, especially since the cloak couldn't have covered them as she was flying.

If they bothered her, though, she didn't show it. She didn't blink. Her blue eyes were wide and eerily bright in the dim light, smile tight and unwavering.

She was looking at me like I was something to be devoured. Like she wanted to peel my face off and wear it over her own.

"I discovered it about a decade ago, you see," she chirped. "It wasn't there two-hundred years ago. I knew it was his right away. He must have come without telling me, must have—" She blinked, like she lost her train of thought mid-sentence. "But I could never open it."

I said nothing.

Drip, as my blood hit the stone floor.

The child's eyes locked to it. His throat bobbed. Evelaena's nostrils flared.

I slid the pendant into my pocket and reached for my blade. I tried not to show it, but I was still leaning against the wall. My head ached with the exertion of forcing my eyes to focus. Fragments of—of whatever I had experienced when I touched the pendant slipped into the corners of my vision without my permission, a gritty, grainy version of the world.

"And the wings," she added, still not blinking. "How *interesting*."

Drip.

My blood hit the ground again.

The child lunged for me.

He was fast. I barely had time to respond before he was on

me, teeth sinking into my arm. I let out a curse and flung myself against the wall, sending him careening to the stone.

Move, little serpent, Vincent whispered to me, hurriedly. *Move. She's coming for you.*

I knew she was. She was coming and I couldn't move quickly enough.

I heard her before I saw her. I whirled around as fast as I could, nearly sending myself back into the stone, lashing out at her with my blades. I caught flesh — her arm.

She drew back, face contorted into a hiss. She wielded a rapier, similar in style to the one Vincent had once wielded. Not a coincidence, I was sure.

I barely managed to deflect her when she lunged again.

My body felt as if it was a half-step disconnected from my mind. My wings, which I had no idea how to disappear, drastically altered my balance. Evelaena was no great warrior, certainly not compared to those I fought in the Kejari — but she was still strong and fast, her movements eerily similar to Vincent's in style. Efficient, precise, graceful — but half a step from bloodlust, sloppier with every drop of my blood.

She was taller than me, but at least I was used to that. I blocked her from above with one blade and used the opening to drive my second into her side.

She snarled and retaliated with a blow so devastatingly strong, my back slammed against the wall.

Pain. A moment of blurred vision. When I focused again, Evelaena's face was right in front of mine, our noses brushing. My arm trembled violently as I blocked her sword between us.

I'd been in exactly this position countless times before. I could use her momentum, force her against the wall. Blade through the heart. Always so satisfying, because this was always where they thought they had me.

But it took a massive burst of strength to do that. I didn't know if I had it. If I tried and failed, I'd expose myself to her.

I didn't have a choice.

I took the shot.

With a ragged scream, I pushed back against her with everything I had, reversing our positions against the wall. She hadn't been expecting it—her shock worked to my advantage. Good. I was glad someone still underestimated me.

I did not hesitate. I drew back my blade, ready to plunge it into her chest—

Agonizing pain ripped through me.

I couldn't even place it, at first, only that I knew it was some of the worst I'd ever felt, like fire and steel at once.

I staggered backward, whirling to fling away my attacker.

The child went rolling across the ground.

I tried to turn and tripped. My body wasn't cooperating with me. I glanced down and realized that he had stabbed my already-wounded wing. It now dragged on the ground, hindering my movements.

Fuck.

Evelaena.

She was already lunging for me. I raised my weapon to meet her—

Too late.

She was on top of me before I could react.

Slender, clawed fingers grabbed my face, nails digging into my cheeks.

"Such a rude guest," she murmured.

She smiled at me, and then slammed my head against the ground.

2 5

RAIHN

Oraya hadn't come back to our rooms.

I watched her up there for almost an hour, just sitting in that tower staring at the horizon. I'd give her space when she wanted it—I owed her that, didn't I?—but that didn't mean that I was about to leave her unguarded. I remained until my exposed skin stung and my eyes began to ache, but eventually, I had no choice but to get back to the room.

When I left, Oraya had still been at the top of that tower.

I peered between the curtains for the fifteenth time this morning, wincing as the sun hit still-tender burns.

Even in stolen, three-second glances, Lahor managed to look even more pathetic in the daylight. Downright grotesque. At least at night, there was a kind of ancient romanticism to it, the moonlight suggesting outlines of what it might have looked like, long ago.

But there was nothing sentimental about Lahor in daylight. Just corpses and debris. Starving humans creeping around in the ruins, trying to rob starving vampires. Starving demons attempting to use the sunlight to hunt their prey, flinging their fellow beasts out into the deadly light, letting it cook them alive.

And Oraya was still out there.

"What're you doing?"

Mische's voice was sleep-slurred. I glanced over my shoulder and closed the curtains to see her rubbing her eyes, blinking blearily at me. Her hair had only gotten wilder as it had grown longer. One side was now comically smooshed up against the side of her head.

"Oh, you know," I said, keeping my voice casual in my deliberate non-answer.

"Past sunrise."

"Mm."

Mische glanced around, blinking sleep away. Realization dawned on her. "Where's Oraya?"

I didn't answer. Peered through the curtains again. Winced and flicked them closed.

That was all the answer Mische needed. All at once, she was awake.

"She's gone?"

"We—had gone out sightseeing."

"We?"

I shot Mische a glare. "What's that supposed to mean?"

"I'm just surprised she wanted to go anywhere with you."

"I—"

I cornered her.

I abandoned that train of thought.

"It doesn't matter," I muttered. "I was with her for a while. But then she wanted to be alone. So I gave her what she wanted."

"But she still hasn't come back?" Mische said hesitantly.

A few seconds of silence. The possibility hung in the air, obvious, even if neither of us would state it right away.

Mische whispered, "You don't think she…"

Ran. Betrayed you.

Oraya would have had the perfect opening for it. An unfamiliar city. The cover of daylight. No guards here that would stop her. Brand new wings to carry her away.

197

I swallowed, rubbing the center of my chest.

Tonight, I had seen her smile—really smile—for the first time in more than a month. And Goddess, it did something to me. It was like witnessing a rare natural phenomenon.

And when I'd watched her fly tonight, alight with such joy, only one thought had rang out in my mind:

I never knew something could look so beautiful flying away.

I peered through the curtains and imagined Oraya fading off into the distance of that sun-bleached blue sky, never to be seen again. Imagined her finding some new, wonderful life, somewhere so far from here.

"You think she—she left?" Mische asked, finally, like it took her all this time just to put words to it.

I thought of Oraya curled up with her knees to her chest in those ruins, those sobs coming out of her like deep water drawing from a rift in the earth.

My fingers tightened around the curtains at the thought of it.

Did Oraya run?

I fucking wished she had.

But the pit of tension in my stomach said, *Something isn't right.*

"No," I said. "No, I don't think so."

I closed the curtains and turned back to Mische.

"Let's go."

26

ORAYA

I forced my eyes open.

Pain shocked my body, but I couldn't place where it was coming from, only that it was overwhelming.

It was dark. I struggled to make out forms in the shadows. The only light emanated from two Nightfire lanterns above an unlit hearth. It smelled like mold and dust and civilizations long dead. No windows, only stone. A few half-decayed pieces of broken furniture. A strong, cold draft from somewhere I couldn't place.

Evelaena stood before me, holding the Taker of Hearts.

"I was wondering what had become of this," she said.

Shit. She'd gone through my possessions. I cursed myself for bringing it at all—at the time, it had seemed much safer to keep it with me rather than leaving it unguarded in Sivrinaj. Now, it seemed foolish.

I tried to move and was rewarded with a stab of pain so sharp it left me breathless. I twisted my neck and drew in a strangled gasp.

My hands were tied together in front of me. But those weren't the restraints that kept me immobile—no, those were the

199

nails driven through my wings, which had been stretched out along the brick wall. My blood, bright crimson, ran down the leathery black in streaks that echoed my Heir-red marks.

Cold, unrelenting terror fell over me. I tried to spirit them away—but how did one do that? Raihn hadn't told me. Wishing them away, even desperately, did nothing but make my heart race in panic.

I drew in a deep breath, trying to calm myself as my eyes continued to adjust to the darkness. Several of Evelaena's child companions were scattered about the room, too, standing against the wall or curled up on the broken furniture. I jumped as I caught movement out of the corner of my eye, and turned my head to see one of the youngest-looking ones crawling on the ground near my feet, lapping at drips of blood falling from my wings.

"Get the fuck away from me," I spat, kicking at the girl like a stray cat, and she gave me an appropriate hiss before skittering away.

"Don't speak to my children that way." Evelaena moved swiftly, with all of Vincent's smooth grace. She still wore the bloody dress from our fight. She was close enough now that I could see the burns on her hand. When she carried the sword, she did so with a wad of fabric around it, now stained black with her blood. She couldn't wield it, either.

Her lip curled as she glanced down at it. "I wondered where this had gone. If the usurper had taken it or managed to destroy it. Turns out, he just gave it to his wife."

Something glinted in the darkness as she leaned closer to me —the pendant, now dangling around her neck. Her dress was open low, the mottled scar tissue forming a grotesque halo around the moon.

Her head cocked, eyes predator-sharp. "Can *you* wield it, cousin?"

"No one can wield it but him. You know that."

Evelaena laughed, high and manic. She leapt closer still, her free hand coming to my throat, then sliding down—over the bare skin of my upper chest, where she'd opened up my leathers to reveal my Heir Mark.

"I had to see if this was real," she said. "Tried to scrub it off you while you were out."

If only it was so fucking easy.

"Get off of me," I hissed, but she only pressed harder against my chest, making the nails tug at the delicate skin of my wings.

"I thought it would be me," she said. "*I* was Vincent's closest living relative. *I* spent my whole life training to be queen one day. Do you think it's easy? Learning how to rule all by yourself?" She thrust the sword behind her, wildly gesturing to her child soldiers. "I needed subjects to rule! Do you know how hard it was to bring this damned place back from the dead? And I was all alone! *All alone!*"

Her voice cracked. The scent of something burning hit my nostrils. The dim cold light hit Evelaena's chest, revealing that the pendant was burning her, too, where it lay against her skin. Every time it swung back against her, she winced.

"But then there was *you. You,* who he kept alive. *You,* who smell so—so *human.*" Her nostrils flared. She leaned closer still, our bodies now nearly flush.

Every muscle stiffened.

Too close. Too fucking close.

"*Get off of me,*" I snarled.

Nightfire. There was Nightfire in this room. I just had to reach for it, call to it. Even if my own refused to come to me. I'd done it before. I—

"Why do you deserve this? You, a human?"

And then the next thing I knew, Evelaena's mouth was at my throat.

Pain, as her teeth dug into my skin.

A wave of sickening dizziness as her venom hit my veins.

I gasped, flailing out against her, my knee coming up to strike her and failing to make contact. Her grip on me was impossibly strong. With every gulp of blood she took from me, my vision blurred.

It was Evelaena's mouth on my skin.

The Ministaer's.

My old lover's.

Panic set in, artificially dimmed by the venom. I was trapped. Helpless. Heir Mark or no. Wings or no.

Evelaena released me, throwing her head back and licking blood from the side of her mouth.

"You *taste* human," she hissed. "You look human. You smell human."

My head lolled. I forced myself back to consciousness through the fog of the venom.

Think. I had to think.

"And it was *you*." She laughed, hoarse and raw. She straightened, and the pendant fell against her chest, and again, she flinched.

She froze, going abruptly still. Her eyes gleamed with tears.

"I always thought he meant to leave me alive," she said, barely louder than a whisper. "Always thought it was his plan. That he chose me. But—"

Her hand clutched the pendant, white-knuckle tight, blood bubbling between her fingers.

Suddenly, I understood.

She didn't just flinch because of the pain of the burns. But she had experienced what I did when she touched that thing. Pieces of Vincent. Distant shards of his memory.

His memory of the night he had tried to kill her, a five-year-old child. And had failed. Not because he intended to. Not because he meant to spare her. But because he had killed so many children that night that he was a little sloppy, and she wasn't important enough to risk going back for.

And for an odd moment, I understood her so completely that it twisted a knife in my heart. She was obsessed with Vincent. She loved him because he was her only tenuous connection to power and hated him because of what he had put her through. She survived for centuries by building up fairy tales around him, around Lahor, around a crown she might wear one day.

And now she was realizing that she had meant nothing to him.

There was no plan. No secret. No fate.

Just a careless, bloodthirsty man and motives that did not make sense.

I saw myself in Evelaena as clearly as if I was looking into a mirror. Both of us built and broken by the same man. She had prayed for fate and gotten feckless luck. I had hinged my life on luck and gotten secrets.

I got power. She got nothing.

But at least she could get revenge.

You are not like them.

Vincent's words echoed in my head. I hated him for them. And yet, in this moment, I latched onto them with ugly certainty.

He was right. I wasn't.

I was one of the most powerful vampires in the House of Night. In all of Obitraes. I had that power, even if I didn't know how to access it. It was in me.

This bitch did not get to be the one to kill me.

An idea solidified in this understanding—a risky one.

"You're still his blood," I whispered. "Whether he recognized that or not."

She scoffed, but I went on, "I don't want bad blood between us, cousin. You deserved more. And I—I would give you the sword. If you want it."

She hesitated. One of the children, a little girl, stood, interest piqued, her fair gaze spearing me—like she saw what I was doing.

"You're owed that much, don't you think?" I said. "For what he did to you?"

Evelaena's eyes fell to me, then the sword in her hands. And then back to me again.

They shone with lust. Evelaena was a creature driven wild with starvation—for blood, for power, for love, for validation. The only reason I was alive right now was because she had so gorged herself the night before, but the hint of blood lust still visible in her face right now was due to a much deeper hunger, one that had been following her, I suspected, for two hundred years.

She didn't even know what she wanted to do with me. Love me, hate me, eat me, fuck me, kill me. Hell, all of those things, maybe.

This seemed like a revelation.

I'd spent my entire life fixated on all the ways vampires were different than me. I'd been so certain that all my confusion and frustration was because of my fragile human nature.

But Raihn was right. Vampires were every bit as fucked up.

I didn't even need to be that good of an actress. Evelaena was desperate to believe me.

"You can't wield it now," I said, "because it's mine. It belongs to the Hiaj Heir."

I nodded down—to my chest, and the tattoo pulsing across it.

"But," I said. "I could transfer ownership to you."

"I'm not foolish enough to let you hold that blade."

"You don't have to," I said. "Just let me touch it. That's all. And it's yours."

She went still—that unnatural vampire still. I could see the calculation behind her eyes.

She'd kill me anyway, of course. That was what she was thinking. She wanted it all—the companionship, the Heir Mark, the sword, the crown, my blood. She wasn't willing to give up any of those things after centuries of constant sacrifice.

"Fine," she said.

She brought the sword closer to me, holding it out, while maintaining a strong grip on it over the cloth.

"I need my hands," I said.

Her mouth thinned. Still, she nodded to one of her children. The little girl, the one who had been watching me so warily, approached me with a little dagger. Her abrupt slice through the binding cut my wrist, too.

Hands free. That was something. Not enough. But something.

I gave her a weak smile and gingerly pulled back the cloth wrapped around the blade. The red glow seemed much stronger than usual now, warming my face and reflecting in Evelaena's eyes, which were wide and unblinking.

I stared at it. My father's blade, supposedly carrying a piece of his heart. Just being this close to it again made me feel as if Vincent was standing just over my shoulder, forever out of sight.

If you are, I thought, *you'd better help me here. You owe me that.*

That's a rude way to speak to your father, Vincent replied, and I almost scoffed aloud.

I took a deep breath and opened my palms over the blade, just an inch or two from the surface. I closed my eyes and tried to look very, very serious.

I was bullshitting so fucking hard.

Use this moment, Vincent commanded in my ear. *This may be an act, but it might be the only time you get to prepare yourself.*

He had a good point. I used this moment to connect to the forces around me, feeling the room.

Feeling the Nightfire.

I was probably too weak to generate it myself right now, or at the very least too inconsistent to be certain I could, but... I could feel it pulsing in those torches, the energy familiar, if weak and distant.

I could work with that.

All I needed was a few seconds of distraction.

I opened my eyes to meet Evelaena's.

"It's done," I said. "Try it."

She looked wary. "Are you sure it worked?"

"This is powerful magic. It knew you were blood."

Telling her what she so desperately wanted to believe. The flare of desire in her eyes showed me she'd bought it.

The little girl was still giving me that wary stare, and she tugged on Evelaena's skirt, as if in silent protest.

Evelaena ignored her as she unwrapped the sword.

"Take its hilt," I said. "It's ready to accept you."

She was definitely going to see through this. How could she not?

But hope was a strange, potent drug, and Evelaena was at its mercy. She took the hilt and drew the sword.

For a moment, nothing happened. The room was utterly silent. A slow smile of glee spread over her lips.

She started, "It's—"

—And then she let out a shriek of pain.

The steady glow of the blade flickered in erratic spurts. The scent of burnt flesh filled the room. The sound Evelaena was making rose from a moan to a scream, but she wouldn't release the sword—or maybe the sword refused to release her. Several of the children ran to her side, pulling at her in panic. The rest hugged the walls, watching wide-eyed.

Move, Vincent roared. *Move now!*

One chance. One opening.

Fear is the fucking key to it, Oraya, Raihn had screamed at me, during the Halfmoon trial.

He had been right. The key was all the ugliness, all the weakness I refused to look at. Everything the sword had pulled up in me. Everything that had hurt me.

I reached deep.

Deep into my heart and my past and the memories.

My rage, my grief, my confusion, my betrayal. I took all of it. I ripped it all open inside myself.

Beneath it all was sheer power.

The brightness of the Nightfire seared my vision. Evelaena's screams were so loud, so constant, they faded to a distant din beneath the blood rushing in my ears. Her form was difficult to make out around the fire, but she was stumbling, unable to control herself, still clutching the sword.

I leaned forward, ignoring the pain as the nails tugged at my wings, and grabbed her.

She was half limp. She turned to me, wide-eyed, and in that split-second, I saw exactly what she must have looked like as a five-year-old child, the night that Vincent had driven his blade through her chest.

For a moment, she looked at me like I might save her.

I didn't. I pried the sword from her hands.

The moment my own closed around its hilt, the pain took me. I thought I couldn't feel pain anymore, compared to what had been done to my wings. I had been wrong. This was deeper than flesh. Deeper than nerves.

For a moment, I wasn't here anymore. I was in a dozen different places at once.

I was in a ruined tower in Lahor.

I was in Sivrinaj, in a colosseum full of screaming spectators, kneeling before a goddess.

I was in the Nightborn castle, sitting at my desk.

I was in my private training arena in the castle, training with my daughter, my daughter who needed to be better than this if she was to have any hope of surviving this world.

I was lying in the sands, my daughter holding me, death looming over her shoulder.

Stop.

But the images kept coming—more than images, sensations. I lost my grip on the world around me. The tide swept me away.

STOP STOP STOP STOP—

Focus, Oraya.

It wasn't Vincent's voice in my head this time. It was my own.

You have one chance. Right now. Take it!

I barely managed to claw myself back to awareness. The sword hurt to hold, but I refused to let it go.

I cut through the ropes binding my legs and stumbled forward. Pain flooded me as my full weight pulled against my wings.

The Nightfire had overtaken the room. Several of the children now climbed up the debris on the side of the walls, trying to stay away from the flames. Evelaena had pushed herself to her hands and knees, crawling toward me, a sword clutched in her burned-up hands.

No time to figure out how to get rid of my wings.

I pushed off against the wall and screamed as the delicate flesh ripped free.

I flung myself at Evelaena, pinning her to the ground. Her sword went sliding across the floor.

She reached for me. "Cousin—"

I didn't let her speak.

I drove Vincent's sword into her chest, right through the scar he had left two hundred years ago—straight into her heart.

She went slack beneath me, her eyes filling with betrayal before going vacant.

My breath was labored. The Nightfire still clung to the corners of the room.

I tried to get up—

Someone struck me from behind. I went toppling to the ground. The little girl, the same one who had been staring at me, leaned over me, red dotting her face.

She lifted her knife in both hands over her head, ready to bring it down.

I tried to counter, tried to—

A blast rocked the room. My vision blurred, dimmed.

A moment or minutes or hours passed.

I forced my eyes open.

Raihn leaned over me, brow furrowed with concern.

I was hallucinating, clearly, or dreaming again. Someone pried my hands free and I let out a choked cry.

"It's alright," Raihn murmured, leaning close to me.

I hated these dreams, the ones where I dreamed of the way Raihn had once looked at me, when we fought together in the Kejari. Like his heart was outside his body.

Made it hard to reconcile all he had done to me, when he looked at me that way.

"You're safe," he whispered, as he gathered me in his arms, and I faded away.

27

ORAYA

I opened my eyes from a mercifully dreamless sleep. My head was throbbing, and my body hurt even worse.

Coarse linen rubbed against my cheek. I was in a plain little bedchamber. A desk, a chair, a crooked table. Behind me, someone was moving around. I could hear the snap of a fire, and the hiss of something boiling, and the smell of something delicious.

I tried to roll over and was met with a stab of pain so sharp I let out a little strangled sound that was intended to be a *"fuck"* but instead sounded more like *"ffermmkk."*

Footsteps circled the room, approaching me.

"Well look at you," Raihn said. "So bright and cheerful when you wake up."

I tried to say, "Fuck you," and coughed instead.

"Oh, I still heard that."

He sat at the edge of my bed. It was so rickety that his considerable weight made the entire thing shift to one side.

I choked out, "Where are we?"

"One of the Crown homes in the east. It's, uh… seen better days. But it's safe. Quiet. And closer than Sivrinaj."

"How long have we been here?"

"Little less than a week."

I started, and Raihn raised his hands. "We kept you sedated for a while. Trust me, that was for the best."

I didn't love the idea of Raihn's men carting around my unconscious body for a week.

As if he could read my face, he said, "Don't worry. It was just me."

That did feel like a relief, though I didn't want to examine too closely why.

"Where are the others?"

"Mische is here. The Bloodborn are in Lahor with Ketura and her guards, getting it under control."

Lahor. It all came back with overwhelming detail. The fire and Evelaena and the sword and—

"I killed Evelaena," I said, not quite intending to speak aloud. "She—"

"Strung you up in a basement. Yes. I know."

The basement.

The tower. The sword. The—

Panic. I touched my chest, eyes going wide.

"I found something in the tower. I found—"

"This?"

He reached for the bedside table and withdrew a carefully wrapped object about the size of his hand, flat and circular. He opened the cloth covering, revealing the moon pendant. The last time I'd seen it, it had been covered in Evelaena's blood, but now it was pristine.

"You were crawling for it when I found you. Even half-dead." He quickly covered it and set it back on the table, wincing and rubbing his hand. "The minute I tried to touch it, I realized what it was."

"I don't know if I *do* know what it is. Just that it's…"

"Special."

"*His*. It was his. More than that. It was… It has to do with whatever Vincent was trying to hide."

This certainty came to me with an unexpectedly strong flood of satisfaction. There was so little I understood about my father. Finding even one puzzle piece seemed like a triumphant victory, even if it only led to more questions.

"Probably," Raihn said. "All the better that Septimus doesn't know about it. I'm glad it's here, with us, instead of with him."

He seemed shockingly unconcerned with it. My eyes narrowed.

"I'm surprised it's still here, and that you didn't fly off to Sivrinaj with it. This was what you were looking for, wasn't—"

"You were fucking dying," he snapped. "I had more important things to worry about than your father's games."

He clamped his mouth shut, like he'd just said something he didn't intend to. "That'll burn," he muttered, and rose to go stir the pot over the stove.

More important things.

He returned, carrying a plate piled with steaming meat and vegetables.

"Here. Eat."

"I'm not hungry," I said, even as my mouth watered.

"It's delicious. You want it. Trust me."

Arrogant.

But my stomach rumbled. I had to admit, the smell was… incredible.

I took a bite and almost melted back into the bed.

Mother fucking damn him.

I took another bite, and another.

"Was I right?" Raihn said, infuriatingly smugly.

"Mm," I said, between bites.

"I'll take that as, *'Delicious, Raihn. Thank you for this meal cooked with love, and also for saving my life.'*"

A joke. It was a joke.

Still, my chewing slowed. I set aside the plate—already almost half empty—and turned to Raihn with a hard stare.

He must have thought I ran away. It would've been a reasonable assumption.

"You came to find me," I said.

His smile faded. "Is that really so surprising?"

"I thought you'd think I just—"

"Oh, I did think."

"But you still came after me. Why?"

He let out a sound between an exhale and a scoff.

"What?" I said.

"I just—nothing. Just turn around so I can check your wings."

My wings.

The thought made the blood drain from my face. Oh, Goddess. I'd been so disoriented, the pain so constant, that the terrible reality of what had happened to them hadn't yet sunk in.

They had been *nailed through*. Many times.

He settled behind me. "Give me some room back here."

I obeyed, wincing as I edged forward on the bed, my legs folded beneath me. He let out a breath through his teeth, and my stomach turned.

My new wings—the only gift of these last horrible months. Shredded.

I choked out, bracing myself for the answer, "How do they look?"

"I'm glad you killed that depraved bitch. If she'd been alive when I got there…"

He didn't need to finish the sentence.

My throat was thick. "So it's bad?"

"She nailed you to the fucking wall."

"I couldn't spirit them away. I couldn't—"

"It's hard to do. Harder than getting them out, and nearly impossible if they're injured, even for those who were born with them. I should have made sure I taught you that before I left you. That was stupid of me."

His voice softened at that, and I winced at it.

"I don't need pity. Tell me the truth." My words wavered a little, despite my best efforts. "They're ruined, right?"

Silence.

Horrible silence.

The bed shifted. Raihn leaned around me, turning my head by my chin so I was looking into his face.

"That's what you think? That you'll never fly again?"

My face must have said enough.

I might've expected his expression to soften, but instead, it grew harder, like I'd offended him.

"You're made for the sky, Oraya. Never let anyone take that away from you. Of course you'll fly again." He released me and returned to my back. Under his breath, he muttered, "Like I'd ever let that happen."

My exhale was shaky with relief.

"So they'll heal?"

"It'll take some time, but they will heal. They already look a hell of a lot better than they did."

They will heal. I had never heard three more beautiful words. Raihn said them like he'd will it into truth if he had to.

I heard rummaging behind me, and the sound of something unscrewing—a jar, maybe? I tried to look over my shoulder with limited success.

"What's that?"

"Medicine. You're due."

I couldn't turn enough to see what Raihn held—at least not without more pain than I was interested in—but I eyed the slight glow against the bedside table. It was good stuff, whatever he'd gotten.

There was a long, awkward silence.

"Do you mind if I—?" he asked.

Touch me. He'd have to touch me.

"I could get Mische if you want," he said, "She's out right now, but—"

"No," I said curtly. "It's fine. You've already been doing it, anyway."

"It's going to hurt, probably."

"It's fi—"

My body seized. My vision went white.

"*Fuck*," I breathed.

"Thought it would be better if you didn't have warning."

Oh, I recognized that line. I half-smiled, half-grimaced as he moved on to another cut.

"So this is revenge," I said. "I understand now."

"Got me. You did a good job patching up my back, though. I'll return the favor. Promise."

A lump rose in my throat as I thought about that night for the first time in months—the night Jesmine had tortured Raihn for hours in the wake of the attack against the Moon Palace. So much about the memory now felt... different. More complicated.

"Must have been hard for you that night," I said.

"Getting stitched up or getting tortured?"

"The questioning. You didn't break."

Jesmine's methods were... thorough. Honed to perfection for their intended purpose, and that purpose was getting information out of unwilling participants.

"I wasn't lying," he said. "I wasn't responsible for the attack on the Moon Palace."

I peered over my shoulder and shot him a flat look.

He huffed a laugh. "I guess I've earned that face. But I'd come too far to let one woman with a knife bring me down." Then, after a pause, "Well. *That* woman with a knife. Met another one who was a whole different story."

I bit my lip as he applied another well-timed dab of medicine, but the pain was a welcome distraction.

"So has it been worth it?" I asked. "Being the Nightborn King."

His hands paused. Then resumed.

"Does it count as bad bedside manner if you're the one in bed? Trying to make us both equally uncomfortable?"

I shrugged and immediately regretted the way the movement jostled my wings.

"Fine," he said. "I'll keep it interesting for you, since I know you need the distraction. Was it worth it? I saved the Rishan people from two centuries of subjugation. I took back what was rightfully mine. I got revenge upon the man who killed thousands of my people. I even get to wear a crown in front of the pricks who once treated me as a slave."

All things I expected him to say. All things that I knew were true.

"That's what I would say to anyone else who asked," he said. "But it's not anyone asking. It's you. And you deserve the truth, if you want it."

He moved on to another wound. I barely felt it.

I'd regret it if I let him keep going. I knew that whatever he said to me would hurt. Would be complicated.

And yet, I said, "One honest thing."

"I don't know if it was worth it." The words came fast, low, in a rough exhale, like they'd been pressing on the backs of his teeth for far too long. "The night Neculai lost his throne, I just wanted to burn it all down. I never wanted... this. Feels like it's all cursed. This crown. Maybe the only way to survive as a ruler of this place is to become just like the ones who came before you. And that—that terrifies me. I'd kill myself before I let that happen, and I hope that if I couldn't, you'd do it instead."

It was more of a confession than I expected. I had to force the lightness into my voice as I said, "I already did that, remember?"

He laughed humorlessly. "I told you that you should have let me stay dead."

"And what about that? Would that have been worth it?"

Another question I immediately knew I shouldn't have asked. Another wound, another stab of pain.

"To die, rather than killing you?" he said quietly. "Yes. That would have been worth it. Even I had to draw a line somewhere. And you're the line, Oraya."

Mother, I was a fucking masochist. Asking questions with answers I didn't know what to do with.

He cleared his throat, as if to scrape away the uncomfortable sincerity of those confessions. "I need to adjust your wings. Can you lift them a little?"

I tried to do so, wincing. What I'd intended to be a stretch became an awkward lurch, and the bed creaked as Raihn's weight fell back.

"Careful, princess. You're going to take my eye out."

"They don't listen to me," I snapped.

"You're just adjusting to having two new, giant limbs stuck to your back. When I first got mine, I could barely even walk properly. Just kept drifting to the sides because the weight threw me off."

I couldn't help it. That image made me chuckle.

"Sure, laugh," he grumbled. "We'll see what your walking looks like soon. Here. Alright if I help?"

I hesitated, then nodded.

"It's hard at first to figure out how to isolate the right muscles. But…" Gently, so gently, his hands moved to the underside of my wings, where they met my back. "You're stiff. If you relax your muscles, they won't fall off. I know it feels like they will."

His hands slid up, applying gentle pressure along the way, coaxing them to spread. My instinct was to move them myself, but Raihn said, "Don't you dare. I don't want to get stabbed in the eye again. Just… relax."

Another stroke, at that tight knot of muscle. I twitched as his thumb ghosted over my skin.

He stopped immediately.

"Did that hurt?"

I didn't answer right away. "No."

No. It was the opposite of hurt. Awkwardly so.

"Do you want me to stop?"

Say yes.

But it had been more than a month since I had felt safe. Longer than that since a touch had felt… comforting.

I found myself answering, "No."

He resumed, slow, running along the muscle. Even through the thin layer of my shirt, I could feel the warmth of his hands. The roughness of his callouses.

"Just let go of it," he said softly. "Let me support the weight of them. I've got you."

As if he could hear the inner fight I was having with my subconscious. And slowly, slowly, with the help of his hands braced beneath my wings, the muscles relaxed.

"There you go," he said. "Not so hard."

I didn't speak, mostly because I didn't have words for how good it felt to have someone else bear some of that burden. I hadn't realized how heavy it was until the weight was lessened.

Suddenly, I was exhausted.

Raihn's touch traveled farther up—where the limb gave way to the delicate, softer skin of the wing.

I stiffened. Right away, he withdrew his hands. "Did I hurt you?"

I was so grateful he couldn't see my face. It felt hot.

"No. It—it's fine."

He hesitated. Then his hands fell back to my wings, light and gentle.

"Open for me," he said.

I didn't even have to tell my body to obey. They just... unfolded beneath that barely-there touch, like flower petals.

"Beautiful," Raihn murmured, as his fingertips ran all the way up the soft, sensitive underside.

This time, the pleasure was unmistakable. No longer hidden beneath the surface, no longer ignorable. This was intense, a shiver that ran up my spine—up my inner thighs, into my core. Like his mouth had once felt on my throat or my earlobe.

Like desire incarnate, echoing in my entire being.

My exhale trembled.

Touch had become something consistently violent, consistently painful.

Not this. This was...

Fuck, it was dangerously good.

In Raihn's sudden stillness, I knew he had realized what I was feeling.

"Good?" he asked, voice thick.

217

Asking for permission. Because like me, he knew that this was far more treacherous than pain. Pain was simple. Pleasure was complicated.

If I told him to stop, he would, without question. And if I was a stronger person, I would have done just that.

I wasn't a stronger person. I was weak.

"Yes," I said. "Don't stop."

He let out a tiny sound that sounded unintentional, almost a groan. His fingers continued their dance, fingernails slightly dragging against the underside of my skin, my body acutely aware of every stroke—like he knew where all of my nerve endings were and exactly how to caress them.

My breath was growing shallow, my face flushed.

He hit upon an especially sensitive spot, and I let out an involuntary, choked sound—a whimper.

He laughed softly.

"There, huh?"

Goddess. Yes. There.

He lingered in that spot, swirling around it. The pleasure rolled over my entire body, every nerve reacting to those little touches—wanting more. Begging for it. My teeth clenched, biting back whimpers. I didn't know why I tried. Surely he could hear my heartbeat.

Smell my arousal.

When he dragged his fingernails across my skin, the almost-moan that slipped from my teeth was too sudden to control.

He made a returning sound, too, something between a growl and a groan, and suddenly I was slumped back against him, the hard muscle of his body against my back.

"I dream about that sound." His mouth was so close to my throat. I could feel his voice vibrate on my flesh, right against the scar that he'd left. "Do you know that?"

His fingers danced along my wings again, and I barely even tried to hide my moan this time.

My breasts ached, sensitive against the fabric of my shirt. I wanted the clothing gone—mine, his. I wanted his skin. I wanted his breath. Mother, I craved that. I craved it so much that right now, I couldn't even hate myself for wanting him so much.

And yet, I didn't want it to go any further than this. This touch, his mouth near my throat, and his body close to mine.

"When I went into that room," he murmured, "I thought you were dead. I thought I lost you, Oraya. I thought I lost you."

His voice was far too raw, like an open wound, cracked and bleeding. It touched me in places I didn't expect. Places more sensitive than his hands on my wings.

He was my enemy. He would kill me if he had the chance.

He was my enemy.

"Would be a relief for you," I said. "A lot of problems solved."

He went rigid. Suddenly, his hand was at my face, tilting my head back to meet his eyes. They were furious.

"Stop saying things like that."

"Why?" I whispered.

Knowing I was taunting him.

Knowing I was, once again, asking a question I didn't want the answer to.

His forehead lowered. Our faces were so close—I could feel his breath, shallow and quick.

"Because I'm so tired, Oraya."

His mouth brushed over the tip of my nose. Almost a kiss. Not quite.

"I'm so tired of pretending. Tired of pretending I don't think about you every night. That I've ever wanted anything—"

His throat bobbed, and he closed his eyes, as if he needed a moment to collect himself. His fingers found that spot on my wings again, dragging across it so agonizingly slowly, and I let out a trembling breath that made him lean a little closer, like he wanted to capture that sound on his lips.

"I'm exhausted, princess," he groaned. "So damned tired."

It sounded like a plea—like he was begging me for an answer, a solution. And I hated that I recognized it because I felt it too.

It was exhausting, to be this sad all the time. To feel so angry.

To resist, constantly. Just as tiring as carrying the wings on my back.

A part of me wanted to give in. Let myself feel something more than nothingness or sadness or anger. Let him touch me, taste me, fill me. Fuck him until I didn't feel anything but pleasure.

It had worked before. For a little while.

But so much had changed since then.

Because when I closed my eyes, I wouldn't see pleasant visions of Raihn's naked body or his kisses or his affection.

I would still see his bloodied form on the ground. I would still see him killing my father.

I would still see my blade in his chest.

I pulled away, just enough to put some distance between us, and I saw Raihn's expression settle into serious understanding—a mirror of my own realization, reality seeping in.

The haze of pleasure and comfort was starting to fade. I already mourned it.

"I was selfish," he murmured. "The day we had together, I was willing to let you use me to escape. I did that knowing that if you knew the truth of why I was there, you'd hate me for it. And that—that was wrong. I thought I'd die in that ring, and it would be over, and you would never know. But—"

It was amazing, how fast it happened. Like a flame drenched in frigid water.

The sudden wave of anger was coldly all-consuming.

"And what the hell was that supposed to be?" I said. "Was that supposed to be a mercy? You dying for me?"

His face shifted, a line between his brows. "I—"

"I dream about my blade going into your chest every fucking night, Raihn."

Too much. Don't show him this.

But it was too late. The words poured out of me, hot and scalding.

"You *made me kill you*," I ground out. "You made me do what you couldn't do. For the second time in my life I—"

I bit down on those words, so hard my teeth drew blood from my tongue. I turned away. But it was too late to avoid seeing the realization fall over Raihn's face, as he touched his chest, right where my blade had pierced it.

Shame flooded me.

I'd almost—

Mother, what the hell kind of daughter did that make me? What kind of queen?

"Oraya," Raihn started, and I cringed, bracing for his words.

But then a knock rang out at the door.

He didn't move. I could feel his eyes staring into my back.

Another knock, louder.

"Raihn?" Mische's voice came from the hall. "Are you in there?"

Still silence.

Then, he finally rose. I didn't look up, though I heard the door open, and Mische's bright greeting. "Oh! You're up!"

I couldn't look at her. I didn't want her to see this, too.

"What is it?" Raihn's voice was hushed.

A beat of silence, as Mische, undoubtedly, put things together.

"It's from Vale," she said, matching his tone. "There's... a problem in Sivrinaj."

Raihn let out an exhale that was a wordless curse.

"I know, right?" she sighed. "Those fucking bastards."

2 8

RAIHN

"Those fucking bastards," I muttered.

"Mhm," Mische agreed.

I read the letter again, fingers crumpling the parchment around Vale's words.

The tentative peace after my performance at the nobles' meeting could only get us so far, apparently. There had been rumblings of unrest near Sivrinaj, with some of the smaller Rishan nobles not only refusing to send their troops, but actively undermining Vale's efforts.

I had my fair share of flaws, but naiveté wasn't one of them. I knew that sooner or later—probably sooner—this was going to happen.

Vale didn't directly spell out that he thought Simon Vasarus was responsible. But I knew what my suspicions were. Figured, we'd deal with Oraya's spurned would-be Heir and then have to go deal with mine.

"So."

One word, and I already was dreading what Mische was going to say next.

"What was that?" she asked, very casually.

"What?" I said, even though I knew *what*.

"What I walked in on."

I had a headache. I didn't want to think about what that had been, mostly because I myself didn't know. I didn't want to think about Oraya's moans, or her skin, or that brief moment of vulnerability. Or the hurt in her eyes.

"Nothing," I grumbled.

"Didn't look like nothing."

"It was a mistake."

All of it.

You made me do what you couldn't, she'd said—with actual tears in her eyes, an expression so raw and open. She had no idea, I was certain, how transparent she was, all that pain floating right to the surface.

I felt so stupid. So unimaginably stupid.

Until this moment, I hadn't realized what I'd done. Here I was thinking that I'd made this great noble sacrifice. Thinking that I had saved her—or tried to, even if my plan had gone... differently than I'd hoped.

I hadn't. I'd just given her something else to have nightmares about.

"I'm going to leave tomorrow," I said. "At sundown."

I didn't look up from the letter—an attempted signal of *I-don't-want-to-talk-about-it* to Mische—but of course, it went ignored. I could still feel her disapproving stare.

"Raihn—"

"Nothing to say, Mish."

"Bullshit." Then again, for emphasis, "Bull. Shit."

"You've got a way with words. Anyone ever tell you that?"

"Look at me." She snatched the letter from my hands, stepping in front of me. Her eyes were so big that I could practically see fire reflected in them, sometimes, when she was really pissed.

"So what's your plan?" she said. "What's the next step?"

"Oh, I don't know." I thrust a palm at the letter. "Go behead all of my enemies and see if there's a kingdom left when I'm done, I suppose."

"First of all, you aren't going to be able to do anything with all of this power until you stop resenting it."

I made a choking sound that was almost a laugh. It took every shred of my self-control to keep my mouth fucking shut because nothing good was about to come out of it.

Stop resenting it.

I loved Mische—loved her deeply—but the fact that she could even say that with a straight face infuriated me. Of course I resented it. I'd been forced into this position—forced into it partially *by her.*

"And second," she went on, her face and voice softening, "you can't just run away from her. She needs you."

I scoffed again at that. This time, the sound was more pained than angry.

"She needs someone, Raihn," Mische said. "She's... she's really alone."

That part... that was true. Oraya did need someone.

I sighed. "I know. But—"

But that person should not be me.

It felt silly to voice that. I couldn't bring myself to, not in those words, even though it now seemed clearer than ever.

"Don't abandon her," Mische said. "She isn't Nessanyn. It's not going to end the same. She's stronger than that."

I shot Mische a warning look. Strange how even after hundreds of years, the mere mention of Nessanyn's name was like a finger against a crossbow trigger, sending a bolt of regret through my chest.

"No. Oraya isn't like Nessanyn."

"And you aren't Neculai."

"Damn right I'm not," I muttered, though I sounded less convinced than I'd like. I wasn't like him. So why did I feel him shadowing my every move these last few months?

"Let her in, Raihn," Mische said, softly.

I rubbed my temple. "I don't even know what you're talking about."

"Bullshit. Yes you do."

I caught my snappish response in my teeth — *isn't that a little hypocritical coming from you, the girl who locks up every time anyone tries to ask you anything fucking real?*

But that was a childish response. None of this was about Mische.

Maybe it wasn't even about Oraya.

"Everyone has abandoned her," Mische murmured, her eyes sad. "Everyone."

"I'm not abandoning her." My words were sharper than I'd meant for them to be. "I made vows. I'm not doing that."

Your soul is my soul. Your blood is my blood. Your heart is my heart.

I'd been struck by it even that night, the way those words felt rolling over my tongue. With so much weight.

It would be so much easier if this was the game that I tried too hard to convince everyone else it was. But I knew, deep down, the truth of what this was. I could lie to everyone else, but I wasn't good at lying to myself, not even when I wished I could.

I turned away, studying the rolling dunes outside the window, my arms over my chest. The view was beautiful, but within a few seconds it blurred to the image of Oraya's pained face. Her face the night of the Kejari. Her face on our wedding day. Her face when she'd sobbed at the top of that tower in Lahor. Her face just now, on the verge of tears.

I had fucked up.

From the first moment I'd seen Oraya, ready to throw herself into a pack of drugged vampires to save her blood vendor friend, I'd been fascinated by her. I told myself it was just curiosity at first — totally practical interest in Vincent's human daughter.

That pretense didn't last long. No, I'd never been very good at lying to myself. Never even bothered trying to tell myself that the only reason I kept Oraya around was because of what she could offer me.

"I thought I could," I said, finally, not looking away from the dunes. My voice caught in my throat a little. "Thought I could — I don't know."

Save her.

Those weren't the right words. Oraya didn't need to be saved. She just needed a soul beside her on the dark walk to her own potential. Someone to protect her until she was strong enough to save herself.

I settled on, "I thought I could help her. Keep her safe."

"You can. You are."

"I don't know about that." I turned. Mische had fallen back into the armchair, her knees drawn up to her chin, her eyes wide and rapt. No one listened quite like Mische.

"I hurt her," I choked out, "so fucking badly, Mish."

The wrinkle between Mische's brows softened.

"You did," she said softly. "So what are you going to do about it?"

I had thought I'd known the answer to that question. I'd give her everything that had been taken away from her. I'd hand her the power that Vincent had tried to keep away from her her entire life. I'd protect her. Defend her. Arm her.

It felt like the only right thing. And the world didn't deserve Oraya—but what a magnificent thing she could become.

I wanted to see that. What the hell was the point of any of this if I couldn't do that? Right this one wrong?

But now, doubt crept into the dark corners of those thoughts.

Maybe I shouldn't be the one doing any of those things.

I turned back to the window.

"I'm going back to Sivrinaj on my own," I said. "Oraya shouldn't travel that fast yet. I'll have some of Ketura's men escort you two back later."

Mische leapt up. "What? You are not heading back there alone, Raihn."

"Work on her magic with her. You're better at that than me, anyway. And when Ketura gets here, she can teach her how to disappear her wings."

"Raihn—"

"I don't have time to wait, Mische," I snapped. Then I let out a breath, and said, more gently, "Do this for me, alright? Watch out for her. Like you said. She needs someone."

226

Mische's face softened, though I could still see the conflict in it—torn between letting it go and pressing.

"Alright," she said at last, though she didn't sound convinced.

I LEFT AS SOON as night fell the next day. I said goodbye to Mische, who vocally and emphatically disagreed with my decision to leave early. I shut down the argument fast.

When I went to Oraya's door, no one answered my knock.

She was in there, of course. Nowhere else for her to go. And anyway, I could smell her. I could always smell Oraya's blood, the pulse of it. I could hear her in there, too—faint rustling of blankets on the bed.

I knocked again.

Third time, I decided, I'd just let it go.

I knocked one more time, and—

"What?"

Downright vitriolic. I couldn't help but let a little smile tug at the corner of my mouth. *There she is.*

I opened the door and peered in. She sat on the bed with a book, cross-legged, her wings slightly unfolded behind her.

I took a careful assessment of her in that split-second—eyes, skin, wings, wounds.

The wounds looked better than they had the night before. Wings looked a bit more relaxed, too. I'd practically ached on her behalf yesterday, just feeling the strain of those muscles. The tension, I was sure, long predated the wings. Oraya was always trying so hard to bear all that armor. I knew she'd been holding those shields up for twenty years.

I was staring. Oraya looked unamused.

"What?" she barked, again.

I smiled at her. "You're so charming, princess."

She stared at me.

"I'm leaving," I said.

She blinked twice, a little too fast. Her face changed, grumpiness shifting to —

My brow twitched.

"Look at that face," I said. "If I didn't know any better, I'd say you were worried."

"Why?" she asked, voice tight. "Where are you going?"

"Back to Sivrinaj."

"Why?"

I gave her a tight smile that was more of a baring of teeth. "Because Rishan nobles are fucking pricks."

Could practically hear Cairis scolding me for even giving her that much information — information that could be used against me.

Her expression shifted again. Disapproval. Hell, maybe hatred. She tried to tamp it down and failed, of course.

"Oh."

"Mische is staying here with you, and some of the guards." I nodded to her wings. "Keep those out for now. Ketura will be here in a few days. She can teach you how to get rid of them. Not hard once you get the hang of it."

She stared at me, wrinkle between her brows, saying nothing.

"Try to contain your excitement at my departure," I said flatly.

I glanced at the table. An empty bowl sat there — scraped clean. I couldn't help feeling some satisfaction at that.

Oraya still said nothing.

I wasn't quite used to her being so quiet.

"Well, that's it," I said. "Take care of yourself. See you in a few weeks."

I started to close the door, but she said, "Raihn."

I stopped mid-swing. Peered back in. She had leaned forward slightly, her lips pressed together, as if in protest against whatever thrashed behind them.

"Thank you," she said. "For fixing my wings."

My fingers tightened around the door frame.

As if that was something to thank me for. Common decency.

"Like I said, you were made for the sky," I said. "Would be an injustice to let that be taken away."

The faintest hint of a smile brushed her mouth, a glimmer of sun through the clouds.

Then it faded as her eyes went distant. I wondered if she was thinking of Vincent.

She blinked that expression away fast.

"Safe travels," she said flatly, turning back to her book.

I gave her a faint smile. "Thanks."

I left around midnight that night, armed to the teeth with two of Ketura's guards with me. Not enough, Vale would've said, but I'd rather leave the rest for Oraya and Mische. Both of them were forces to be reckoned with, certainly, but Oraya was injured and Mische... well, it seemed like I saw more burn scars on her arms every time I looked at her.

I looked back one last time before we flew away. Immediately, my eyes floated up—to the second floor of the little cottage, where a set of moon-silver eyes stopped my heart in its tracks, just like they did every damned time.

Oraya leaned against the window frame, arms crossed. When my gaze met hers, she lifted one hand in an almost-wave.

It felt like some kind of small victory.

I waved goodbye to her, and then I was gone.

PART FOUR

HALFMOON

INTERLUDE

Time is cheap for vampires.

The slave learns this quickly. As a human, he'd felt every passing second — missed opportunities slipping by, as if swept away by an eternally rushing river. Humans mourn time, because it's the only currency that really matters in a life so short.

There are many things about his new life that the slave despises. But of all he grieves for his fading humanity, the loss of time's mark is the most devastating. A life in which nothing means anything is not a life at all.

Years blur by like wet paint drowned in the rain, drenching a forever-blank canvas. The vampires of the king's court revel in this agelessness. Centuries of life had dulled the common pleasures, making their tastes extreme and cruel. Sometimes, humans are the subject of this cruelty. Other times, human lives are too short and fragile. Turned vampires, then, are the next best thing — durable, longer-lived, but every bit as disposable as the humans they once were.

The slave is nothing special. He is not the only Turned among the king's collection. He is not even a particular favorite. Time and boredom had driven the king to accumulate a well-curated menagerie of entertainment, men and women of every build, appearance, origin.

The slave does try—truly try—to hold onto his humanity.

But it slips away from him, day by day, anyway. Soon he cannot remember how long it has been since he was Turned. When he thinks of his life from before, it feels as if he is thinking about an old friend—distant, fond memories.

He watches the sunrise every day until the rays of light bite into his skin.

Days became weeks became years became decades.

Later, he will try and fail to describe in words the extent of his degradation during that time. To those who surrounded him, he was a collection of skin and muscle, an object, a pet, not a person. When this is what you are told for years, it becomes easy to believe it. It becomes easier to survive if you believe it.

Only one person treats him differently.

The king's wife is a quiet woman with big, dark eyes. She rarely speaks, and she rarely leaves her husband's side. In the beginning, the slave assumes she is just the same as all the others. But later, he begins to see her as a fellow victim of her husband's cruelty—silent camaraderie in his blows, his ownership, his commands.

It stays that way for a long time.

Then, one day, he finds himself alone with her. He had been beaten badly that day, punishment for some imagined disobedience. When the others leave the room, he remains behind, bandaging his wounds with the rote routine of something he has done a thousand times before and will do a thousand more.

She remains, too.

She does not say a word. She just takes the bandages from him and winds them around the injuries he cannot reach.

He pulls away at first, but she is gently persistent. Eventually, he relents. When she is done, she rises and leaves without a word.

He has forgotten what it feels like. A kind touch. It hurts more than one might think. He can feel her hands on him for the rest of the night. It terrifies him, because he knows now he cannot forget it.

It starts like that.

They inch closer, over months, years, comforting each other in the wake of the king's cruelty. It takes months before they speak to each other.

But the words matter less than the kindness. The line was crossed that first night, that first gentle touch.

Everything after that feels inevitable.

In a dark world, eyes naturally find the light. She becomes the brightest thing in his.

By the time their silent meetings become meandering conversations, they had already long since jumped from the cliff.

By the first time he kisses her, mouth still stained with blood by her husband's hand, they are already rushing towards the ground.

By the time they make love, they are so desperate for companionship, they don't even care about the inevitable crash.

29

ORAYA

T ime went on in mundane placidity.

It seemed silly that this house should feel so empty without Raihn. Mische talked constantly, and was extra talkative now that I was her only companion—at least, the only one that actually engaged with her, Ketura's guards forever stoic. Still, I couldn't shake this feeling of a missing puzzle piece, a silence between breaths that I wished would be filled.

We fell into an easy routine—healing, training, resting, repeat.

Mische was a good teacher, though training with her reminded me too much of the time we had spent working on our magic together during the Kejari. Then, Mische had only been one half of my instruction. The other had come from Vincent, whose teaching style had been the opposite of hers in every way —rigid commands and control to counter every instance of Mische harping on about opening one's heart and soul. To return to one without the other highlighted the shape of his absence... a wound that, unlike the ones on my wings, felt like it would never heal.

In our rest time, we examined the pendant. Mische was not

only a talented magic user, but well-read in sorcery and magical history. Still, even between the two of us, we couldn't make much sense of what the thing was or what it did. I was the only one who could touch it, though it wasn't especially pleasant—making Vincent's presence feel far too close, even more than his sword did. The best Mische could figure was that it was just a piece of something larger—perhaps a key, or a compass, or a device intended to enhance the power of something else. Not a power in itself, she theorized, but something designed to unleash another. But even these thoughts were just guesses, frustratingly rooted as much in luck as in fact.

At nightfall and dawn, Mische tended to my wounds, which continued to improve dramatically with each passing day. None of the treatments were as painful as that first one. None, thankfully, were as... pleasurable, either.

One day, as she observed the remaining wounds, she remarked, "You already look so much better! This stuff must be worth whatever Raihn went through to get it."

"Whatever he went through?" I repeated.

"It wasn't easy to find. But he was determined." A pause, then, more tentatively, "He was so worried. We thought..."

I thought I lost you, Raihn had said, the words shuddering along my skin.

I was suddenly very uncomfortable with this line of conversation.

"He's got to protect his asset," I muttered, even though the words tasted bitter—even though I knew it wasn't true.

Mische sighed, dabbing at the last wound on my left wing. "Raihn has a lot of flaws, Oraya," she murmured, "but he knows how to love."

I didn't know what to say to that.

I wasn't sure what it meant that I couldn't think of anything at all.

"YOU'RE BLOCKING IT," Mische said, for the fifteenth time that day. I gritted my teeth and tried to ignore her.

Since I'd received my Heir Mark, my magic had become undoubtedly more powerful. I could feel it constantly thrashing under my skin. But with that power came more volatility than I knew how to control. Like every time I used it, I had to tap into something viscerally painful.

Right now, the pressure built, sharper and sharper, like a blade slowly parting skin.

"Keep going," Mische said. Her voice was distant over the sound of my blood rushing in my ears. "Don't let go of it!"

A bead of sweat dripped down my nose. Despite Mische's commands, I could still hear Vincent in my ear, too: *Focus. Control. Willpower.*

Lately, his voice had been an unwelcome visitor.

The Nightfire sputtered and roared, threatening to either spin out of control or wither away completely, as I balanced on the edge between shutting myself off and falling into a pit of emotion I couldn't confront.

Where do you want me to go? Vincent whispered. *I'm a part of you. And isn't that what you've always wanted?*

Once, I had wanted nothing more than I wanted to be Vincent. Even now, a part of me still wanted it—even knowing how he had lied to me, knowing what he had done to my family and his, knowing the brutality he had inflicted upon people just like me for centuries.

I was ashamed of it.

Ashamed? Vincent said. *I made you everything that you are, and you say that you are ashamed of me?*

That one was a memory. One of the last things he had said to me.

The Nightfire flared, spinning out of control. Mische took a step back. I struggled to wrangle it. Struggled to fight back the war of shame and guilt in my head.

But when I was using magic, everything came so much closer to the surface. It was Vincent's magic, after all—his blood that gave me this power, his Heir Mark that intensified it. I could not wield it without feeling his presence breathing down my throat.

"Keep going!" Mische urged, though I could barely hear her.

My eyes burned against the blinding white of the Nightflame. In that light, I saw Vincent's bloody face in those final moments —always so real, no matter how many times I tried to forget it.

The voice in my ear whispered his final words. *So many regrets in the end. Never you.*

I couldn't do this. Goddess, I couldn't do this—

STOP.

I severed myself from all those unwelcome memories.

The Nightfire guttered out.

Suddenly, my knees were in the damp dirt. My breath was painful, coming in deep, raspy gasps.

"Oh, gods." Mische knelt before me, her hands at my shoulders—I leaned against them without meaning to, silently grateful for the stabilizing force.

"You're alright," she murmured. "It's alright."

I didn't know why her voice sounded like that—so pitying— until something wet hit my splayed hand. I blinked down at it, confused, and another spot joined it.

Tears.

Fuck.

My face grew hot.

"I'm fine. It's—let's just go again."

I stood and turned away, swaying a little on my feet. It was hard to pull myself together once I'd started to break. Like all that pressure was building up right under the surface. That was how I'd ended up sobbing in front of Raihn. And now Mische. Great.

"I'm fine," I said.

Mische said softly, "You don't have to be fine."

She said it so simply. Like it was just a truth, nothing to be judged or disagreed with. I knew that she believed it, and in this moment, I loved her fiercely for that.

Even if I couldn't bring myself to.

I had a kingdom relying on me, and a crown waiting for me, and people who needed me to become something better than this *immediately*.

And what had I done? Lodged a single failed attack? Found a pretty little necklace I couldn't figure out how to use?

"Oraya…"

Mische touched my shoulder. I didn't turn—I couldn't show her my face. Perhaps she knew this, because she didn't try to make me, only offering me that one touch—so light I could move away if I wanted to.

"Magic is like… a living thing," she murmured. "I guess it makes sense that it comes from the gods, because it's just as fickle and temperamental as they are. Yours feeds on your emotion. It makes you reach into things that are… hard right now. But one day, the things that are the most painful are going to be sources of strength."

I glanced down, at Mische's hand on my shoulder and the several inches of her wrist visible beneath her sleeve. The scars covered nearly all her exposed skin.

Had they been that bad before? Or had she just been incessantly trying, and failing, to use her magic ever since her god abandoned her?

Maybe my profile revealed the question I didn't ask, because she removed her hand and pulled her sleeve down as I finally turned to face her.

"Don't think I don't understand what it feels like to—to lose something," she said.

When I'd first met Mische, it might have been easy to dismiss her as some pretty, vapid thing. But every so often, I glimpsed something so much harder under the surface. Now, that shadow passed over her face. A glint of blade-sharp steel hidden in the flower garden.

"Can I ask you a question?" I said.

She hesitated. Then nodded.

"What was it like to Turn?"

Her face darkened.

"It was hard," she said. "I would have died if Raihn hadn't found me."

"He saved you."

That shadow parted, just enough to let a little sad smile slip through. "Mhm. He saved me. I don't really remember it. One minute I'm very sick in the middle of the desert, and I'm—" Her expression shuttered, and she cut herself off. "Then I'm waking up in some shitty inn with a giant, grumpy stranger. That, let me tell you, was a hell of a confusing moment."

I could imagine.

"You were a priestess," I said carefully. "Right?"

The smile faded. She tugged at her sleeve again and didn't say anything for a long, long moment.

"I'm sorry," I said. "That was—"

"No. No, it's fine." She shook her head, as if pulling herself from her haze. "Yes. I was. A priestess of Atroxus. It's just... it's hard for me to talk about, sometimes." She gave me another weak smile. "Hypocritical of me, right?"

"No," I said. "It isn't."

"Magic is... I know some people think it's just another discipline, but I think it lives close to our hearts. I think it draws right from our souls. Mine has always been close to me. And I—" Her jaw snapped closed, eyes shining.

"It's alright," I said quickly. "I shouldn't have asked."

It was downright painful to see Mische on the verge of tears.

But she laughed and wiped her face with the back of her hand.

"This is what I mean, Oraya," she said. "We've all got our reckoning. My Turning wasn't my choice, and it broke me. Raihn's was his, and maybe it broke him even more. Maybe the others don't let you see the shards. Maybe they don't show you the things they mourn. Doesn't mean it's not there. Doesn't mean they don't feel it. And your father—"

Her face went serious now, fiery-fierce. Her hand fell to mine, clutching tight. "Your father, Oraya, felt all those things, too. He was just as broken as the rest of us, and he was so determined not to acknowledge it that he flayed you with those sharp edges and then berated you for having skin instead of steel."

My throat was tight. Grief and fury surged up it before I could stop myself.

"Don't talk about him that way," I said. But my words were weak and pleading.

Mische just looked at me sadly. "You and Raihn are always trying to be like them," she said. "I don't understand it. You're better than him. Don't forget that, Oraya. Embrace it."

She was wrong.

But she didn't give me time to tell her so before she threw her arms around me in a brief, fierce hug. "We'll try again tomorrow," she said, released me, and strode back into the house without another word.

DAYS PASSED. Our routine continued. Ketura arrived from Lahor, tired and battle-weary. She told us that the city had fallen into significant disarray with Evelaena dead, and it had taken some time to get things under control there.

"It was already in significant disarray," Mische pointed out, which was very true, and I shuddered to think of how much worse it could have gotten.

Ketura added another teacher to my daily training routine, teaching me how to appear and disappear my wings, now that they were healed enough. She, at least, provided a more familiar instruction compared to Mische's cheerful style—harsh, barked commands that made me appreciate just how brutal of a commander she must be to her soldiers. Still, she was effective—a week later, and I was semi-reliably able to conjure and spirit away my wings on command.

But uneventful as this time was, day by day, the signs of Mische's unease slowly grew more obvious. I'd often catch her staring out the window, a little wrinkle between her eyebrows, rubbing the scars on her wrists.

I'd be lying if I said I didn't feel it too. It was too quiet, like we were trapped behind glass, frozen in artificial tranquility, while darkness encroached on the horizon.

One day, when Mische finished tending to the much-improved wounds on my wings, I said, "I think it's time for us to go back to Sivrinaj."

She paused before answering, "Raihn told us to wait until he sent for us."

I scoffed. "And have you heard from him?"

That was an intentionally stupid question. I knew she hadn't—her quiet anxiety told me that. I told myself this was why I knew, and not because I'd been watching for his letter just as closely.

Mische looked torn.

"You want to go," I said. "So let's go. What, Raihn's king now so he gets to tell us both what to do? Fuck him. I'm the queen. My say counts just as much."

I said it very confidently, even though we both knew it wasn't that simple.

Still, at that, she cracked a smile. "I like that attitude."

I knew she was going to agree. This was, after all, the girl who had run off and joined the Goddess-damned Kejari in order to force Raihn's hand. But maybe it was a testament to her friendship with Raihn, and her respect for him, that she still had to think about it for a long moment.

But her impatience won out.

"Fine," she said eventually, just like I knew she would. "You're right. We can't just wait around here forever."

30

ORAYA

Raihn didn't look happy to see us.

He hadn't been expecting us to turn up when we did, clearly, even though Ketura had written before we left. The journey was long, especially because we traveled on horseback instead of straining my wings by flying the whole way, for which I was, reluctantly, grateful. We arrived at Sivrinaj nearly a week later, tired and travel-stained, and taken to Raihn's study to wait for him.

When he opened the door, followed by Vale, Cairis, and Septimus, he paused in the frame for a moment, as if caught off-guard by our presence.

We stared at him, too, just as shocked by his—because he was covered in blood.

It clearly wasn't his. Spatters of red-black dotted his face and hands, smeared on his fingertips, clinging to his unbound hair. He wore the fine clothes that he always donned in the castle, though they were disheveled, wrinkled on the sleeves where he'd pushed them up to his elbows.

It wasn't hard to piece together what he'd just been up to. He had rebels to deal with. Rebels needed to be questioned—and punished. Raihn, I knew, was not the type to let others deal with his dirty work.

I'd grown so accustomed to seeing the different masks he'd worn over these last few months—the charmer, the king, the cold-blooded tyrant. Now, at the sight of him like this—blood covered, hair wild, that just-killed sheen in his eye—a visceral familiarity wrenched through me. Like we were in the Kejari all over again.

I wondered if he was thinking the same thing, because the slow, wolfish grin that spread over his lips echoed the one he used to give me in those trials... even if, this time, it took a little too long to reach his eyes.

"You two," he said, "weren't supposed to be back yet. I tell you to do *one thing*, and that thing is just *don't do anything*, and you still can't bring yourselves to listen to me?"

Mische's nose wrinkled. "You look disgusting."

"If I'd known you were coming, I'd have taken a bath."

"No. I don't think you would have." She looked him up and down. "Long day, huh?"

The smile softened. "Long week. Long month."

Then his gaze shifted to me. For a split second, it was just as exposed, revealing just a glimpse of too many emotions. Then the mask was back up, the role reassumed.

"I take it you're feeling better."

"Better enough."

He eyed my wings. His face remained blank, but I still saw the faint glimmer of concern—felt it like I'd felt like his hands on them.

He wasn't the only one staring.

Vale, Cairis, and Septimus were transfixed by those wings, too, and didn't bother to hide it. Nor did they hide their wary curiosity, like they were trying to reconcile something that didn't make sense.

The wings were a symbol of my power. Vincent only left his visible when he needed to remind the world he was the King of

the House of Night. And mine were a near-perfect replica of his
—that deep black, that blinding Heir red.

I'd made it easy for them to ignore my Heir Mark, hiding it
beneath high-necked clothing. But right now, there was no
ignoring the wings.

Septimus smiled, taking a puff of his cigarillo.

"You do carry them better when you're conscious," he said.

I didn't like thinking of Septimus seeing me unconscious.
Raihn didn't seem to like it much, either, because he took a step
closer to me, as if putting his body between us.

Mische glanced between all of us quietly, noting the obvious
awkwardness, before another cheerful grin broke over her face.

"We're starving," she said. "Can we eat?"

It took a few solid seconds after Mische's declaration for me
to realize that a vampire had said the word "starving" in my presence and not a single one of them had so much as glanced at me.

Maybe I really was becoming a vampire, after all.

Raihn wiped the blood off his face with the back of his hand,
or tried to, largely unsuccessfully. He scowled down at his blood-
smeared hand with wrinkles on his blood-smeared forehead, and
said, "I've worked up a bit of an appetite, too."

"If you'll excuse me," Septimus said, breezing by us. "I'll pass
on dinner. Busy night, I'm afraid."

He paused at the doorway, looking back at me.

"Good to see you doing better, Oraya," he said. "We were all
very worried."

Sometimes it seemed like the man didn't even have footsteps.
He was simply gone, without so much as an echo behind him.

RAIHN DIDN'T EVEN CLEAN up before we all went to the dinner
table. I considered not attending—I still didn't like to be around
feeding vampires, vampire blood or no—but when I realized that

Vale, Cairis, and Ketura would be there, the logistical benefit was just too great to pass up. I'd spent far too long wrapped up in my own grief and anger to actually do anything useful. And sitting at dinner with Raihn and his highest-ranking advisors was useful.

I was, of course, directed to a seat beside Raihn, though he barely looked at me when I sat. He seemed to be deliberately paying less attention to me, which was awkwardly noticeable. It had the obnoxious effect of making me more aware of him than I already was.

The others were given elaborate plates of bloody-rare meat, and, of course, enormous goblets of blood, which Mische chugged down immediately—royal table manners be damned. Raihn disappeared for a few minutes as the servants laid the table, then returned.

I eyed him. "Thought you were going to clean yourself up."

Flecks of vampire blood still covered his face.

He winked at me. "Don't pretend you're offended by a little bloodshed."

But I knew a message when I saw one. Raihn was letting himself be seen as the slaughterer. Someone who killed and didn't even care enough to wipe the remnants of his victim off his face afterwards.

So... he didn't trust his own inner circle. Interesting.

A few minutes later, my plate was brought out and set before me. I somewhat dreaded digging into the near-raw meat that the others had been given. But I also wasn't about to highlight all the ways I was different by turning it away, either.

But at my first bite—

Sun fucking take me. I must've been hungrier than I'd thought, because this was incredible. I barely stopped myself from letting out an audible noise—surprise, pleasure, or both.

I could feel Raihn's eyes on me. I glanced at him. He looked oddly smug. "What?"

"Nothing," he said casually, and turned back to his food.

The realization dawned on me.

Oh, for fuck's sake. So he was a good cook. So what.

I didn't give him the satisfaction of acknowledging aloud how delicious it was.

Didn't stop eating, though, either.

"So." Raihn leaned back in his chair, taking a long swig of blood. "Cairis. You had something you wanted to talk about."

Cairis glanced around the table, then pointedly at me, and then at Raihn. "Here?"

"Here. I think Vale will be interested in your idea."

Vale looked like he was already dreading whatever this was going to be. His wife, on the other hand, seemed like her interest was piqued. She was a very openly curious person, and I appreciated that. Maybe because it was a deeply human trait. I wondered how much she understood of this conversation—she was a foreigner, and her Obitraen, from what I'd heard, was not very strong yet.

"If you insist," Cairis said, and turned to Vale. "We need an event."

Vale stared flatly back at him. "An event."

"Something big. Something with a lot of flash. Something to provide an excuse for us to invite all the nobles to Sivrinaj and flaunt the king's significant and awe-inspiring power, and whatnot."

Vale looked unconvinced, and Cairis leaned across the table.

"Wars aren't just fought on the battlefield, Vale."

"Unfortunately not. But I'm not thrilled to hear what any of this has to do with me."

"The event will be your wedding celebration."

Vale let out a breath through his teeth and an immediate, forceful, "No."

"Come on, Vale." Raihn arched a brow. "You don't want the best party planner in Obitraes throwing your wedding for you?"

Despite Raihn's joking tone, I got the impression that no one was really giving Vale—or Lilith, for that matter—a choice in the matter.

Vale gave Cairis a dagger stare. "We're already married."

"So what? It's just the celebration. Besides, does it really count without all the... sparkle?"

Cairis waved his hands in the air, as if to demonstrate the proverbial *sparkle*.

Vale looked pissed.

Lilith looked around with a wrinkle of genuine confusion between her brows, like she was putting a lot more effort than her husband into understanding this.

"Why us?" she said, in heavily accented Obitraen.

"Wonderful question." Cairis took a long sip of wine, then set the goblet down hard. "Because Vale, unlike the rest of us dogs, is a true Nightborn Rishan noble. He has a name that commands respect among the Rishan who have the most... we'll call it apprehension... about the king's rule." He smiled. "And a wedding is always a nice, non-political celebration, isn't it?"

I'd seen the aftermath of enough vampire weddings to know that was certainly untrue.

"No," Vale said, returning to his food.

"I'm not giving you an option on this one, Vale," Raihn said. So very deliberately casual, in all the ways that told me nothing was casual about this conversation.

Vale set down his fork. He stilled, staring unblinking at Raihn.

"Lilith is foreign and Turned," he said, between his teeth. "This isn't the high-ranking political marriage you seem to think it is."

"Unfortunately," Cairis said, "it's the best we've got."

Vale's eyes, amber gold, fell to me. "Is that really true? We have the king's own marriage we could celebrate."

Raihn's calculated disinterest fell away like a discarded cloak. He sat up straight.

"That," he said, "isn't an option."

And thank the fucking Mother for it. I'd sooner kill myself than put myself at the center of that kind of spectacle.

Anyway, everyone at the table knew that that would be a terrible idea. I was no great political mind, but even I knew that presenting my marriage to Raihn as anything other than straight-forward and settled would be a mistake. The fact that I was still breathing already cast doubt upon Raihn's ability to rule.

And besides, I was supposed to be something closer to a slave than a wife. Not a prize to be celebrated, but an enemy to be humiliated.

Even Vale knew this. He winced a little, as if mentally bracing for the response.

"And you know exactly why." Raihn's voice was harsh, leaving no room for argument. "This isn't a debate. You are doing this."

Vale's self-control briefly warred across his face, but his temper won out. "You know what they're like. I refuse to put Lilith at their feet."

Raihn let out a bark of a laugh, such a cruel and vicious sound I felt it up my spine. "*They?*" he spat. Suddenly he was on his feet, palms planted on the table, eyes brighter than flames. "You are one of *them*, Vale. I saw you be one of *them* for the better part of a fucking century. And you had no problem with their behavior then. But now you have a Turned wife, so every-thing has changed? Now it affects yours, so you can be moved to care? Don't feed me that bullshit."

No performances here. That was all real. More real, I suspected, than Raihn wanted it to be.

Vale's body was rigid. Tension drew tight in the air, all of us balancing on its edge. I was half certain that Vale was about to lunge across the table at Raihn. My hands drifted to my blades on instinct—ridiculous, because what was I going to do, leap to Raihn's defense?

But then Lilith jumped to her feet, shattering the breathless suspension.

"Stop," she said. "This is a stupid fight."

I wasn't expecting it. My brows lurched without my permis-sion. Mische let out a laugh that seemed mostly unintentional.

Lilith looked around the table before her gaze settled on Raihn.

"The House of Night needs this?"

The anger drained from Raihn's expression when he looked at Lilith.

"Yes," he said, voice immediately softer. "I wouldn't be doing it otherwise. I promise you that."

No more performances here, either. The truth. It should have been surprising, for a vampire king to speak to a former human foreigner with more respect than his high-ranking noble general. And yet it didn't surprise me at all.

Lilith considered this, nodding slowly.

"I am not afraid," she said.

Vale grabbed her hand, as if trying to drag her back to her seat.

"Lilith—" he grumbled.

But despite her fractured Obitraen, Lilith's tone was final, her stare not breaking from Raihn's. "If it is what the House of Night needs," she said, "then we will do it. That is it."

31

RAIHN

I liked Lilith. At least she had balls. It took them, to stand up and yell at a bunch of vampires speaking a language you barely even knew.

After dinner, everyone filed out to their rooms. Vale remained glued to Lilith's side, his hand around hers. For a moment, I watched the two of them.

I'd had my assumptions, when Cairis had told me that Vale was coming back from Dhera with a brand-new Turned bride. I'd seen that story before. No, most vampires didn't decide to marry their wards, but that didn't change too much in my mind. Give someone endless life, and then take whatever you want from them afterwards. An eternity of servitude, sex, devotion.

I knew that story very, very well. Especially when written by people like Vale.

Even if maybe—maybe—he seemed like he actually loved her. Admittedly, I hadn't been expecting that.

I came up behind them in the hallway, where Vale was whispering to Lilith in Dheran.

"Mind if I cut in?"

The look Vale gave me probably had been used to gut disobedient warriors on the battlefield.

"Of course," he said.

"Ketura wanted to talk to you."

"Can it wait?"

I smiled. "Better not to keep her waiting. She might bite."

Excuses aside, that was true.

Vale glanced at Lilith, and I said, "I have a few minutes. I can escort Lilith back to her room."

He still didn't move.

Fair enough for Vale to be protective of his wife—he was right for that. But the suspicion in his expression went beyond your typical possessive newlywed behavior. Fitting suspicion, maybe, for someone who lived in Neculai's court for so long— even if in a very different capacity than I did. Neculai took everything for himself, willingly or not.

One might've thought it would be a little satisfying to be looked at with that kind of wariness by a noble. Instead, it made me deeply uneasy.

"She'll be safe," I said. A little bit of a lilting joke. A little bit of genuine reassurance. "Promise."

Reluctantly—and with a small nod from Lilith—Vale left.

I gestured down the hall, and Lilith and I set off in silence.

She definitely was an unusual woman. I fought a bemused smile when she spent the entire length of the first hallway staring at me outright—not just the typical curious glances, but actually *staring*, and doing absolutely nothing to hide it.

"You'll walk into a wall if you don't look where you're going," I said, in Dheran.

At that, she almost *did* walk into a wall.

She smiled. "You speak Dheran."

"A little out of practice," I said.

Goddess, I hadn't spoken my own mother tongue in centuries. The syllables now felt uncomfortable on my tongue. Maybe because I felt like a very different man when I spoke them.

Her brows lowered, as if in deep thought. "Because you're Turned. Vale told me that."

I really did struggle to stifle my laugh at that one. Cairis had complained about her bluntness, but I found it oddly refreshing. I'd never once had someone so directly say something so rude.

At my reaction, her brows lowered. "That was impolite," she said, though she said it as if it was a guess, like she really wasn't sure how to read the expression on my face.

"No. It's true. I was born in Pachnai. Very human, at the time. And you're from...?"

"Adcova."

"I haven't heard of it."

"No one has."

"Do you like what you've seen of Obitraes so far?"

"It's... it's unlike any place I've ever been. It's beautiful and dark and intriguing—" Her eyes went far off, staring straight ahead, as if far past the wall at the end of the hall and beyond. "I imagine I could spend a lifetime here and not see all it has to offer. The history in this place, and the—"

She cut herself off. "I don't mean to ramble. I apologize."

"Not needed."

It was nice to see someone enthusiastic about something. The idea of seeing so much beauty and potential in Obitraes was foreign to me. A little refreshing, in a romantic kind of way.

"Has it been difficult to leave your home?"

"No," she said. "I never belonged there."

"And the other transition?"

Again, she stopped walking. This time she didn't resume, staring at me hard.

"Forgive me for what I'm about to say," she said. "But why are you talking to me?"

At that, I couldn't help but laugh.

"You *are* blunt."

She tucked a strand of wavy hair behind her ear. "I've grown up knowing I would live a very short life. It's more efficient to be direct."

"I appreciate it. Turns out near-immortality makes people far too long-winded."

We continued walking, and I went on, "As long as we're being blunt, I'm just surprised because when I heard that Vale, a vampire noble, had Turned a human woman to bring back as his wife, I expected a very pretty, very polite, very subservient little thing."

"I'm none of those things," she said.

She was, objectively, pretty, if not my taste. But no, definitely not subservient or polite.

"I'm no good at games, Highness," she said. "I'd like to know what your concern is. Are you worried that I'll embarrass you at this—this celebration?"

I hadn't thought about that, but... maybe someone really should make sure she didn't get to talk to anyone important and easily offended.

I was unsure how to word my next question—unsure how much I wanted to show this woman I barely knew. Just the fact that I was having this conversation with her revealed more than I felt comfortable showing.

"You will find," I said at last, "that most vampires don't think especially highly of the Turned."

"I've gathered that."

"Many vampires don't have especially benevolent reasons for Turning a human. My maker was no exception. So, since you like to be blunt, I'll be blunt, too. If you don't want to be here, Lilith, you don't need to be here. If any of this has been against your will—"

"No." She bit out the word fast, then laughed, like I'd just said something ridiculous. "No. It's not like that. Vale Turned me to save my life."

I didn't find this especially convincing. *They always say that,* I wanted to tell her.

Do you want to live? Neculai had asked me. And I'd said yes, too. I'd begged for life. Like a fucking fool.

"Sometimes it can start that way," I said. "But—"

"I'm here because I want to be here," she said firmly. "Vale treats me with nothing but respect and affection."

I'd been watching closely, and I had never seen anything that contradicted that. But I was still skeptical. Vale was the same man who had witnessed horrific abuse on Turned slaves in Neculai's court, and had treated it as nothing but normalcy.

"Good," I said. "I'm happy to hear that. Just know that if anything changes, you will never be trapped. Not here. Not in my court."

A faint smile flitted across her mouth. "I appreciate that. More concern than I thought I would get from the king."

She stopped at a set of double doors. "This is my room." Then she bowed her head. "Thank you for walking me."

I waved away the bow. "Of course."

I started to turn away, but Lilith called after me, "Highness."

I glanced back over my shoulder.

"You're distrustful of Vale," she said.

That was very true, and also something I was absolutely not going to admit out loud. "Vale is my highest general and I give him all the trust befitting that position."

She looked unconvinced. "You dislike him, then. Why?"

Ix's tits, this woman.

I smirked. "I'm sure Vale has his reservations about me, too."

Lilith didn't answer, and that was answer enough for me.

"You'll learn eventually that it's a strange thing to be so long lived," I said. "So much can change in a couple of centuries. But you carry all that shit with you, anyway. Centuries worth of it."

She smiled a little. "Not so different from humans."

I shrugged. "Maybe not."

I turned away again, uninterested in sharing more uncomfortable honesty. "Goodnight, Lilith. Thank you for indulging my curiosity."

32

ORAYA

The castle looked different. I couldn't remember if it had
been this way when we'd left, or if it had changed in the
time we had been away. Either could be true. Before, I
was in such a haze of grief and anger that I could barely process
the world around me.

Now, as I wandered around the twilight-empty halls of the
castle, I wondered if it had always been this... bare. So different
than when my father had ruled this place, all the Hiaj art
stripped away. I'd expected that they would quickly be replaced
with Rishan art, Rishan trophies, Rishan artifacts—all the same
preening signals of power, just with a different kind of wing.

But Raihn hadn't done that. He'd left the walls bare. The
whole castle was empty, as if trapped in the space between an
exhale and an inhale.

Maybe that was what drove me out into the human district
that night. Nothing about my home looked familiar anymore, so
perhaps I was looking for something familiar out in those dilapidated streets—after all, they had forged me just as much as the
castle had.

Or maybe I just really needed to go kill something that deserved it. I'd accept that answer to.

But when I got there, the human districts had changed too. They were... quiet.

I hadn't been out here in months, not since Raihn and I had come during the Kejari. In the past, whenever I'd neglected my duties for more than a couple of weeks, the district would be crawling with vampires. I expected to find a killing field ripe for a harvest.

Instead, perplexingly, I found no one at all. Not a single hunting vampire. Nothing.

After a few hours, I sighed and leaned against the wall. Reluctantly, I slid my blades into their sheaths.

Was I actually disappointed that I wouldn't find anyone to kill tonight? That was selfish of me. I should be glad.

I *was* glad.

And confused. A little suspicious.

A welcome gust of wind cooled the sweat on my skin. It sent a wooden sign across the street clattering against the brick building. My gaze fell to it—to the sign that read, *Sa ∂ r ʾs*, but perhaps had once said, *Sandra's*.

A familiar, shitty little pub.

I rubbed my dry tongue against the roof of my mouth. Suddenly, the taste of cold, foamy, absolutely fucking terrible beer sounded... strangely appealing.

I stood up, stretched, and decided I could handle a detour.

I DIDN'T KNOW what the hell I was thinking.

I kept my leathers buttoned all the way up to my throat— more than far enough to hide my Heir Mark—and drew my hood up tight. My wings were gone. I had no sharp canines. Most importantly, I wasn't a vampire.

And yet, I still felt so out of place. Every time someone casually glanced my way, I had to resist the urge to run.

The pub was packed—even more than it had been when I'd come here with Raihn. It smelled of sweat and beer and burning candles. Voices all melded together into a single rush of laughs and jokes and flirtations and ill-fated bets on cards.

I had been surprised the first time I came here, to see how relaxed the patrons were. It had seemed foolish for a human in Obitraes to do anything but live in constant fear.

Now, they seemed even more carefree. And this time... maybe I couldn't fault them for it. I'd spent hours wandering these streets in search of dangers to protect them from and had found none.

Maybe that was worthy of celebration.

Still, their behavior felt foreign to me. If some tiny part of me had come here searching for familiarity, I hadn't found it. I had some human blood, but I was nothing like these people—even if a part of me wished I was.

"Hey, pretty girl, you here alone?" a young, copper-haired man said, sidling up to me, and I shot him a dagger stare that made him make a face and immediately turn away.

I realized after he left that I'd had my hands on my blades.

For fuck's sake. What was I doing here?

You don't belong here, little serpent, Vincent whispered in my ear. *Here among the mice.*

Even in my head his voice was so disgusted by them, so dismissive. I could hear it so clearly, because I'd heard that tone from him countless times in life.

It set my teeth on edge. My fingers tightened at my sides.

Fear is a collection of physical responses.

I forced my breath to slow, my heart rate to lower.

If Raihn could do it, I could certainly do it.

I managed to fight my way to the bar by wielding some mixture of appropriately stomped feet, pointy elbows, and my ability to be small enough to slip between the hulking bodies of sweaty bearded men.

Ugh. Humans did sweat so much more than vampires.

When I made it to the bar and the barkeep, a wiry old man with deep set, tired eyes, turned to me, I froze.

Seconds passed. The barkeep looked increasingly pissed with every one.

"Well?" he pressed. "We're busy, kid."

"Beer," I choked out finally.

The barkeep stared flatly at me.

"One…one beer?" I tried.

"Two beers," a deep, very amused voice corrected from behind me.

Familiar warmth encircled me as a large body leaned against the bar beside me. I recognized him long before I looked at him.

How the hell did he find me here?

Raihn murmured in my ear, "You brag about winning the Kejari, but you don't know how to order a beer?"

My face heated.

"Not a very useful skill," I grumbled.

"Really? I've found it very useful."

The barkeep returned with two mugs of foamy brown liquid, and Raihn slid a couple of coins to him with a jerked half-nod of thanks. It had been long enough since I'd seen this version of him that it was jarring all over again. He wore a dark cloak and a slightly yellowed white shirt unbuttoned distractingly too low, his hair messy and unbound. Everything about his body language mirrored those around us. Casual, rough, unpolished.

Unmistakably human.

Still, I noticed he kept his hood up this time. Maybe he trusted his disguise a little less than he used to.

He took the two mugs and gestured to a little semi-secluded table across the room, not far from the spot he and I had sat the first time we came here. The place was so crowded that he practically had to fight his way through—though, of course, he managed to do it with a lot less overt aggression than I had.

Helped to be huge, apparently.

"Why are you here?" I asked, as soon as we were at our table.

His brow twitched. "You planned on drinking alone? How depressing."

"Were you following me?"

He set the mugs down and raised his palms. "Easy, viper. I'm here for the same reasons you are. The seductive allure of piss beer. Good to know it's grown on you."

He smiled, and I didn't.

"So it's just a god-chosen coincidence that you've shown up here?"

"Your sarcasm is so subtle, princess. Elegant and refined. Like fine wine. Or this beer." He took a swig, made a face, and let out a refreshed sigh. "What, you think I've been spying on you?"

"That's exactly what I think."

"So what if I have? You think Mische is that shitty of a body-guard, that you could slip out into the human districts and no one would know?"

Embarrassingly, it hadn't even occurred to me that Mische had seen me go.

"So you *were* tailing me," I said.

"No. I knew you could handle yourself. This part, you and I ending up here at the same time... that actually *is* luck. I come here a lot. Missed it while we were gone."

I did have to admit I believed that. A part of Raihn existed out here that didn't exist in the Nightborn castle. Maybe... maybe just like a part of me existed here that couldn't there, too.

I sipped my beer and winced at the bitter taste.

"Ugh."

"Hasn't gotten better with time, huh?"

"No."

And yet, I took another sip. I wasn't sure how something could taste so good and so bad at once.

"So." He took another swig of beer. "It's been quite awhile since you had a nighttime patrol out here. How'd it go?"

I knew a leading question when I heard one. The way Raihn was watching me out of the corner of his eye as he drank his beer told me enough.

My eyes narrowed.

His brow raised.

I leaned across the table.

He leaned back against the bench, hands behind his head.

"If I didn't know better," he said, "I'd say that expressive face of yours is accusing me of something."

"What happened out here?"

"What do you mean?"

Oh, Mother damn him. He was playing with me.

"You know what," I said. "It's…"

"Quiet," he provided. "Peaceful."

"There's no one to kill."

He chuckled and leaned closer, his face only a few inches from mine, and murmured, "You sound so disappointed, my murderous queen."

My gaze fell to his mouth as he said that—fell to the little smile that curled its edge, something softer and more playfully affectionate than his usual performative smirks.

I knew the way that smile felt against my lips. Knew how it tasted.

This thought struck me without permission, visceral and uncomfortable. Even more uncomfortable than that was the longing that came with it, a sudden, deep pang, like the drawing of a bow across the mournful string of a violin.

I leaned back, putting a few more inches of distance between us.

"No," I said. "It's a good thing. It's just—"

"The place should be filled with criminals by now, since you, the heroic savior of the human districts, have been a little distracted."

I glowered, because I knew he was teasing me, but nodded anyway. "Yes."

He took an aggressively casual sip of beer. "Has it occurred to you that maybe the human districts now have *another* protector?"

"You?" I didn't bother to hide my disbelief. "What, you're telling me that you sneak out here every night to go inflict vigilante justice on these poor bastards?"

On one hand, it was ridiculous. Raihn was the Nightborn King, after all—not as if he should have the time to go skulking around in the human districts every night. Then again... was it really any more unbelievable than that person being me?

He set down his mug.

"You're thinking too small, princess." His voice was low, like he didn't want to be heard. "You talk about vigilante justice, but I don't need vigilante anything anymore. That's what it means to rule a kingdom. It means the ability to change things."

The little curl still clung to the corner of his mouth, like a permanent shield, but his eyes were serious. Vulnerable, even.

Realization slowly dawned.

"You—"

"I made the necessary commands and the necessary changes to make sure that the human districts are, and always will be, safe. Yes."

"How? It was always forbidden to hunt in the human districts, but—"

"But it happened anyway. Why?"

I didn't answer.

He gave me a sad, knowing look. "Because no one *actually* cared. Because no one enforced those laws. No one guarded the perimeters after dark. No one punished those who disobeyed. Well... no one except for you."

A sour knot formed in my stomach. I thought of those districts I would hunt, night after night, always catching at least one more culprit. Thought of what my father had showed me, mere days before he died. All those humans soaked in blood, pinned to the table. Nothing but food.

"You mean Vincent," I said. "He was happy to just let the human districts be preyed upon."

Even now, I half expected to hear his voice in my ear—an explanation, a defense, a rebuke. But there was nothing. Not even my imaginary version of my father could justify his choice.

And that's exactly what it had been. A choice.

Raihn was an unpopular king who had been in power for mere months, all of them tumultuous, and he had still managed to make the human districts far safer than they were before.

Vincent just never cared to. Even with his human daughter, he never cared to.

"Not just Vincent," Raihn said. "All of them. Neculai was no better."

I swallowed thickly.

"He always told me," I said, "that nothing could be done."

Nothing could be done about so many things. My family in Rishan territory. The humans in the human districts, even the human districts of Sivrinaj. Even my powerlessness could only be solved with a wish from Nyaxia.

A wry smile flitted across Raihn's mouth. "They have a way of bending reality, don't they? Making it exactly what they say it is."

My knuckles were white around my mug. The words flowed over my tongue before I could stop them. "I feel like—like such a fucking *idiot*. Because I never questioned any of it."

I didn't want to see the pity in Raihn's eyes. I kept my gaze glued to the table as he murmured, "I never questioned any of it, either. For a hell of a lot longer than twenty years. But that's what happens when one person gets to shape your entire world. They can make it into whatever they want, and you're stuck inside those walls, whether they're real or not."

How could he sound so calm about it? I was desperate for calm.

"And they just get to die?" I spat. "They just get to escape the consequences?"

The hatred in my words took me by surprise. I should have been ashamed to think such a thing—that Vincent's bloody death had been the easy way out, cheating us all out of answers.

I wasn't, and that scared me.

My eyes flicked up to meet Raihn's. Warm and red in the dim lantern light, they held no hint of the pity I'd expected. Instead, they were fierce and steadfast.

"No," he said. "We get to use the power we got from them to make this kingdom into something they fucking despise. What's the point of any of this if there's nothing to actually fight for?"

There had always been a snide, petty part of myself that had doubted whether Raihn's grand declarations were just another performance for my benefit.

In this moment, I knew he was telling the truth. I knew it because the determination—the spite—in his eyes mirrored the glimpses of it I saw in myself.

It was a sudden realization, a truth snapping into place to reveal an uncomfortable portrait. The simple thing had always been to hate Raihn, to tell myself that he was my enemy, my captor, my conqueror.

But Vincent had spent my entire life telling me convenient lies. Maybe I didn't have the stomach for it anymore.

Maybe the complicated truth was that Raihn was more like me than anyone ever had been. Rishan Heir or no.

He leaned a little closer. Those eyes drifted from mine— running over my forehead, my nose, my lips.

He murmured, "We need to talk about—"

SMACK, as his forehead whacked against mine, making me see stars.

"Fuck," I hissed, jerking back and rubbing my head. Raihn did the same to his as he peered over his shoulder, annoyed, as the same young man who had approached me earlier held up his hands apologetically.

"Sorry, sorry!" He took in Raihn's considerable size, then made the very nervy decision to clap him on the shoulder. "That was an accident. Crowded in here. Didn't mean to get in your—"

Then the man's face changed. The smarmy smile faded. His eyes widened, and just kept going, until they were comically perfect circles.

He stumbled backwards, nearly tripping over two of his companions.

"Highness," he breathed.

My heart sank.

Fuck.

Raihn's face fell as the boy dropped clumsily to his knees, his hands raised.

"My king, I apologize. I—I apologize. I'm sorry. I'm so sorry."

Raihn ducked his head, wincing, as if he could make the boy unsee what he had recognized. But it was too late.

And just like that, the room turned.

It took a few seconds for people to realize, but once they did, the silence spread through the crowd like the blanketed fall of night. Soon every set of eyes was trained on Raihn, all wide, all terrified.

And for one moment, Raihn's gaze fell back to me—utterly devastated. Just a glimpse, before he quickly swept it away under a mask of nonchalant ease.

He rose and raised his palms. "No harm done," he said. "Didn't mean to cause a commotion."

He glanced around at the room, now pin-drop silent, half the patrons on their knees and the other half looking too terrified to even make themselves bow.

"We should go," he muttered to me, and took my hand.

I didn't even pull away as he led me out the door, the crowd parting around us like they couldn't get away fast enough.

33

ORAYA

R aihn didn't talk for a long time when we returned to the city streets. He was walking fast and I matched his pace, not sure where we were going. He adjusted his hood, looking straight ahead, not so much as glancing at me.

But he didn't have to.

I felt a pang of sympathy for him. He had few pieces of his human identity left. I knew how much he valued the shards he could salvage. As much as he tried to pretend it was all about shitty beer, I knew otherwise.

I shouldn't care. I knew I shouldn't care. Yet I just kept walking beside him.

"Sorry," he muttered, finally, once we had walked a couple of blocks.

"It's nothing."

It wasn't nothing. Not really.

"I guess I can't go back there for a while," he said. "But at least..." He stopped short, and I realized that we'd come to the same boardinghouse he'd brought me to before. He flashed me a wry smirk, barely visible under the shadow of his hood. "At least we have some other safe havens."

The man at the front desk was, once again, asleep—at which I could've sworn Raihn breathed a sigh of relief. He led me up to his apartment. The place looked the same as it had the last time we were here, though a little messier—more papers scattered over the desk, a used wine glass beside the basin, the bedsheets a little rumpled.

I eyed those bedsheets longer than I meant to.

Raihn sat down at the edge of the bed and fell back over it, sprawling out as if collapsing from exhaustion. Then he caught my eye and grinned.

"What?" he said. "You want to join me?"

A teasing prod, of course. And yet I could imagine it so clearly. How his body had felt beneath me. How he'd smelled. How he'd tasted.

What he'd sounded like when he came.

How he'd held me when I did.

I hated him for touching me the way he had back at the cottage. Just brought all those unwelcome thoughts back to the surface.

"You ever have companions up here?" I asked.

What the hell?

Why did I even ask that?

I made a mental note to never drink again.

His smile broadened, brow furrowing. "What?"

"Nevermind."

"Are you asking if I fuck other women in this bed?"

"*Nevermind*," I grumbled, turning away.

But he caught my hand, fingers gently intertwining with mine —not pulling, though, just hanging there between us.

"I'm married," he said. "In case you forgot."

Despite myself, I almost smiled. "A difficult marriage. No one would blame you for seeking some easy pleasure."

What are you doing, Oraya?

He scoffed. "Easy pleasure. Like there's such a thing." His fingers drew a little tighter—pulling my palm closer, drawing my fingers between his, the slide of his rough skin against mine sending uncomfortable shudders through other parts of my body.

His eyes didn't leave mine.

"I like a little fight," he murmured. "Besides, she's ruined me for all others. My own fucking fault, though. I knew it from the beginning."

His hood had fallen back, dark red hair fanning behind him on the bedspread. His shirt, partially unbuttoned, revealed a triangle of his defined chest and a hint of dark hair. The muscles of his throat shifted as he swallowed, perfectly in time with the slight shudder in my breath—like he sensed my desire, and was reacting to it.

He was lonely. I was lonely. Both of us were mourning the worlds we'd thought we'd known.

At least this time, I was willing to admit to myself that I was tempted. Maybe that was why I was willing to dangle my fingertips close to the flames.

"Hard pleasure, then," I said.

"Only good if it hurts," he replied.

I took a step closer to the bed, so my legs were pressed against the mattress—Raihn's knee between them, nearly brushing the apex of my thighs.

I'm fucking exhausted. So tired of pretending.

Even then I'd been pretending. Pretending I didn't feel what he did. The hunger.

He sat up slowly, the movement making his knee slide forward. I could have stepped away, but I didn't. Instead I settled onto it, pulling myself partially onto his lap—the pressure of his leg, and the roughness of his clothing and mine, sending a little spark of pleasure up my spine.

I lifted our intertwined hands, tilted so his thumb was facing me, and before I knew what I was doing, lowered my mouth to it.

His skin was salty and clean. Even his hands held that scent of *him*—that scent of the desert and warmth. I slid my tongue over the rough pad of his thumb, drawing a slow exhale from

Raihn. I held his gaze, unblinking, and he didn't relinquish it, meeting the challenge. He wasn't even breathing.

I wasn't sure why I did what I did next. My body just acted without me.

I bit.

He let out a hiss of surprise, but the spark in his eyes wasn't one of pain or anger.

I let more of my weight fall onto his knee, my hips shifting.

Hot, salty, iron-tinted liquid flowed over my tongue.

Raihn's blood was... was...

Mother, it was exquisite. Even the few drops that rolled over my tongue were intoxicating, sweet and savory and rich, seductive as wine and sugar.

It staggered me, the rush of it sending me spiraling. Before I could stop myself, my tongue pressed against his skin again, cheeks hollowing.

Raihn's other hand had migrated to my shoulder, then my throat, then my face, his other thumb now stroking my cheek. My eyes closed, as if my entire body wanted to focus more fully on the pleasure of it. And yet, I knew he was watching me.

He let out a low, rough chuckle. I felt it shiver through my entire body—my core, my spine. The sound jerked me back to this world, pulling me from the haze of his blood.

I released him and jerked back. Perhaps I was half vampire, but my teeth weren't especially sharp—the gash I'd opened was far less graceful than the two delicate little scars he'd placed on my throat, an ugly jagged line of pearling red-black.

My embarrassment rose to the surface too, congealing like his blood.

What the hell had I just done?

If Raihn was surprised, or offended, he didn't show it.

"You have a little..."

His other thumb swept over my lower lip, pressing over the plump curve of it. His smile faded into thoughtfulness as it lingered there.

"You're full of surprises, princess," he murmured.

Mother, I was never ever *ever* drinking alcohol again.

I released his hand abruptly and he quickly darted it to my back to keep me from falling backwards, since I was still precariously balanced on his knee, my weight now entirely supported on him.

"Easy. Let's not get too overwhelmed."

"I don't know why I — I didn't mean — "

His brow twitched with amusement. "It's alright to be curious."

"I don't know why I just did that."

My face was warm, which was even more embarrassing.

He shrugged. "Sometimes it's no use to question our more primal instincts. You're half vampire, Oraya. You're still learning the ways that affects you."

I'd known it for months, and it still hadn't gotten any less jarring to hear it said aloud. It didn't help that Raihn looked so... amused about the whole thing.

"So... good, I take it?" he said.

I couldn't bring myself to say aloud that good was not a strong enough word.

I had tasted Raihn's blood before — when we'd fucked, and again, during the wedding. Even then, I had been surprised by its appeal. And then with the blood at Evelaena's party...

"I — " I cleared my throat. "I tasted blood by accident. At Evelaena's ball. And it was..."

That had probably been human. Taken from someone who had no choice in it. Taken from someone who had paid for it with their life.

My face must have grown solemn, because Raihn's did, too. "You liked it."

"I didn't think — "

"Half vampires are rare. All of them have different traits. It makes sense that blood would taste good to you." His thumb stroked my cheek again — an easy motion, like he was doing it without thinking. "It doesn't have to mean anything. It's just how your body reacts. Doesn't mean you support it, or that you have to drink it."

"You tasted... different."

A pained smirk flitted across his mouth.

"Mm. That can happen."

I didn't even know what question to ask, or if I could find the right words—if I even wanted to hear it confirmed aloud.

You did taste... different, Raihn had told me. *I thought it was because of how I feel about you.*

As if he saw me putting those pieces together, he murmured, "It doesn't have to mean anything. Just your body."

Fucking figured that my body had to react to Raihn, of all people. Just had to make this situation even more complicated than it already was.

He removed his hand from my back and examined his thumb, still bloody.

"But if you wanted to experiment," he said, "we could do that in better ways than this."

He lifted his chin a little, as if to present his throat.

I scoffed. "You'd offer me your throat? That's stupid of you."

"Maybe. But you do have a fucking exquisite mouth, and an even better tongue."

Goddess. Now he was definitely teasing me.

"Oh, fuck you," I muttered.

"And there she is," he chuckled.

I let out a breath, trying to shake away the lingering sensation of Raihn's taste and his overwhelming proximity. I felt like his scent now covered me, like condensation clinging to glass.

I stood up, grateful to put some space between us.

"You said there was something we needed to talk about," I said. "Why are we here?"

His face twisted into a scowl. "Ugh. You want to talk work."

I SAT on the little dining table across the room while Raihn talked. He leaned casually against the bedframe—somehow the thing supported his weight—and managed to look completely nonplussed by our entire interaction, which I couldn't tell if I found admirable or annoying.

"So," he said. "The wedding."

"So you're going to tell me what that's actually about?"

He gave me a half smile. "That obvious, huh?"

I shrugged. "Call it intuition."

"We have problems, as you know. The Bloodborn."

"No matter my commands, they haven't been letting up on their viciousness," he said. "Some areas have been totally devastated by their actions."

"Hiaj areas."

"They're all my kingdom." He cocked his head. "So you've been keeping track of things."

I shrugged again. It was my kingdom, too. It was my job to pay attention.

"And we're no closer to finding this... god blood."

I thought of the pendant, safely wrapped and hidden in my locked bedchamber. Mysterious as it was, it hadn't actually given us any information, no matter how many books we read or spells Mische and I threw at the thing. We had, embarrassingly, no clue what it even was.

Raihn winced. "No. It doesn't seem like it. On top of that, I had to rush back to Sivrinaj because of rebellion from a few of the Rishan nobles. As you know."

He tried to hide his annoyance—deeper than annoyance—and failed. I watched him with a wrinkle between my brows.

"They really hate you."

He scoffed. "Of course they do. Many of these people were friends of Neculai's, and they saw me..."

Did he know that he always bit off his words whenever he talked about those days? His eyes slipped away, staring at the floor.

"They were never going to accept me as king," he said. "It's just some of the smaller ones, for now. But the one I'm really concerned about has been too quiet. Simon Vasarus."

I recognized that name. "You killed his brother, that first meeting."

"The very same." Raihn's gaze flicked away. The look on his face—it was too familiar. He didn't need to outright tell me who this man was to him. I understood.

"He's coming to the wedding," Raihn went on, and that tone, too, told me everything I needed to know. He didn't just hate this man—he was afraid of him.

"Why?"

"Because he has a bigger army than I do, and I need to make nice with him until I have a better solution." His lip curled, the disgust palpable in his voice.

A better solution. Me. Of course.

"The god blood," I said.

He let out a long breath, pacing to the desk. He pressed his palms to the wood and leaned over it for a long moment, as if deep in thought.

"I've invited the House of Shadow to this party," he said.

My brows leapt. I'd seen Shadowborn royalty a few times. It was rare to invite them to Nightborn events, but not unheard of. Raihn was a new king. It would make sense that he would be extending these kinds of diplomatic ties—and that the Shadowborn would be interested in indulging their curiosity.

"The Shadowborn King hates the House of Blood as much as we do," he said. "He doesn't want the Bloodborn taking over the House of Night and creeping closer to his borders. The Shadowborn might be the quietest of the Houses, but they're formidable warriors, too. And their mind magic…" He shrugged, as if to say, *What else is there?* "They're powerful. I've made the connection to the Shadowborn King personally. He's sending one of his sons. If I'm able to pull the right strings, present the right image, I could gain their alliance."

It was a stretch. True alliances between the Houses were rare. Vampires were independent and self-serving creatures. But then again, if anything could motivate an alliance between the Houses of Shadow and Night, it would be aggression from the House of Blood.

"That'll be some tricky political maneuvering," I said.

Raihn laughed wryly. "Don't I know it. But Cairis is right. The wedding is an opportunity to present an image. And I do know the power of that."

That, I knew, was true.

"I need outside assistance. Need the image of a strong alliance. The Rishan..." He shook his head, jaw tight. "The old nobles won't be convinced by anything other than a major show of force. I need to show them I'm just as powerful as Neculai was."

"What does Cairis think of this plan?"

"He knows that I've invited the House of Shadow, but doesn't know why. No one knows."

I blinked in surprise — at the reveal, and that he was willing to share that with me.

"Why not?"

He didn't answer right away.

"The Rishan rebels," he said, finally, "knew more than they should have. Little things. Nothing major. It's circumstantial. But I know how to trust my gut."

My brow furrowed as realization dawned on me. "You think you have a traitor."

He gave me a look that I knew meant confirmation.

"Do you know who?" I asked.

Again, he didn't answer. But my brain was moving now. Raihn's inner circle was so small. Cairis and Ketura... he must trust them completely, because he had left Mische in their care at her most vulnerable, the ultimate expression of his confidence. And Mische, of course, would never betray Raihn.

That left...

"Vale," I said. "You think it's Vale."

Vale was a noble. Vale had known Raihn two hundred years ago, when he was nothing but Neculai's slave. Vale had seen

Raihn at his weakest. In vampire society, it was hard to come back from that.

Raihn said nothing. But again, I could see the confirmation he didn't say aloud.

"What will it take?" I said. "To convince the House of Shadow to ally with you? They won't want to give you that kind of power. Not enough to go up against the House of Blood and your own little traitors."

"They won't skimp. Not when it comes to putting the Blood-born in their place. And if I manage to gain the respect of the other Houses, that should be enough to make my own detractors shut up." His brow twitched. "And earn the respect of the Hiaj, maybe, with your help."

I scoffed. "You're a dreamer."

"Couldn't have made it this far if I wasn't."

He was giving me a certain look that I immediately recognized —like he was sizing me up for something. It reminded me of the Kejari, and the look on his face before he'd asked me to be his ally.

My eyes narrowed.

He let out a short laugh. "What's that face for? What did I do?"

"When you look at me like that, I know to brace myself."

He touched his chest. "Ouch. You were about to be very happy about what I was going to say next, actually."

"I doubt that."

"Let's call it a challenge." He stopped a few paces short of me, a smile tugging at the corner of his mouth. "Here's the thing, princess. Once I have the support of the House of Shadow, Septimus's strange little side projects won't matter as much. Which means, I won't need you anymore."

I blinked at him in surprise. I wasn't sure if I was hearing what I thought I was.

"We get through the wedding," he said. "You help me present the image of the powerful Rishan conqueror. I gain the support of the House of Shadow. And if I do that, then you're free."

Free.

The word stuck in my mind, like sap in the gears of a machine.

I just stared at him.

I had never been beyond the boundaries of the House of Night. Hell, up until less than a year ago, I had never even been beyond the borders of Sivrinaj, at least not in a time I could remember. My life had always been one of confinement—confinement in my room, in my fragile human body, in Vincent's rules and expectations, in… in whatever this was, between Raihn and I.

I'd heard of this. Animals who had been held in captivity for so long they didn't know what to do with an open door.

"The Hiaj are just as much my subjects as the Rishan are, and the humans," Raihn said softly. "I'll treat them fairly. I hope I've shown you that I would."

As much as I hated to admit it to myself, he had.

"This place has taken everything from you, Oraya. Even things it had no business asking for, when you were far too young to give them. You're young. You're beautiful. You're powerful. You could do whatever you want. You could build whatever life you dreamed of." I forced my gaze up from the table to meet his. "You deserve to be happy."

Happy.

The thought was laughable. I didn't even know what happiness meant.

"What if you let me go and I just turn around and wage my own war on you?"

He laughed. "A valid possibility."

More than valid. It would be the only course of action expected of me by those that followed me.

"It's stupid of you to let me go."

"Some people have been saying it was stupid of me to keep you alive at all. I guess I'm a stupid man."

I stared at him, brow furrowed, jaw set, picking apart his

casually pleasant expression as if I could make sense of this by peeling back every layer of his skin.

"I don't understand," I said, finally.

It was the only thing I could think to say, and it was embarrassingly true.

"Think on it. See where that vicious imagination of yours takes you." He leaned closer—and I couldn't be sure, but maybe I imagined the slight sadness in his eyes, hidden beneath the crinkles of his amused smile. "Freedom, Oraya. You should've had it your whole life, but better late than never."

34

ORAYA

reedom.

Raihn's words echoed in my head long after our meeting and into the days beyond. They lingered behind my every thought as I went through the motions of my routine—training, pacing, eating, reading. Raihn stayed out of my way for those next weeks, probably because he—like just about everyone else—was preoccupied pulling this ridiculous wedding together. The Nightborn castle was abuzz with chaotic energy, dozens of servants running around to sweep away the remaining evidence of the coup's disorganized mess and replace it with grand symbols of Rishan power—fit for a bloodthirsty, powerful king of one of the most bloodthirsty, powerful empires in the world.

The day before the wedding, I wandered the deserted halls of the castle on my own. It was eerily quiet, after the near-constant flurry of activity these last two weeks. On the eve of the wedding, the work had been done. Everyone was holed up.

I relished the quiet of these hours.

I wandered into various libraries, sitting rooms, meeting rooms, studies. Places I had never been allowed when this place was really my home. All were empty—until I rounded a corner into one of the libraries, dimly lit with the faintest dregs of sunlight beneath the velvet curtains, and stopped short.

I immediately backed away, but a smooth voice said, "You don't have to leave."

"Sorry," I said. "Didn't mean to interrupt."

The scent of cigarillo smoke pooled in a room this small. Vincent would've been appalled to have it staining the pages of these books.

Septimus gave me a pleasant smile. The fire was lit, back-lighting his silhouette, making his platinum hair seem downright golden.

"Not at all." He gestured to the other chair. "We haven't gotten to catch up in a while. Join me."

I didn't move, and he chuckled.

"I don't bite, dove. I promise."

It wasn't exactly Septimus's bite that I was afraid of. Actually, the days when teeth were my biggest worry now seemed a little quaint.

His clothes were disheveled, his shirt unbuttoned just enough to reveal a hint of darkness at his chest. His eyes seemed more golden than usual, more threads of amber in the silver, though perhaps that was just the reflection of the fire and the darkness that bracketed them.

"You look tired," I said.

"Does Raihn like you because you have such a way with flattery?" He gestured to the chair again. "Sit. Soak up the quiet before this place becomes a hellscape of peacocking nobles tomorrow."

I hated to agree with Septimus, but —*ugh*.

Still, it was my curiosity more than anything that brought me across the room. And, fine, maybe it was a little craving for mortal pleasures that led me to accept when he offered me a cigarillo. I turned down the match, though, lighting it myself with a little spark of Nightflame.

His eyebrows rose slightly. "Impressive."

"You watched me fight in the Kejari and lighting a cigarillo is what impresses you?"

"Sometimes the little things are harder than the big things."

He slid the matches back into his pocket. I watched his hands in the movement. Watched the tremble of his little finger and ring finger on his left hand. Constant, now.

Bloodborn curses. Was that a sign of his? The symptoms varied. Some were near-universal—the red eyes, the black-scarlet veins underneath thinning skin. The insanity, of course, at the very end. Everyone knew that the Bloodborn turned into little more than animals—like demons, stuck in a perpetual state of frenzied bloodlust, incapable of thought or emotion. But even that was often whispered about. The Bloodborn were protective and secretive. They hid their weaknesses well.

"It's nice to see you wandering about on your own," he said. "Out of your cage, for once."

"I'm not caged."

"Maybe not now. But you were. A pity. Raihn is the only one around here who recognizes what he has in you. Vincent certainly didn't."

Strange, how so much of my own mental narrative lately had been stewing in anger over Vincent's behavior, but even the slightest comment against him from someone else, and I was biting back defenses in my teeth.

"I have a blunt question for you," I asked, and Septimus looked a little delighted.

"I love blunt questions."

"Why are you here? Why are you helping Raihn?"

He exhaled smoke through his nostrils. "I told you what my goal is."

"God blood." I let the words drip with sarcasm.

"Oh, such venom. Yes, dove. God blood."

"So you can what? Flaunt your power to all the other Houses? You'd risk fucking with the gods for that?"

At that, he laughed—a sound like a snake slithering through the brush.

"Tell me, Oraya," he said, "how did it feel to grow up a mortal in a world of immortals?"

When I didn't answer, he took another drag of his cigarillo. "I'll guess. Your dear father always made sure you knew exactly how weak you were. Exactly how good your blood smelled. Exactly how fragile your skin was. You probably spent your entire short life cowering in fear. Yes?"

"Watch it," I hissed.

"You're insulted." He leaned forward, eyes glinting amber in the firelight. "Don't be. I respect fear. Only the foolish don't."

I scoffed, inhaling my cigarillo, enjoying the burn through my nostrils.

Septimus's brow twitched. "You don't believe me?"

"I'm not so sure *you* believe you."

He chuckled, his gaze slipping to the fire. "I'd like to tell you a story."

"A story."

"An entertaining one, I promise. Full of all the darkest pleasures."

Despite myself, I was curious. He arched his brows at me, taking my silence as tacit approval.

"Once upon a time," he began, "there was a kingdom of ruin and ash. The kingdom was beautiful once, a very long time ago. But then, some two thousand years ago, the people of this grand kingdom pissed off their goddess, and... well, that's not the sad tale I'll tell you tonight."

The smirk faded from his lips. With the firelight reflecting so harshly on the cut panes of his face—hollower, maybe, than they were a few months ago—he resembled a statue.

"No," he said. "I'll tell you a tale of a prince of the House of Blood."

Oh. About himself. That figured.

"The kingdom of the House of Blood had suffered for two millennia now, its people destined to die early deaths that afford them little dignity," he went on. "The Bloodborn are a proud people. They don't allow outsiders to witness the ugliest parts of themselves. But trust when I tell you that the death of a Blood-born curse is an ugly one. While the other two vampire king-doms thrived, building empires on the backs of their goddess-gifted immortality, this kingdom clawed its way along, trapped in a cycle of endless life and eternal death. Surviving, but little more."

I took another drag of my cigarillo. Septimus's was untouched now, dangling between his fingertips.

"But," he said, "some time ago, the king fell in love. The king's lover was young and optimistic. Despite the woes of her kingdom, she believed that things could change. The king... he was no romantic. It's no easy task, understand, to rule over the dust of a crumbling nation. He was a powerful man, but power could not stop his people from dying or his kingdom from with-ering or the other vampires from spitting in his face." A wry, humorless smile twisted his lips. "But love. A powerful drug. Not enough to convince him. Not enough to make him the optimist his young wife was. But enough to make him think a dangerous word: *Maybe.*

"So the king married his lover, and not long after, she was with child. It is during this time that, as is often tradition with royal families, the king and queen visited a seer."

I leaned forward a little, curious. I'd heard that the House of Blood often employed seers, though not much about what they often learned from them.

"But insight from seers, as you might know, can be a bit... spotty. While it's tradition for expecting highborn women in the House of Blood to visit a seer, the results of those sessions are usually vague, ego-stroking affairs—predictions of great skill or loyalty or intelligence, that kind of thing. So this was, perhaps, what the king and queen were expecting when they visited the seer that night. Instead, what they got was a prophecy."

I scoffed. I couldn't help myself. Septimus laughed and raised his palm.

"I know. They have quite a reputation. But this seer was trustworthy—while her predictions were somewhat vague, they were never untrue. When she completed her ritual, she was shaken. She told them that their son would either save the House of Blood, or end it. The king was troubled by this news, but the queen was ecstatic. She barely heard the foreboding warning, only the hope for the future. Her son was destined to save their kingdom."

I stared flatly at him. "So we're sitting here so you can tell me all about how you're the destined savior of the Bloodborn."

The corner of his mouth curled. "You don't know how to enjoy the twists and turns of good storytelling, dove." He cleared his throat, and continued. "Months pass, and soon the House of Blood has a new little prince. The king and queen adored their son. They showered him with everything a child could want."

I shifted uncomfortably in my chair. It was practically unheard of for vampire parents to treat their children with obvious love. I'd witnessed the Bloodborn literally disassemble their opponents in battle. The thought that their leaders could be so softly affectionate... it was foreign to me.

"The years passed, and the boy was raised to be loyal, strong, intelligent, insightful. He was trained in the arts of magic, of war, of battle, of courtly manners. He was... the very best of us."

Septimus did not look away from the fire. The expression on his face was hard to read—mournful, angry, affectionate, all at once.

The realization fell over me: he wasn't talking about himself, after all.

"The decades passed, and soon, the Bloodborn prince was ready to take up his mantle as the god-chosen hero of the House of Blood. So he gathered his best general and his best men, and he went off on his mission—to find Nyaxia, prove his people's loyalty, and earn back her love for the House of Blood.

"He did, in the end, find the land of the gods. And he and his men did complete several trials to earn Nyaxia's affections, though they cost him many lives. And then he scaled the most treacherous mountains of the gods to find his goddess one final time, to beg for her forgiveness for the sins of his great-great-

great-great-grandfathers, to swear his fealty to her, and to free the House of Blood from its curse."

Septimus's face had gotten colder, crueler, the smile at his lips looking as if it had been chipped from ice. He leaned closer, the remnants of his last drag blowing in my face with his next words.

"And do you know, dove, what that miserable cunt did then?"

He didn't wait for an answer. Didn't breathe. Didn't blink.

"She laughed at him," he said. "And then she killed him."

The words came down like the blade of a guillotine.

"She left his general alive — though forever tainted — and sent him back to the House of Blood with the prince's head."

Septimus's eyes slipped back to the fire. "I have only heard my mother cry once," he murmured. "Only once."

Understanding dawned on me.

"He was your brother," I said.

"One of them. My parents were unusually fertile for a vampire couple. I had seven siblings. Six brothers. One sister."

Had.

He let out a humorless laugh. "The sister is alive. Not that that's much comfort to my parents. Maybe they're still off in the House of Blood right now, trying to make another male heir. Still hoping that prophecy of theirs might come true somehow."

He lifted his cigarillo to his lips.

"Do you know what that makes me, dove? That makes me the last resort. So, you see..." A wry smirk, and he let out a long, slow stream of smoke. "I understand what it feels like to not have time. You and I, we don't get centuries to play our games like they do. And I think it makes us better. More ruthless. More willing to do what needs to be done."

He moved closer, still — so close that I felt the urge to lean back in my chair, put some more distance between me and the hungry look in his eye.

"And I am willing to do whatever needs to be done."

I didn't like the way he was looking at me. I'd learned young to recognize when vampires were looking at me with desire —

though this wasn't about desire for my blood or my body. This, somehow, seemed even more dangerous.

"I should be going," I said. "Get some rest before—"

I started to rise, but Septimus caught my arm.

"My bet has always been on you, Oraya," he said. "And if I have to choose, my bet will stay with you. All I ask for is loyalty."

I fought hard to keep my face still. To reveal nothing.

Septimus was choosing his words carefully. But I knew what he was offering me. Knew what he was implying.

And for better or for worse, I knew that if I accepted his offer, he would hand me the crown to the House of Night. Yes, it would be a dangerous offer, the crown attached to more puppet strings than even Raihn's.

My father, I knew with sudden certainty, would have taken this deal.

Months ago, I would have denied that. I had looked at the deal Raihn made and snidely, haughtily declared that Vincent never would have lowered himself to such a thing. Never mind that Vincent had proven himself more than capable of taking extreme measures. Never mind that Raihn had been backed into a position where he had no other options—backed into that position to save me.

I couldn't consider those things then. It was easier to ignore uncomfortable truths. Now, uncomfortable truths were the only kind that remained.

Vincent would have taken the deal. Used the Bloodborn like a weapon to cut out Raihn's knees from beneath him. Sold whatever he needed to sell to get power. Dealt with the consequences later.

He had, after all, already done such things before.

A few months ago, I wanted nothing more than I wanted to be Vincent. Run his kingdom. Be worthy of his blood. Win back his crown.

I looked down at Septimus's hand, slender fingers curled around the cigarillo. His little finger was tucked in, mostly hidden, but I could see the tremors nonetheless. Both hands, now.

"I know better than to make a deal with a desperate man," I said. "Besides, you're right. I am tired of being caged. I recognize bars when I see them."

I stood and put out my cigarillo in the ashtray, not breaking Septimus's silver-gold stare.

"Thanks for this," I said. "See you at the wedding."

35

ORAYA

The dress was indecent.

Cairis had picked it, surely. Everything about the design was flawlessly deliberate. The patriotic colors of the House of Night, blue and purple rendered in layers of rich, rippling silk. The asymmetrical neckline, which echoed the style of Rishan men's jackets—matching, I was sure, Raihn's. The silver trim and metal accents, chains over my shoulders and hanging down my back. The long train. The tight cut, revealing too much.

And of course, the mantle, tight dark fabric that went over my shoulders, buttoning all the way up to my throat—designed, clearly, to hide my Heir Mark.

Cairis sent in half a dozen young women to help me dress and attend, it seemed, to every part of my body—my hair, my skin, my eyes, my lips. I protested at first, practically snarling at the first poor girl who came at me with a brush. But they were persistent, and eventually I came to realize it wasn't worth fighting. I let them surround me in a flurry, and when they were done, they left just as suddenly, leaving me swaying in front of the mirror.

I should have hated the version of myself I saw.

I wasn't so sure that I did.

Without the mantle, the gown was even more revealing than the one I'd worn at the Halfmoon ball, which had scandalized me at the time. I toyed with that mantle now, picking at the intricate silver embroidery. Beautiful, of course. And the Oraya of not long ago would have appreciated it—something thick to cover my arms and chest and throat, one more layer between my heart and the rest of this brutal world.

I undid the buttons one by one and let the fabric fall from my shoulders.

My Heir Mark pulsed, glowing slightly in the dimness of the room. Maybe my human eyes, much more sensitive to the difference between light and darkness, were more aware of that than those of my vampire counterparts. It seemed to fit the dress so perfectly, the neckline framing the wings of red ink across the span of my shoulders, the plunging V revealing the spear of smoke between my breasts.

It would be safer to wear the mantle.

Cover my throat. Cover my Mark. Make myself small and unnoticeable. The cynical part of me could say that Raihn's circle wanted me to cover it because it made him seem more powerful, but I knew the truth was more complicated than that—knew that the Mark also posed a significant risk to me, a target painted right over my heart in a room full of stakes.

And maybe a part of myself was happy to hide it, ashamed of what this Mark meant—even as I still longed so fiercely for the man who had worn it before me.

Even though that man would have hidden it from me my entire life.

It had been a long time since I'd really looked at myself in the mirror. My body was starting to look healthy again, the muscles more defined on my shoulders and arms, the high slit of the skirt revealing a graceful swell of thigh. I turned around and looked at my back. The dress dipped low without the mantle's cape, leaving it bare. The firelight played over the topography of my skin—tight over newly-developed muscles, stronger than they ever had been even at my peak physical fitness, marred by a few scars from a lifetime of fighting.

I was as strong as I was before. Stronger, even. My body showed it.

I faced forward again, running my gaze from my feet to my face. My face—serious and stoic. Big silver eyes. Low dark eyebrows. Cheeks that were starting to fill out. A mouth that was too thin and serious.

I looked like him.

The resemblance struck me all at once, suddenly undeniable. The coloring was all different, of course, my hair night-black compared to Vincent's blond. But we had the same icy pallor to our skin. The same flat brow, the same silver eyes.

He spent an entire fucking lifetime lying about what was plainly painted on my face.

But then again, that was our entire relationship. He'd raised me to look at the bars of my cage and call them trees.

And then, finally, my eyes drifted down, past the curve of my jaw, to the very exposed column of my throat. To the two sets of scars there—one I had asked for, one that I hadn't.

When I went to the door, I left the mantle on the floor.

36

RAIHN

I'd give him this: Cairis was a hell of a party planner. Somehow, within a court plagued by unpopularity, indecision, power struggles, and two ongoing civil wars, he'd still managed to throw together a wedding celebration that looked as if it was held by the grandest of Nightborn dynasties. He'd transformed the castle into an embodiment of peak Rishan leadership. One would never guess that two weeks ago, the place had been stripped bare, caught awkwardly in the transition of a coup.

No, it now looked just like it had two hundred years ago, just newer—right down to the flower arrangements. Someone else might have been surprised that he'd remembered all that detail, but I understood it. I'd been right there beside him, after all. Lots of time to study the details when you're desperate for something to distract you through the worst nights.

I couldn't afford to be distracted right now, even though I wanted to be. Neculai Vasarus would not have been distracted— he'd be reveling in this shit. I wasn't him, but still, I slipped into the role the same way I slipped into the too-tight jacket Cairis had dressed me in—awkwardly, but with enough confidence to make it look like second nature.

The position of every single muscle was intentional—the straight back, the raised chin, the loose, casual grip on my blood-stained wine glass, the steely stare with which I surveyed the ballroom.

The feast had begun. The nobles had started to arrive. All was, so far, going as it should. I kept waiting for someone to flaunt their disrespect. It didn't happen.

But Simon Vasarus still had not arrived.

Neither had Oraya, though I'd been assured by an openly irritated Cairis that she was coming. Nothing was easy with that woman. It was kind of comforting.

I leaned against the wall and took a sip from my glass. Human blood, of course—it had to be human blood for an event like this, Cairis was insistent upon that—but all from well-compensated blood vendors, and blended with vampire blood and deer blood. More blood vendors would be joining the feast later in the night to offer fresh delicacies too. I'd tripled their pay when no one was paying attention, and commanded Ketura to keep a close eye on them. I knew she'd do it. Ketura was prickly, but unlike most members of my court, she didn't seem to view my views on humans to be some sort of semi-endearing, semi-irritating eccentricity to be managed.

I'd rather they not be here at all. But change, I had to remind myself, came in small steps. This party had to convince a lot of important, terrible bastards that I was one of them.

So far, it was looking the part.

The blood was sweet and flat, slightly bitter with the added alcohol. Biology meant that human blood would always taste good to me—no moral stance could change that. It seemed like a fucking injustice that human blood, even taken against someone's will, would always taste good, while a perfectly seasoned steak now tasted like ash unless it was bloody-rare.

Still, since the Kejari, even human blood didn't hold the same appeal. It tasted... one-note. Either too savory or too cloying.

Since the Kejari.

No, since a certain cave, and a certain woman, and a slew of tastes and sounds and sensations that I'd probably be chasing for the rest of my damned life.

I swirled the blood around in the glass and my eyes fell to my thumb—the faint jagged mark on the pad, mostly healed.

I didn't want to admit how many times I'd looked at that mark these last few days.

How many times I'd thought about the exact sensation of Oraya's tongue against my skin. And fuck, the look of primal pleasure on her face—that was something I could drink up for the rest of my life.

It was pathetic, the things I clung to with her. The soft, hungry press of her tongue. The lash-flutter of pleasure. The moan when I'd touched her wings, the way her legs had fallen open, the way her back had arched—the way she'd fucking *smelled*, so aroused, like she—

Ix's tits. What was wrong with me?

I snapped myself out of that train of thought with another long drink. I wished there was more alcohol in it. I craved beer. Human beer.

Another set of nobles arrived and bowed before me. I gave them impassive stares, polite greetings, and waved them away, accepting their submission as I should—like a king who expected nothing less.

They glided across the ballroom to pay their respects to the couple of honor. Vale accepted their congratulations as I had, while Lilith stood somewhat awkwardly at his side. Cairis had told her, a little rudely, not to talk if she could at all help it, and she was following his orders for the most part. Still, every time a guest walked away, she would whisper in Vale's ear excitedly—no doubt peppering him with constant questions.

Vale didn't seem to mind, though. Seventy years with the man and I'd never seen him smile so much.

I watched them, frowning, brow furrowed.

"You're staring."

Mische's voice almost made me jump.

I glanced at her and did a double take.

She grinned, spinning around.

"Right? Cairis let me pick it out myself."

She looked like a literal ray of sunshine. Metallic gold fabric wrapped around her body, the skirt layered and flaring more than typical House of Night style usually dictated. It had no embroidery, no accents, but what it lacked in decoration it made up for in that brilliant color, extra striking against the bronze of her skin. It was sleeveless, the neckline open. She wore a pair of long black gloves that reached her upper arms — I couldn't help but linger on those, knowing why she was wearing them.

Even her face glittered — gold over her eyelids and dotting on her cheeks, complementing her freckles.

I'm sure she expected some kind of dismissive joke. But maybe I was an old sap after all, because I couldn't bring myself to make one. It had been a while since I'd seen Mische shining. It was nice.

So I said, honestly, "You look fantastic, Mish."

She beamed, cheeks glittering.

"I do, right?"

I chuckled. "So humble."

She shrugged. "Why should I be humble?"

Hell, why should she?

She looked me up and down. "You look... uh... *kingly.*"

Her tone, rightfully, did not indicate that to be a compliment.

"That's the idea."

"I think it's nice. I mean, it's very polished. You look really... clean."

I was very conscious of all the eyes on me. It was too easy to be myself with Mische. My words could be casual, but my body language had to stay consistent — I was the Nightborn King.

And yet, at this, I had to clench my jaw hard to swallow my laugh.

"Clean," I choked.

Mische threw up her hands in a gesture of, *Well, what the hell do you want me to say?*

"You *do.*"

"Thank you, Mische. When I have all these nobles blowing smoke up my ass, it's nice to have you to bring me back down."

She patted my shoulder. "You're welcome."

Then she followed my gaze—to Vale and Lilith, now whispering and chuckling to each other like they were the only ones in this ballroom.

A soft smile spread over Mische's lips. "They're cute," she said.

"Mm. Cute."

Maybe. I wasn't sure I was convinced yet.

Her eyes narrowed. "What's the grunting for?"

"Nothing."

She knew, of course. For a moment, we both watched them.

"I think it's real," she declared at last. "I think he loves her."

I gave her a look. She gave me one back.

"What? You think that because he did some bad things two hundred years ago, he's not capable of love?"

Capable of loving a Turned woman? Capable of loving a *human?* I fucking doubted it. Even if the evidence before me was, I'd admit, disconcertingly compelling.

"Maybe," I said.

"I've got to believe in love, Raihn. The world is sad enough."

My eyes slipped to the other side of the ballroom, to the one painting that still remained from Vincent's reign. That lone Rishan man, falling to his death, reaching for something that was never going to reach back.

I made a noncommittal sound and then cleared my throat, straightening my back.

"I don't need to be nannied over," I said, motioning to the banquet tables. "Go eat. If I know you, you've been mentally undressing that feast since you walked into the room."

She giggled. "Maybe a little."

She moved to kiss me on the cheek, and I quickly moved away, disguising the movement as me picking up my wine glass again.

Because Simon Vasarus had just walked into this party, and suddenly, I was infinitely aware of every appearance.

Still, even with that distraction, the flicker of hurt on Mische's face twisted in my gut.

"I have to be careful," I muttered, casting a pointed look. She followed my gaze, and her face hardened.

"Is that him?"

The words were cold with hatred.

I didn't answer. I rearranged every muscle into the careful facade—a facade, I distantly realized, of Neculai. I didn't allow myself to look directly at Simon. But I could feel his stare on me. Could feel him approaching. Sensed his proximity like I was being stalked.

I hated that he made me feel that way.

"Go," I said to Mische, more firmly than I meant to, but suddenly the last thing in the world that I wanted was for Simon to notice her existence.

She slipped away to the banquet table, and I remained, perfectly nonchalant, as Simon and his wife, Leona, approached me. The room seemed to quiet—everyone knew what they were witnessing. Out of the corner of my eye, I saw Cairis move so-very-casually into position behind me. Vale's gaze, too, seared through me like a spear.

"Highness."

That voice, and that word, brought me back two-hundred years. The way he'd used it on Neculai—always with such syrup-sweet deference, always a *thank you* for some gift or some invitation or some feast. Sometimes a *thank you* for me.

At last, I allowed my gaze to turn to them.

Simon was old now. He had been almost as old as Neculai back in those days, and centuries had passed since then. Still, he was a vampire, not human—his age showed only in a few streaks of silver in his hair, in the distant, ageless coldness in his eyes. He'd survived some hard times. Maybe he was leaner than he was back then, but then again, it was never his size that made him a threat.

His hair was longer now, falling to his shoulders. He kept the beard, in similar style to Neculai, even after all these years—a few flecks of gray mixed in with the brown. He'd gotten new clothes for this occasion, it seemed. He was well dressed, as was Leona, a tall, slender, raven-haired woman at his arm.

Even though I had braced myself, seeing them so close drew forth a violent reaction—a physical sensation that seized me in a firm, sudden grip.

It had been a long time since I had experienced fear this way, so primally. I wrenched it back immediately, but maybe it was too late—for a moment I was so fucking sure he had to have smelled it on me.

I shoved that fear down deep, deep, and poured my hatred all over it. I thought of Oraya and her furious face and the way she spat in the eyes of things that could kill her with a flick of their fingers.

I couldn't lie to myself and say I had all that courage. But I could pretend I did.

I gave Simon and Leona a pleasant, lazy smile. "Welcome, Simon. Been awhile. I'm glad you could make the journey at last."

I could practically feel Cairis's glare at the back of my head for that snipe. But hell, let Simon deal with a little bait. See if he snaps.

"It's an honor to be here tonight," he said.

And then they bowed.

Low bows. Proper bows.

The entire room seemed to exhale.

I regarded him coldly as he rose.

I was supposed to hope that Simon did not remember me very well. And maybe he didn't—I was just one slave after all, one unremarkable body to be used. For the sake of my position as king, it was in my best interest to hope that these powerful people didn't remember those days as well as I did—that they did not remember what I looked like on my knees.

Pettily, a part of me now hoped he *did* remember, and I hoped he was thinking about it just now, when he bowed to me.

"Apologies that we haven't made it to Sivrinaj sooner, Highness," he said. "An old man gets stuck in his old ways."

Neculai still would've killed him without thinking twice for spurning his invitations, and I really, really hated that I didn't have that option.

My voice came out in a low, cold growl as I said, "You're very fortunate I'm in a forgiving mood."

A damn near perfect mimicry of Neculai.

Simon betrayed nothing, but I didn't miss a faint flicker on Leona's face. Just a hint of disgust.

Cairis touched my shoulder, pulling me away. "Look," he murmured.

I glanced at the entrance, where the servants now gave polite bows.

The House of Shadow.

It was easy to recognize them immediately—by the dark, heavy, tight-fitting clothing, the wisps of shadow that followed their movements.

This was the real test. I straightened and left Simon and Leona without another word, crossing the room to receive the Shadowborn prince.

We bowed to each other—his a little deeper than mine.

The prince was older than I was, but he was very boyish in appearance. His hair was chestnut-brown and slightly curly, puffed up in a way that suggested it had evaded many attempts at styling, or maybe that he'd spent a very long time getting it to look that way.

I cleared my thoughts, eternally conscious of the Shadowborn's mind abilities.

"You throw an incredible party," he said, as he straightened. "My father will be disappointed he couldn't make the trip."

"No expense too great for my general's wedding."

"I have to admit, I expected to see... well, not to be morbid."

He chuckled, shaking his head. "I expected to see something much drearier. We hear stories."

The Shadowborn were known for being cold and unfriendly, but I wasn't sure what to make of this man's overly familiar attitude—though the entourage with him certainly seemed to fit the stereotype much more than he did.

I kept my smile pleasant and cocky and just the right amount of cruel.

"We had our pests," I said. "Nothing we couldn't put down. I'm sure you've had your own in the past."

"Of course," he said cheerfully. "Never needed the Bloodborn to help us with ours, though."

I almost let my surprise show at that, catching myself just in time.

"Like I said." I lowered my voice. "We have our pests. The Bloodborn had their uses, but—"

I glimpsed movement over the prince's shoulder, at the entrance. I allowed myself to get distracted.

How could I fucking not?

I could've sworn that I wasn't the only one—that the room went damn near silent.

Or maybe I imagined it.

Maybe I just imagined that the entire world stopped when my wife walked into the ballroom.

37

ORAYA

It surprised me, just how unafraid I was.

I'd gotten through the church's ball wearing nearly as little clothing as this, yes, but I thought that there would be something different about walking into this particular party, in this palace, so similar to all the parties I'd never been allowed to attend. Always reminded that they were nothing more than traps for me.

But I walked into that ballroom with my throat exposed, and I didn't feel afraid. The vampires stared at me, and I didn't feel afraid. I showed off the Mark I was supposed to hide, and I didn't feel afraid.

Maybe it was because there was something different in the way they looked at me now—not like another blood vendor or a curious forbidden delicacy.

They looked at me like I was an actual threat, and I liked that.

My eyes found Raihn immediately, even through this massive crowd, like somehow I'd already known exactly where he'd be.

He was staring right at me—staring with an intensity that made my step falter a little. He was dressed much like he had been the day he'd had to receive the nobles, which was to say, uncomfortably polished. Our outfits, of course, complemented each other's, his silver-trimmed, dark-blue jacket an obvious mate to my gown. His image was perfectly befitting that of the powerful Nightborn King.

It looked fake.

But not his stare. That was... too revealing. He shouldn't be looking at me like that here. Not with all these people watching.

I recognized those with him right away—House of Shadow royalty. I wasn't about to interrupt that.

I turned away, breaking our stare. Strange how all these eyes on me meant nothing to me. But Raihn's... my fingers fell to my chest, over my quickening heartbeat.

"Gods!" Mische was beside me in a flurry of gold and the scent of lavender. "You look *incredible!*"

She was holding a glass of blood in one gloved hand and some kind of meat-and-blood filled pastry in the other. She looked like the embodiment of sunshine—so dazzling it actually stunned me.

Her eyes were round as she looked me up and down and leaned close.

"Is this... did Cairis pick this?"

"The dress? Yes."

"But the—"

She stared pointedly down at my chest—my Mark.

"The top piece was uncomfortable," I said. "I decided not to wear it."

A sly smile spread over her lips. "You've got such balls. I love it."

I took in Mische's dress, the gold shifting and glittering under the Nightfire lights. It was so... un-vampiric. So unabashedly *her.* I couldn't imagine a single other soul wearing it as well.

"You look good, too," I said, even though *good* was too weak a word for it.

My gaze slid across the room again over her shoulder—to where Raihn was talking to the Shadowborn prince. The prince's eyes kept wandering away from him and landing on Mische.

Poor Raihn. Such an important conversation, and he couldn't even keep the man's attention. Then again, could anyone blame him?

"Looks like the dress has earned you some admirers." I nodded to the prince across the room, and Mische turned to follow my stare—

—And froze.

Her smile faded. Her cheeks, normally flushed, went ashen beneath speckles of gold.

The difference in her was so sudden and stark that it had me startled. "What's wrong?"

She didn't answer. Didn't move.

I touched her shoulder, as if to physically pull her out of her trance.

"Mische," I said. "What's wrong?"

I let more concern creep into my voice than I'd meant to.

She turned abruptly back to me. "Nothing. Nothing. I just—I suddenly have a headache. I think I need a drink." She set down her nearly full glass and turned away, then turned back to me, like she couldn't decide which direction to go. Her eyes were wide and frantic. "Don't tell Raihn I'm—just tell him I—I needed more food."

"Mische—"

But she'd slipped back into the crowd before I could get her name out. I started to go after her, but someone caught my shoulder. I jerked away and turned around, a snarled word already halfway to my lips.

Standing before me was Simon—Raihn's troublesome Rishan noble.

I recognized him right away, even though we'd never met. He strongly resembled the brother Raihn had killed during that first meeting. But even aside from that, his real tell was that his entire being reeked of vampiric noble entitlement. I knew the type well.

He extended a hand.

"May I have a dance?" he asked.

I'd already taken two strides away from him, my back to the wall.

"I don't dance with people who touch me without permission."

Raihn had to kiss this man's ass, maybe, but I sure as hell didn't. Besides, I had a role to play: *I'm the brute king, and you're the prisoner wife who hates him.*

Simon's smile—a cryptic curve of his lips that seemed to hint at all kinds of unspoken secrets—didn't falter. "It was rude of me to do that without introducing myself. I'm—"

"I know who you are."

Delight sparked in his eye. "Did your husband tell you about me? How flattering. We've known each other for a very long time."

I made a noncommittal noise of agreement and began to turn away, but he caught my arm, pulling me back.

I yanked it away.

"Do not," I snarled, "touch me."

But if he was fazed, he didn't show it. "Like everyone else, I admit I wondered why he kept you alive. Now, seeing you up close, I think I understand."

I didn't like this man. I didn't like the way that his very presence made me feel like I had a year ago—like a piece of meat to be consumed, an indulgence to be coveted. I gave him a smile that was more of a baring of teeth.

"I'm the exotic prize," I said, my voice dripping with sarcasm.

Simon laughed. "You are. Rishan kings have always enjoyed collecting beautiful, curious things." His gaze slipped back to Raihn, still engaged with his conversation across the room, and it shocked me how the way he looked at Raihn was exactly the same as the way these nobles had always looked at me—the same hunger, the same entitlement.

As if Raihn felt that stare as much as I did, he glanced over at us.

303

His haughty false smile for the Shadowborn prince's benefit fell away.

"Not so very long ago," Simon murmured, conspiratorially, "Raihn was the pretty exotic thing. Did he ever tell you about that? Probably not."

I'd spent my whole life as a pawn in petty games of power. I knew how to recognize when I was standing in the center of a board. Simon was using me to toy with Raihn. Using me to humiliate him, two hundred years later, as revenge because Raihn had the audacity to become something more powerful than him.

I despised him.

Simon's fingertip grazed my bare shoulder.

I caught his wrist.

Not what a subservient slave queen would do.

Not that I gave a fuck anymore about that.

"He told me all I needed to know," I said, and I found a little satisfaction in the momentary flicker of Simon's smile—a *how-dare-you* falter.

Good. How fucking dare I, indeed.

Suddenly, a large form was between us, one hand on my shoulder.

The smile that Raihn gave Simon was barely even the facade of anything but a threat—wide enough to expose the sharpest points of his teeth.

"She's mine," he said. "I don't share."

I'd never heard Raihn's voice like that—like the grinding of bars barely holding against something much worse.

He didn't give Simon the chance to say anything more. Instead he swept his arm around my shoulders and led me away, towards the center of the ballroom.

Feeling possessive? I wanted to say, but before I could, he growled, "Stay the fuck away from him. If you want to hurt me, do it in other ways."

It was perhaps the only time Raihn had spoken to me like that—in a command. And yet, though my instinct was to lash out at him for talking to me that way, something else beneath the hardness of his tone made me pause.

I stopped walking and looked at him, and he did the same. His expression was a stone wall. Then something shifted. Softened. Did I imagine that he looked almost apologetic?

He glanced around the room, as if remembering all over again where we were. He straightened his spine and smoothed out his expression.

He extended his hand. "Dance with me."

"I'm a bad dancer."

His mouth tightened, like this reaction was amusing. "I thought Cairis prepared you for this."

I wasn't sure if anyone could call whatever Cairis did "preparation." He'd sent someone in to give me a few cursory dance lessons — *"So you don't embarrass us all!"* — and I'd let them snap at me for a few hours before I chased them out of my room.

A choked snicker escaped Raihn's lips. "Oh, that face tells me exactly how that must have gone."

"I'm a bad dancer," I grumbled again.

He stepped closer, his voice lowering. "Maybe. But you move beautifully. And you move even better with me. And I need an excuse for why I've just been standing in the middle of the room fighting with you."

"I thought you wanted me to fight with you in public. I thought I was supposed to be the pissed-off Hiaj captive."

"In that case," he murmured, taking my hand, "just keep wearing that face and we'll be fine."

His touch was so gentle in contrast to the roughness of his hands. Warm — warmer than it seemed like a vampire should be. But then again, Raihn's skin had always seemed a little warmer than most.

Every primal instinct within me screamed, *"Danger!"* at that touch.

Yet when he began to move, I moved with him.

3 8

ORAYA

The orchestra, as was common at Nightborn parties, was enhanced with magic, the music layered to inflate through every crevice of the massive room. It made the sound deep and rich, filling me up from the inside.

In this moment, the music swelled, sweeping up into the beat of the next arrangement. It was a slow, dramatic song, with a rhythm that echoed the beat of a heart, all seductive strings and aching organ notes. A dance designed to be an excuse to bring two bodies together.

Raihn slipped one hand into mine, the other settling at the small of my back. I flinched a little at his touch against my bare skin, but hid it quickly.

The dance was a challenge. The same part of myself I'd unleash at the start of every Kejari trial rose up to meet it.

I'd sell the hell out of this thing.

Raihn swept me into our first steps. Clumsy at first—just for a half step or two. But it surprised me how quickly we fell into a rhythm, even with our bodies this close together. The steps that had seemed ridiculous and unintuitive when fed to me by Cairis's dance instructor now felt like instinctive responses to each of Raihn's movements.

"See?" he murmured in my ear. "Look at that. You're a natural."

"I'm just stubborn," I replied. "Don't like to pass up a challenge."

He chuckled, a low, breathy sound. "Good. If you're going to play the game, can't quit just when it starts to get interesting."

"I don't know what you're talking about," I said, too sweetly.

Raihn pulled away just enough to raise a skeptical brow at me, just as he launched me into a twirl, caught me, dipped me. When I arched my back, a shiver rippled up my spine as his fingertips traced the shape of my Mark — just brushing the swell of my breasts.

"Oh? Then what's this?" he murmured.

He straightened, sending me deeper into his embrace. The warmth and size of his body enveloped mine. The rhythm of the music had slowly begun to accelerate, mimicking the rush of a seduction. Maybe it was the pace of it, and the matching cadence of our steps, that reduced the rest of the ballroom to nothing more than inconsequential blurs, cocooning us together.

Maybe.

I wished he'd picked a different song.

"The mantle was uncomfortable," I said. "I decided not to wear it."

His lips curled. "You're such a shit liar, princess."

Another dip. I returned from it viciously, like a counter to a strike. It turned out the two of us did know how to move together, after all. Our footsteps matched each other's like blades, a mirror to countless sparring sessions.

"Maybe I'm tired of hiding," I said.

"Some kings in my position might call that a threat."

The beat grew faster, faster. What had begun as slow and seductive now was the racing heart of the moments before a kiss. When he pulled me back to him, the full length of my torso pressed to his, our bodies battling to keep up with each other's next step.

I'd been physically close to Raihn since the wedding. More than I'd wanted to—every time we sparred, every time we flew together. And yet it was this dance, fully clothed, that felt so… sexual. Like the push and pull of the night we had been together, our flesh fighting for dominance, finding agonizing pleasure in every defeat or victory.

And when he watched me now, I felt it just as I had then. Like nothing in his centuries of existence mattered more than making sure he wrung every shred of pleasure from me.

Another spin. Another violent crash into his arms, too fast to stop myself, too fast to keep our noses from nearly touching. I felt the slight, silent shudder in his exhale and wondered if it was from exertion. Felt the brush of hardness against my lower stomach and knew it wasn't.

"A threat?" I said. "Could've sworn you liked the dress."

Dip. This time he lowered with me, forcing my body to arch against his.

"Oh, I do," he murmured. "The dress is an act of war. But you've always looked fucking fantastic in blood."

His mouth brushed the angle of my jaw as we straightened. My entire being responded to that brief touch, awareness limiting to skin-against-skin.

"You don't go into battle without armor," I said. "This is all just another trial, right? Just as much of a fight as the Kejari."

He chuckled, scarlet eyes sparkling.

"Damn right it is. So who's the enemy?"

I laughed, short and rough with effort, as he launched me into another series of steps. Our dance had gotten vicious now, quick, like a battle gone brutal.

"What's so funny?" he asked.

I tilted my head up to whisper into his ear. "*Everyone* is the enemy. That's what's funny."

"I've seen you survive worse odds."

The force of the next spin flung me against him, the speed of the music forcing me to keep up. The pace was frantic, exhausting, but I wasn't about to surrender.

His fingers played at that little dip in my spine, right where my skin met the fabric, as if trying to stop himself from sliding beneath it. I could feel it in the strain of his muscles that I knew better than to think was from exertion alone—no, Raihn was strong. Moving was nothing for him.

Holding himself back, though? That was hard.

And worst of all, I knew he sensed it in me, too. The same desire that he'd brought to the surface of my skin the night he had touched my wings, and the night I had tasted his blood.

And that, I knew, was what drove him wildest of all, earning the lust in his eyes, the flare of his nostrils.

"So should I be afraid?" he murmured, the smile fading on his lips. "Are you going to kill me, princess?"

An echo of the past. A shade of the future.

I thought of Septimus's offer.

It would be so easy, to drag Raihn to a dark corner of this crowded ballroom, kiss him, drag his hand between my legs, let him feel my desire for him. I could take him away. Let him slide this dress off my body. Let him spear me against the wall, fuck me while I sank my teeth into his throat to dull my screams.

And what a distraction it would be, when I buried the knife strapped to my upper thigh into his chest. Right where I did it last time.

It would be the perfect time to make a move, with all the power of the Rishan here to be slaughtered.

The music rose to its crescendo. I leaned close so he could hear me over the roar. "I already did. I don't know why you keep giving me chances."

The room was so loud, his voice so low, and yet I heard nothing but his words: "I'd spend a lifetime at the tip of your blade, and it would have been worth it."

I blinked. Something in his voice snapped me out of the haze of our flirtatious game. I pulled away just enough to look at him, a question on my lips, even though I couldn't articulate exactly what it was.

But Raihn just smirked at me. "Grand finale. Ready?"

The music was deafening now, throbbing in every curve of my body, drowning out words and thoughts. Before I could protest, he launched me into the finale of the dance, and I was in too deep now to let us falter here—my pride, if nothing else, dictated that. The end was frenetic and savage, and I threw myself into it with all the fury of our battles—and just like he had the final night of the Kejari, he met every step, never faltering.

And in the end, I was back in his arms, inches from falling before he caught me, my back arched in a graceful dip.

The last notes of the song swelled through the ballroom. My breath was heavy. Raihn's hand was planted firmly between my shoulder blades, mine around his neck. A few loose strands of his hair tickled my cheek.

Everyone was staring at us.

As the rush faded, it sank in what we must look like.

"That was stupid," I said. "Cairis will be pissed at both of us."

Raihn grinned. It was such a disarmingly pure expression, like it didn't belong in a place like this at all. "So what? Let them talk."

He helped me back to my feet, but the movement was a little off-balance. He half-stumbled as he straightened. I caught his shoulder to steady him.

"Took that much out of you?" I muttered. "You're out of shape."

"Maybe more than I thought."

But I couldn't keep the wrinkle from my brow. I left my hand on his arm. He was swaying slightly—I could feel it, even if it wasn't visible. Was he *drunk?* Raihn was a big man. That would take a lot of alcohol, far more than I'd seen him drink tonight.

"Are you alright?" I whispered.

He hesitated before shooting me another easy smile. "Perfect."

I pulled my hand away and stepped back. Raihn did the same, assuming, once again, his role of Nightborn King. It was such a smooth transition, such a perfectly rendered disguise, that no one else would notice the slight stumble in his next step, nor the flicker of confusion across his face.

But I did.

I started to follow him, but Cairis swooped in. He, unsurprisingly, looked irritated.

"Excuse me, Highness. I need to speak with you."

With a firm hand on Raihn's shoulder, he ushered him away. A protest caught in my throat—even though I didn't know why I wanted to stop him, or what made me so uneasy.

Even if I'd gotten the words out, it wouldn't have mattered. The crowd swallowed them immediately, and Raihn didn't look back.

39

RAIHN

Maybe Oraya was right, and I was more out of shape than I'd thought, because that dance had taken more out of me than it should have. For those few minutes, the rest of the party had become a blur, time and music and the sounds of the crowd fading to a distant din. How could it not, when I was so singularly focused on her?

But when Cairis led me away, that feeling lingered. My thoughts were fuzzy and slow, a half step behind. When I looked around and realized that we'd left the ballroom, wandering outside under the cooling night air, I startled a little. I didn't even remember walking through the rest of the party.

Cairis was saying something, but I'd managed to miss whatever it was.

"Wait." I held up a hand, then pinched the bridge of my nose. "I—go back. I'm sorry. What are we talking about?"

He let out a small laugh.

"One dance with her and you can't even think straight anymore, hm?" His voice lowered. "I told you to be careful about that."

My head was suddenly throbbing. I didn't especially feel like being scolded.

"I'm allowed to dance with my wife," I said shortly. "What did you want to talk to me about? I have things to do."

I imagined Oraya in that ballroom, surrounded by vampire pricks who'd just found a new reason to be interested in her. Suddenly the image of Simon standing over her, his hand on her arm, was infuriatingly vivid.

Cairis's mouth thinned as he cast a disapproving glance back to the party, light spilling from the open doors and multi-paned windows. The entrance was farther away than I remembered it being—when did we walk this far?

He sighed. "That's the problem, Raihn. You think we're all stupid."

It took a few seconds for the words to sink in. When I turned back to Cairis, brow furrowed in confusion, my eyes struggled to focus on his face. I couldn't get the sharp rebuke out of my mouth.

"Surely you must think more of my intelligence than that," he was saying, hands tucked into his pockets, eyes drawn to the ground. "You keep saying that she's just a prisoner. But I'm not blind. And no one else is, either. *Everyone knows.*" His gaze lifted to me, a wrinkle between his brows. "It's sweet, Raihn. But it wasn't just *you* who sacrificed for this."

His voice sounded like he was underwater. The world tilted, the stars behind him smearing against the sky.

I opened my mouth to argue with him, ready to unleash the appropriate verbal storm of a disrespected Nightborn king, but instead, a sudden wave of dizziness had me falling back against a stone wall, barely catching myself.

He caught my shoulder. "Are you feeling alright?"

No.

The truth solidified through my sluggish thoughts.

This wasn't alcohol or exertion. Something was very wrong.

I forced my head up to look at Cairis, expecting confusion or concern on his face.

Instead, what I saw was pity.

Guilt.

"I'm sorry," he said, voice low. "I just can't go back to the way it was, Raihn. I can't stay with you until that happens. I just —I can't. I need to pick a winner. You have to understand that."

Realization ignited through increasingly sticky, drug-addled thoughts. What Cairis was admitting to. How many drinks had I let him hand me tonight, accepted without question?

I never even considered him.

That fucking *bastard*.

I conjured my wings, trying to fly, trying to move fast enough to prepare for the onslaught that I knew was coming. But my body betrayed me, just as my advisor had.

I fought the drugs until the last moment, even as my vision faded at the edges, my stomach roiling, my head pounding. I fought it even though I couldn't even keep track of how many soldiers—Rishan soldiers, my own Goddess-damned men— poured from the darkness, surrounding me, grabbing me. I managed to strike a head, a throat, an arm.

But whatever Cairis had given me drained my consciousness ravenously, second by second.

I fought until I physically couldn't anymore.

Until the chains wrapped around my wrists.

I forced my head up to see that distant ballroom light, now little more than smears of gold in my failing vision. I tried to crawl to it.

But by then my body had failed me.

In another distant world, the clock rang out in ominous solitude, a thunderous *GONG* echoing through the bloody night.

I didn't hear it chime again.

40

ORAYA

The music had gotten louder, more chaotic. I couldn't hear myself think over it. The alcohol had flowed freely. The blood, too. The blood vendors had arrived, a dozen humans who had clearly been chosen for their appearance just as much as their blood. All were dressed in finery no human in Obitraes could possibly afford—dressed by Cairis, I was sure. Some were obviously professionals—I even recognized a few from Vincent's parties. Others seemed new. One sat on the lap of the Shadowborn prince, her cheeks and chest flushed, eyelashes fluttering as he nipped at her throat, his hand wandering up between her legs. Her bodyguard—one of Ketura's—stood beside them, clearly struggling to fulfill her job of watching over the human without making awkward eye contact.

That was the difference between this party and Vincent's: every one of the blood vendors had a bodyguard. I recognized these ones. They were among Raihn's best. And this was what they had been chosen for tonight. Not guarding Raihn. Not serving the Shadowborn guests. They were watching over these humans—humans that, under my father's rule, would have been considered disposable.

It was Raihn's order. He'd probably gotten pushback over it. Vampire nobles didn't like to feel like they were being chaperoned while they nibbled on beautiful humans.

I took a sip of wine that I immediately regretted. I subtly spat it back into the cup. Vampire wine was strong. I had the nagging sensation that I had to keep my awareness intact.

My mind, involuntarily, wandered back to Raihn, and that little stumble, and that flicker of confusion.

I glanced around the room and didn't see him anywhere. I didn't see Mische, either, even though her dress would've made her stand out. Vale and Lilith were still at their table, not partaking in the dancing, Lilith looking curious and Vale looking like he was very ready to go to bed.

Everyone else was engaged in... debauchery.

I found myself fidgeting. I let my hand fall to my side, brushing the hilt of my blade strapped around my thigh, just to check that it was still there.

"Quite a party, isn't it?"

I glanced up. Ugh.

"I don't think I've ever seen you not smoking," I said.

Septimus smiled. It was the same smile he had given me the first night I met him—the kind designed to loosen lips and undergarments.

"Afraid I've run out," he said. "I'd offer you one."

"I don't like to have too many anyway. Addiction is for the weak."

He took a sip of his wine. "Oh, how she wounds."

He had a smear of red at the corner of his mouth. Apparently, he'd been having plenty of fun with the blood vendors tonight.

My gaze fell across the ballroom, where a set of open arched doors led into the castle. Simon's wife was heavily occupied with one of the young male blood vendors, while Simon approached her and whispered something in her ear. She turned back to him and laughed, offering him the human's wrist.

Mother, I fucking hated them. Meeting them once was more than enough. They seemed far too happy.

Perplexingly happy, actually, for two nobles who'd just had to bow to a former slave.

"I have to admit," Septimus said, "though I knew you had many talents, I never thought you were much of an actress."

I said nothing, still watching Simon across the room, brow furrowed. An uneasy sensation tingled at the back of my neck.

Something just seemed…

"Actress?" I said to Septimus, half-listening.

"The dance," he replied. "To be honest, I'm not sure what you would have to gain at this point by making Raihn believe that you want him."

That got my attention. My gaze flicked back to him, and he chuckled.

"My, you *are* an actress," he purred. "Look at that little startle on you."

"I don't know what you're talking about," I said.

"Don't play stupid with me." The smile didn't move. But his eyes narrowed, glinting like sharpened steel. "I know you're a very smart young woman. Though…" He set down his glass and leaned closer, his breath warming my cheek. "No, I don't think you are much of an actress, after all."

His hand grabbed my forearm, hard enough that his sharp thumbnail pierced my skin, and I jerked away.

GONG.

The clock struck.

In a lifetime here, I'd never heard it this loud—as if the entire room inflated to take it into its lungs, the marble and stone and glass vibrating with it. The music only grew louder, as if emboldened by it.

Across the room, Simon and his wife rose, abandoning the half-limp blood vendor. They went to the door leading from the ballroom.

Why the hell were they doing that alone? Why would they be allowed to go anywhere in this castle?

Suddenly I didn't even care about the blood running down

my arm. "Excuse me," I muttered, and set off across the room before Septimus had time to say anything.

Everyone was drunk. The dance floor was little more than a mostly dressed orgy. Some of the Rishan attendees were slumped on the ground, laughing hysterically to themselves with blood running down their chins.

Simon and his wife had disappeared down the hall.

GONG.

I followed. The ballroom was so hot that the moment I stepped from the room, I met a rush of cold air. The hall was quiet. Distant footsteps faded ahead. I glimpsed Leona's purple silk skirt disappearing around the corner.

"How noble of you," a silken voice said. "Charging after your lover's captor, blades drawn. How sweet."

I didn't even notice I had drawn my blades.

I turned. Septimus stood in the doorway, his hands in his pockets, that eternal smirk on his lips. Behind him, the arched door framed a tableau of decadence in the party beyond.

I wasn't about to wait for whatever snarky bullshit he was going to say next. I started to move—

But just as quickly, his hand was out of his pocket, fingers lifted.

Pain shot through me. My body seized. I glanced down— down at the cut he'd made on my arm, just minutes before.

I couldn't move. Red mist slowly thickened around me—my own blood, turning against me. I wasn't anticipating it. Mother, Septimus was a strong magic wielder. Stronger than most others I'd encountered in the Kejari. Then, I could at least fight through some of it.

Now, I was frozen, choking on air, as he stepped closer.

"You could have had everything, dove," he murmured—and for a moment he looked so deeply disappointed, so confused. It was perhaps the only genuine emotion I'd ever seen on his face.

I tried to choke out, *What are you doing?*

But only managed a garbled, "Wh—"

GONG.

The world dimmed at the edges of my vision, just in time for me to see blood-soaked chaos break out in the party beyond as Bloodborn soldiers turned on Ketura's men. A wave of animal-istic shouts rose to overtake the music, swords through flesh, teeth through throats.

But none of it was louder than Septimus's voice as he cradled my face.

"I told you I only make winning bets, Oraya," he whispered. "I'm sorry this time it wasn't on you."

He flicked his fingers.

CRACK, as my body contorted.

GONG.

Everything went black.

41

ORAYA

Consciousness didn't want me back. I had to claw for it with my teeth and fingernails, and even then, I only managed to reclaim tatters of it.

The floor, moving beneath me.

Hands on me. Hands all over me.

Don't fucking touch me.

I tried to say it aloud, but my throat, my tongue, wouldn't cooperate.

Someone was pulling at my skirt, sliding their hand up my thigh. My instinct was to kick them. Instead, I tamped the impulse down and remained limp, buying myself a few seconds to gather my senses.

I was... where? I was still in the castle. I recognized that rose-stale smell.

"—Should've killed her by now."

"Can't. You know we can't."

A man. A woman. Both Bloodborn—I recognized that accent. Desdemona.

"Get that off," she snapped.

"Trying," he hissed.

The hands sliding up my skirt weren't lecherous.

He was trying to take my blades.

Quickly, I reassembled the fuzzy memory of what had happened. Septimus. Simon. The coup. The blood all over the floor.

Raihn stumbling a little as he walked away from me.

Suddenly I was wide awake, my blood cold.

Raihn. Leaving with Cairis.

He could already be dead.

The Bloodborn man managed to unbuckle my dagger.

"Fucking fi—"

As he loosened his grip on me to lift the sheath, I grabbed the hilt and slammed the blade into his chest.

Black blood sprayed me across the face. He went flying back. It wasn't fatal—I didn't have enough strength behind the movement.

But it was enough to earn me time.

Desdemona was on me immediately. I had to be quick—I'd never seen her use blood magic, but that didn't mean she didn't have the ability. I couldn't be stronger than her, so I had to be faster. But even that was difficult, my movements a little too sluggish as they fought the aftereffects of Septimus's sedation.

My back slammed against the wall as Desdemona countered me. My blade buried in her side, deep.

She barely flinched, her eyes not leaving mine.

Shit.

We both knew I was fucked. She smiled as she drew her weapon back.

But then, she hesitated. Her next strike wasn't for my throat, my heart—it was for my leg.

Her momentary pause gave me the window I needed to slip her grip, just enough that she only nicked me.

The realization hit me—my greatest advantage. Septimus could have killed me himself, easily. Desdemona could have killed me right now. Neither of them did. That was an intentional choice.

Septimus still wanted me—or at least, wanted my blood. He wouldn't kill me. Not yet.

He'd just keep me locked up like a slave. He'd make me another tool to be leveraged.

And why the hell wouldn't he? That's all I'd ever been. A thing to be used at the convenience of others, or a risk to be mitigated.

Not a force in her own right.

Fuck that.

Nightfire bloomed to life in my hands, clinging to the edge of my blade. Desdemona wasn't prepared. She stumbled, her hands flying up to protect her face.

I went straight for her heart.

Maybe Raihn was right. Maybe my half-vampire blood meant I was capable of more than I'd ever let myself dream. Because it felt like I didn't even have to push all that hard— the dagger slid right into her flesh like it was meant to be there.

I did not take time to relish this.

I kicked her off my blade and spun around. The familiar burning had already started in my veins. Her companion had recovered, his hand lifted, pearling droplets of my blood floating around us.

The two of us lunged at each other and tangled in a mass of limbs and teeth and steel. The burn of his magic grew stronger, stronger. I had never managed to stave it off for this long. I let it fade to a faint buzz in the back of my mind—simply made every strike stronger to compensate for the force of it, fought harder to cut through the resistance.

I wasn't thinking about anything anymore.

I was angry.

I was fucking *furious*.

I didn't call upon the Nightfire to consume me—it came to me all on its own.

And when it did, the licks of white-blue obscuring my vision, the only thing that remained was my opponent's shocked face against the tile of the floor, my knees around his torso, my blade raised.

I brought it down.

He went silent. Countless minuscule drops of my blood spattered to the ground like misty rain.

My heaving breath ached in my lungs. Adrenaline had my heart pumping fast, coursing through every vein. The Nightfire still burned and burned.

I stood. I was shaking slightly. I noticed this only with faint recognition. I was still so angry I couldn't speak. Couldn't think.

Couldn't think except for one word, one name:

Raihn.

I glanced at the table, which had the male Bloodborn's arm slumped against it, like he had been reaching for something in his final moments. Just beyond his grasp was a long object, wrapped in white silk. Immediately, I recognized it. They'd taken it from my room.

Vincent's sword. The Taker of Hearts.

This time, I didn't hesitate. I sheathed my blades and unwrapped the sword. When my hand closed around the hilt, it didn't hurt at all. Mother, how could I ever have thought it hurt? This wasn't pain. This was power.

This is what you were always meant to be, my little serpent, Vincent whispered in my ear.

I flinched at the sound of his voice—so much more real whenever I touched this sword.

But he was right.

This is what I was always meant to be. And he'd hidden that from me. He'd stifled me. He'd lied to me. He gave me his power and then spent twenty years making me small and afraid and telling me how weak I was.

And yet, as I drew the blade, a lump of painful grief rose in my throat.

I was everything I was meant to be.

My father's daughter. Victim and protégée. Greatest love and ruination.

I did not know how to reconcile all those things. Suddenly I no longer cared to. It didn't matter what he had wanted of me.

I had his power.

Nightfire rolled up the delicate blade like the sun setting blaze to the horizon.

I didn't even have to consciously call to my wings. Suddenly they were out, and spread, and the air was rushing around me as I roared out the door and into the hall, the wind burning away the tears in my eyes.

WHERE ARE YOU?

I had been taken to the basement of the castle. I slipped into the tunnels that so few people knew how to navigate like I did—the tunnels that Vincent had hoped might one day save him from a coup just like this one. Sounds of bloodshed echoed in the walls, as if the castle itself was moaning and screaming in its final death throes. Some of the doors I passed had blood seeping beneath them, dark and slippery on the stone landings.

I ran, and ran, and didn't stop—didn't stop to think, didn't stop to question why I was sticking my throat out to save him. I didn't know. I wouldn't know. All I knew was that the truth of it stood before me, an inevitable action.

Where are you?

The castle had dungeons. But Raihn was a king. Not only a king, but a king who was reviled by the man who intended to take his crown.

I knew exactly what Simon thought of Raihn. Turned. Slave. Tainted. He thought Raihn was only fit to be used by people like him—not the other way around.

Simon needed a show of strength. He wanted to put Raihn in his place in front of everyone. Just like Vincent had once lined the city with Rishan bodies on stakes.

Vampires didn't kill for practicality. They killed for joy. Retribution. Spectacle. Fear.

You don't do that in a dungeon. You don't do that quietly in a back hallway.

Where are you?

I ran up the stairs. My thighs burned.

I kept thinking of Vincent, and all those Rishan wings pinned to the walls of Sivrinaj.

All the times he'd hung some poor bastard who defied him out in front of the castle.

Where are you?

I kept going up, up, up.

Because I knew where Raihn was—or at least, I prayed I did, the guess clinging to my gut with the desperation of hope.

I reached the top of the final staircase and flung the door open. A wall of hot, dry air blew my hair back.

The top floor of the castle—a ballroom, a wall of windows, and a balcony. Beyond the windows, the night sky, pink with oncoming dawn, opened before me, the reflection of the moon and stars spilling over the black marble floor, polished as a mirror.

For a moment, it was all so fucking beautiful—the untouchable beauty of the moment before glass shatters.

A number of people were in the room, their backs to me.

And there, beyond the glass, silhouetted against the sky, wings forcibly spread, was a figure I recognized immediately—even from this distance, silhouetted.

The following seconds happened slowly.

The Nightfire around me swelled and billowed.

The Rishan soldiers turned to look at me.

I tightened my grip on the Taker of Hearts. My palms burned, but I wanted to lean into it. It fueled me.

Now you understand.

Vincent's voice sounded a little proud. A little sad.

Power hurts. It requires sacrifice. Do you want to change this world, little serpent? Climb the bars until you're so high no one can catch you.

I told you that once.

I know because I did it, my daughter. I know.

My eyes settled on Raihn's form, strung up by chains.

When the Rishan soldiers lunged for me, I was ready for them.

42

ORAYA

I had always been a good fighter. But this—this was like breathing, effortless, innate. I didn't have to think. I didn't have to plan. I didn't have to compensate for my weakness.

I was the Heir of the House of Night, and I was the daughter of Vincent the Nightborn King, and I was every bit as powerful as both those things suggested.

The Taker of Hearts was an incredible weapon. It shredded bodies and pierced ribcages like they were made of sand. Now I understood why Vincent might have been willing to sacrifice his soul for this kind of power. Why Septimus was willing to tear Obitraes apart for something even greater.

I was drunk on it.

I didn't remember killing them. I was only vaguely aware of the bodies collecting beneath my feet. My wings erased the barrier between the ground and the sky, helping me move faster and dodge quicker and fling myself exactly where I needed to be. Blood covered my face, dripped into my eyes, tinting the world black-red.

Another gust of wind as I fought my way to the open doors of the balcony. Sivrinaj spread out beneath me, a sea of ivory curves, the Lituro River slithering through it all like a glass serpent.

The Taker of Hearts cut through the next Rishan who came at me in seconds.

Did he strike me? I wasn't sure. I didn't feel it.

I didn't care, either way.

A strange sensation in my back—not pain, not quite. I turned. The man's sword was bloody, dripping with crimson. "Half-breed bitch," he snarled, but my sword stole the rest of his words.

Good, Vincent said. *They deserve it.*

The last man, the one who had been handling the chains, lunged for me. I lowered the Taker of Hearts and let it slice through his leg, sending him stumbling, howling, to the ground.

I didn't let him fall fully. Hoisted him up, even though distantly, I recognized my muscles burned. Pressed him to the wall.

The last one *here*. The last one between me and Raihn. But I wasn't fucking done. I was hungry. I was *angry*.

"Simon," I snarled. "Septimus. Where are they?"

The man spat at me and tried to swing at me. He hit something, I wasn't sure what.

Fine. If he didn't want to talk, he didn't want to talk. Like he'd be important enough to know that information, anyway.

I skewered him and tossed him from the balcony.

I whirled around, ready for the next attacker. But instead of battle cries or gasps of pain or clattering steel, I heard only my own pounding heartbeat.

And—

"Hell of an entrance, princess."

The voice was hollow and hoarse.

I blinked the red from my eyes. The haze of my blood rage fell away, a sudden cold enveloping me at the sight.

Raihn.

Raihn strung up with silver chains against the wall of the castle. His wings were out and nailed through, blood clumping in the elegant feathers. Blood spattered his face and smeared his once-fine clothing. His hair was free around his face, clinging to his skin.

He'd fought like hell. One look at him told me that. Drugged or no.

I crashed back to the earth with staggering force. Suddenly, looking at Raihn like this, I did not feel powerful, despite the trail of bodies I'd left in my wake or the sword in my hand or the Nightfire at my fingertips. I did not feel powerful at all.

He gave me a weak, lopsided smile.

"I can't possibly look *that* bad."

I sheathed the blade at my side and strode across the balcony. Up close he looked even worse—some of the chains were screwed right through his skin.

I swore under my breath.

They were going to let him burn. Let the dawn kill him, slowly, right in front of all of Sivrinaj. The most humiliating way for a vampire to die. In Simon's mind, he wasn't even worthy of a real execution. Executions were for threats.

"Cairis," Raihn rasped. "It was Cairis. The traitor. Can you fucking believe that?"

Then he laughed, like something about this was hysterically funny.

"Don't do that," I snapped.

I heard voices in the distance. Many of them.

Shit.

My attack wasn't exactly subtle. They'd be coming for me. Coming for Raihn.

He heard it too, his head tilted towards the noise. Then back to me.

"This is going to hurt," I muttered. I didn't have time to be gentle. I yanked the first chain free from his wrist, a fresh spurt of blood dribbling down his arm.

"You can leave me," he said. "I'll be alright."

I laughed. It was an ugly sound. "Like hell you will."

"You're hurt, Oraya. There will be a lot of them."

No joking anymore. No cocky remarks.

Raihn was right. I was injured. Probably badly. Now that the adrenaline faded, everything hurt. I tried not to think about it, but I was getting dizzy.

A lump rose in my throat.

"I already came this far," I muttered, moving faster as I grabbed another chain and pulled it. One wing slumped down, pain spasming across his face at the extra weight yanking on his other side.

The voices were getting louder. Fuck.

I pulled away the second chain on his left arm, freeing it.

"Here. You've got an arm now. Help me," I spat, moving to the other wing.

He did, wincing as he tugged against his right side.

The voices were on this floor now, or closer.

"Hurry," I said.

"Oraya—"

"Don't you dare tell me to leave," I spat. "We don't have time for that."

Only his ankles left now. Both wings were free, and both arms. I dropped to my knees to get one ankle while he reached for the other.

Goddess, we had seconds. Less.

"Oraya."

I didn't look up. "What?"

CLANG, as metal fell to the ground.

"Why did you come for me?"

I paused for a split second we didn't have.

I didn't even ask myself that question. I didn't want to look too hard at the answer, a confusing knot in my chest.

"We don't have time for this." I yanked his final restraint free with one last clatter.

I stood, and Raihn tried to take a step forward only to slump against me. I nearly caved beneath his weight.

Over his shoulder, I watched a flood of Rishan and Bloodborn soldiers pour around the corner. More than I could fight in this state, even with the Taker of Hearts at my side.

Raihn noticed them too, then stumbled to the railing.

I looked at his wings, broken and useless. At his injuries. Down at the drop below. At the soldiers.

Then, finally, at his face.

He was bathed in pink gold as the sun crested the horizon, making his eyes gleam like dark rubies. The right side of his face was already starting to blister under the force of the sun. His hair was so red beneath the dawn—redder than I'd ever realized it was, closer to human blood than vampire.

An arrow whizzed by his head.

As the first soldiers breached the doorway, I grabbed Raihn and held him close.

"You are so impossibly beautiful," he murmured in my ear.

And then I spread my wings, and we hurled ourselves over the edge of the balcony.

PART FIVE

WAXING MOON

INTERLUDE

T he cruel truth is that it is harder to survive when you have
something to care about.

The slave and the queen have little in common. When they
talk, it is often about the king, long conversations to help themselves cope
with his behavior and moods. Most often, though, they do not talk at all,
instead using their meager time together to retrace ugly touches with
tender ones, replace pain with pleasure, like plants desperate for water.

One cannot underestimate the power of such a thing. It is enough to
build a connection that deceptively resembles love.

And who is to say it isn't? It feels like love. It tastes like love. It
consumes him like love.

Perhaps these two people would not have found any reason to be with
each other in any other world.

But in this one, they became each other's only reason to live.

The slave quickly learned that it was far harder to care about something than it was to care about nothing. For the first decades of his impris-
onment, he curated his apathy like an art. Now, in a matter of weeks, it
shatters. Every strike hurts more because of the way she reacts to it. Every
debasement is more shameful because she witnesses it. Every act of violence

against her sends him closer to a line he knows he will not be able to return from—no matter how she begs him for restraint.

Who wins? she asks him, tears in her eyes. Who wins if he kills you?

So the years pass, and the slave does not fight.

But that kind of hatred never fades. It just festers. For years, decades. It consumes his heart like a fungus, until he can no longer remember a life before it.

The king grows more paranoid, more desperate for power, as rumblings of rebellion build in the distance. The Kejari approaches, an open door for all the king's greatest enemies. As the world beyond his walls spirals further from his control, his desire to control the world within them grows more merciless. He requires constant distraction. Constant reminders of his own power.

The fungus grows.

The idea starts as a little knot of rot buried deep within. It spreads so quickly that even the slave cannot tell when it becomes more than a fantasy—only that one day, it is no longer a possibility, but an inevitability.

The slave starts paying attention to the whispers of the city. He learns of a promising Hiaj warrior, a man who makes no secret of his brutal commitment to his brutal intentions.

The first trial of the Kejari, the slave is allowed to attend alongside the king.

He sits behind the queen and watches her adjust her hair to hide the bruises around her throat.

He watches the bloody colosseum below as the blond vampire hacks apart his enemies with the same ferocity he would use to hack apart the world and take what he wants from it.

He watches the king, and the fear he tries to pretend does not exist.

And the slave, at last, sees an opportunity.

The kingdom is already drenched in oil.

He is more than willing to provide a match.

43

ORAYA

I had no idea where we were going.

It was impossible to fly well with Raihn's weight dragging me down, even though he did try — unsuccessfully — to help. But that was probably for the better. We dropped low quickly, hiding between the buildings of Sivrinaj while I frantically tried to keep us airborne. I managed to get us to the edge of the human districts before we crashed down on cobblestone streets.

Raihn, despite his injuries, somehow managed to get up quickly, limping along the walls of crumbling brick buildings. As soon as I got to my feet, I tucked myself under his arm to help support him.

I squinted up at the brightening, cloudless sky above.

"We need to get you inside," I said. "Fast."

I looked around, searching for an empty building to take shelter in, but Raihn kept dragging us forward, jaw clenched.

"I know where we're going," he said.

"Your apartment? You'll never make it. We'll find —"

"We're going," he snapped.

I was ready to argue with him again, but he shot me a look—stony, determined—that made my mouth close.

In these hazy minutes between night and dawn, it was quiet on both sides of Sivrinaj—vampire and human. But soon, I knew, we would attract attention in the human districts under a rising sun. We made it a block and a half before I spotted the first set of eyes peering through a bedroom window, hidden hastily when I met them.

"People will see you," I muttered. "We have to find somewhere faster."

"No." The word came between clenched teeth. Raihn was moving slower, leaning heavily on the walls—and clinging, with limited success, to the shadows they cast—but he still dragged himself forward. "We're close. One more block."

Mother, I didn't know if we would make it that far.

It felt like an age later that the building came into view, and I felt his breath of relief at the sight. But by then, dark burns marked his cheekbone on one side, slowly spreading across his face.

His steps were so, so slow. I was caving beneath his weight. The sun was rising higher.

"You're close," I said quietly. "A little farther."

We were so fucking close.

And then, mere feet away from the door, he collapsed.

I dropped to my knees beside him, dragging him as far into the shade of the buildings as I could. Every inch was difficult—he was heavy, and I was hurt.

"Get up," I said, trying and failing to hide how scared I was. "Get up, Raihn. We're so close."

He grunted and tried to stand. Failed, falling back against the wall.

What was I going to do? I couldn't carry him. The sun encroached quickly. I tried to shove him as far into the shade as his hulking body could fit.

A door opened and closed, and my hands went to my sword—

I looked up to see a large, balding man standing over us.

He looked familiar, though at first, I didn't recognize him. Then it hit me: the man from the apartment building. The one who was always asleep at the desk.

My mouth opened, but I didn't know what to say—whether to snarl at him to stay away or beg him for help. No disguises today. We were so obviously vampires. So obviously helpless.

A million possibilities ran through my mind as to what a human would do when faced with two stranded predators.

The man spoke before I could. "I'm no fucking fool. I know who you are."

He approached, then paused when I visibly flinched away, positioning myself between him and Raihn.

His eyes were... kinder than I'd expected. "You got nothing to be afraid of. Neither of you."

He nudged past me, knelt down, and grabbed Raihn's left arm. "You take the right," he said.

He was helping us.

Goddess, he was actually *helping* us.

I did as he said, supporting Raihn's right side. Between the two of us, and Raihn using the last of his strength to assist us, we got him into the apartment building. The keeper kicked the door shut behind us, yanking the curtains closed with his free hand.

The moment the sun was gone, Raihn let out a sigh of relief.

"Better," he managed. "Much better."

"Sh," I said. I didn't want him wasting his energy on words when there was still a staircase to tackle.

But without the sun, he immediately had more strength, mostly able to get himself up the stairs, even if he had to lean on us for support. When we made it into the apartment, he immediately sank onto the bed.

The human man stood in the doorway, arms crossed.

Raihn lifted his gaze to him. "Thank you."

But the man just held up a dismissive hand. "This place has changed. Don't think that people here don't know why." He glanced between us. "I don't know what happened here, but—it's none of my business. Let me just say, I hope that things continue the way they have been. And if getting you up here helps make that happen…" He shrugged and stepped back from the door. "I'm gone for the day and locking up behind me. If anyone asks, I didn't see a thing."

And with that, he shut the door, leaving Raihn and I alone.

I glanced at Raihn. His throat bobbed, but then he collected himself and turned to me, surveying me up and down. I was holding my abdomen. The wounds that I was in too much of a frenzy to pay attention to before were now far more noticeable. But they wouldn't kill me.

Raihn stood and hobbled across the room.

I jumped to my feet.

"Where the hell are you going?"

"Ix's tits, princess. Just across the room. I'm fine. Just the sun that was getting me."

That wasn't true. Though, at least he could move. That was something.

He shot me a bemused look as he opened a desk drawer, rummaging through it. "Sit down and stop glowering at me like that."

"Why?"

He laughed. "Is that really too much of a command?"

I sat, reluctantly, as he returned and sat beside me. His breath was heavy and rattled slightly. Blood stained the bedspread already — mine, his.

He undid his coat an extra button. It was now ripped and stained, his hair wild around his face, his sleeves pushed up to his elbows. My once-fine dress was torn and soaked in blood.

Everything refined about our appearances from earlier tonight had been washed away in bloodshed.

"Thank you," he said softly. "Thank you for coming for me."

My throat was tight. I didn't like when he talked like that. Reminded me too much of the way he thanked me after I'd let him drink from me. Too genuine.

"Simon talked about you like you were—" My lip curled. "Like you were nothing. Fuck him."

A brief smile ghosted over Raihn's lips, a little pained, because we both knew that my distaste for Simon was not the only reason why I had saved Raihn. But he didn't push me.

"I have something for you," he said, and held out a small, unassuming package, wrapped in plain fabric.

I didn't take it.

"It's not going to bite you," he said. "I've owed you a wedding gift for quite some time."

"And you think *this* is the time for gifts?"

The corner of his mouth tightened. "I think this is the perfect time for gifts."

I wasn't sure why I still hesitated. Like that little twinge in his voice made me think that whatever this was, it was going to hurt.

I took the package, laid it in my lap, and unwrapped it.

A time-stained notebook and a loose pile of parchment fell free.

With a slightly shaky hand, I took the top paper and unfolded it, revealing a scribbled portrait in faded ink—a woman with dark hair, gazing off into the distance, face partially tilted from the viewer. It was old, the ink blotchy, a few drops of water damage blooming on the page. It reminded me of another faded ink drawing—a ruined skyline in a city far away from here.

"What—what is this?" I asked

"I think," Raihn said softly, "this is your mother."

A part of me already knew it. And still, the words cracked open my chest, releasing a wave of emotion I wasn't prepared for.

Vincent had drawn this. It was his hand—I recognized that drawing style.

Vincent had drawn *her*.

I set aside the portrait gently. Beneath it was a tarnished silver necklace with a little black stone charm. I held up the necklace and placed the stone next to my hand—next to the ring I wore on my little finger. A perfect match.

My chest ached fiercely. I set down the necklace on top of the portrait. The notebook remained in my lap, unopened.

"How?" I choked out.

I couldn't bring myself to look at him.

"Slowly, that's how. The castle held hundreds of years' worth of records and notes. Vincent wrote a lot down, but not much of it made sense."

That sounded right. Vincent had liked to write, but was also paranoid about sharing information. Whatever notes he would have left behind would have been intentionally vague, difficult to understand by anyone other than him.

"I took everything that was from around twenty-four years ago," Raihn went on. "Tackled a little of it every day. Just me. No one else knows."

Mother, the time that must have taken. Combing through all those hundreds or thousands of notes himself.

My eyes stung.

I picked up another piece of paper. This one was a letter—or an incomplete piece of one. It wasn't Vincent's handwriting, which I knew now by heart. This was messier and softer, the letters upright and looping.

"Who—" The word was strangled, so I had to stop and start again. "Who was she?"

"I have more questions than answers, too. I think her name was—"

"Alana."

My fingers traced the name at the bottom of the letter. And yet, I felt its familiarity in my bones, too, from some time before that. Like I was remembering the echo of it being said in a little clay house, decades ago.

Then my hand drifted to the top of the letter. *To Alya*, it read. *Vartana. Eastern districts.*

Goddess help me. A name. A place. Vartana was a small city, east of Sivrinaj. The letter itself meant little to me, something that looked to be about healing spells and rituals from a magic I didn't understand, but—*names*.

"From what I gathered," Raihn said, "she lived in the castle for a while. I don't know how long. At least a year, based on the time differences here." He tapped the date at the bottom of the ripped-up letter, then the earlier one on the paper beneath it. That one appeared to be a journal entry of some kind—a list of ingredients. Plants. Some I recognized, some I didn't.

"I think," he went on, "she was a magic user. A sorceress."

My brow furrowed. "Of which god? Nyaxia?"

Even when I asked the question, I knew the answer. My mother was human. Some humans could wield Nyaxia's magic, but none of them became especially skilled in it, certainly never more than vampires.

Raihn gently pulled apart the pages, leaving us at the final parchment. This one, unlike the others, wasn't a letter or journal entry. It was a page torn from a book—a diagram of moon phases. At the bottom was a small, silhouetted symbol—a ten-legged spider.

"That's a symbol of Acaeja," he said.

Acaeja—the Goddess of the Unknown and Weaver of Fates.

Realization rolled over me as I thought of what Septimus had said about my father. That he'd searched for the god blood. That he'd used seers to help him do it.

Sun fucking take me.

My eyes snapped to Raihn, and he raised his brows in silent confirmation that he'd had the same thought I did.

"What did she do for him?" I asked.

"I don't know. I—I wish I knew. Months of searching, and this is all I have."

He sounded frustrated with himself, embarrassed to be offering me so little. And yet, I felt downright gluttonous with all I'd just been given.

I had a name. Goddess, I had a *face*.

And I had a million questions and a million possibilities.

I picked up the first parchment again—the drawing. My fingertips traced the old ink lines.

He drew this. He drew *her*.

Why, Vincent?

Did you love her? Did you kidnap her?

Both?

But I heard no voice in my head. Why would I even be able to conjure a fake version of him that was anything but secretive, when that was all he had ever given me in life?

Or maybe his voice had left me, because he knew I didn't want to hear anything he had to say.

My eyes stung, my throat tight. My thumb caressed that parchment, back and forth. Raihn's presence beside me felt far too close and yet not close enough.

"She looks like you," he murmured.

Something about the way he said that hurt. With such admiration. Like there was no greater compliment.

I traced the cascade of dark hair over her shoulder, the straight angle of her nose, the eerily familiar thoughtful down-turned slope of her mouth.

"I wish I could give you more," he said softly. "More than a name. More than a few scraps of paper."

"Why?" I choked out. "Why did you do this?"

I knew. In my heart, I already knew.

Raihn drew in a long breath, and loosed it slowly. "Because you deserve so much more than what this world has given you. And I know—I know I was a part of that. I took away your ability to get those answers. This isn't enough. I know it isn't. But..."

His voice trailed off, a little hopelessly, like he was reaching for words but couldn't find any. I couldn't find any, either, past the painful gratefulness that swelled in my chest, pulling tight. Yes, Raihn was right. He had taken away my ability to look Vincent in the eye and demand answers.

But even this, mere scraps of a past, was more than my father had ever given me. It meant something. It meant more than I wished it did.

I could feel Raihn's stare, even though I kept my gaze dutifully to the bedspread, ashamed of what he might see within it.

"There's something else," he said.

A faint rustling sound as he reached into his pocket. Then he placed a velvet pouch on my lap. It was heavy for its size, a faint metallic jangle ringing from within as it settled.

Money.

My eyes shot up to meet his. A mistake, because the sadness on his face was so bare, so open, that it startled me.

"What—" I started.

"Gold," he said. "The material matters more than the currency. Anyone in any of the human nations will take it from you. It's enough to last you. I was going to send more if you ever needed it, but—"

I stood abruptly, pushing the paper and the pouch off my lap and onto the bed.

"I don't—"

"Just let me fucking talk, Oraya." Then, more softly, "Just... please. Please let me say this to you."

I wanted to look away from him, now, but I couldn't. Those rust-red eyes, glistening a little too much beneath the lantern light, held me captive.

"At the mouth of the Lituro, near the outskirts of the human districts, a man is waiting for you right now. He has a boat. He'll take you to the trading islands off the coast. There, you can get on a ship going anywhere in the world."

My lips parted.

It had all been prepared. A man waiting for me. The money. This notebook, wrapped and ready, waiting for me.

Raihn had never intended to make my freedom dependent upon the support of the House of Shadow.

He was always going to let me go.

"I—" I choked out, but he stood, barely wincing at his injuries, unblinking eyes never leaving mine.

"*Go*," he breathed. "Go somewhere far away. Go to the human nations. Go learn about your magic. I'd tell you to go become something fucking incredible, Oraya, but you already are, and this place doesn't deserve you. It never has. And I sure as fuck don't."

I opened my mouth again, but Raihn's words came faster now, stronger, like he was pulling them from somewhere deep within.

"I never apologized to you the way I should have. Because everything you've ever said about me has been right. Because you've always seen the Goddess-damned truth, even when I was ashamed of it. What I did to you was—it was *unforgivable*." He spat the word, as if disgusted by himself. His fingertips brushed his chest, right where my blade had once pierced his skin. Because I knew, exactly, where that mark had been. "So I won't ask for your forgiveness. I'm not going to stand here and tell you how sorry I am. What fucking good does that do for you? I don't want to ask you for anything. I want to give you what you should have had a long time ago. Because you..."

The air seemed to have left the room—left my body, leaving me standing there, frozen, not breathing, not speaking, as he stepped closer. Closer. My chin tipped up to maintain our eye contact.

Mother, those eyes. They looked like fire now, glistening, wet with tears that didn't quite overflow.

"You are everything," he choked out, voice ragged. "Everything. So go, Oraya. Go."

My throat was thick. I swallowed past the lump, my jaw tight.

All I could think was: *Fucking fool.*

If he had the House of Shadow as allies, that would be one thing. But Raihn had no allies anymore. Not the Bloodborn. Not even the Rishan. He needed the power I could give him more than ever, now. It was his only chance at making it back to the throne, and certainly his only chance at keeping it.

He needed me more than he ever had.

"You have nothing but me," I said. "And yet, you'd let me go?"

"I have nothing but you," he murmured. "So I am letting you go."

The words left me dizzy, like the entire world had shifted in a direction my body didn't know what to do with. Raihn was so close to me that I could feel his body heat, a sensation that now felt as familiar to me as my own skin. And I could see the way his jaw worked and muscles strained, as if uniting against a primal force that begged to close the distance between us.

How did I recognize that so easily?

Why did it feel so familiar?

I was silent for a long moment.

Then I reached around him, snatched the pouch of coins from the bed, and thrust it against his chest, hard enough to make him let out a surprised *oof*.

"I can't fucking believe you," I snarled.

His face shifted in the beginnings of surprise.

"Everything has just gotten interesting," I said, "and you think I'm just going to run away? When there's a fight to fight? When that piece of shit has *my* crown?" I stepped closer, even though it was dangerous, even though that put us so close that our bodies were nearly aligned, my head tipped up to hold his stare, a sneer over my nose.

"Fuck you, Raihn," I whispered. "*Fuck you.*"

He took me in for a long moment, unblinking.

And we broke that suspended silence at the same time.

I didn't know who moved first. The kiss was like a thunderstorm over the summer desert—a torrent that swept in all at once, obliterating the heat, so all-consuming that suddenly you remember nothing but the rain.

All at once, he was everywhere.

44

ORAYA

The bag of coins made a distant *THUMP* as it fell to the floor, Raihn's hands abandoning it for my body.

He kissed me like he was starving. Kissed me the way he had fed from me in a cave once, many months ago—desperate and deep and full of hunger, like I was the only thing tethering him to the world. And Mother, I felt that way, too, like I was grasping hold of something solid for the first time in so long.

Like I had come *home*.

I had told myself I'd forgotten what it was like to kiss Raihn.

That was a lie. A body doesn't forget a thing like this—it was carved into my muscle memory, a piece of myself that had awakened from some dormant state. He kissed me with not just his mouth, but his whole body—just like he fought, with every muscle rearranged to the task, centered around me alone.

This dress was so fucking thin.

The silk let me feel everything. His hands, large and rough, trailing down my body like he wanted to memorize every muscle, drink up every curve. The warmth of him, so close I could've sworn I felt the throb of his heartbeat beneath his skin. His cock

—Goddess, his cock, hard and thick and straining between us already.

Yes, the silk let me feel everything. It let me feel how much Raihn had wanted this, for so long.

It forced me to feel how much I'd wanted it, too.

Lust pooled low in my stomach, my breasts peaking against the too-flimsy fabric of my dress and Raihn's hard chest beyond it, the apex of my thighs tightening. My body remembered what it was like to kiss him, yes, but it remembered more than that, too. It remembered what it felt like to fuck him. Like a missing piece replaced.

And now, it wanted that. It begged for it. When Raihn's hands slid down over the curve of my backside, brushing the sensitive flesh at the top of my inner thighs, my breath hitched.

The sound he made in return, barely audible, rolled through me like thunder.

The wave of desire made me suddenly dizzy—desire, though, with a darker edge, sharp and dangerous, forged in the anger I'd held so close for so long.

In one abrupt movement, I pushed him down to the bed. He fell against it roughly, the frame squealing in protest against his sudden weight. I started to crawl over him, but a wince flitted across his face, and I hesitated, noticing again the extent of his wounds—brutal, even if they were already starting to heal now that he was out of the sun.

"Don't you dare stop, princess," Raihn rasped, reading my face, the wince giving way to a twisted half smile. "Please. I don't care if it fucking kills me."

His calloused fingertips brushed my cheek, sweeping dangling black hair behind my ear.

"Only good thing about the last time it happened was that you were the last thing I saw."

His voice still had that lilt to it, light and joking, but the smile had faded. Nothing light about that. Nothing light about his touch, either. All of it was steeped in such agonizing tenderness.

It made my chest hurt. Made my eyes burn.

349

It—it made me *angry*.

I wasn't ready for that. Not yet. Not when the remnants of my anger were still so sharp in my veins, the dregs of it tearing at the wounds they'd opened these last few months.

He started to sit up, reaching for me, but I pushed him back to the bed.

"No," I said.

Confusion flitted over his face.

"Don't move," I said. "You don't get to control this."

The confusion melted into understanding. Even that, at first, was too affectionate, too soft, until he replaced it with a slow smirk curling over his lips.

I pressed down on his shoulder again, firmly, in a command to stay put. Then I shifted my attention to his clothing. I started at the buttons of his jacket, undoing each knot of silver across his chest. With each one, the blue silk fell away, exposing bare skin —a landscape of swells and dips of muscle, rising and falling heavily beneath his breath, covered with fresh wounds and old scars and soft dark hair that narrowed as I worked down his abdomen.

I'd hated that costume from the moment I saw it on him. And that's exactly what it was: a costume, trying to make Raihn into one of the people who had once subjugated him.

That wasn't who he was.

It now seemed so sickeningly obvious, I wondered how I'd ever even questioned it. No, the version of him that I revealed with every opened button, every new expanse of imperfect, once-human skin...

This was *him*.

I finished with his jacket, and he helped me by lifting his shoulders as I pulled it off of him and tossed it to the floor. I lowered myself over his chest, tracing his muscles with my fingertips, pausing over his nipple as it hardened beneath my touch, then tracing down, over each raised ridge of abdomen, to his stomach and the darkening trail of hair leading to his trousers.

And Raihn, ever obedient, did not move, though I could feel his ravenous stare. Not even when my hands fell to his waistband, unbuttoned it, and set him free.

The first time I'd seen his cock, I'd been shocked that such a thing could be considered beautiful—and yet, this time, too, it was the only word I could think: *beautiful.*

His entire body tensed when I wrapped my hand around it. It twitched a little against my touch, his abs tightening. I watched the bead of liquid at its head swell.

He wanted me. He wanted me so much he wasn't even breathing anymore, his hands tight around the bedspread. And Goddess, the ache between my own thighs was getting harder to ignore. So easy, to just crawl over him, let him slide inside me.

Too easy.

There was no such thing as easy pleasure.

I wanted him to suffer for this.

I lowered, brushing my lips over the tip of him, tongue darting out against the salty sweet of the liquid on his skin.

Raihn drew in a sharp hiss. His entire body tensed, straining, like it was taking everything he had not to lunge across the bed and grab me.

Still, he didn't move.

I softened my mouth against him, this time in a slower, longer lick—still gentle, gentle enough that I knew it would be torturous.

This time, his exhale had a hint of a groan to it.

"You're vicious," he murmured.

He had lifted his head just enough to watch me, his gaze predatory, like he'd rather die than blink.

An intense wave of familiarity passed over me at this—me leaning over him, him watching me, and that look of such barely restrained lust.

Should I make you beg? I had asked him then.

I swept my tongue over him again, slow, and he let out another hitched exhale.

"You told me once you would beg for me," I murmured.

Another brush of my lips.

"So do it."

I didn't break eye contact. His sparkled with vicious delight.

"Let me touch you," he rasped. And Goddess, yes, he was begging, every word desperate. "Let me feel you. Even though I don't deserve you. Please."

I slowly crawled over his body, until my hips were aligned with his. My dress was hiked up, silk pooling at my upper thighs — I knew we were both so agonizingly conscious of how close we were, as I let my hips lower just enough that his length brushed my folds. I bit down hard on my own moan at even that momentary, barely-there touch.

I wouldn't let him see how much I wanted it.

I lowered myself to my elbows, leaving us inches apart.

"And?" I said.

His gaze glinted with pleasure, like a cat enjoying a game of chase. And yet, beneath that feral delight, something deeper lingered. His fingertips raised to my cheek. Not quite brushing it. Still obeying.

"Let me make you the queen that you are. Let me guard your body, your soul, your heart. Let me spend the rest of my fucking pathetic life at your mercy. If I need to die, then let me do it by your hand. Please."

My chest ached, nearly as fiercely as my desire did.

My hips shifted, and I felt him twitch again, that tiny movement making my breath tremble.

"And?" I whispered.

He loosened a shaky exhale, the smirk twisting his lips. "And for fuck's sake, princess, I'm begging you, let me go to my knees for you."

We lingered like that, our bodies so close to total intertwinement, and yet not touching at all.

And then I whispered, "Fine."

The thread of self-control snapped. If Raihn's injuries slowed him down, he didn't show it. His mouth crashed against mine, rolling over and pushing me down to the bed, his hand running up my body as if the last minutes of not touching me had been torturous.

And then, just as quickly, his weight was gone. Instead, he was off the bed, grabbing my legs and sliding me down.

And just as he promised, he went to his knees.

I couldn't help but watch him, transfixed, as he gently pushed the silk of my skirt up around my hips, pushing open my thighs. In the presence of gods, he had not looked so reverent.

His gaze slowly raised to meet mine.

"Is this acceptable, princess?"

My brow twitched. "Princess?"

He laughed, low and rough. "Queen."

He started at my inner thigh, his kisses so gentle they almost tickled, lifting my leg and placing it over his shoulder.

"My queen," he whispered again, the words pressed to my skin with each kiss, trailing farther up the sensitive flesh of my inner thighs.

Mother help me. My thighs opened, making more room for him, my body conscious of nothing but the anticipation of his touch, his kiss.

When it came, right where I wanted it, he was gentle at first, pulling aside my delicate lace underwear and planting soft kisses along my slit.

So light. So gentle. And yet the shock of pleasure wrung my body tight, my back arching.

He hummed his approval against my skin, the vibration echoing through my core.

"Better," he murmured. "Better than I remember. Better than your blood."

Another touch of his tongue, this one a little firmer, ending it in a long, lingering kiss.

I clenched my jaw against the whimper of pleasure, my hands clutching the bedspread. Mother, I wouldn't give him the satisfaction. Not yet. Even if it killed me.

Another touch, another gasp, another shock of pleasure.

Keeping my moans quiet now took herculean will, my teeth so tight I distantly thought they might crack.

More. The word was on the tip of my tongue. But I wasn't asking Raihn for anything now.

"Let me worship you, Oraya," he whispered, and something about the vibration of my name on his lips against the most sensitive parts of me made me shiver. It was wrought with such utter desperation. I had told him to beg. He was begging. "And let me taste you when you come. Please."

His tongue met me firmer now, in a long lick up the length of my slit, swirling around my bud with just the faintest brush of his teeth.

Goddess help me. I—I couldn't—

A strangled moan escaped me, breaking free from my attempts to swallow it.

His mouth still to me, Raihn met it with a groan of equal strength, like the sound was water to a man dying of thirst.

"Again," he whispered. "Please."

And Mother help me, I couldn't have denied him. Not even if I'd wanted to. Because that sound broke the remaining vestiges of Raihn's self-control, and suddenly his slow, languid work became fierce and desperate.

He worked at me like his singular purpose in life was to wring the most pleasure from my body—his mouth now firm and unrelenting, strokes hard and definitive, moving from my entrance, to my clit, and back, kissing and suckling. My hips ground against him, chasing his movements—I couldn't help it, couldn't control my own muscles anymore.

"Good," he murmured. "Just like that. Let me help you."

Yes, I thought, blindly. *Yes, yes, yes.*

And I didn't realize until his growl of pleasure that I was saying it aloud, over and over again—giving him the answer he had been asking for. Giving him everything he wanted as he gave me everything I needed. My hands had found his head, tangling in red-black waves, unsure whether I was pulling him closer or pushing him away.

Closer, I decided, as his tongue worked at my clit in just the right way, as his fingers slid inside me, as his curse of pleasure shot up my spine like a bolt of lightning.

I loved his voice. I couldn't even deny how much I loved his voice.

That was my last thought, before the wave of pleasure consumed me, wiping them all away.

When my orgasm faded, I was breathing heavily. A faint sheen of sweat covered my skin. My muscles felt loose and shaky. And yet, when I opened my eyes to see Raihn, naked, climbing back onto the bed, desire already stirred again.

He looked so damned beautiful—the lantern light playing over the bare panes of his body, marked by time and wounds and scars and a life well lived, flames reflecting in the lustful rust-red of his eyes, locked to me as if nothing else existed.

Seeing, as always, more than I wished he did.

Seeing, as always, *me*.

Suddenly I felt so wildly exposed, even though he was naked and I was fully clothed. The facade of my games had collapsed. The final heat of my anger had fizzled away like a candle dying in the night.

I blinked and felt a tear streak down my cheek.

Raihn settled beside me. He wiped the tear away with his thumb.

"I hate you," I choked out. But the words weren't an admonishment. They were weak, sad, bare.

They did not say, *I hate you because you killed my father.*

They said, *I hate you because I let you hurt me.*

I hate you because I grieved you.

I hate you because I don't.

There was no hurt in his eyes. No anger. Only gentle, affectionate understanding. I hated when he looked at me like that.

Or maybe I hated that, too, the same way I hated him. Not at all.

He kissed me on the forehead.

"I know, princess," he whispered. "I know you do."

His lips moved down, to the bridge of my nose. My eyes closed against his kisses, a little damp with my tears.

"You have destroyed me," he murmured. "And I have hated every moment of it, too."

The truth of those words swelled in my chest, unbearably heavy. He said them in the same voice he'd said our wedding vows.

I opened my eyes to find his staring directly into mine. The shades of them—so many disparate colors, coming together to create something of such beauty—stunned me.

"Let me kiss you," he whispered.

Begging, still.

"Yes," I whispered.

He tasted faintly of my own pleasure, but more distinctly of him—foreign and familiar, sweet and bitter. This kiss was not like our battle from before. This was an apology, a plea, a greeting, a goodbye, a million words rolled into several endless seconds in which time died between us.

I hate you, I thought, with every new angle, every searching stroke of his tongue, every soft apology of his lips. *I hate you. I hate you. I hate you.*

And with each kiss, I breathed the words into him, even as I pulled him closer, even as I let his body fall over mine.

Raihn's mouth trailed down, over my jaw, my throat. Lingering there for a moment—over two sets of scars—before moving down farther still, to my shoulder. Only then did he lift himself up, fingers playing at the strap of my gown.

"Let me see you," he rasped. "Please."

I nodded.

He slid the straps from my shoulders. He kissed each new expanse of skin as he peeled back the silk—over my shoulder, my breasts, my hardened nipples, the curve of my waist, my hip, my upper thigh. And finally, he pulled the crumpled silk free and flung it off the bed, gaze already transfixed on me, naked and exposed before him.

It wasn't cold. Yet goosebumps broke out over my skin.

He let out a rough laugh.

"What?" I asked.

"I just—" His mouth returned to me, lingering at my peaked breasts in a way that made my breath tremble.

"I just don't have fucking words," he whispered, as his lips traveled higher, taking a meandering path back to mine. "I don't have words for you."

Words were overrated, anyway. I was grateful he didn't have any, because the ones that jumbled in my chest were confusing and difficult.

"Good," I whispered, and kissed him.

Our bodies intertwined again. The length of Raihn's cock against my leg made my thighs inch open. His hands over my body grew more frantic, like he wanted to take in all of it at once.

Mother, I wanted him. I wanted him as open and exposed and vulnerable as he had made me.

A little wordless sound escaped my throat, and Raihn's lips curled against my mouth.

"What, princess? What do you want?"

A genuine offer. Like he wanted nothing more than to give me what I needed.

Goddess, so many answers to that question.

I want you inside me. I want you to fuck me until I don't remember my own name. I want to watch you come undone the way you just watched me.

I want you.

But what came out of my mouth was, "I want your blood."

45

RAIHN

At first, I thought I'd heard her wrong. But no.

I want your blood.

Those words, coming out of those perfect lips. Those perfect lips that had lapped my blood from my thumb weeks ago—those lips that I'd dreamed about ever since, thinking about them with my hand around my own cock with the curtains drawn in the day.

My head was foggy. So much about this last day had felt like a dream. But hell, did I mind all that much, if this was the hallucination I got? Oraya next to me in bed, naked, the light caressing her flawless moonlight-pale skin in a way that made me jealous.

Oraya in bed, naked, asking for my blood.

I could smell her arousal, thick and sweet. Could hear her heartbeat, hard and fast like a rabbit's.

But even sensing her neediness—neediness that I was desperate to fulfill—I still could have spent an eternity just kissing her. Just making love to that poisonous, perfect, beautiful, dangerous mouth.

I never thought I'd get to kiss Oraya ever again. Now, I

358

couldn't bring myself to question it. I just wanted to take whatever she'd offer me.

And in exchange, give her anything—everything—she desired.

A faint flush rose to Oraya's cheeks. I wondered if she knew that she blushed, and easily. I didn't want to tell her, because I didn't want her to stop.

"You want my blood," I repeated.

And still, she didn't so much as blink as she said, "Yes."

Sun take me.

Yes, Oraya wanted my blood, alright. She'd wanted it for months. And I was damned lucky that this was how I got to give it to her.

I rolled over and grabbed her dagger from her pile of clothes.

"No poison in this thing, right?" I said.

She shook her head.

Good. That would have been an embarrassing way to go.

I drew the tip along the side of my neck, just hard enough to break the skin with a fleeting stab of pain. Immediately, the warmth of blood bubbled to the surface, trickling down my throat.

I sheathed the dagger and tossed it aside again, turning back to Oraya.

"You have it, princess," I said. "My blood. As much of it as you want. Yours by right, after all."

Because I'd already promised it to her, months ago.

I give you my body, my blood, my soul, my heart.

And from the moment her tongue had touched my skin that night, the moment the words left my lips, I knew that I meant them. They were true, even if she didn't want them to be. Even if she didn't return it.

I was hers.

Oraya's stare was hard and steady, those moon-bright eyes spearing me more sharply than any blade. Her throat bobbed. Her gaze lingered on my throat—on the streaks of red-black blood.

The scent of her arousal—her hunger—thickened in the air. My cock twitched in response to it.

"Sit up," she said.

My brow quirked. I did as she ordered.

She swung her legs over mine, straddling me. My hands fell to her hips. The closeness of her, her scent, her warmth, so much stronger than a vampire's, left me momentarily dazed.

Immediately, I knew what this was. A recreation of that night in the cave.

Goddess fucking help me.

I was destroyed. I was done.

For a moment, she stared at me, the two of us meeting each other's gazes, unblinking. A knot tightened in my chest. I recognized that look—fear mixed with the hunger. Fear of herself, and her own desires.

My thumb traced a circle on the bare skin of her hip.

"You're safe, Oraya," I whispered. "Alright?"

Her eyes narrowed at me a little, as if calling out my bullshit. And though I hadn't meant to lie to her—now, or ever again—I understood it. Because nothing about this was safe. Oraya and I and this monstrous, beautiful, terrible thing we'd created between us was so fucking far from safe.

She leaned forward, pressing her breasts to my chest, hands braced against my arms, and brought her lips to my throat.

First, she licked up what had dripped down my neck, starting at my clavicle and traveling up, ending with a little twinge of pain as her mouth pressed to the open wound.

And then she drank.

My breath was a little shaky, my fingers tightening into her flesh. My muscles tensed.

No one had ever fed from me since... since Neculai, or Simon and the other nobles he had loaned me out to. I'd never, ever allowed it since then, not even with consensual lovers long after. My skin didn't scar as easily as Oraya's did. Those fangs didn't leave any marks on my throat. But centuries later, I still felt them. I'd never let anyone open those wounds ever again.

My body remembered that, tensing in anticipation, even if my mind knew differently.

But from the moment her mouth touched my skin, I knew right away it was different with her.

I thought she would make me remember, even briefly, those old wounds. Instead, every stroke of her tongue repainted them with something new.

This wasn't Neculai or Simon or any other of the countless unwanted invasions to my body.

This was *her*. Oraya. My wife.

It was almost funny at first, how tentative she was. Her tongue lapped awkwardly against the wound like a kitten at milk, like she didn't quite know how to drink. Still, my flesh seemed to open for her, as if I was intrinsically made to give her this.

"You don't have to be gentle." I couldn't help it—a hint of amusement slipped into my voice. "You won't hurt me."

Alright, maybe the weight of her body against my wounds did hurt a little—but I wasn't going to complain about those breasts against my chest.

She pushed deeper against my throat, taking my advice to heart. With a long, rough inhale, she drew in a mouthful of my blood, and swallowed.

Her exhale was a groan against my flesh.

Fuck, I echoed it.

I hadn't known if Oraya had venom. I would have thought she didn't, without the fangs. But this—this did something to me. Something very different than what the venom of other vampires had, drugging me in sickening ways.

I didn't know if it was venom, or her tongue, or just the intoxication of having her naked body straddling mine. Suddenly, nothing in this world mattered except for her, and her mouth, and the scent of her desire, thickening with every passing second.

Her tongue rolled against my throat again, with a tiny sound of pleasure I didn't think she realized she had made. My head tipped back, giving her better access. Her body had melted against mine. Her back arched, thighs opening.

I was so hard it was physically painful. The only thing I was conscious of other than her mouth and her exhales of pleasure was the fact that her slit was so fucking close to my cock, it would take barely a tilt of her hips to lower herself onto me.

She was drinking so fast that she choked a little, pulling away with a tiny spatter of coughs. I tilted my head just enough to look at her, and the pure lust on her face—eyes heavy-lidded, lips swollen and parted, a trickle of red-black smeared at the corner—left me vaguely dizzy.

"Good?" I murmured.

Instead of answering, she kissed me.

My blood tasted salty and iron-strong. Different than hers had—not nearly as good, but better for the fact that I was lapping it off her tongue. The kiss was demanding, not waiting for breath, her tongue slipping into my mouth as she forced my head back.

Her hips lowered. Her sex ground against my length in one long roll, making my fingernails dig into her skin, a low wordless sound rolling from my throat.

"So you have my blood," I murmured. "What else do you want, princess?"

Another roll of her hips answered my question. Fuck. I had never known what it was to need someone before I met her. I had always thought that kind of talk was silly and overdramatic.

No. I needed Oraya. *Needed* her, like another bodily function.

I knew what she wanted. She knew what she wanted. But I knew she couldn't bring herself to say it aloud. The final vestiges of our game, shaky gates still in place between us.

So she whispered, against another desire-drunk kiss, "Beg."

It was so damned easy to beg for her.

I pushed down on her hips—just enough so that my tip sat at the slick of her, so sensitive that I felt it tighten at the presence of my cock.

"Let me in," I rasped. "Let me inside you. Let me feel you come around me. Let me watch you. Please."

She let out a strangled sigh, pressed her mouth against mine, and lowered herself onto me.

When I disappeared into her wet warmth, everything else fell away.

Immediately, a sound tore from her throat, a mangled moan, and Goddess, it was the most incredible sound I'd ever heard. I thought I'd made myself forget it, put it out of my mind forever.

Stupid of me to even try. And hell, why would I want to? I wanted to drown myself in her. Drown myself in her sounds, her breath, her body—her blood.

She moaned again as she lifted herself off me, lowering again, again, hips rolling, helping me hit where she wanted me. Goddess, I loved it—loved the way she used me. My body still hurt, uncooperative in letting me take her the way I wanted to, but she was more than willing to take what she needed.

My hands trailed her body, memorizing the shape of every muscle, every expanse of skin, from the taut shape of her waist to the full softness of her ass. I kissed her, hard, swallowing all those breathtaking sounds—offering her all of my own.

Our pace was frantic now. Neither of us had patience for this. I wanted everything, and I wanted it now. With every time she took me inside her, grinding against me, allowing me to reach the deepest parts of her, I only wanted more.

I wanted to brand her.

I wanted her to brand me.

My hunger for her was suddenly insatiable, driven to a frenzy by the sensation of her sex around me, the scent of her desire, the taste of my own blood on her lips and the tantalizing scent of hers beneath that sweat-slicked skin.

She broke our kiss, gasping a curse against my lips as I drew her down against me roughly in one particularly deep thrust, her body spasming—and fuck, I almost lost it right there.

"Raihn," she whimpered.

"Take it," I rasped out. Knowing, somehow, exactly what she wanted. "All of it. It's yours."

She let out a fractured sound between a sob and a sigh of relief, and lowered her mouth to my throat again, drinking deep as she rocked around me.

When she pulled away again, blood smearing her lips, I chased her, desperate to taste her again however I could. But instead, she lifted her chin—exposing the elegant column of her throat.

I paused, a sudden absence of movement that made her tighten around me in protest.

She couldn't be offering—couldn't be asking me to—

"Take it," she said, throwing my words back at me.

My jaw closed. Tightened. It was almost—almost—enough to cut through my haze of lust.

I knew what this meant for her. Knew, too, that the chemical draw of my blood and our sex and everything else between us was probably just as addling to her as it was to me.

I didn't want to be something else she regretted.

"Are you sure?"

I barely managed to form the words.

She lowered her chin just enough to meet my eyes. What I saw within them stripped me bare. Far deeper than the lust.

"Yes," she whispered.

No hesitation.

I didn't even have words to give her after that, just this animalistic growl that came out in a mangled burst as I pulled her closer. Her hips resumed their rhythm, drowning us both in a sea of pleasure that couldn't be matched, except—

—Except for when my mouth came to her throat.

Her skin there was delicate. Smooth, save for the little scars —two old, two newer. Just as I had once before, I kissed both of them, tenderly, offering some softness before I let the sharpness of my teeth settle over her vein. I could practically taste the beat of her blood beneath, hot and sweet.

My bite was quick, firm, piercing the skin in a single painless strike before withdrawing.

She drew in a little gasp, her hands clutching my shoulders, walls tightening around me.

Her blood flooded my mouth, thick and rich. Nothing had ever tasted like this—like her, at her rawest essence, every nuance and contradiction. From the first moment I had tasted it, I had known it would change me forever.

Better than any wine. Any drug. A pleasure I'd be chasing for the rest of my life.

Maybe it was the sensory overload of the sex, or maybe the venom just worked particularly quickly. Because I scented the sudden spike in Oraya's arousal rising to an unbearable crescendo. A moan vibrated through her, and I could taste that sound with my next swallow, with every stroke my tongue worked across her skin.

Her pace grew faster now, harder. My fingernails dug into her, leveraging whatever remained of my strength to help her through each thrust.

"Don't stop," she begged, the words fractured by ragged breaths. And thank the fucking Goddess she said it, because I couldn't—I was fucking gone.

It was too much. Everything culminated. Pressure built at the base of my spine. I could feel her getting close, too, her muscles coiling, her strokes growing frantic and her fingernails dragging deep over my back and shoulders.

I needed to feel her come even more than I needed it myself.

I wanted to give her everything.

I tore myself away from her throat, the taste of her blood still thick on my tongue. For one endless moment, her eyes met mine —and so much honesty passed between us, both of us exposed with only our flesh and our desires and our primal impulses.

"Yours," I ground out. "It's yours."

My blood. My body. My soul.

I had given her all of that a long time ago. I even had given her my life.

And I'd do it all again.

I urged her head down as our bodies writhed around each other, rushing to the end. She accepted eagerly, her mouth falling to my throat again, drawing in a deep mouthful of my blood.

I felt her swallow, and then, a moment later, felt her climax take her. A desperate cry, one she didn't even try to stifle, rang out against my skin—long, whimpering, holding fragments of torn-up curses and pleas.

"Raihn," she choked out, like she was hurtling through oblivion and desperate for someone to anchor her.

I knew that, because I felt it, too.

I know, I wanted to say. But my own orgasm stole the words, my cock buried deep inside her, muscles seizing. She was shaking, whimpering, as her body tensed through wave after wave of aftershock.

I held her, and filled her, nestling my face into the space between her throat and shoulder as we both relinquished ourselves.

For a few incredible seconds, everything disappeared in a hazy, soft mist of her.

When the world returned, it all felt... different.

I'd had plenty of sex before. Some bad, some good, much of it ill-advised. But this didn't feel like sex. It felt like a religious ritual—like finding faith.

Oraya had collapsed against me. A sudden wave of exhaustion hit me—and with it, a fresh awareness of the pain of my wounds, which I'd strained something fierce in all the activity. Not that I could bring myself to be too broken up about it.

Her breath was deep and hard. My hand fell to her back, rubbing softly.

Finally, she sat up. She licked my throat with a little flick, cleaning off the rest of the blood. I tipped her head back and did the same, relishing the final tastes of her. The shift of her hips with the movement reminded me that I was still inside her. Another kiss, another minute, and I could've had her again.

But that blood-and-sex-drunk weariness had settled over me, and I could tell Oraya was fighting it, too.

I fell back onto the bed, turning on my side and gently guiding her down to the blankets as I slipped from her.

She curled up on her side and I folded around her, our bodies fitting easily together.

Already, I sensed her heartbeat slowing, her breath calming.

Already, my own eyelashes were fluttering.

I kissed her shoulder, her cheek, settled down in a nest of her hair. Her scent surrounded me. Oraya had always smelled so damned alive—not the scent of incense or withered flowers like so many vampires, but the scent of spring.

I felt the overwhelming urge to say something to her, even though I wasn't sure what that would be. But Oraya's hand fell over mine, and that touch somehow seemed to mean more than all the words put together.

Maybe for the best, because sleep took me so fast, they slipped through my fingers like sand, anyway.

46

ORAYA

I awoke to soft kisses over my cheek, my ear, my neck.

These last months, waking up always felt like a battle, as if I was being dragged back to the land of the living kicking and screaming.

This was not a battle. This was a gentle summons, sweet and tender.

I felt, for the first time in so long, safe.

Safe, for the first time since...

Since... the last time I had woken up like this. In Raihn's arms.

It took several seconds for my awareness to come back to me. I was naked, in bed, in Raihn's arms. I was sore from the battle I'd fought to save his life and then from the fucking we'd done when I refused to leave him.

His kisses trailed to my throat, a tiny stab of pain as they brushed the wounds where I'd let him drink from me.

Mother, I still tasted the tang of his blood on my own tongue.

Every piece of this seemed more outlandish than the last. A month ago—hell, weeks ago—I would have been appalled with myself.

Instead, I felt... strangely at peace.

I opened my eyes and rolled over. Raihn propped himself up on one elbow, watching me. A familiar little smirk clung to his lips.

"Evening, princess."

Funny, how intimate those two words sounded. Maybe it was just the way his voice sounded rolling over them, seductive and warm and just a little bit shy.

I murmured, "Hello."

What else was I going to say?

The smirk softened. "Hello," he whispered.

My gaze trailed down his bare body, taking in the expanse of muscles and scarred skin—pausing, for just a moment, at his cock, partially hardened—before returning to the crisscross of wounds over his abdomen and sides. I questioned my sanity as I took them in. They seemed so much better than yesterday, when Raihn had barely been able to move.

Following my gaze, he said, "The blood helped. A lot." His lips brushed over my forehead. "Thank you."

I squirmed a little at the way he said that. So sincerely.

"Of course," I muttered. Like it was what I'd planned all along. If I'd been thinking logically, it *did* make sense to let Raihn drink from me—I'd seen before how much it helped him heal, and he'd needed that desperately.

But I couldn't even lie to myself. I hadn't offered my blood to him out of a sense of practicality. I'd offered it to him out of blind, maddening desire—desire to have more of him inside me, and more of myself inside him.

And Goddess, it had been—it had been—

I cleared my throat to avoid getting lost in that particular cascade of distracting thoughts.

I twitched as his fingertips traced my abdomen, tickling over my belly button.

"Looks like it helped you, too," he said.

I blinked down at myself, brow furrowed. The cuts were still there, yes, and still sore, but they no longer bled. They looked as if they'd been healing for several weeks, not for twelve hours. It rivaled the effects of a healing potion.

"Is that... normal?" I asked.

"Not sure if anything about either of us is normal," he said.

Well. That was true.

"Heir blood, if I had to guess," he went on. "Maybe combined with your half-human lineage. I don't know. But I'm not about to question it."

His touch ran over one of the shallower wounds, tracing a lightning-crack scar of pink flesh. For the briefest moment, his face darkened, before settling again as he turned back to me.

"Oraya," he said softly, "I—"

I wasn't prepared for this. For his heartfelt words. I had no regrets about last night, but I couldn't open myself up for him again today. Touch was one thing. But words... words were complicated.

"We need to go back to the castle," I said.

I was brisk and businesslike. Just as I had once been with him when we strategized together in the Kejari.

Raihn's mouth closed. Understanding fell over his face quickly. He was a half-step behind me, but he slipped into the same role just as easily.

"I know," he said.

That was it. No questions, no hesitation. Anyone might have laughed in my face for even saying it, but I felt a twinge of satisfaction that he had already been thinking the same thing.

Maybe it was a death sentence to go back there. Anyone else would have advised that we flee Sivrinaj, and not come back unless we had an army to bring with us.

I knew what Vincent would have said:

Don't feed yourself to the wolves, little serpent. Know when your bite isn't strong enough.

But of course Raihn already accepted it as simple truth that we needed to go back, and immediately. Because his inner circle was still in that castle—*Mische* was still in that castle. He would not leave her there, especially not in Simon's clutches.

I wouldn't, either. It was never even an option.

I knew, even without him saying anything, that Raihn was thinking about Mische, because I could see the pained expression fall over his face—one part fury, one part agony.

My hand fell to his arm, firm and comforting.

"We'll get her out," I said. "And in the meantime, you know she's putting up a hell of a fight."

A faint hint of a smile, which immediately dimmed.

"That," he said, "is what I'm afraid of."

Raihn hated Simon, but I'd come to realize he was also afraid of him. Genuinely afraid, the way I had been afraid my entire life. I wondered if my fear seemed as outlandish to Raihn as his fear did to me. As undeserving of his time.

My fingers tightened around his arm. "You are better than him," I said, more viciously than I'd intended. "Fuck him. We are going to destroy him, Bloodborn army or no."

So easily, that *we* rolled off my lips.

The corner of Raihn's mouth twitched. "There she is."

He sat up, face hardening into an expression I'd seen many times before—the same look that would come over him during one of the Kejari's trials. A kind of bloodthirsty focus, like he'd been presented with a very entertaining puzzle.

"So, princess," he said, "that leaves us to figure out how to get back into the castle we just barely escaped alive. Now that we've established that we're fucking insane."

Two of us. A castle full of Rishan and Bloodborn soldiers. Most of whom were probably frantically looking for us. Septimus, presumably, still would want me for my blood. Simon needed to kill Raihn, and quickly, if he wanted to get his own Heir Mark. The nobles would support him due to his history alone—if out of nothing more than distaste for Raihn—but that goodwill would only last so long if Simon never managed to get a Mark of his own.

"Bad odds," I said. But I found myself suppressing a smile.

"Oh, you look dismayed," he said wryly.

I shrugged. "Reminds me of old times. It's been a while since I've been underestimated."

"We know just how much you love that. Going up against impossible odds."

Despite myself, I smiled. "You loved it too."

"I'll admit it."

He flopped back on the bed, hands behind his head. "So. If I remember right, this is the part where we come up with some kind of brilliant, twisted plan."

It was indeed. And my mind was blank.

I fell next to him, staring up at the crooked wooden planks above us. A spider swung from beam to beam, crafting a silver-silken web. It was a chaotic thing, near-invisible threads strung messily into the shadows, functional but far from beautiful. Like fate itself, I supposed.

For a few long moments, we thought.

"So what do we have?" Raihn said.

Then, to start answering his own question, he said, "We have us."

"A human and a usurped king," I said, flatly.

"No. Two Heirs who won the Mother-damned Kejari."

Fair point. Raihn and I had individually managed to fight through incredibly unbalanced battles in the Kejari, and done even more together. What's more, our power had grown exponentially since receiving our Heir Marks. Sure, mine was still difficult to control, but I'd used it to kill Goddess-knew how many soldiers to save Raihn.

Somehow it had seemed... easier then, lost in a frenzy for blood.

All my life, Vincent had admonished my emotional impulsivity, teaching me that stoicism and focus were the only paths to mastering my magic. Yet I'd never felt more powerful than I did in those moments, totally out of control of myself.

I couldn't let myself think about that too much now. How easily Raihn being in danger had unlocked something primal in me.

Mische in danger, I hoped, might unlock the same viciousness.

The corner of Raihn's mouth quirked, albeit with a humorless edge that I suspected foreshadowed his own viciousness.

"Honored you have such faith in us, princess," he said. "And after all this time."

He got out of bed and crossed the room. I eyed his backside —I couldn't help it—as he leaned over the bureau and rummaged through it. When he turned around, something sharp and glittering glinted in his hands, nestled in silk.

I recognized it before he returned to the bed. My brows leapt.

Vincent's mirror.

"You have it," I breathed.

"I got it out of the castle as soon as I could. You think I was about to let Septimus keep it? Or leave it lying around where *you* could find it and bring another round of Hiaj soldiers to my doorstep?"

I was almost offended. Almost. It was a totally reasonable concern.

Either way, I was wildly grateful.

I traced the edge of the shard with my fingertips, watching a little sliver of my reflection.

"So this gives us Jesmine," I said.

Raihn gave me a sidelong glance. "You trust her?"

A valid question to ask, in the wake of a coup. Raihn couldn't trust his own nobles. And hell, I couldn't trust many of mine, either—but for better or for worse, Jesmine had been nothing if not loyal. She never had to follow the orders of her king's human daughter, who she'd never even liked much anyway. And yet, she had, without hesitation. That counted for something.

"I do," I said.

But whatever Hiaj forces I might have were far away from Sivrinaj, now. And we didn't have time to raise an army before we moved.

I looked across the room, to the pile of my belongings that

had been strewn over the floor yesterday. I slid from the bed and stood. I was endlessly aware of Raihn's stare running over my naked body. There was a strange kind of satisfaction in that, I had to admit. Strange kind of pleasure, too.

I rummaged around in the pile of bloody silk and pulled out the Taker of Hearts.

Even sheathed, I could feel its magic burrowing under my skin. Not long ago, that had been uncomfortable, almost painful, like my flesh was too weak for it. Now? I could sense power in that discomfort—heady and a little disorienting, like vampire wine.

I could feel, too, my father's presence in it. Like he was standing right over my shoulder, silently critiquing my grip.

"And we have this," I said.

A weapon that Vincent had used to kill hundreds—thousands, even—of incredible warriors over the years. A weapon powerful enough to defend a throne for two hundred years.

A weapon powerful enough to destroy one of the last true great Rishan cities.

My stomach turned at that thought. I lifted my gaze to meet Raihn's. No more joking in it now. Not even desire. No, he was utterly serious, mouth set. I wondered if he was thinking about the same thing I was—the ashes of Salinae, and the role this weapon may have played in making them.

"Nothing to scoff at," he said quietly.

The pride I'd once felt in being able to wield this weapon soured slightly.

No. Nothing to scoff at. I'd taken down dozens of Simon's men with this thing—and that had been alone. With Raihn beside me? Hell, we could almost fight our way through that castle by ourselves.

Almost.

As if reading my mind, Raihn said, "If we were taking them by surprise, we might be able to do it by brute force. But not tonight, when we're the most wanted people in the House of Night."

I settled back at the edge of the bed. Raihn and I were silent, thinking.

He was right. Brute strength wouldn't work. But I hadn't won the Kejari by being the strongest, anyway. I'd won because I had spent my whole life learning how to survive in Obitraes despite what I was or wasn't. Learning tricks that could get me farther with less.

Tricks like…

My lips curled slowly.

Even before I looked up, I could hear the smile in Raihn's voice. "I think I recognize that face."

I said, "We have one more thing. We have me."

47

ORAYA

Vincent had taught me how to stay alive. That meant learning how to fight, yes, but it also meant learning how to flee.

My father had created a castle perfect for a man who knew, one day, his greatest threats could come from within his own house. The tunnels were extensive, confusing, and disjointed. Septimus was aware of some of them—my own foolishness had seen to that. But he couldn't know all of them, let alone guard them.

The hard part would be making it there.

I was certain that Vincent had created multiple avenues into and out of the castle. Unfortunately, he hadn't trusted me with any of them—in hindsight, it made sense that he didn't want to give me ways to sneak away from him. Still, he'd given me instructions on one way out. One way that was so unpleasant, he could feel confident that I wouldn't use it unless my life was in imminent danger.

Much had been written over the years about the Lituro River. Visitors had spun plenty of poetry about the way it wound through the dunes like a streak of silver paint beneath the moonlight. Some claimed it represented the lifeblood of Nyaxia herself.

I imagined that maybe, out there in the desert, it was indeed a thing of majestic beauty.

However, in the heart of Sivrinaj, it was as much piss as it was water.

Sewage had to go somewhere. In the city, most figured it was easiest for it to go right into the river. Hell, many people decided to skip the washroom altogether and put it there directly.

Many, many, many people.

I was certain of this as the water—if it could be called that—swallowed me up.

I couldn't hear much underwater, but I certainly could make out Raihn's appalled, garbled curse as the piss water surrounded us.

I forced my eyes open and then immediately regretted it. I couldn't see anything under there, anyway.

Our heads broke the surface at the same time. Raihn shook his hair out like a dog, sending spatters of rancid liquid over my face.

I wrinkled my nose. "Ugh. Watch it."

"What? Is that too much piss for you?" He pointedly looked around. "Not sure that's the problem, princess."

I flicked a handful of water at him. Despite his attempted dodge, it caught him squarely in the cheek, which I appreciated. He scowled, but didn't protest, like he knew that he deserved it.

I lifted my chin to motion down the river—where the back of the castle stood, looming over us in shadow. We'd picked a secluded area of the river, bordering the human districts, to jump in without being seen, but the activity up ahead was visible even from this distance—a smattering of torches and Nightfire, and the thrum of distant voices. Even the castle was unusually well-lit, the windows pulsing firelight that revealed hints of distant silhouettes within.

It reminded me of the way this city had looked the night of the Kejari's finale—the night Raihn had taken over.

"I won't be able to see underwater," I said. "It's straight ahead. Then to the left once we get closer to the castle. One of the grates leads inside and connects to the tunnels. Stay close to me."

"*One* of the grates?" he repeated. I understood his point—the castle was enormous, and had a dozen sewage grates on its western side alone.

I was so young when Vincent had showed me this, and it had been from the inside out, not outside in. I didn't remember exactly which one. Luck would, hopefully, be on our side.

I winced. "I'll... have to try a few."

He laughed softly. "It's not fun if it's too easy."

That was one way of looking at it.

"Ready?" he said.

I glanced down at the rancid muck.

No. No I was not.

I was glad that Raihn had packed a few different sets of leathers for my grand escape. I'd have to burn these.

But aloud I just said, "Absolutely."

Together, we ducked beneath the water.

I WASN'T the best swimmer. Raihn was fast, but he had to keep stopping to let me catch up to him. Worse, I couldn't see anything—even in the few seconds I could force my eyes open at a time, I saw nothing but cloudy darkness. Raihn and I stole silent gulps of air at the longest intervals possible, especially as we approached the castle. Guards were everywhere, both Rishan and Bloodborn, though they appeared to be wildly disorganized. Most rushed around yelling at each other rather than standing watch.

They were, we pieced together, trying to find Raihn, and they were certain they'd do so out in the city as he attempted to flee — not at their doorstep as he came crawling back to the castle.

Fair assumption. This was not what most rational people would do. Let alone by swimming through sludge.

And it was, indeed, *sludge* by the time we made it to the castle, the liquid too thick to be called "water," sticking to my skin and hair every time we rose to take a precious gulp of air. The smell was so putrid that even those seconds above the surface weren't such a treat anymore, no matter whether I breathed through my nose or mouth. I could *taste* it.

At one point, I caught Raihn eyeing me, a pursed smile at his lips, like he was trying very hard not to laugh. I scowled at him, and he shook his head. Even silent, though, I could hear the words: *That fucking face.*

I had to be grateful for the sewage, though — at least it disguised our scents, especially mine. Even when we swam mere feet away from soldiers on the streets above, we passed undetected.

When we finally reached the turn where the river met the castle's aqueducts, I thanked the Goddess under my breath. We had to fight a surprisingly strong current to make it up to the castle, since the channels had been constructed at a slight downward angle to ensure the constant outward flow of waste. Clinging to the side, allowing the stone wall to shield me, I poked my head above the water to examine the grates ahead.

I could not even remotely remember which one led into the tunnels.

I dove again, throwing myself against the first set of iron bars. Raihn swam beside me, helping me pull at the metal.

Not the first. Nor the second. When we rose for another quick breath, the voices of the soldiers were even closer.

Fuck. The longer we stayed in one place, the greater our risk of being seen. I didn't know how much longer we had here before someone would wander too close.

Please, Vincent, this had better be the one.

We slipped under the water and threw ourselves against the next set of bars.

And maybe the Goddess or my dead father were looking out for us, after all, because this one ground into movement immediately.

The door was awkward, designed to be pushed out from the inside instead of entered from the outside. Raihn held it open for me to wiggle through, and I did the same for him as he squeezed between the metal rods. No easy feat against this current, stronger than ever this close to the castle sewers.

Inside, Raihn had to grab my arm and use his body mass to keep me from getting swept away. By the time the tunnel started to rise, we were practically dragging ourselves along the slime-slicked walls. My muscles screamed. My lungs burned, desperate for air. I clutched the strap over my chest, suddenly very afraid that the current would sweep the Taker of Hearts off my back.

When the floor finally rose and we could stand, I choked out, "Thank the *Mother*."

"That," Raihn muttered, "was fucking vile."

He wiped sludge from his face as I leapt out of the water and dragged myself up a steep step at the side of the tunnel. The air was hot and stagnant, and it absolutely reeked of shit.

It was still a Goddess-damned perfumery compared to where we'd just come from.

Raihn followed me, the two of us now standing on a raised pathway along the edge of the sewer. It was very dark in here. I conjured a little ball of Nightfire in my palm, and blue light bathed Raihn's face.

I snickered.

"What?" he said.

Here he was. The Nightborn King. Drenched, wearing ill-fitting, cheap leathers, face completely covered in shit save for the domino mask of "clean" skin he'd wiped around his eyes.

He read my face and sighed. "Because you look so fucking fantastic, princess. Ix's tits. Let's get going. Where's this tunnel?"

Right.

That was a good question. I shuffled along the wall, hand pressed to the brick—rough, old, slimy. More or less how one would expect stone that had been marinating in centuries worth of wet excrement to feel.

"It was around here somewhere," I muttered, feeling around the bricks. "Under one of these arches—"

My fingertips snagged on something. At first, I thought it was just a crack in the bricks, but a second pass and a closer look with the Nightfire revealed otherwise—no, it was an outline.

"Here," I said.

"I've got it." Raihn threw his weight against the door. He strained against it for a few seconds, face contorted, before giving up and leaning against the wall. "You're sure this opens in this direction?"

Fuck. I certainly hoped it did. Otherwise, we were screwed.

Vincent was so thorough. I couldn't imagine that he would go through the trouble of creating such an elaborate path out unless he also planned to use it as an emergency path back in, too, if he needed it.

But... only if *he* needed it.

"He'd have made sure that only he could use it," I said. "Maybe I..."

On a hunch, I grabbed my blade from my hip and swiped the tip over my palm, opening a delicate river of red. Then I pressed the bleeding wound to the door, cringing slightly at the sting of the slimy surface against the cut.

My first thought was, *I am definitely going to get an infection from this.*

My second was, *This isn't going to work.*

But those words barely had crossed my mind before the door opened before us with a growl of grinding stone, revealing a narrow, dark tunnel lit with Nightflame lanterns.

That was... quick. And easier than I had thought it would be. Easier than using my blood to operate Vincent's magic ever had been before.

I stared down at my bloody palm. I could feel Raihn's gaze on me—making the same observation, no doubt.

"Looks like the door wasn't just for him," he said.

I swallowed thickly.

Did you really think, Vincent whispered in the back of my mind, *that I wouldn't account for you, too, my little serpent?*

I flinched. Once, I'd craved his voice so fiercely. Now, it brought with it a wave of complicated emotions.

It didn't make sense. He'd hidden these paths from me, along with my magic, my blood, and my past. And yet—he had loved me enough, too, to offer me this safety precaution alongside his own.

So did he trust me, or not? Or did even he not know?

"I don't know," I said curtly. "Maybe it's just recognizing his blood in me. Let's go. It's this way."

I drew my father's sword from my back, trying and failing to ignore the overwhelming wave of his presence that hit me the moment my hand closed around the hilt, and started walking before Raihn could say anything else.

Not that he tried.

THE TUNNELS WERE POORLY MAINTAINED, narrow, and winding, a side effect of them being kept in absolute secrecy—they'd been built around the existing infrastructure of the castle by an extremely limited team of workers, and then never maintained afterward because Vincent did not want to risk a single soul knowing about them. After a hundred years or so, they were starting to show their wear. Even though Raihn and I were already under the castle, it took a good long while of walking before the tunnels began to look a bit more like the hallways I'd grown more familiar with.

Soon, we scaled sets of crooked stairs, leading us up into the building itself. Muffled, harried voices echoed through the walls —all of them frantic, even if we couldn't make out the words.

"Sounds like they're having a wonderful time," Raihn muttered, as the unintelligible voices of warriors yelling at each other faded away behind us.

"Not sure that you're in a good position to go judging someone else's coup," I said, "seeing how yours has gone so damned well so far."

He laughed softly. "Fair point."

We reached the top of this set of stairs, the tunnel now splitting off into two directions. I kept my voice low, conscious of how thin the walls could be in some parts of this ancient building.

"We're behind the second-floor library right now." I pointed to the left path. "That one's yours. It will take you to the dungeons. Just go down, and to the right."

Raihn eyed the other path. "And that's yours?"

I nodded. It would take me up to the upper floors of the castle—up to my rooms.

My rooms, where I had hidden Vincent's pendant.

Only I knew the convoluted path up to the top level of the castle. Only I could carry Vincent's blood-bound artifacts. So that meant I had to be the one to go up to get it—because, of course, we couldn't leave that in Simon or Septimus's possession. We may not know what it was, but we knew it was too important to lose.

Which meant that Raihn would need to go to the dungeons to rescue Mische by himself, at least temporarily, until I could join him.

We'd talked this through at length. We couldn't both go to both places, which would attract attention too quickly. Our only chance at achieving both goals was splitting up, albeit temporarily.

Still, now that our paths diverged, I couldn't help but hesitate

—my eyes lingering on Raihn's body, where I knew his leathers hid evidence of still-healing wounds.

Despite myself, I was starting to doubt that this was a good idea.

"Are you sure you can do this?" I said.

His brow twitched. "Are you worried about me?"

"I'm being practical."

"I'll be just fine. I can handle a few of Simon's guards. I'm the Nightborn King, remember?"

"I remember having to save your ass from 'a few of Simon's guards' about thirty-six hours ago."

His smirk faltered, like this was a legitimate sore spot for him. Raihn may try to play the unflappable king, but I knew he really, really didn't like to lose. "That wasn't a fair fight," he said. "They drugged me. And surprised me. I look forward to the rematch."

I was unconvinced.

"Besides," he said, "if it all goes poorly, I just need to stay alive for a few minutes until you can come save me all over again, and I'll even let you gloat about it all you damn well please."

It was a little appealing. A little. Still, I couldn't shake the knot of unease in my stomach.

Maybe Raihn felt some of what I did, too, as he gazed over my shoulder to the right path, stairs disappearing into shadow.

"Be quick," he said. "In and out. Simon doesn't deserve the honor of killing you."

I scoffed, like this prospect was ridiculous. My bravado, though, was a little less convincing than Raihn's. Yes, I'd killed dozens when rescuing Raihn. Yes, I'd won the Kejari. But I still had a lifetime's worth of fear of vampires ground into me. A hard thing to leave behind.

"Stop wasting time," I whispered, and started to turn away, but he caught my arm.

When I looked back at him, there was no more teasing in his face. No false confidence. His hand reached out to brush the angle of my chin, so briefly I didn't even have time to react to the touch.

"Careful, princess," he murmured. "Alright?"

I held that stare for a moment longer than I meant to.

"You too," I said. "Be careful."

And with that, we each slipped into our own shadows.

48

ORAYA

The hallways nearest to my room were the riskiest. I avoided the path I had taken the day that I'd escaped down to Vincent's office, but I was still very aware that Septimus had known about those tunnels. Though the path I was on now didn't directly connect to the one I had taken then, I couldn't be sure how much else he had discovered. By the time I reached the top level of the castle, I was moving very slowly, barely breathing, listening for any guards while simultaneously being silent as a ghost.

I didn't hear much activity out there, unlike on the lower floors. The only thing in this wing was my room and Raihn's, neither of which were the actual king's quarters. Simon and Septimus had managed to launch their coup successfully by catching Raihn off-guard, but that didn't mean they had any more manpower than he did. They'd have to use their forces sparingly, focused where they were most needed.

I had to hope that neither Simon nor Septimus thought they were needed up here.

I waited at the passageway to the main hall for several long seconds, ear to the door, before moving. When I heard nothing, I slipped through, sword in hand, promptly closing the passageway behind me.

The hall was empty. Silently, quickly, I moved along the wall, rounding one corner and then another until I came to our hallway.

Emptiness would have been too easy.

Two guards waited for me.

Both of them, thankfully, were Rishan, not Bloodborn—no blood magic to deal with. They recognized me right away, but I didn't give them time to react before I lunged for them.

Two of them. Once, that would have been intimidating. Now, it was a relief. Only two? I could handle two.

As if awakened by the promise of imminent bloodshed, the Taker of Hearts warmed in my hands, the red glow of the blade flaring.

I thought about Mische, as the two men started for me.

I thought about the way their chosen master had abused Raihn, and the marks he had left long after the ones on his body had faded.

And suddenly, it wasn't so hard to call upon my magic, the cold white of Nightfire mingling with the hot bloom of Vincent's sword.

The last time I'd used it, I'd barely gotten to appreciate what an incredible weapon it was. This time, when the blade plunged through the first soldier's chest, barely meeting resistance, burns of searing white spreading across his chest, I had to admire it.

It had never before been quite so easy to kill.

The second man staggered back in shock when he saw how quickly his companion fell. But to his credit, he wasn't a coward. After a momentary stagger, he was coming at me again, sword drawn.

That half-second pause, though—that was enough.

I stepped aside, using his own momentum to throw him against the wall. It was awkward to use the sword when I was so accustomed to using my dual blades. I had to force my body to fight in a completely different way, mimicking Vincent's steps

387

instead of leaning on my own. In that moment of hesitation, he opened a slash across my cheek that left me hissing in pain.

I could so perfectly envision how Vincent would have countered. I'd witnessed it many times.

My execution wasn't perfect, but it got the job done.

When I pulled back, my breath heavy, the Rishan was slumped against the wall, the Taker of Hearts skewered through his chest.

I withdrew it, not bothering to wipe the blade. Not that I had to—it was as if the weapon absorbed it, as hungry for bloodshed as I was. My Nightfire simmered. Already, I was thinking about wherever Raihn was right now—thinking far too vividly about him being overtaken in the dungeons, surrounded by soldiers, getting strung up again the way he had during the ball—

I went to my door and tried the knob.

Locked. Of fucking course.

I knelt, examining the locks. All four required keys.

Could I... melt them, the way I had the day I escaped? Or...

I glanced down at my sword, coated with the beading remnants of blood. It seemed ridiculous to try to stab a lock into submission. Then again, if any weapon could do it...

My gaze fell to the blood on the blade.

Then the bodies it had come from.

I went to the nearest slumped corpse. There, on his belt, was a little ring of silver keys.

Considering stabbing a door before I even looked for the keys. Goddess fucking help me. I was grateful Raihn wasn't here to see this.

With some brief fumbling, I unlocked three of the four locks. It was only on the fourth one that it occurred to me:

Why was my room being guarded?

And why was it locked to begin with?

This thought only hit me as I pushed open the door, only to immediately dodge a vanity chair swinging at my head.

"Fuck," I spat, hitting the ground in just the right way to disturb the worst of my wounds.

"*Gods!*"

Thump, as the wielder of the weaponized chair let it fall to the ground.

I rolled over, wincing, to see Mische standing over me, her hands covering her mouth, eyes wide. She was still in her gown from the party, though it was now wrinkled, her makeup smeared.

"I am *so* glad you're alive!"

She dropped to her knees, looking like she was about to fling her arms around my neck, then went suddenly serious, brow contorted.

"What the hell are you doing here? And why do you *smell* like that?"

Once Mische's questions started, they didn't stop.

"Where's Raihn?" she asked, as she helped me up. "How did you get in here? Did you see what's happening outside? Is there an army coming?" And then, again, like the first time wasn't enough, "Where's Raihn?"

"We can talk and walk," I said. "We don't have much time."

Though, Goddess, I was happy to see her.

I lowered to grab my sword, which had fallen in Mische's wild chair attack, and when she saw it, her eyes bulged.

"Is that—"

"Yes."

"*Gods*, Oraya. You've actually *wielded* it?"

For some reason, Mische's disbelief was the thing to make my own set in all at once, a wave that I'd been suppressing for the last two days.

It had been... a very, very strange two days.

"It's... yes." I didn't know what else to say, so I just cleared my throat. "Let's hurry. Guards might be coming or—"

"There were only those two."

Mische put aside her shock, her face going serious.

The pendant.

Right. I went to my vanity and yanked open the top drawer.

"Why are you here?" I asked. "Why aren't you in the dungeons?"

A beat of silence.

"Let's just go," she said, going to the door, her back to me. "You said we don't have time."

I paused. There was a note to her voice that seemed... odd.

But she was right. We didn't have time. I rummaged through one drawer of my vanity, then another, my heart rate rising.

It had been in here.

The pendant had been in here.

I was certain of it. I had been very careful about where I put it. I checked on it every night. But in the drawer was only a nest of useless fucking silks.

No pendant.

Not even a hint of its magic.

"Goddess fucking damn it," I muttered.

"What?" Mische asked.

"Did someone come in here?"

I ripped open another drawer, just in case I was wrong, even though I knew I wasn't.

"Before me? I've only been here for a day. It took a few hours for them to—"

I slammed the drawer shut, hissing a curse.

They'd found it, then. They'd searched this room. Of course they had. Septimus was a prick, but he wasn't stupid.

It was gone. If it was in this room, I'd feel it.

I didn't have time to think about what that meant. Not when, with every passing second, Raihn could be having his ass handed to him down in that dungeon.

I returned to Mische, who stared at me with a wrinkle between her brows. She had questions, I knew, but like me, she knew now was not the time to ask them. She went to one of the Rishan corpses and grabbed the sword from his still-rigid hand.

I'd fought alongside Mische several times now. But it still seemed a little strange every time I saw her with a weapon, mostly because she was so competent with them, and that seemed at odds with a personality like hers.

The two of us crept down the hall, moving swiftly and silently along the walls.

We just needed to get back to the tunnel and get back down to Raihn before—

It was the worst luck.

Horrifically, hilariously terrible luck.

A figure arrived at the top of the stairs at the exact same moment that we rounded the corner. We had no time to hear his steps and backtrack.

Our eyes locked. Ours to his. His to ours.

Fuck, I thought.

Mische went so still it was like she stopped breathing.

Before us stood the Shadowborn prince.

49

ORAYA

It took me a moment to recognize him. I'd only seem him from across the room at the wedding, and I'd been distracted then. Highborn vampire men tended to have the same sort of look about them—the high cheekbones, the smooth skin, the sharp eyes, the dangerous allure designed to lure in prey. The Shadowborn prince had all those things in abundance. A beautiful, dangerous person who fit in seamlessly among all the other beautiful, dangerous people.

It was only once I saw the diadem upon his head of thick hair, and the style of his clothing—fine, tight-fitting brocades— that it clicked into place.

A little smile of recognition spread over his lips, too, though his gaze fell to me only for a moment before sliding behind me— lingering on Mische.

What the hell was he doing here?

If I'd given even the slightest thought to where the Shadowborn prince had gone when the coup broke out, I would have assumed that he'd fled the city. What interest would a Shadowborn have in remaining to watch the Nightborn tear each other apart?

Then again... why *wouldn't* he want to watch that? Vampires. Shrewd and bloodthirsty, so easily entertained by violence. So enthralled by the idea of their enemies on their knees.

And why wouldn't Simon want him to see it all, if it meant a chance at gaining the respect of a powerful Obitraen leader?

Smart of him. Because the prince was valuable.

If I was a better diplomat, maybe I could have seized this opportunity. I could imagine Raihn doing so skillfully—putting on just the right mask to show the prince what he wanted to see.

But I wasn't Raihn. I wasn't Vincent. I looked at this prince and saw nothing but a threat, every nerve in my body screaming, *Kill him!*

Doing that would be foolish. A political nightmare. But—

The prince stepped closer, his eyebrows raising.

"Well," he said, "this is—"

A smear of bronze-and-gold streaked past me. The brush of a body knocked me momentarily off balance.

The next thing I knew, Mische was on top of the prince, and blood was everywhere.

I had never seen Mische fight like this, not even in the Kejari. It was animalistic, not her typical light, quick movements, but vicious and brutal. The two of them tangled on the ground, limbs flailing, wisps of shadow magic making it impossible to make out what was happening.

I dove after her a split second after she moved. But by then, their fight was already a mess of gore. First Mische was on top of him, stabbing wildly, red-black blood spattering her face and then mine as I rushed over to them.

Then, just as I was within striking distance, he slammed Mische to the floor, snarling as his dagger inched closer to her face.

All thoughts about diplomacy or alliances or impending war disappeared.

I threw myself against him, wrenching him off her. He recovered fast, recoiling, turning on me. I had my sword ready to charge through his chest—

But before I could, Mische leapt on him.

It was an incredible strike, even by the standards of vampire speed and strength. Accurate, quick, powerful.

She didn't even hesitate as her blade breached his breastbone. It was so gracefully beautiful that the ugly slam of his body against the wall startled me.

She'd driven that sword all the way through him, and she still just kept pushing—pushing that blade against the wall, the two of them inching closer. Her face was unrecognizable, a mask of fury, remnants of her gold makeup settling into lines of pure rage.

The Shadowborn prince did not blink as he died.

And when he was gone, his eyes just kept staring right through her.

She still kept pushing, even though the blade was now buried in the wall. Her once-stunning golden gown was now drenched in black.

The silence was suddenly deafening, save for Mische's heaving, shaking breath. She was trembling violently.

I touched her shoulder.

She drew in a gasp and stumbled backwards, her hands clapping over her mouth. The sword remained stuck in the wall, through the prince's body.

"Oh gods," she breathed. "I—oh gods. What did I just—"

She had just murdered a prince of the House of Shadow.

Cold fear settled over me.

I stuffed it down, far beneath more pressing matters.

"We can't worry about that—"

But Mische whirled to me, and something about the look in her eyes gave me pause.

I recognized that look. It went deeper than the frenzied shock of an unexpected kill.

Perhaps I had worn a similar expression the night I had run to Vincent's bedchamber in tears, after my lover had raped me.

My mouth closed.

I thought of the expression on Mische's face when she had seen the prince at the wedding. And I knew, I didn't have to ask.

But she still choked out, "It's—he's the one who—"

The man who had taken her as a teenager. Who had Turned her against her will. Who had abandoned her to die when she got sick.

Now I understood why Mische was brought up here, to these rooms. Somewhere comfortable and attractive, rather than unpleasant dungeons. She was a gift returned to her maker. A token to keep the foreign prince's favor.

My gaze fell to the prince's body, which slowly sagged against the blade skewering him to the wall. I resisted the overpowering desire to spit on his corpse.

Diplomatic issues be fucking damned. I couldn't bring myself to be sorry.

I grabbed the hilt of her sword and yanked it from the wall—and the corpse, which went sliding down to the floor with a dull *thunk*. I held the weapon out to her.

"Raihn needs us."

It was all I needed to say.

She blinked, clearing almost-tears. Her jaw set. She nodded and took the sword, the prince's blood dripping onto the tile floor.

"Let's go," she said.

WE MOVED SWIFTLY through the tunnels. I prayed that I would find Raihn at our rendezvous point—the juncture of the two paths, where we had last separated. But when we flew down that last set of stairs, nothing met us there but two darkened hallways.

Dread clenched in my stomach. But I didn't hesitate.

"That way," I said to Mische, and the two of us swept down the next path, the one that would take us down to the dungeons.

I knew what we were charging into before we reached the door. Mische heard it before I did, with her superior ears—but the sounds grew louder quickly, a distant thrum of banging and grunts through the walls.

I knew what violence sounded like.

Soon we were both running, abandoning stealth for speed. By the time we made it to the door, there was little doubt of what was going on beyond it. It took palpable effort to force myself to slow down as we slipped through, the tunnel letting us out into a hall just beyond the dungeons. The sounds of steel and flesh echoed against the stone walls.

Three long strides, and I was around the corner.

Movement. Guards. Steel.

Bodies.

Blood.

Raihn.

I barely took the time to observe all this before I was throwing myself into the fight.

My sword found one guard's back, aiming straight for the heart. The blade cut through the flesh so easily, with so little resistance. Raihn flung the body off him, meeting my eyes for only a split second before he had to turn his attention to the other soldier lunging at him.

That moment, though—it was enough to convey so many things, a million shades of relief.

Raihn, injured as he still was, had been struggling against half a dozen guards—more, maybe, before we had gotten there— even with the help of his Asteris.

Now, that changed.

I'd forgotten how good it felt to fight beside Raihn. How intuitively we understood each other. How he watched my body even without watching, anticipating every move, complementing it. It was like slipping back into a comfortable jacket.

Strike after strike blended together, my awareness fading

save for the next move, the next opponent. My Nightfire flared at my blade and Raihn's Asteria surged at his, our light and dark intertwining.

Alone, he had struggled. Together, we were devastatingly efficient.

Minutes and the final body fell.

I pulled my blade from the still-twitching guard and turned to Raihn.

He swept me up in an embrace before I could even open my mouth, his face burying into the space between my neck and shoulder.

And then, just as quickly, he released me, leaving me swaying.

"What was that for?" I said.

"Your endless charms," he replied.

Then he saw Mische and stilled. His eyes widened at the sight of her blood-covered gown.

"Where *were* you?" he said.

But she just smiled and shook her head, as if shaking away the vacant look that had been there moments ago. "Later. Good to see you, too."

She was right. We didn't have time. We were lucky that Simon's forces were split in too many directions right now, but it was only a matter of time before either the bloodbath upstairs or down here attracted more attention.

The cells were built into the walls and barred with thick, solid metal doors, with only a small slit looking in. Raihn was already rummaging through the bodies, groping for keys, and when he found them, he tossed them in the air with satisfaction.

Then he went to the first door, swinging it open to reveal a highly disgruntled-looking Vale. He was still wearing his wedding finery, though it looked like he'd put up a hell of a fight, the silk torn and blood-spattered.

"Lilith," he blurted out, desperately, like the name had been thrashing behind his teeth for hours.

Raihn had been so sure Vale would be the one to betray him.

But looking at him now, the possibility seemed incomprehensible.

Raihn's face went serious, like he was having the same thought. He went to the next door and unlocked it, releasing an equally disheveled-looking Lilith. Vale was on Lilith immediately, cradling her head as if inspecting her for damage, while she muttered "I'm fine, I'm fine," under her breath.

Meanwhile, Raihn opened the third door, releasing Ketura, who just looked pissed. The first words out of her mouth were, "That fucking prick."

I wasn't sure whether she was talking about Simon, Septimus, or Cairis, but in any event, I agreed.

"That fucking prick indeed," Raihn muttered. "But later. Let's get the hell out of here."

Vale and Ketura armed themselves with the guards' discarded swords, and I led us back down the hall to the tunnels, carefully closing the door behind us. I had no doubt that it wouldn't take long for Simon's men to piece together who was responsible, going by the Nightfire burns and the evidence of Asteris on the bodies we'd left behind.

We had to get out of Sivrinaj, and fast.

We moved swiftly through the tunnels. When we were nearing the sewers again, the sounds from the castle within grew much louder, footsteps echoing through the stone with renewed urgency, garbled raised voices shouting commands.

"That about us?" Raihn muttered.

"Probably," I said.

I flung open the passageway to the sewers and held it open for the others, then sealed it behind us. Jumping into the muck wasn't any less disgusting the second time, but running from imminent danger did have a way of making it a little more tolerable. Still, I couldn't argue with Mische's gagged curse as we hit the water.

As the traitors in the castle roused to our presence, ready to tear apart the city to look for us, we swam.

We swam for our damned lives.

50

ORAYA

I wasn't used to flying for this long. My wings ached. More than ached—they *burned*. My body was depleted. As the only human—fine, half-human—my stamina wasn't as strong as the vampires', and a week of nonstop travel was beginning to get to me, especially since I had never done this much flying at once.

I was grateful, at least, that I didn't need to carry anyone. Raihn carried Mische, and Vale carried Lilith for the latter half of the trip. As a Turned Nightborn vampire, Lilith did have wings, which were a beautiful speckled amber that matched the color of her hair. But she wasn't a strong flier yet, and while she did her best to fly for most of the trip, eventually it was just faster for Vale to carry her.

I could see Raihn watching me too closely, looking for signs that I needed the same. But I was the Heir of the Hiaj vampires. I wouldn't let anyone carry me anywhere if I could help it. I could deal with a little pain, even if it had me cursing silently to myself every time we landed or took off.

When the wall of sandy stone emerged from the darkness,

the moonlight illuminating a patchwork of cave structures, I practically wept with relief.

"Is that it?" I asked. "That's it, right?"

Mother help me, please let that be it.

"That," Raihn said, sounding as relieved as I felt, "is it."

My legs felt like jelly when we landed, nearly collapsing beneath me in the soft sand. Goddess, the idea of flopping over in it honestly sounded appealing. We had only rested during the strongest hours of direct sunlight, even traveling — albeit slowly — when the sun was weak enough that the vampires could shelter themselves with layers of protective clothing. I was exhausted.

But I locked my legs and forced myself upright. I'd never seen the cliffs before — they really were an incredible sight, bone-white stone rising from the desert sands, punctured with holes and openings that led into an elaborate cave system. They were taller than I'd imagined, stretching all the way up to the sky like they were reaching for the moon. They looked oddly like bones — a flat expanse of ivory skull and eye sockets.

Most people stayed away from this area. The heat and humidity were brutal out here, and the cliffs a perfect habitat for hellhounds and demons. What's more, it was highly isolated out in Hiaj territory, a hundred miles from the nearest city.

What reason would anyone have to be out here?

Unless, of course, you were a fugitive.

"Well, I think this is you, princess," Raihn said, hands on his hips. "Go on over and shout hello. We'll kill whatever runs out at you."

I approached the nearest opening, squinting into the dark. I conjured Nightfire in my palm, though the white flame did little to illuminate that darkness — unending darkness, the kind that swallowed up light itself. It reminded me of Vincent's wings. Reminded me, I supposed, of my own.

"I don't know about that," Mische said from behind me. "Looks... ominous."

"I wouldn't go in that way," a smooth voice called from above, distant against the desert breeze.

I looked up to see a slender figure standing in the mouth of an upper tunnel, leaning against the wall. She wore all tight-fitting black—Nightborn leathers—and her ash-brown hair, bound in a single long braid, flew out with the wind.

"Demons everywhere," Jesmine said. "Better to come up this way, Highness."

I WASN'T TOTALLY convinced that Jesmine and Raihn weren't going to stab each other to death the moment they were left alone. After seeing the wounds on Raihn's back, I honestly wouldn't have blamed him if he did. But as Jesmine led us through the tunnels and into the settlement she'd built here with those that remained of the Hiaj army, she was surprisingly respectful of him, despite a few wary glares.

The tunnels were dark and hot. I imagined that baking clay must feel a whole lot like this. But they were also hidden, and they were shelter. It was no wonder that I'd had such a hard time communicating with Jesmine, even through Vincent's mirror. Aside from the fact that the thing would never be perfectly cooperative with my blood, Jesmine was in such a remote location that I had to imagine we were stretching the range of that magic.

Remote, in this case, was good. Remote was exactly what we needed.

It was unnerving to see what had happened to the Hiaj army over these last few months. What I had always known as an all-powerful regime of warriors had now been reduced to a few hundred men and women sheltering in caves. Others, Jesmine explained, had dispersed into the kingdom, taking shelter elsewhere after the armory battle—while her most loyal forces remained here, hiding, waiting.

The caves were dim for my human eyes, though they were sparsely lit with Nightfire lanterns. Warriors had erected tents in the offshoot tunnels, claiming some semblance of privacy for themselves, while common areas had been staked out in the main paths. It stank in here, the heat rotting the carcasses of the vampires' prey—foxes, wolves, the occasional deer, and even a demon or two, though I couldn't imagine how repulsive that must've been. Surely an act of total desperation. I'd been trained to recognize hungry vampires my entire life, and these ones were hungry indeed, their eyes tracking me as Jesmine lead us through the camps.

Still, the way they looked at me, even on the cusp of starving, was... different now. They noticed my human blood. Smelled it. That was biology. But they didn't look at me as prey anymore. Maybe the red ink on my chest had something to do with that.

Jesmine took us to her private dwelling—a collection of objects stored in a dead-end enclave, covered with a demon-hide flap. She'd stacked a few crates to create seats and pushed several more together for some semblance of a desk, upon which she'd spread a number of papers, most of them scribbled and bloodstained. It reminded me of what Vincent's office had looked like, near the end—chaos. This, I supposed, was what it looked like to lose a war.

Jesmine settled on top of the desk, long legs crossed. Up close, in more light, I could see that her once-fine leathers were now in rough shape, the fabric torn and patched. Several buttons were undone, revealing the top of the long scar between her breasts.

I'd admit it: I hadn't thought much of Jesmine when Vincent promoted her, seeing little more than her sultry voice and low-cut dresses and delicate, well-tended beauty. Now, looking at her like this, my image of her from back then seemed laughably two-dimensional. I wasn't sure that I liked Jesmine, but it was hard to deny that I respected her.

She looked us up and down, one by one—me, Raihn, Mische, Ketura, Vale, Lilith.

Then she said, "You all look like you crawled out of a sewer."

"Fitting observation," Vale grumbled.

Mother, I couldn't wait to get out of these clothes. I'd gotten used to my own stench, but I had no doubt that it was putrid. Probably like someone who had drenched themselves in shit and then moved nonstop across the baking-hot desert for a week.

A little smile curled at the corner of Jesmine's mouth.

"I'm well aware of the tunnels," she said. "Probably smart of you to use the most unpleasant one."

I didn't want to admit to her that the real reason we had picked the "unpleasant one" was because Vincent hadn't trusted me enough to show me any others.

"We made it here alive," I said. "That counts for something."

"I'd say it counts for everything." She leaned forward, her violet eyes like Nightsteel in the darkness. Her face was such a perfect mask of deadly beauty that it stunned me.

"Now please, Highness," she said, "tell me we're about to take back our damned kingdom."

In response, I found myself smirking.

"Why else would we come all this way?"

I HAD TOLD Jesmine some of what had happened when I contacted her before the rescue, and her own sources—still extensive, and still very effective, despite her current circumstances—had apparently filled in more. But I briefed her on all of it just the same. She listened in silence, expression growing harder and hatred sharper. By the end, her fury was palpable.

"And now a Bloodborn prince and a Rishan imposter sit on the throne of the House of Night," she spat. "Vincent would be appalled."

Vincent would also be appalled to see me standing here alongside the Rishan Heir. Actually, a lot of my behavior these last few weeks would have appalled Vincent. But I tried not to think about that at this particular moment.

"Not for much longer," I said. "How many men do you have here? How many more could you call back?"

Jesmine's lips thinned. It took her a moment to answer, like it pained her to admit this. "We've lost many. I don't have enough to retake Sivrinaj directly. Not with the Bloodborn there." Her gaze fell to Vale. "Though if you wanted me to get rid of the Rishan, that would be another thing."

Vale made a wordless sound of disgust, his nose wrinkling, and Jesmine laughed softly.

"Vale Atruro," she purred. "What an honor to meet a legend. What were you, Neculai's... third-best general?"

"First best, now," he said tightly. "Others are dead."

"Such a shame," she muttered.

I wasn't sure who would get my bet if the two of them lunged at each other.

"Trust me, you'll be grateful to have him." Raihn gave her a wolfish grin—the kind designed to expose fangs. "Vale, how many Rishan men can you get? Loyal ones, I mean. Simon doesn't have them all."

Vale gave Jesmine a chilling smile. "Enough to take what little remains of the Hiaj."

Jesmine practically hissed, and Raihn sighed.

"You know what I'm asking," he said.

Vale's gaze slipped back to Raihn, slipping into serious thought. After a long moment, he said, "A thousand. Maybe more."

Raihn looked back to Jesmine, brows arched. "Well look at that. A thousand here. A thousand there. Sounds like an army to me. Maybe even a good enough one to take back Sivrinaj."

Ketura looked sickened by this idea. "An army of Hiaj *and* Rishan?"

"An army of whoever the hell is willing to help us get the Bloodborn out of this kingdom and the crown out of Simon's hands," Raihn said. "Does anyone here object to that?"

A long silence. No one voiced it, but we could all feel plenty of objection in the air.

"Of course," I said, "there's option two. Which is to simply let them have the crown and wait for them to inevitably come root us out. If that sounds more appealing to anyone."

"Them?" Jesmine said. Her eyes narrowed at Raihn. "What about *him*? What you describe is exactly what we have been living these last months. Why should I put my soldiers' lives on the line for his throne?"

"I never considered the Hiaj my enemy," he said, and she scoffed.

"You considered us an enemy even before you killed our king. You destroyed the Moon Palace. You ask for my help to fight against usurpers, but you're a usurper yourself."

Raihn's jaw tightened. "I told you many times, Jesmine, that I had nothing to do with the attack on the Moon Palace. And you're such a damned effective torturer, how could I lie?"

This wasn't going anywhere good.

"Enough," I said. "This is an order, Jesmine. It isn't just Raihn's throne that we're reclaiming. It's mine, and I don't want Simon or the Bloodborn anywhere near it."

Her eyes flicked between Raihn and I.

"So this is a formal alliance."

It felt a bit odd to hear Jesmine, of all people, putting it in those terms.

"An alliance that goes both ways," I said. "We help him. He helps us. We take back the throne, and the Hiaj are free again. No more hiding. No more fighting."

It sounded like a sickly-sweet dream aloud. Jesmine looked at me like I was a toddler espousing the beauty of rainbows.

"And," I said, "I am queen just as much as he is king. When we've reclaimed our kingdom, I intend to rule beside him as such."

I could feel Raihn's eyes on me. Could practically hear his voice: *Really, princess? You're finally taking me up on my offer?*

Fine. Apparently I was. And hell, why shouldn't I? If I was

going to ally with him to get Septimus out of this kingdom, I might as well put my ass on that throne, too.

The silence was suffocating. Jesmine didn't show shock the way most people did. She just stared at me like she kept trying to make puzzle pieces fit together that were incompatible. I could feel it from the others, too—on me, on Raihn. I wondered if this was the first they were hearing about this arrangement, too.

Finally, Jesmine said, "Understood, Highness."

It would never get less uncomfortable, hearing her call me that. But I tried to take this in stride, as Vincent would have, like it was nothing more than a given—of course a general would obey her queen.

"You will work with Vale and Ketura," I said. "Devise a strategy for raising our joint army and using it to retake Sivrinaj. The quicker, the better."

I felt like such an imposter.

But she obediently inclined her head. "Yes, Highness. It will be challenging. But not impossible."

"Challenging has never scared us before."

I found myself glancing at Raihn. Because of course, he and I were the "us." I had never fought beside Jesmine before—never would have been allowed to, and Jesmine would have never deigned to lower herself to it. But Raihn and I... we had done the impossible together countless times over.

The little smile on his face said, *There she is.*

Then I looked to the rest of our sorry group—all in their dirty and stained fineries from the wedding, more than a week ago, now. Not that they looked much better than Raihn and I, in our ill-fitting, disgusting leathers. A pathetic sight.

"But that can wait a couple of hours," I said. "Is there somewhere we can..." There was no other way to put it. "...wash the shit off of us?"

Jesmine's nose wrinkled slightly. "That would be a relief for everyone. No offense intended."

None taken.

"There are hot springs in the lower levels of the caves," she said. "Alliah, my second, can show you. And she'll find some clothes for you, too. Something less... marinated."

Thank the fucking Mother for that.

I wasn't the only one who thought so. Mische audibly groaned at the mention of springs.

"But Highness," Jesmine said, as the others began to file out of the room, "if I may have just a few more moments of your time."

I nodded, allowing the others to leave. Only Raihn hesitated, until I gave him a small nod, and he followed the others out.

She waited until the footsteps faded before she stood, her arms crossed over her chest.

"So," she said. "Is that real?"

I knew what she was asking, and I knew why she was asking it. I would too, in her position.

"Yes," I said. "It is."

"Pretty trouble," she said. "I warned you of that, once."

Yes, well. Raihn was definitely trouble. Even now, I couldn't deny that. But maybe he was the kind of trouble I needed. Right now, he was the kind of trouble all my people needed.

I should have had a very diplomatic, queenly response for her. Instead, I just said, "Sometimes we need a little trouble to get shit done."

A short laugh. "Perhaps." That smile faded, her face going steely. "You have my full loyalty and respect, Highness. Even if your decisions are not the ones I would make. In light of recent events, I want to make that clear."

After seeing the way Raihn's people had rebelled against him, I was so grateful for this, I could've hugged her. Yes, I knew this loyalty was borne of nothing but my relation to Vincent, complicated as it may be. But loyalty, no matter the source, was more precious than gold.

"I wanted to speak to you, too," I said. "About something that Septimus has been working on."

She listened as I told her about Septimus's claims of the existence of god blood in the House of Night—and his claims that

Vincent had known, and perhaps even harnessed it. I told her about the pendant I had recovered from Lahor, and the unfortunate fact that it was likely now in Septimus's clutches. With every sentence, her brows rose slightly higher—the only change in her expression.

"Do you think this could be real?" I said. "Did Vincent tell you about it?"

Because surely, if he was going to entrust knowledge of a secret, powerful weapon to anyone, it would have been Jesmine, his Head of War—right?

But she was quiet, a regretful expression passing over her features—like a distant reflection over glass.

"Your father," she said finally, "was a very secretive man."

I wasn't expecting this shade to her voice—sad, and a little vulnerable.

"But he trusted you," I said. "Didn't he?"

She laughed, short and humorless. "Trusted me. Yes, perhaps. As much as he trusted anyone."

I was confused by this. Because when he was alive, I had envied Jesmine and Vincent's closest advisors. I had envied them because they had a level of respect from him that I thought was beyond my reach. At least, until I won the Kejari and bound myself to him, matching his strength with a Coriatis bond.

My confusion must have shown on my face, because her brow quirked. "This surprises you."

"I just... I always thought that you two had a..."

I wasn't sure how to word it.

"You thought because I was his Head of War, and because he was fucking me, he told me things."

I wasn't going to put it that way, exactly, but...

"Well, yes," I said.

A pained flinch, there and gone again in less than a second. "Me too," she said. "For a while."

The tone in her voice was so uncomfortably familiar. I'd always assumed she'd gotten some part of him I never could—not the sex, of course, but the trust. It had never occurred to me that she was chasing him, too. Hell, it had never even occurred to me that she had even cared enough to want that intimacy from him.

The question slipped out before I could stop it. "Did you love him, Jesmine?"

I half expected her to laugh at me for asking. It seemed like far too personal a question. But instead, she seemed to actually consider this.

"I loved him as my king," she said at last. "And perhaps I could have loved him as a man, too. I did in some ways. Maybe I wanted to in more. But he could not have loved me."

Why? I wanted to ask. Because Jesmine seemed like the epitome of everything a man like Vincent should love. Beautiful. Brilliant. Deadly. Powerful. If he had ever chosen to marry, I couldn't have imagined a better match for him.

A tight smile flitted across her lips.

"Loving someone else is a dangerous thing," she said. "Even for vampires. More dangerous still for a king. Vincent knew that. He was never going to open himself up to more weakness. And he already had exposed himself enough with the love he had for you."

The words struck deep, and I wasn't prepared. My jaw tightened. A raging monsoon of emotions knotted in my chest, all of them contradictory.

I so desperately craved to hear that Vincent had loved me.

And yet, I was so angry to hear it, too. Yes, maybe he had loved me. But he had still lied to me. He had still isolated me. He had still hurt me.

Maybe he had loved me. Maybe I got what Jesmine wanted and never could have. Was I supposed to be grateful for that alone?

What if I couldn't be?

I just said, "Well. You said it. He was a secretive man."

Jesmine nodded slowly, in a way that said, shamefully, she understood.

Then she cleared her throat. "So no," she said. "He never

talked to me about this... god blood. But that doesn't mean he didn't have it. On the contrary, I think it seems like exactly the sort of thing he would do. If it existed, he would have found it."

"If that's true," I said, "then I sure as hell hope he hid it well. Somewhere Septimus and Simon can't find it. Even if the pendant—"

I winced, as I did every time I thought of that damned pendant, cursing myself for ever letting it leave my sight.

Jesmine's lips thinned, clearly imagining all the same terrible scenarios that I was.

Defeating Septimus and Simon would already be a challenge. If they had any surprises for us, we would be fucked.

"Vincent was a very cautious person," she said. "Especially when it came to weapons. If he had it, he never would have left it accessible by a single key, no matter how well-hidden that key was. And even still, I think he would have multiple failsafes. Split it into multiple locations, for example."

Goddess, I hoped so. At this point, I wasn't even holding out hope of finding this god blood—if it existed—myself. I just wanted to make sure Septimus didn't have it.

"Here's hoping he hid it well," I muttered, and Jesmine laughed bitterly.

"Men and their secrets," she said. "We spend a lifetime trying to unravel them, and once they're gone, we're still at their mercy. Yes. Better hope Vincent hid his well."

In-fucking-deed.

51

RAIHN

I could not fucking wait for a bath. It was hard to play the convincing role of the confident Rishan king to a bunch of my greatest enemies while coated in two-week-old shit.

Jesmine's second, a straight-backed, wary-eyed woman who looked like she was debating whether to stab us with every step, showed us to the springs. It was amazing that such a thing could exist out here in the desert—I had to admit that the House of Night, for all its many faults, was a place of great natural wonder. The springs were located deep in the tunnels, where the dry air turned damp and steamy. The water was a perfect teal blue, illuminated by shocks of bright light running up the cave walls—which seemed far too beautiful to just be minerals and algae. The caves separated down here, running into many little offshoots. Convenient for privacy, which I think everyone was glad for after so much nonstop travel together.

"Well," Mische sighed, the moment our guide left us, "this is *amazing*."

She stretched out her arms, as if already imagining diving in.

I watched her out of the corner of my eye. I knew Mische, and I knew that something had been wrong since we left Sivrinaj. Hell, I could tell from the moment I saw her in the dungeons —those big eyes practically bursting with tears. Not a hint of those, of course, during the journey. It would be easy to mistake Mische's outgoing attitude for emotional openness. She may be chatty, but she was damned good at hiding all the things that mattered.

Oraya had told me about the Shadowborn prince—that Mische had been the one to kill him. It was a diplomatic headache, but one I could put off dealing with for a while. I was more concerned about what Oraya didn't tell me. And I knew there was something. Her stilted, "You should talk to Mische, when you can," said that well enough.

But Mische made sure I never got that chance. We had been moving so fast that I'd barely gotten a private moment with her since we fled, and every time I tried, in our rare moments of rest, to speak to her alone, she'd run off with some harried, half-baked excuse.

Now, I turned to her. "Mische, before you go—"

"Later," she said, without so much as looking at me. "Bath now." And she was gone into one of the caves before I had time to argue with her.

I wished I could say I was surprised.

Ketura and Lilith excused themselves immediately too, clearly just as eager to wash themselves off. Vale, though, lingered for a long, awkward moment as I gathered the clothes our guide had brought.

I peered over my shoulder.

"If your goal is to make this as uncomfortable as possible," I said, "you've achieved it."

Vale's jaw tightened. He still said nothing. Still didn't move, either.

Amazing. The man's wife was off naked in some hot water after a week of travel and zero privacy, and he was still standing *here*. I dreaded to think what this would be about.

"What, Vale?"

"I wanted to—" His gaze slipped away, examining an apparently fascinating pile of rocks. "I appreciate the rescue."

So this was what a noble looked like when they had to say "thank you."

"You're more useful to me out here than you are in there," I said, hoping this was the end of that conversation.

But he still lingered. His eyes snapped back to me. "I'm no fool. I know that you must have wondered. But if you need confirmation of where my loyalties lie, I hope finding my wife in that prison cell gave them to you."

Ah. Now I understood.

I straightened and turned to him. Vale's chin raised slightly, all traces of his earlier uncertainty now gone. Even covered in shit, he was every bit the Nightborn noble.

Sometimes, vampires' agelessness seemed like a cruel joke. Two hundred years had passed since my time under Neculai's control. And yet I looked the same, and Vale looked the same. Every time I looked at him, I saw him as he was then. I saw him just watching as it all happened. Maybe if he'd had lines to his face or gray hair or aging eyes, I might've found it easier to forget that this was the same person.

But there he was. Vale. One of Neculai's nobles.

And yet, I knew that what he was telling me was the truth. I'd known it from the moment I opened Lilith's cell door and saw him run to her. If Vale had remained loyal in the face of threats against her... that was true loyalty.

I gave him a rueful half smile. "You can't blame a man for wondering."

He pursed his lips. "No. I can't. What you said before the wedding was the truth."

I didn't show my surprise, but it struck me anyway. Even as a king, I never thought I'd hear anything even close to "you're right" from Vale.

"Things are..." His gaze momentarily flicked down the path Lilith had followed, before returning to me. "Things are different than they were. In those days, I was more committed to the House of Night than I was to anything. It was the only love I knew. I let it define me, and that meant letting Neculai define me. I did not question the things he did, or the way he treated those beneath him. What my king said was truth. And when he treated his Turned slaves as possessions, I didn't question that, even if I didn't agree with it."

It was harder than I wished it was to hear this. I didn't like addressing that time directly—not ever, but especially not with Vale, of all people. It just made me painfully conscious of everything he had seen.

"And to be clear," he went on, "I *didn't* agree with it. Not then. Not now. But you were right. Not agreeing was not enough. I was complacent. And if it had been Lilith—"

"It never will be," I said.

He inclined his chin. "I know that as long as you are king, it never will be."

As long as you are king.

We both knew neither of us could say the same for Simon. Or Septimus.

I'd never thought of Vale as the romantic type. Back in Neculai's court, he had been just like all the others—maybe not as abusive, but just as power hungry. Even when I'd called on him to fight for me, I'd figured it would be his pride and ambition alone that brought him back. Two hundred years ago, his vision for the House of Night had been simplistic in the way all vampire aspirations were: Be bigger, be stronger, and above all, be more powerful.

Maybe now he was looking for something more. Maybe he had found it.

It didn't make me forget who he had once been. But it made me respect the person he had become a little bit more.

And perhaps that was why I found myself saying something a little dangerous to him. Something that undermined the image I presented even to my most "trusted" inner circle.

"Any kingdom that Oraya rules," I said carefully, "would also be safe for Lilith. If it comes to that."

Vale stiffened, and I briefly wondered if I'd made a mistake by saying this. Hundreds of years had cemented his hate for the Hiaj

But maybe people could indeed change.

Because Goddess help me, Vale's face did soften with reluctant understanding.

"If it comes to that," I said again.

The message clear:

If I die, and you want this kingdom to be what you dream it could be, then support her.

Vale nodded.

"I understand," he said.

And then he bowed. Not just a little polite one, like he had often given me since arriving here. A deep bow, one that lingered for several seconds, offering true fealty. Not for any audience. Just for us.

A strange feeling came over me at this sight. A weight on my shoulders, heavy and dizzying.

He straightened. We regarded each other for a few awkward seconds, as if both readjusting to this freshly re-established power dynamic.

Being a king was bizarre.

"If that's all," I said, "I'd like to go wash the sewage off of myself."

Vale almost smiled. Almost. "Likewise."

I FOUND a secluded offshoot in the caves and stripped down. My clothes practically cracked when I peeled them off, leaving flakes of dried-up Goddess-knew-what on the damp stone ground. These leathers were a back-up set from my apartment in the human districts, and they fit poorly, too tight around my shoulders and chafing at my wings during all the flying. I let out a borderline-sexual groan of pleasure to get them off my body.

There was nothing borderline about the noise I made when I walked into that pool, though. Ix's fucking tits. Paradise did exist, and it was here. The water was still and hot and clear. It didn't even smell, not even a little.

Amazing.

I conjured my wings and stretched them out in the water, lowering myself to submerge them completely, flexing the weary muscles. Then I dunked my head under the surface and remained there, submerged in blissful warm darkness, until my lungs started to ache.

When I came up again, I was aware of her immediately.

That smell. Steel and Nightfire and a hint of spring.

I didn't even have to turn around.

"Enjoying the view, princess?"

52

ORAYA

'll admit it. I had been staring.

It was impossible not to. He looked like a Mother-damned painting, standing there with that uncannily teal water pooled around his waist, the blue algae glow settling into every line of his form, tinting his wings with yet another shade in their already endless complexity. And then, of course, there was his Heir Mark—glowing red in the darkness, the whorls of shadowy strokes stretching across the muscled expanse of his back, trailing down his spine all the way into the water.

I hadn't looked at that Heir Mark closely since the night of the final trial. I found it almost as striking now as I had then, though in a very different way.

He turned and glanced at me over his shoulder, one eyebrow quirked.

"Water's fantastic."

I just said, "Turn around."

He paused before obeying. "There are other caves," he said, "if you want privacy."

Respectfully. He understood that just because he'd seen me naked before, didn't mean he was entitled to see me again.

417

But I stripped off my rancid leathers, leaving them in a heap beside his. It was so comfortably warm down here, just hot enough to raise a sheen of sweat to my skin, and yet it still felt fresh and clean and comfortable. And the water itself—Goddess, when I stepped into it, I practically moaned.

He chuckled. "I made that sound, too."

Still, he kept his back turned.

I dunked my head under the water, swimming submerged for a few strokes before surfacing again near Raihn. The water here was up to his waist and my ribcage. His hair clung in wet whorls to his upper back, water pearling into beads on his tan skin. I found myself struck by the scent of him. He'd always had a distinctive smell, but lately, even beneath the disgusting scent of grime, it had gotten over-whelming to me—a constant, lingering awareness whenever he was in my proximity. I'd chalked that up to the fact that we all probably smelled something fierce while traveling, though I'd never noticed anyone else's scent like Raihn's. But, even with the sweat and sewage washed away, it was just as strong—the sky and the desert, even when submerged in water.

Was this, I wondered, what vampires felt like all the time? This aware?

My eyes fell to his Heir Mark. The red ink pulsed with the slow, steady beat of his heart, faint wisps of red smoke rolling from each stroke. The scarred flesh beneath it was raised and rough, though the lines of the Mark were smooth and clear. Once he'd claimed his power from Nyaxia, nothing could have kept that Mark hidden. I couldn't even imagine how badly he must have burned himself all those years ago to hide it to begin with.

The Mark stretched across his back, all the phases of the moon rendered in delicate brushstrokes, framed by spirals of smoke. The spear traveled down his spine, fitting perfectly between his wings, down to the dimpled small of his back. Until now, I hadn't realized just how similar his Mark was to mine.

The arrangement was different, but we both had the smoke, the moons, the same elegant red strokes.

Strange, that these Marks supposedly branded us as innate enemies. And yet, they were obvious mates to each other.

My fingertips traced the lines, following them across his upper back, around his wings, down his spine. I couldn't help but wince a little at the rough texture of the scar beneath them. Mother, that must have been terrible.

His shoulders stilled for a moment at my touch.

"What do you think?" he said. "Suit me? I don't actually get to look at it too often."

His voice was flippant. And yet I heard what lingered beneath it. Knew that there was nothing flippant about Raihn's feelings towards this Mark.

"It's beautiful."

He scoffed slightly.

"You don't like it," I said. Not a question. It was true.

He glanced over his shoulder again, giving me a glimpse of his profile, before turning ahead.

"You're too perceptive for someone with such bad people skills." Then, after a moment, "It reminds me too much of him. Doesn't seem fair, sometimes, for him to have marked me this permanently. I don't want anything of his on me."

"It's not his. It's *yours*."

My fingertips ran up his spine again, this time following the swirls of smoky red. I had never met Neculai, never seen his Mark, but I couldn't imagine this one on anyone other than Raihn. Every small detail of it seemed crafted to complement his body, the flow of his muscles, the shape of his form, even bending and reforming around his scars.

"Your skin," I murmured, pushing aside tendrils of wet hair to follow the strokes near his neck. "Your body. Your Mark."

He didn't say anything for a long moment. I was very conscious of the way goosebumps rose on his flesh beneath the trail of my touch.

"May I turn around, princess?" he asked.

The tone was teasing. The question was real.

The corner of my mouth twitched. "Queen. Remember?"

I could hear the smile. "Of course. My queen."

The "my" made it something more than a joke.

"I'll allow it," I said.

He turned.

His gaze drank me in slowly, starting at my hair, my eyes, my face, and then trailing down over my shoulders—lingering at my breasts, peaked and wet, exposed above the water that pooled around my ribcage.

But he lifted his eyes to my Mark, over my throat, shoulders, and chest. He reached out to touch it, his fingertip tracing the lines just as mine had done to his. I wanted to hide the way it made my skin pebble—made my breath grow a little uneven.

His eyes were heavy lidded, unblinking. With the blue reflection of the water and the algae, they looked almost purple.

"Can't imagine it looked this good on Vincent," he murmured.

I wondered if he was seeing the same thing in my Mark that I had just seen in his—all the ways it complemented my specific form. I hadn't noticed that before. Like Raihn, I had seen the Mark as something that belonged to someone else, superimposed onto my skin.

It wasn't until right now, looking at it through the lens of Raihn's, that I considered the differences. The way the wings across my chest were a little smaller, more delicate, than Vincent's, following the shape of my clavicle. The way the smoke speared down between my breasts, following the lines of my body and mine alone.

"I never thought it looked right on me," I admitted.

Like it was a costume. Something that never should have been given to me.

"I think it suits you perfectly." His touch trailed down—down between my breasts, feather-light over the sensitive skin.

"You said it yourself. Your title. Queen. This Mark belongs to you." His lips curled. "Your skin. Your body. Your Mark."

Somehow, it didn't sound like a platitude when Raihn said it. It sounded like the truth.

His gaze lifted, those deep red eyes piercing mine. His touch stalled, lingering on my chest.

"Did you mean it?" he said. "What you told Jesmine."

He didn't need to specify what he was talking about.

When we reclaim our kingdom, I intend to rule beside him as such.

I felt, all at once, much more naked than I had thirty seconds ago.

"I'm not going to risk my life and the lives of what little army I have left just to put your ass back on that throne without taking some of it for myself," I said.

Somehow, I could tell he knew my dismissive tone was a little forced.

He rasped a low laugh.

"Good," he said. "I'd be disappointed otherwise."

"It has nothing to do with you," I said, before I could stop myself.

An infuriating, stubborn smile clung to his mouth. "Mhm. Of course not."

"I'm still not sure that you're not going to fuck me over," I grumbled—just because I felt like it was what I *should* say, even if the truth of it was now obvious, even to me.

But his thumb came to my chin, gently tipping my face back to him. His stare was steady, uncomfortably direct.

"I am not going to fuck you over," he said.

Firmly. Like it was nothing more and nothing less than fact. It *felt* like fact, when he said it like that. And the truth was, I believed him.

I didn't want to give him that satisfaction, though. So I narrowed my eyes.

"*Again*, you mean," I said. "Fuck me over *again*."

His lips twitched. "That face. There she is."

Then the smirk faded, revealing something so much more serious, something I wanted to wriggle away from. I didn't, though—I met his stare, let his thumb hold my chin.

It was frightening to give someone your trust.

More frightening still to give it for a second time, after they broke it the first.

"One honest thing," I murmured.

And he didn't hesitate as he said softly, "Never, Oraya. Never again. And not just because I don't have a chance in hell of taking Sivrinaj back without you. But because I wouldn't want to, anyway."

I thought of what was ahead—two armies that hated each other now forced to work together to take on a greater evil. For a moment, I couldn't help but consider what myself from a year ago would say if presented with all of this.

She would fucking laugh.

No. She would refuse to believe it altogether. That version of Oraya literally would not be able to comprehend any of it. Not Vincent's death, or his lies. Not the Heir Mark on her skin, or her wish to a goddess, or the idea of allying with the Rishan Heir.

She certainly would never believe that I could be standing here now, naked, in front of Raihn—not only a vampire, not only a Rishan, but her greatest enemy—and not feel even a little bit afraid.

At least, not afraid for her physical safety.

Another fear settled, though, deep under my skin.

"Do you really think we can do this?" I murmured.

He contemplated this.

"Yes," he said finally. "Yes. I do."

He traced my Heir Mark again, a line of concentration between his brows.

"At the very least," he said, "I sure as hell believe that you can."

I wanted to laugh at him.

I wanted to weep.

Because I knew he meant it.

My fingertips touched his chest—damp skin, rough with

various little scars and the soft texture of dark hair. Right over his heart, where my blade had pierced that night.

"Funny, how things change."

He tipped my chin up. And I didn't have time to move or react before he kissed me, slow and deep, his soft tongue gently caressing mine as my lips parted for him like leaves opening toward the sun.

It was the kind of kiss that made doubts wither. The kind that made it easy not to think about difficult realities—even if it hinted at a more frightening one that I hadn't yet accepted.

Our mouths parted, but our noses still touched, as he murmured, "Been wanting to do that constantly for the last week."

Goddess, me too. I wasn't sure what had changed the night we were together, but it was like my body had awakened to a whole new sense. It was a little shameful, actually, how I craved him. I was constantly aware of his proximity, his scent, his gaze. I could feel it when he looked at me, even when I didn't meet his eyes. And every time we had lain beside each other in our sparse, very much non-private moments of rest, I had to stop myself from closing the distance between us.

It was dizzying. It was terrifying. It was addictive.

I hated it. Fucking hated it.

...But maybe also liked, just a little bit, that he felt it too. I could practically sense his heartbeat, slow but quickening, hot beneath his skin. And I could very literally sense his cock, hardening in the space between us, nudging my hip.

I took a certain satisfaction in the fact that his desire was so much more physically obvious than mine. I could pretend my peaked breasts were from the cooling water on my skin. Could pretend my own quickening heart was from the anticipation of what we were about to do.

Yet something about his shaky breath over my lips told me he knew the truth, too.

I moved a little closer, hardened nipples brushing the hair of his chest.

"That wasn't what you were *really* thinking about."

His lips curled. I could taste that smile as he kissed me again, this time softer, nipping at my lip.

"One of the things," he admitted. "Not all of them."

His hand lowered to my breast, his thumb circling the peak. It responded to him immediately, tightening beneath his touch, my breath hitching.

"Don't think I'm the only one," he murmured.

Another kiss.

"You're arrogant," I said.

Even as I was chasing his lips again. Chasing that kiss like an addict. Practically grinding myself against him.

Pathetic.

But I didn't feel ashamed.

"A little," he replied, before cupping my face and kissing me again—this time harder, more viciously, something much more akin to the storms of our other torrential trysts. And I let it sweep me away, my desire devouring my pride as his arms folded around me and mine encircled his neck, pulling myself flush against him.

The nagging need that I'd been managing to ignore for the past week was suddenly all-consuming. Utterly devastating.

And hell if I even cared. It was better to be lost in this than to be lost in all our difficult concerns.

His hands glided over wet skin, like he was eager to refamiliarize himself with my body. My thighs parted, the warm water agonizing against my growing need, and my legs folded around his waist. He cradled me, lifting me up, making it easier for me to cling to him. His head craned, allowing me to control our kisses, fervent and unbroken.

My slit met the rigid length of him, and I let out a little strangled sound against his mouth.

"Fuck, Oraya," he breathed, the words butchered as my back met stone.

I needed him. Goddess, I needed him now. No more waiting.

But he paused, pulling back slightly, eyes meeting mine.

"This alright?" he said, in panting breaths.

At first, I wasn't even sure what he was asking.

Then I realized: I was pinned here, between his body and the rocks.

Every other time we'd been together, he had been so careful to make sure he never trapped me. Make sure I always was free to get away if I wanted to.

Not long ago, the idea of ever having sex with anyone again in a position where I couldn't extract myself immediately was inconceivable. And yet, here I was. Not even noticing that he'd trapped me, with a rapid heartbeat that had nothing at all to do with fear.

I reached around his body, dragging my fingernails down his back—lingering at the delicate flesh and soft feathers where his wings met his skin.

It was a guess, really, as to whether he felt those nerve endings the way that I did. But his entire body reacted to that touch. His breath shuddered. His wings—those majestic wings—shivered, unfolding slightly, big enough to cocoon us both in a sheet of black-red. His cock twitched, hips pushing a little against me in a movement that seemed totally involuntary.

I smirked. "I know I'm still in control."

His eyebrow quirked. "No objections," he murmured, and kissed me again.

Just as I tilted my hips, opened my thighs, and he sank into me.

Goddess fucking help me.

He hit so deep from this angle, that very first thrust setting my body alight like a match.

I didn't realize I'd made a sound until his mouth covered mine and he whispered, "Careful. Others are close."

Oh, I heard that taunt in his voice—saying that just as he swirled his hips, grinding against my clit.

I bit down on my moan, and choked out, "Then you'll have to be *so* quiet, won't you?"

I dragged my fingers down his back again—giving him the

same challenge he gave me, and relishing the slight growl that came from low in his throat.

He didn't have a retort for me. I had unleashed him. Just as I'd wanted. Just as I needed.

All that pent-up tension, from the battle and the travel and a week spent in agonizing, untouchable proximity, burst free.

He kissed me hard, viciously, as his strokes took me—seizing full advantage of the control he had in this position, unrelenting, fast, deep.

This wouldn't last long. Not for me, not for him. That was fine—we were too impatient for that. Who knew how long we had left to live. We would burn ourselves hot and quick.

And Mother, I loved it.

My skin was so warm, the pleasure so intense, I thought I might die here in it. And Goddess, what a fucking way to go. Moans and screams and pleas and curses bubbled up in my throat, driven closer to the surface with every one of his thrusts.

I needed more, needed release. I tilted my hips to urge him deeper, though there was nothing I could do but take him—and I did, gladly, openly, clinging to him and clawing at his back for support.

His mouth broke from mine, moving to my ear.

"This," he rasped, breath hot and ragged. "This is what I was thinking about, Oraya. I missed you."

I missed you.

Strange, how much those words hit me—how much I understood them, even if I couldn't bring myself to say them back.

I missed you.

A week without touching him, and I missed him. Months without his friendship, and I missed him.

It wasn't about a week. It wasn't even about sex.

It was about everything before that. Repairing some chasm that had opened in our relationship. Finding, terrifyingly, how much we had mourned what had been lost in that gap.

I had missed him, too.

But I couldn't voice it. And I was grateful that he didn't give me the chance to, anyway, because his strokes were unrelenting, the pleasure building to a crescendo that was—Goddess it was—it was so much that it almost *hurt*, and—

I tightened my legs around him, pulling him against me, forcing him to go up in flames with me.

I buried my face against his shoulder when I climaxed, stifling my scream against his skin, because I couldn't choke it down anymore. Distantly, with the crescendo of pleasure, I felt a brief stab of pain—pain, as his teeth sank into the space between my neck and shoulder. Not feeding—stifling himself, too, his groan instead ringing out in shudders across my flesh.

In the wake of it, I felt weak and dizzy. And yet, so very at peace.

The water was warm.

That was the first sensation that returned. All this pleasant warmth. Warmth of the water. Warmth of Raihn's body, surrounding me. Warmth everywhere.

He kissed the mark he'd left on my shoulder. "Sorry."

"I think I scratched up your back."

A breathy chuckle. "Good."

That's how I felt, too. *Good*. Let us leave something on each other's corpses.

He drew back enough to look at me, tracing my face. He had little beads of water in his lashes, which glittered as his eyes crinkled in an almost-smile.

It occurred to me that this might be the only time I got to be alone with Raihn before we threw ourselves into a mission that would probably kill one or both of us. The thought made a lump of unspoken words rise in my throat.

Instead, I kissed him—hard enough that there was no use for words, anyway.

I felt him start to harden again within me, my thighs tightening around him.

I whispered against his lips, "We might not get privacy again."

Because the moment we left this bath, we would be leaders

again. We would be reclaimers of a lost kingdom. We would need to think about the future. There would be no time for the present.

I wasn't ready to leave.

He smiled softly. "Mm. Probably not."

My hips rolled against him, breath hitching at the now-rigid length inside me.

Goddess fucking help me. How did he *do* that?

"Might as well take advantage," I murmured.

"Just practical," he said, swallowing the words in his next kiss, and that was the last we spoke.

53

RAIHN

I was glad that Oraya and I had made the most of our time alone, because we didn't get any more of it after that. Everyone understood that time was of the essence. The faster we struck, the better our chances at seizing Sivrinaj while Simon's hold over it was still shaky. Jesmine and Vale clearly hated each other, but they made surprisingly effective allies. Both now understood what it was like to be the underdog, and both understood the mindset of the upper class. They emphatically believed that now was not the time to try something risky and sneaky—this was the time for a dramatic show of strength. The only language, they insisted, that Simon and those who followed him would understand.

I hated having to speak that language. But I wasn't too obsessed with the moral high ground to not stoop to their level. No point in thinking about the chances. Oraya and I had defeated worse odds before—seven times, in fact, in seven trials. How much harder could this possibly be?

The answer, it turned out, was much harder.

I was a good fighter, but before these last few months I'd had virtually no experience in battles—not fighting them, and certainly not leading them. Jesmine and Vale, however, excelled at the ruthless strategy of warfare. The moment Oraya and I had given the commands, they leapt into action. Immediately, we were swept into a whirlwind of preparations—plans, maps, strategies, weapons, inventories, rosters of soldiers and diagrams of loyal forces. Letters were sent. Maps were drawn. Tactics were plotted.

We would prepare for a week, and then we would march, the forces that Jesmine and Vale had summoned joining us along the way. We'd move quick, before Simon's army would have the time to head us off. It was a convenient incidental benefit that we wouldn't have time to doubt ourselves, either.

Hell, Oraya and I had been throwing ourselves against impossible odds for close to a year now. Why stop now? And in a way, it was oddly invigorating—to do something that felt right and earned again. To do it beside Oraya. It made a lot of things seem easier.

Both of us were grateful for the distraction of work. Maybe we wanted to avoid thinking too hard about what might happen after the battle—about how the Rishan and the Hiaj and the other kingdoms and hell, even Nyaxia herself, might react to the prospect of the Rishan and Hiaj Heirs ruling together. It sounded ridiculous. I know everyone thought it was. Strangely enough, only Vale seemed to take the alliance as settled law. Everyone else tip-toed around it, accepting it but not hiding their skepticism. Even Ketura pulled me aside at one point, asking—ever blunt—"Do you really think she's not going to bury a blade in your back the minute she has that throne?"

Maybe I was a fool for it, but no, I didn't. Oraya had passed up so many opportunities to kill me. If she was going to do it, she'd have done it by now.

And if she did... fuck, maybe I deserved it.

That would be a problem for future Raihn. Present Raihn had more than enough to deal with. Everyone wanted to talk to us. Everyone needed something.

The one person I tried hardest to pin down, though, was the one person who was the best at evading me.

I finally caught her near dawn one day, as she was crawling back to her little tent. I flicked her on the back of the head through bronze curls.

"You're coming for a walk with me."

Mische turned around, startled. Her eyes went round in surprise, then scrunched in something resembling a wince.

She winced when she saw me. *Winced*.

"I have to—"

"I don't want any bullshit excuses, Mische." I pointed to the path ahead. "Walk. With me. Now."

"Is that an order?"

"Is that an attitude? You've been spending too much time with Oraya."

No smile at that. No returning joke. She just said nothing.

Concern twisted in my stomach.

I held out my hand to help her up. "Let's go."

"Don't you have work to do?"

"It can wait."

I didn't move my hand. Just stared at her.

Mische and I had been friends for a very, very long time. She knew when there was no point arguing with me.

She let out a sigh and took my hand.

"JESMINE SAID there are demons out here," Mische said. "We shouldn't go too far."

Mische and I wandered through the more secluded paths in the cliffs, out of earshot of the camps. It was dark here, though not so dark our eyesight couldn't make out what it needed to. Better yet, it was quiet.

I'd missed quiet.

Meanwhile, Mische seemed so uncomfortable she was practically trying to speed walk through our stroll.

I scoffed. "As if I believe you're afraid of demons."

"Why wouldn't I be afraid of demons?"

"I don't know, Mish. Maybe because you ran off and joined the Kejari like it was another day of the week."

That sounded a lot more bitter than I intended it to. Thought I was at a point where I could joke about Mische's actions. Guess not.

Maybe I wasn't the only one, because instead of giving me some kind of smart-ass retort, she buried her hands in her pockets and kept walking.

"That was different," she muttered.

It took me a second too long to understand what she meant. I kept pace beside her, my eyes slipping down—to the scars visible where her sleeve rode up.

My lips thinned. A wave of concern passing through me.

And with it, frustration.

"Mische." I stopped and touched her shoulder. She stopped walking, but seemed reluctant to look at me.

"What?"

"What do you mean, 'what?' I've put up with you every day for fucking decades. Enough."

"Enough of what?"

"You've been avoiding me since—"

"I haven't been avoiding you."

"Oraya told me about the prince."

Mische's mouth remained open for a moment, her half-spoken words dying on her lips, before she closed it.

"Alright."

Alright.

This fucking girl. Mother help me.

"What?" she said. "You're angry. I know. It's a big political problem and—"

I scoffed. Actually scoffed, because what the fuck else was I supposed to say?

"I'm not mad about the prince."

"Well, obviously you're mad. So what the hell are you mad about?"

"Something is wrong with you and you won't tell me what it is."

It was more direct than I should have been. Maybe I was worn down after months of trying to help someone who hadn't wanted to be helped. Between Mische and Oraya, it was exhausting.

She and I stared each other down, silent. Mische's eyes were big and stubborn. Most of the time, they looked pretty and doe-like. People often said that Mische's eyes were her prettiest feature. But they didn't see her pissed off. Then, they were downright terrifying.

She wasn't quite there, yet, but I could see the shadow of it, and that was bad enough.

As if she should be giving me that look. When I was the one following her around getting snapped at for the great crime of worrying about her.

And I *was* worried about her.

"Enough with the bullshit," I said. But the words came out soft—as soft, I supposed, as I meant them. "Tell me what happened."

"I thought Oraya told you already."

Oraya didn't tell me why you've been avoiding me for a week, I wanted to say. *She didn't tell me why you were put in that apartment instead of in the dungeons. She didn't tell me why you look so broken.*

"Oraya told me about a dead prince," I shot back. "I don't give a fuck about that. I'm asking about *you.*"

Mische stopped walking, then turned around. The anger drained from her face, leaving behind something childlike and conflicted that reminded me so much of the way she had looked when I first found her, it made my chest physically hurt.

"She didn't tell you?"

"Do I need to talk to Oraya now to find out what's going on inside that head of yours?"

433

Mische didn't answer. Instead, she leaned against the wall, slid down it, and perched on a pile of rock, her head in her hands.

The guilt was immediate.

I sat down next to her, even though the rocks were so low to the ground that I ended up ridiculously curled up on myself. I peered at her face between tendrils of honey hair.

"Mish," I murmured. "I —"

"It was him."

The three words came out in a single breath. So fast they ran together and it took a minute for me to untangle them.

"Him," I repeated.

And she lifted her head, and she looked at me with those big eyes filled with rage and tears, and I just fucking knew.

Every shred of my frustration fell away. Every single emotion, every thought, every sensation disappeared, save for the utter all-consuming rage.

"*Him?*" I said, again.

She nodded.

The image of the Shadowborn prince unfolded in my mind. The Shadowborn prince, who I'd invited into my castle. I'd talked to him. Laughed with him. Fed him fucking delicacies.

And then, that memory was replaced by another one. Mische, as I had found her all those years ago. Pale and thin and sun-scorched, vomit crusted to her lips, left in the dirt like a discarded toy.

When she was in the throes of her fever, she'd just kept saying, over and over again, "What's happening? What's happening?"

She had been so damned young. Practically a child. And she had been so, so afraid.

That had been a long time ago.

But I never forgot it. Not really. I still saw that version of her sometimes, even though I knew she'd hate it if she knew that. I saw it the night of the Moon Palace attack, when I'd scraped her up off the floor among all that Nightfire. I saw it every time I glimpsed the burn scars on her arms. And I saw it now.

And that man—that fucking *monster*—had done that to her.

I had *smiled* at that prick.

"I shouldn't have killed him," Mische was saying, though I was so furious I barely heard her. "It was careless, I—"

"What the fuck do you mean, you *shouldn't have killed him?*" My fists were clenched so tight they shook. I probably looked ridiculous, hunched over on this stupid little rock, shaking like a madman. "I'd say *I* should have killed him, but I'm glad you got to be the one to do it."

She averted her eyes, staring at the ground. "I just —snapped."

"Why didn't you tell me? The minute he walked through the door, Mische, I—"

"I didn't know," she said weakly. "I didn't know who he was. Not until I saw his face." She shuddered. "I used to think a lot about what it would be like to meet him again. But I used to be afraid I wouldn't remember. It was all fuzzy. I was so sick."

I remembered that well. That first year, after Mische had recovered, she'd had an intense, paranoid fear that any man she met could have been the one who Turned her. She didn't remember her maker's face or name, so, in a cruel twist of fate, that meant he was everywhere—every passing stranger on the street.

"Well." She laughed darkly. "I knew. I knew it right away."

I was quiet. It hurt—actually hurt—to think that Mische hadn't been spared that. I hated Neculai, and what I hated most of all was the innate connection I'd had to him as the man who Turned me. He made himself the center of my entire world not only because my survival hinged solely on him, but also because he had literally created me.

Some intrinsic bond—no, shackle—existed in that relation-ship for vampires. It made you feel small and dirty and ashamed.

I hated that Mische knew what that was.

"He knew me, too, I think," she said. "Well. Not really. I

435

don't think he remembered me. But he... noticed me. Maybe he smelled himself on me."

And she had been up in that apartment. Given to him, probably, by either Simon or Septimus, who noticed his interest in her —who wanted to bribe him to stick around and witness their grand ascension to power. Maybe buy themselves an ally.

I didn't even want to ask. Didn't want to make her relive the answer. But I had to.

"Mish, did he—"

"No," she said quickly. "No. Maybe... maybe he would have, but..."

But he ended up with Mische's sword through his heart.

Good.

And yet it didn't feel like that much of a comfort. He'd already violated her in so many other ways.

"You should have told me," I said. "The minute you knew."

She gave me a skeptical glance, a little pitying. "You needed him, Raihn."

"It doesn't matter."

"It *does* matter. You *know* it matters."

"And let's say I had won his alliance. Then what were you going to do? What was your plan? Just stay in that castle with him for Goddess-knows how long, and suffer through it?"

Mische sighed. Suddenly, she looked so tired. "Maybe," she said. "I don't know. He is—was—important, Raihn. I'm not a child. You're trying to do something big. And even though you won't give me shit about it, I know I pushed you into it." She touched her chest, letting out a wry laugh. "And *I'm* supposed to get in the way of that, now? *Me?* You sacrificed for this. You gave up Oraya, and I know—I know what that meant to you. You gave up your *life*. I wasn't going to stand in the way."

You gave up Oraya.

Those four words hit me in the chest like arrows, one after the other, too quick to catch my breath.

I had fucked up.

Because Mische was right. I had sacrificed in the name of

power. I thought my sacrifices were my own, but that wasn't true. Oraya had suffered the weight of them. Mische had suffered the weight of them.

And now she thought—genuinely believed—that she was less important than that cause.

"It doesn't matter," I said softly. "Alliances. War. Politics. It does not matter. Alright?"

"That's not—"

"Let me talk," I snapped. "Don't you fucking dare regret it for a second, Mish. The House of Shadow wants to come for us? Let them come. It will have been worth it."

I meant it, even though I also didn't want to think about the consequences. At least we had some time before we had to deal with that. As far as the House of Shadow knew, their prince died in the care of Simon Vasarus, not me. We were trying to retake the throne quickly. Whatever diplomatic issues this might cause... we could save that for the next war.

Tomorrow's headache. Not today's.

And even tomorrow, I wouldn't be able to bring myself to be sorry.

"Besides," I said, "maybe we'll all be dead by then and it won't matter."

A smile twitched at the corner of her mouth. "Have you seen what this army looks like? Seems like a 'probably,' not a 'maybe.'"

I scoffed. "And this from the optimistic one."

She laughed. It was weak, but it was a laugh. I'd take it. "Sorry. I'm tired."

Tired. Long-term tired. I understood right away what she meant.

She stared off into the darkness of the tunnels. If I listened carefully, I could still hear the sounds of the camp far in the distance, echoing down the hall. A constant reminder, even out here, of what was coming.

I watched her profile, so uncharacteristically mournful.

"I'm sorry, Mische," I said quietly.

She started to shake her said, but I said, again, "I'm sorry for all of it."

I'm sorry that it happened to you. I'm sorry that I couldn't stop it. I'm sorry you had to fight this alone. I'm sorry that I didn't get to help you kill that fucking bastard. I'm sorry you felt like you couldn't tell me.

I'm sorry I made you feel like it wouldn't matter if you did.

Her face softened. "It's alright."

"No. It isn't. But it will be." I paused, then added, "Maybe. If we're lucky."

She laughed softly, then laid her head against my shoulder. "I think we're lucky," she murmured.

I wasn't convinced, but I sure as fuck hoped so.

I had a million things to do. But I wasn't ready to go. We remained there, in silence, for a few minutes longer.

54

ORAYA

The days and nights blended together in a messy blur of preparations. We worked, and slept, and ate, and worked. The caves grew more crowded as Vale and Jesmine collected the soldiers they had available in the north. In what felt like a miracle, we only ended up with four dead from fights between the Hiaj and the Rishan. I was amazed the body count was that low—though we did, apparently, have a few gouged-out eyes and ripped-off ears, too. Still, compared to the bloodbath we were expecting, it was practically camaraderie.

We moved out fast. Raihn and I had made the trip north very quickly, but it would take us a little longer to move with this many people. Jesmine and Vale had also set up a rendezvous point outside of Sivrinaj, so that the troops summoned from the farther reaches of the House of Night could move directly toward the city. Vale had some Rishan friends who had significant fleets, too, from their lands on the western shores of the House of Night, who would be circling the Ivory Seas to flank us from the ocean.

Would it be enough?

This was the question on all our minds, unspoken, as we

gathered our troops and set out across the deserts. We moved shockingly fast for such a large group of people. The wings helped, but what helped more was the sense of urgency in the air.

The Hiaj were ready to finally reclaim their throne, even if they had to do it alongside the Rishan. And the Rishan were just as eager to get the Bloodborn out of this kingdom.

They actually *cared* about this.

That didn't really hit me until we were halfway across the desert. It was nearly sunrise. We'd have to stop soon. Jesmine said as much to the rest of us, flying as we headed up the group, and Vale had remarked, "They aren't ready."

I glanced behind me at the warriors who followed, flying in swift, neat formation—Rishan on one side, Hiaj on the other.

Despite the hours of travel, despite the sky tinted the dim pink of near-sunrise, Vale was right. They weren't ready to stop. One look at them, and I could see it in their faces: driven determination.

It actually startled me.

I'd never expected more from them than resigned loyalty. Never thought that they could give me, a half-human, more than that, let alone when asked to walk beside an enemy they'd fought for thousands of years.

And yet...

My eyes flicked to Raihn's, and I saw the same amazement, same disbelief, in his face.

"It's cloudy," he said. "We can keep going for a little longer. If they don't want to stop yet, who the hell am I to complain?"

He dipped a little closer to me after that—just close enough for the tip of his wing to nudge mine, the feathers tickling. As if to silently say, *Well, would you look at that?*

We squeezed out maybe an extra half hour of travel that morning. Nothing significant. And yet, when we did finally settle down in our shelters, I couldn't help marveling at how far we'd come.

I still wasn't sure if it would be enough.

But Goddess, it was something, wasn't it?

I HAD NEVER LOOKED at the silhouette of Sivrinaj from this far away before. I'd memorized that skyline from my bedroom window over the years—every spire or dome, every path the sun took over the sky above it. I seared that shape into my soul. I could've drawn it from memory.

But perspective did change things.

From out here in the deserts, the smooth silver waves of the dunes rolled in the foreground instead of the distance. The harsh blocks of the slums framed the city in squares of washed-out, dusty gray. The Moon Palace stood to the east, looming over the skyline, deceptively peaceful for a place that had, not long ago, claimed so much blood. And then the castle—my home, my prison, my target—loomed far ahead, distance reducing it to the smallest of them all.

The castle was not the tallest building in Sivrinaj. But it had always felt like it to me. Larger than anything in life could be.

From out here, it was just another building.

Tonight, we would march for that city.

We were ready. Vale and Jesmine's troops had met us here. Our army had tripled in size since we'd left the cliffs. This stretch of desert had now been transformed into a sea of tents and makeshift shelters to hide from the strongest hours of sun.

We were ready, I told myself.

We had to be ready.

"You should be getting some rest," a familiar voice said behind me. "I hear it's a big night."

I peered over my shoulder to see Raihn peeking through the flap of the tent.

I put my finger to my lips. "You'll wake Mische."

No one got their own tent. We'd rather spend our energy

441

carrying weapons than supplies. That meant the warriors—us included—were packed three or four to a tent for the hours we were forced to rest. Raihn and I spent that time wedged in with Mische and Ketura, trying to sleep while also dodging Mische's flailing limbs.

Raihn slipped from the tent, closing the flap behind him. When my eyebrows jumped, he raised his hands. "Relax. I'm in the shade."

He was. Kind of. The tent blocked the strongest of the light, and it was a hazy day today. The shadows were long now, sunset approaching.

Still seemed like an unnecessary risk. But then again, I also knew there was no point trying to tell Raihn to avoid the sun.

I scooted backward, so I was sitting beside him. He squinted out over the horizon, taking in the same view of Sivrinaj that I'd just been admiring.

"Looks small from out here," he murmured.

I nodded.

"The first time I saw Sivrinaj," he said, "it was when I was dragging myself out of the ocean. I thought I'd crossed into another world. Even the biggest cities I'd been to were nothing like this. I thought, *Thank the fucking gods. I'm saved.*"

I shuddered a little. Raihn, of course, had not been saved. He'd been walking into his own prison.

It was hard to imagine that version of him. The sailor from nowhere, who had never seen anything as grand as Sivrinaj's castle. Just a broken, frightened human man who didn't want to die.

I could remember so clearly the way Raihn's voice had cracked when he'd told me this story the first time.

He asked me if I wanted to live, he had told me. *What the hell kind of a question was that? Of course I wanted to live.*

"Do you wish you'd said no?" I murmured.

I didn't even need to specify what I was talking about.

He took a long time to respond.

"I cursed myself for that answer," he said at last, "for a long,

long time. Death would have been better than those next seventy years. But... maybe there's something to be said for the years that came after that." His eyes flicked to me, crinkling slightly with an almost-smile. "Maybe even the years that come after this one."

The corner of my mouth twitched. His brow flattened.

"What's that face for?"

"Nothing. It's just... a very optimistic thing for you to say."

He threw his hands up. "Well fuck, if we can't be even a little optimistic, what are we doing any of this for?"

It was, I had to admit, a fair point.

"So you think we can do this," I said, my gaze slipping back to the city. "Tomorrow."

Optimism wasn't exactly what I got from his long silence.

"We'd better," he said.

"It's just quiet," I said. "It's..."

"Unnerving."

Yes. Unnaturally quiet, even for the daytime. I would have expected to see more activity visible in Sivrinaj. More barricades, maybe, or more troops stationed beyond the boundaries of the city. But even when we had arrived here, at dawn, it had been still.

"They're bracing for us," Jesmine had said. "They don't have enough men. They need to use what they can to keep the inner city safe, not run out and meet us out here, leaving their other sides exposed."

Logically, that made sense. Vale had agreed. Still... something about it made the hairs stand up on the back of my neck.

"You'd better not be going soft on me, princess," Raihn said, nudging my shoulder. "What, you're scared? *You?* The steel-nerved Hiaj queen?"

I glared at him, and he chuckled.

"That's better."

"I'm not scared. I'm just..."

I looked back at the city. Then at him. Then at the city.

Alright. Maybe I was scared.

I settled on, "I feel the way I felt before the last trial."

Not *afraid*, exactly. Not afraid for myself, at least. I wasn't afraid of a sword through my own gut. But I was afraid of letting my kingdom fall. I was afraid of all I could lose.

I glanced back to Raihn, his face now serious as he gazed out over the skyline, pink sunset light outlining his profile, and suddenly, that fear cut even deeper.

His eyes flicked to mine, and I saw that fear reflected back at me, like a mirror to my own. It stirred a complicated knot of emotions in my stomach, words that I didn't know how to untangle.

He swept a stray strand of hair behind my ear.

"I always admired that about you," he said. "That you fought even when you were afraid. Don't you dare stop now. No matter what happens."

I gave him a wry smile. "You said that then, too."

Don't you dare stop fighting, princess. It would break my damned heart.

"I remember. And it did break my heart when you stopped."

I didn't know what to say to that. I settled on, "Well. At least we're fighting now."

A faint laugh. "We sure fucking are."

"It will be enough." I hoped it didn't sound like I was reassuring myself, even though I was. "A show of strength. That's all they respond to."

Without meaning to, I touched my Mark.

They will never respect you unless they fear you, little serpent, Vincent whispered in my ear. *Show them something to be afraid of.*

It had been a while since I'd heard his voice, even in my head. The sound of it left me a bit off-balance.

As if he'd seen it—because of course he'd seen it—Raihn's hand lingered at my lower back, a steadying touch.

"They won't stand a chance," he said.

But did I imagine that he, too, sounded uncertain?

I turned a little, intending to face him, but the movement just pressed me against his arm. I ended up leaning against his shoulder, laying my head on it.

It was just... nice, to soak up these last few minutes of private companionship. It was different than having sex with him. Different, even, than sleeping beside him. It was somehow more intimate.

His arm folded around me. His face tilted, and when he spoke, I could feel his breath on my forehead. "Just want you to know, Oraya," he murmured, "that you were the best part of it. The best part of all of it."

My chest clenched violently, so sudden and sharp it felt like the aftermath of a blow. The earnestness of what he'd just said cut me open.

But worse still was how much it sounded like a goodbye.

I said, voice tighter than I intended, "You accuse me of going soft when you're spewing that sappy bullshit?"

He laughed, and I scowled. But I still didn't move, settling more comfortably against his body. And when his hand moved down to mine, I threaded my fingers through his like it was the most natural thing in the world.

I wasn't sure how long we stayed like that. Just watching the minutes tick by until the end of it all.

55

ORAYA

T he minute the sun set, Jesmine roused the warriors. The bloodthirsty excitement of the night before was gone. Now, the soldiers were efficient, focused—a set of well-oiled gears grinding to life for one purpose alone. Warriors silently donned their weapons and armor, all ready and waiting. We didn't have much time to strike. Every second counted.

The summoners had been preparing their sigils the entire journey, calling Nightborn demons the moment the sun disappeared beneath the horizon. Now I understood how Jesmine had used so many demons in her attack on the armory, what felt like a lifetime ago—she, wisely, had recruited many summoners to her army. Smart, because demons were far more expendable than people, especially in an army this woefully undermanned. I was grateful for the beasts now, disgusting as they were. We needed the bodies, and while demons weren't as smart as vampires, they were certainly just as vicious.

We didn't bother breaking down our tents, leaving them discarded in the sands, an eerily abandoned sea of debris left in our wake—looking as if thousands of people had simply disappeared into the desert.

We knew that either way, in victory or defeat, we wouldn't be coming back.

Our offensive would be a fourfold attack. Vale's allies' fleets would circle Sivrinaj from the sea, splitting the attention of Simon and Septimus's forces. Raihn would spearhead the airborne assault with Vale, bringing hundreds of Rishan and Hiaj warriors straight to the inner city. The demons and a smaller team of soldiers would approach by ground, breaking down the barricades and cutting a path to the castle, led by Ketura. And finally, Jesmine and I would lead an army into the tunnels, heading directly for the castle itself—between the two of us, we knew Vincent's secret routes through the city better than anyone.

With the sun gone, Sivrinaj had become a ghostly silver outline, ominously lit with the flaring white of Nightfire. Sivrinaj was not usually so bright, not even on festival nights. They knew we were coming, and they were preparing for us.

Fine, I thought. Let them.

The warriors fell into formation, preparing to march. Raihn and I took our positions at the front of the group, Jesmine and Vale beside us.

"I think we're ready, Highness," Jesmine said quietly, then stepped back.

The world seemed to be holding its breath, waiting expectantly. Waiting for me—for us—to lead.

Mother, what a surreal experience. It was suddenly dizzying.

I glanced at Raihn, and I could see the same thought on his face. His brow twitched as he gave me a wry smile.

"I suppose that's us, isn't it?"

"Feels like we should have an inspiring speech," I muttered.

"It does. You write anything?"

I scoffed.

"Shame," he said. "You have such a way with words."

I scowled, and he chuckled.

"Keep that face. That's better, anyway."

My eyes settled on the Sivrinaj skyline. The city that had

kept me captive all my life, now captive itself. My kingdom, ready to be liberated.

I drew Vincent's sword. As it always did, holding it filled me with a wave of cold strength that reminded me so painfully of my father's presence, its power surging through my veins all at once.

I embraced it.

Nightfire rippled up the blade, my magic meshing with his.

You have teeth too, little serpent, he whispered in my ear, and Goddess, he sounded closer than ever. *Show them that bite.*

There, in that city, waited the men who believed Raihn and I did not deserve our crowns. They took this kingdom by force, because it was all they knew how to do.

I was tired of letting people like that tell me what I could be, or what the House of Night could be.

I lifted my sword, the streak of Nightfire blinding against the night sky.

"Let's take our fucking kingdom back," I snarled.

Raihn laughed. "I thought you said you didn't have a speech."

He spread those stunning wings and tilted his face to the sky. But before he could take off, I caught his arm.

"Be careful," I blurted out, before I could stop myself. "He doesn't deserve to kill you."

Raihn's eyes remained crinkled with an easygoing smile. But his hand lingered over mine, thumb rubbing back and forth.

"Give them hell, princess," he said. "I'll see you soon."

I'll see you soon. Such casual words, and such a deep promise within them.

We released each other, and a sudden gust of wind blew my hair back as he launched into the air.

My gaze settled back on the city ahead. Our target.

Behind me, a dull roar built slowly, like distant thunder, as hundreds of winged warriors followed Raihn into the night. I could feel Jesmine's eyes on me, expectant.

I raised the Taker of Hearts, and charged.

56

RAIHN

The wind rushed around me, yanking my hair back. Beside me, Vale matched my pace, our warriors behind us, wings spread, cutting through the air. We were flying fast, headed straight for that castle, hedging our bets on how far we could get before Simon sent men out after us.

From up here, we could see the fleet in the distance, purple sails tinted blue beneath the moonlight, surrounding the coast of Sivrinaj. Distant sparks flashed through the darkness—explosives and magic hurled at the castle. Nothing that would bring down the city, but it was enough to create a distraction, splitting Simon and Septimus's valuable attention and resources.

Far below us, Ketura and her men were reduced to a single wave of destruction. The explosions of Nightfire lit up the night with blinding bursts that drenched Sivrinaj in white, as the demons tore through stone and wooden barricades to free up paths to the inner city. It was, in a way, morbidly beautiful—like a hand sweeping through sand.

It was only a matter of time, though, before the Bloodborn forces flooded the streets to meet her. With the Rishan occupying the sky, she'd be forced to take the brunt of Septimus's troops.

She was ready for it. The crashes of unbridled chaos below shifted into the cacophony of battle, distant screams and clashes of steel mingling with the explosions and demon snarls.

She was evenly matched.

But not outnumbered. Not yet.

I prayed to the Mother it stayed that way.

Vale dipped close to me. "Highness," he said, voice low and serious, and I didn't even have to turn my head to know exactly what he saw by his tone alone.

We'd been rushing toward the castle, seizing as much sky as we could before Simon's Rishan men would come to meet us. We'd made it far, now over the tall spires of the inner city— farther, honestly, than I had expected.

But the easy part had come to an end.

A wave of Rishan soldiers rose from the castle grounds like a thick plume of smoke—a rolling morass of wings and steel blotting out the stars.

My heart sank when I saw that wave of soldiers. Vale had only been able to guess at exactly how many Rishan warriors Simon had been able to accumulate. We'd hoped he was relying more on bravado and illusions than numbers.

This sight dashed those hopes. This was a real army.

Still, attacking by air meant we only had to deal with Simon's limited Rishan forces. We'd prepared for this.

I scanned the lines, looking for the man I was really after— the only one I had to kill to end this, once and for all—but I didn't see Simon anywhere in that sea of faces.

That surprised me. I was so certain he'd be at the front of the pack, ready to demonstrate his dominance. Hell, I thought he'd want to make sure he was the one to kill me himself.

My gaze lifted beyond the onslaught of incoming men, to the silver spires of the Nightborn castle rising above the bloodshed.

Or maybe he was cowering in his tower, waiting for me to come to him.

I could make that happen, too.

Simon's soldiers gained speed, whipping through the air like arrows. And we didn't slow, either, bracing to meet them head-on.

If they wanted a fight, they'd get a fight.

"Ready yourselves!" Vale bellowed, silver wings spreading beneath the moonlight, his own weapon bared.

An expanse of steel raised as our opponents charged for us, neither group slowing, neither group hesitating.

I was fucking ready.

I lifted my sword, and we dove into the wall of death.

57

ORAYA

I didn't know that the tunnels extended this far beyond the castle grounds. I knew that Vincent hadn't trusted me with everything, but sometimes, the extent of all he had withheld still threw me. He had always told me that the passages were through the castle grounds only. But Jesmine led us through a little shack on the outskirts of the city, and through a trap door in its dirty, fully furnished bedroom that led down into the tunnels.

I didn't even have time to be bothered by this now. Of course Vincent wouldn't have told me about tunnels beyond the grounds. He wanted me to stay exactly where I was, safely within the walls of his castle.

Why should I be surprised?

We moved swiftly, though the tunnels, narrow as they were, were inefficient for this number of people. We'd prepared ourselves for potential confrontation down here—we couldn't know how much of the tunnel system Septimus had discovered —but didn't encounter a soul. A stroke of luck. Any battle within these narrow passages would be a disaster.

The halls were too dark for my human eyes, but the Nightfire at my blade lit the way. I didn't consciously intend to run—but my steps grew quicker and quicker the closer we got to the heart of Sivrinaj.

Once we encroached upon the inner city, we started to hear the clashes above.

The sounds started off muffled and dull, the distant rumbles of cracking wood and crumbling stone, the sporadic blasts of explosives. Ketura's troops, traveling over the streets above us, breaking down the barriers between us and the castle with the help of the demons and the Nightfire explosives.

The sound raised goosebumps on my arms—in anticipation, not dread. This was what we were supposed to be hearing. That, at least, was the sound of progress.

Soon, those echoes grew louder as the tunnels grew wider and better lit. We were reaching the inner city, moving steadily toward our final destination.

That was when things started to change.

The noises from above were now loud enough to vibrate the walls, the worst of them sending waterfalls of dust and dirt falling from the ceiling, the Nightfire flames shivering with the impact. A knot of unease started in my stomach, though I told myself that we were expecting things to get harder as we progressed—we were prepared for this.

But when a particularly loud *BOOM* made the ground itself lurch, sending both Jesmine and I stumbling against the walls, we exchanged a wary glance.

Jesmine walked faster, shouting urgent commands to those that followed us, but my steps faltered.

It wasn't the sound, exactly, that did it. It was something deeper, something in the air itself, that I couldn't put a name to. It buried under my skin, more persistent than the anxiety of battle. A force pulsing against my magic. A toxic smoke clinging to the inside of my lungs.

It was silent, it was invisible, and it was everywhere.

Fifty years ago, a volcano on one of the Nightborn islands erupted, killing every living thing on it—every living thing except for the birds, which all disappeared six hours before, flying off in one sky-darkening flock.

Was this, I wondered, what the birds had felt like that day?

I doubled my pace, catching up to Jesmine, then overtaking her. She shot me a look that had me wondering if she'd felt what I did, too. I'd never seen her show anything close to fear. And still, this wasn't fear—not quite—but it was close enough to be almost as unnerving.

"Did you—" she started, but I cut her off.

"We need to get up there." The words flew from my lips before I knew exactly how true they were. "We need to get up there, *now*."

58

RAIHN

I'd lost track of just how many men I'd killed. I was in the Kejari all over again, thrown into senseless, indiscriminate, unending violence.

Maybe I wasn't any better than Neculai, or Vincent, or Simon after all. Maybe I was just another cursed king.

Because I fucking loved it.

I barely felt the scream of my muscles or the bite of my wounds. Something more primal took over. Rational thought disappeared. My magic surged in my veins, grateful for the opportunity to finally be set free, fully unleashed—and this was what it wanted to do. *Kill. Reclaim. Possess.*

I wasn't relying on sight anymore, and that was a gift, because I couldn't see anything even if I'd tried. Through the smears of black blood in my eyes, my field of vision became nothing but fragmented flashes of wings and weapons and steel buried in bodies. The blinding black-white of my Asteris followed my every stroke. Defeated enemies hurtled to the ground like limp rag dolls, falling onto the roofs of the buildings below.

Time, physicality, space ceased to exist. I thought about

nothing but the next strike, the next kill, the next inch of ground I could gain toward that castle—*my* castle.

Until *him*.

The shift was immediate, so strong it actually managed to knock me from my bloodlust—so strong it made my muscles freeze at the most inopportune moment, interrupting my counter against the Rishan soldier attacking me and earning me a vicious cut over my shoulder.

I grabbed the soldier, skewered him, and let him fall to the ground, but I wasn't looking at him anymore. Instead, my gaze flicked up.

Up to the castle.

Simon was there, standing on the very same balcony where he had tried to kill me. Even through the carnage, through the endless bodies, I knew he was there. I knew it because I *felt* him, the way one felt ripples in a pond when something terrible circled beneath the water.

And this *was* something terrible.

I had never sensed anything like this before, but that certainty ground into my bones immediately. I'd awakened something primal in myself, and now, that beast was recognizing a threat—a threat that did not belong, here or anywhere else.

What was that?

I was too far gone to be afraid. I'd spent too damned long fearing Simon and the people like him, even if I refused to admit it to myself or anyone else.

I was pushing through the warriors before Vale even had the chance to call after me. Cutting through bodies, wings, weapons —anything standing between me and him.

I was going to fucking kill him.

He stood on the balcony waiting for me, amber wings spread, sword drawn, hair pulled back tight in a way that emphasized the hard, cruel planes of his face.

I didn't slow down as I flew for him. Instead, I pumped my wings, surging faster, so fast I couldn't see anything but his slow, predatory smile, split seconds before we clashed.

We met in a deafening thunderclap of steel and a burst of magic, my Asteris dousing us in a mantle of black light. Our bodies slammed against each other. His sword met mine, metal screaming against metal.

Immediately, he countered. He was a strong warrior, even after all these years. Despite his age, he met me strike for strike, step for step. Even my magic didn't seem to deter him, even though, spurred by hatred, it poured from every stroke of my blade, punctuating each clash.

I was wounded. I was tired. My body didn't care.

I was going to kill him.

Through the red of my rage and the black of my Asteris, Simon's face looked so uncannily like his cousin's. It was my former master who sneered at me in the seconds between strikes and blocks, taunting me, urging me on.

How many times, back then, had I imagined what it would be like to kill Neculai?

Countless. Seventy years. Twenty-five thousand days to lie there in bed and close my eyes and think about what he might sound like with blood filling his lungs, think about what it might look like to peel his skin back inch by inch, think about whether he'd piss himself in his final moments.

I'd thought about it so many times.

I wasn't the one who had gotten that satisfaction in the end. That had gone to another cruel king. I'd told myself I was alright with that. Let them tear each other apart.

I had been lying to myself.

I had wanted to be the one to do it.

And now, this seemed almost as good.

The first time I struck skin, opening a river of red-black across his arm, I actually fucking laughed—loud and crazed.

That one drop of blood awakened something in me. My next blow was harder, faster, blade seeking out his flesh like a starving animal. When he managed to get in a return strike, I barely felt it, instead using the force of his hit against him.

I was so lost in my own frenzy that it took me far too long to notice exactly what was so off about him. To notice that Simon didn't seem concerned at all, even though I'd wounded him. Not even when I struck him again, sending him staggering back.

I pushed him against the wall, licks of night rolling from my sword, the smell of his blood thick in my nostrils.

This was it.

I wanted to look into his eyes when he died. Wanted that satisfaction.

I wanted to see the fear on his face when he realized that the slave he had abused two hundred years ago was going to be the one to kill him.

But when I met Simon's eyes, I didn't see fear. I didn't see much of anything, actually. They were vacant and bloodshot, glazed over, like he was looking *through* me instead of at me, at something a million miles past the horizon.

A sour drone thrummed in the air, nagging at my magic, burrowing deep into my veins.

I hesitated. And finally, I heard the voice in my head—the one that insisted, *This isn't right.*

My eyes flicked up for a moment, catching movement through the glass window over Simon's muscled, armored shoulder.

Septimus stood in the middle of the empty ballroom, enjoying the view through those floor-to-ceiling windows, utterly calm. He smiled at me, a lazy trail of cigarillo smoke rising between his teeth.

This isn't right.

Simon wasn't moving, even though I had him pinned. The pulse in the air grew thicker, louder. The unnatural ripples that called to my magic seemed to pull tighter, like lungs inflating in an inhale, drawing me closer.

I actually took in Simon's appearance for the first time since I saw him, my head clearing.

He wore old, classic Rishan battle leathers. Finely made stuff. But oddly enough, he'd left the top unbuttoned down to his chest, revealing a long triangle of skin.

Skin marked with black, pulsing veins.

And all those veins led to a chunk of silver and ivory, buried right into the flesh of his chest.

It was so grotesque, so unnervingly *wrong*, that at first, I couldn't make sense of what I was looking at.

And then I recognized it:

The silver was Vincent's pendant, smashed and melted and warped, smeared with Simon's blood.

And the ivory was...

Teeth.

Teeth, welded into the metal.

The memory of Septimus's voice floated through my mind:

I found some, in the House of Blood. Teeth.

What the fuck does one do with the teeth of the God of Death? Oraya had asked.

And in a sudden moment of clarity, I realized: *This* was what someone did with god teeth.

They created a fucking monster.

This thought crossed my mind only briefly, as Simon's face finally broke into a chilling, blood-lined smile, and he unleashed a burst of magic that rearranged the entire Goddess-damned world.

59

ORAYA

I was running.

Running through those tunnels, even though I'd outpaced Jesmine, even though I didn't even know exactly where I was going—only that I was going up, and out, as fast as I possibly fucking could.

We were, thankfully, close to the end. I practically wept with joy when I saw the stairs before me. I dove up them, flinging open the door at the other side—taking only seconds to evaluate where I was, at the foot of the castle. Mother, it was chaos out here, flinging me into a sea of blood and steel and death, Bloodborn and Rishan and Hiaj and demons all ripping each other apart.

I barely paid attention to it.

Instead, I looked up—up to the top of the castle, to the balcony where I had saved Raihn's life not long ago. I couldn't see anything from this angle, but I could feel it, the epicenter of this noxious sensation.

My wings were out and I was in the air before I could question myself.

I'd never flown so fast before. Faster than I even knew I was capable of.

I rose to the balcony, only to immediately be knocked back by—

What *was* that?

It was like Asteris, maybe, but stronger—red, not black. It seemed to rip apart the air itself and reorder it. It lasted for only a moment—at least, I thought it did—but when I regained awareness, my wings weren't working, and I was falling.

With a gasp of air, I righted myself, pumping my wings just in time to avoid hurling myself into a pillar.

I soared back up to the balcony.

Raihn. Raihn, locked in a battle with—Mother, was that *Simon?* He looked so different—not just because of his armor, a stark contrast from the fineries I'd seen on him before, or even because of the whorls of red magic that surrounded him. He *felt* different, like he'd been pushed beyond some boundary that no mortal should cross. Like a part of him no longer even existed anymore.

Every shred of my awareness balked at his presence.

And that instinct reacted viciously at the sight of Simon leaning over Raihn, sword raised, eerie red mist clinging to the blade.

I didn't remember landing, or running, or lunging. Only the satisfying spurt of blood that sprayed across my face as the Taker of Hearts found its mark, skewering through Simon's back, right between his wings.

A deadly shot for anyone, human or vampire.

But Simon, I realized immediately, was not *just* a vampire right now.

He let out a snarl and reared back, dropping Raihn and whirling to me as I yanked my sword from his flesh and danced backward. When his bloodshot eyes fell to me, vacant and vicious, I felt like I was looking into the face of death itself.

And then I saw it:

The... *thing* fused into the skin of his chest. Metal and... bone?

My magic reacted to its proximity. Suddenly, Vincent's presence seemed so much closer—but twisted, enraged.

Twisted, just like the pendant had been twisted, shattered. Melded with...

Teeth?

God teeth, I realized.

Fucking Septimus.

It seemed outlandish. It seemed ridiculous. The horror of it fell over me distantly. I didn't have time to let myself acknowledge it.

He lifted his sword, but before he could bring it down, I lunged at him.

He responded immediately, our blades meeting, each clash more vicious than the last. He was bigger, stronger; I was faster. Still, he kept pace. My body crumpled beneath his blows and the force it required to deflect them. It took all my focus—but I remained perpetually aware of Raihn out of the corner of my eye, crumpled on the ground. When he slowly pushed himself up, I breathed a sigh of relief.

For a split second, before Simon was on me again.

My muscles screamed. His magic rivaled mine, even as my Nightfire poured from my skin, surrounding us. The burns didn't seem to bother him, not even when the flames ate away at the delicate flesh around his mouth and eyes. He just stared through them, and smiled.

An empty smile. A dead smile.

I couldn't remember when his first hit was—my side, perhaps, making me stumble just enough to make it difficult to evade his next lunge. When I looked up again to see his sword raised, I thought, *This is it. The end.*

Just as a streak of black-red came hurling in from his left side, sword drawn.

Raihn threw himself at Simon, the two of them tangling in a dance of destruction.

I hadn't been able to hear anything over the violence and my own breath and heartbeat throbbing in my ears. But as I steadied myself, I chanced a glance down below—to the city of Sivrinaj.

It was a bloodbath.

Our opponents had been holding back. Now the full numbers of Bloodborn forces poured from the castle grounds, seeping through the city streets like a wave of fire. Ketura's men had been beaten back, the squeals of dying demons drowning beneath the screams of dying vampires. Jesmine's forces had risen from the tunnels, only to be met with a formidable force that was expecting them, and far outnumbered them.

And Simon—and whatever terrible, twisted magic he wielded— hadn't even made it down there, yet.

We were fucked.

We were utterly fucked.

We needed to retreat. We needed to retreat *now*.

Raihn had seen what I did, or maybe the dawning horror on my face told him everything he needed to know.

When I launched myself back at Simon, he rasped out, "Go."

The one word he could choke out.

I knew what he meant: *Go to the armies. Go lead them away.*

I didn't even consider it.

We had only one shot at salvaging this, and that was by killing Simon here and now. I wasn't going to run away. I wasn't going to leave this man here to keep my throne and this twisted power he'd gotten from my father's magic.

I'd had enough. My entire life, these people thought they could take everything from me.

And the thought of ceding one more single second to them enraged me.

My heartbeat throbbed in my ears, hot beneath my skin.

This is my kingdom, Vincent whispered, the words pulsing through my skin, my veins, my heart. *This is my castle. Do not let anyone take it from me.*

Mine, my heartbeat echoed.

This was mine.

I would not let anyone take it away. And I sure as fuck wasn't going to let them kill Raihn to do it.

Raihn whirled around as more Rishan soldiers ran from the castle doors, surging for him—distracting him in this critical moment.

Not me. I barely noticed them.

I let my rage blind me, drive me, drown me as I threw myself at Simon.

My awareness narrowed to the satisfying sensation of my blade parting Simon's flesh, the Nightfire swelling and overtaking my body, my magic flourishing in the depths of my uncontrollable rage.

Simon actually flinched, his body lurching.

Someone laughed and it took a few seconds to realize that it had been me. My cheeks split with a smile as he straightened and faced me, all that terrible power focused only in one spot.

I wasn't afraid.

We lunged at the same time, our weapons meeting again, each blow unrelenting. At first, I was lost in the intoxicating haze of vengeance, and I loved it, each wound a shot of alcohol, an unnatural high.

But Simon didn't let up.

Raihn, surrounded by Rishan soldiers, was not coming to help me.

And Simon just kept coming, and coming, and coming.

The first little nagging shard of fear came when he struck me so hard I thought I felt something crack when I blocked his weapon. The pain shot through me in a lightning bolt, stealing my breath.

No time to recover, though. No time to counter.

Because the onslaught continued, that one devastating strike turning to two, three. Soon I couldn't do more than evade, block, stumble backwards to get my footing—

But I'd been knocked off balance. And I had no time to regain it.

The realization that I was fucked was slow and certain.

He opened a wound on my shoulder, my arm, my hip. Each one came with a breathtaking stab of pain, deeper than flesh. His magic, that red, noxious smoke, surrounded us both. The twisted creation in his chest pulsed unnaturally.

I could feel Vincent's cold rage, his need for dominance, thrashing inside me, but it had nowhere to go. The magic of the Taker of Hearts was powerful, but it wasn't as strong as whatever Simon had done to himself.

I leapt backward in a dodge and found myself against the balcony railing. *Fuck.* Nowhere left to go.

A hot breeze surged, blowing my hair back and yanking strands of Simon's from its binding, making him look even more monstrous as he loomed over me, a bloody smile spreading over his lips.

Behind him, Raihn's eyes locked onto me, as he cut through one Rishan soldier, two —

He wouldn't be fast enough.

Mother, I was going to die.

But, oh, what a death it will be.

I wondered if it was Vincent's voice, or mine.

Simon reached out and touched my face, turning it toward his, as if in curiosity.

His smile soured.

"Just a human," he said. "That's all."

A fighter's death, I promised myself, as Simon raised his sword, and I raised mine.

His strike was devastating.

A burst of magic blinded me. A deafening crack left my ears ringing. Something sharp flew back against me, opening little cuts in my cheeks, my arms.

I barely felt them, because the pain was everywhere.

Simon had staggered backwards, doubled over, but it was too late.

I was falling, too. My body went over the railing in what felt like slow motion. The last thing I saw was Raihn, his eyes wide and terrified, as he yanked his sword from a body and ran for me —

He looked so, so scared.

I reached for him, but I was already falling.

Worlds blended together in my weightlessness.

In one world, I couldn't hear anything over the sound of screams and explosions and desperate commands.

In another, I could hear nothing but my father's voice from an old memory. Could feel nothing but his grip, so firm it hurt — but then again, that was Vincent's love, hidden in sharp edges and always just as painful.

I told you not to climb that high, he said, voice harsh. *How many times have I told you, you can't do that?*

I know, I wanted to say. *I'm sorry. You were right.*

"Oraya!"

Raihn's scream cleaved through the air, even through the sounds of a kingdom falling. I forced my eyes open to see smears of blurring color.

He was diving down after me, wings spread, covered in blood, a single hand reaching out for me.

Something about this image looked so familiar, and then it clicked — the painting of the Rishan man falling, one hand outstretched. I'd always thought he was reaching for the gods.

He was reaching for me.

Everything went black.

60

RAIHN

etreat.

I flew over the battlefield, a sea of carnage, Oraya's limp body in my arms. She was covered in so much blood I couldn't even tell where she was injured, only that whatever Simon had done to her had been devastating.

She wasn't dead.

She couldn't be dead.

I could feel her heartbeat, slow and weak. I refused to accept the possibility that it would stop. That was not an option.

She was not dead.

I knew Simon was not far behind me, launching himself down into the fighting. And I knew—I knew the minute he landed, it would be over for all of us.

Retreat.

I found Vale in the midst of the bloodshed, hacking apart a Rishan rebel who plunged from the sky. I didn't recognize my own voice when I screamed his name. He turned and took in Oraya and I in less than a second, his brow immediately contorting in grim dread.

Then his eyes lifted over my shoulder and widened.

Simon.

I just choked out, "Retreat. *Now*. Get as many out as you can."

And I didn't stop flying.

I needed somewhere safe. Somewhere close. Somewhere secret. Somewhere no one would think to look for her. Somewhere she could get help now, *right now*, because I wasn't about to let her die in my arms after everything we had been through together.

Couldn't go back to the camp—no one could help her there, not fast enough.

Couldn't get back to the rendezvous point in time.

Couldn't go anywhere in Sivrinaj, where Simon and Septimus would be looking for her.

My thoughts did not make sense. I didn't know how or why I chose our destination. It wasn't a conscious choice. Just the memory of a name and a place scribbled on a twenty-five-year-old letter, and blind hope, and sheer fucking desperation.

Some distant part of my subconscious made the decision without me, while I could think about nothing but Oraya in my arms, and her limp body, and her heartbeat—growing steadily slower, weaker.

Vartana was not far from Sivrinaj, just a few cities over. It was a small town, barely noticeable from above—the kind of place you only went to if you had a reason. I half-surprised myself when I landed, clumsily, in the dusty streets of the human districts.

They had to help her. They had to.

I was in the town square. It was quiet here after nightfall. I barely glanced at my surroundings—the brick buildings, the packed-dirt streets, the fountain well at the center of the square. A young couple was perched at its edge, probably interrupted from some midnight tryst, staring at me in wide-eyed shock.

I was only distantly aware of what I must've looked like, landing in front of them, clutching Oraya's bleeding body. Wild-eyed, enormous, covered in blood.

The man pushed the woman behind him slightly, the two of them staggering back.

I just choked, "Help. I need help."

The name. Fuck, what was the name?

"Alya," I blurted out. "Alya. There's someone here by that name. A healer. Or there used to be—"

I couldn't even string a Goddess-damned sentence together.

What was I doing? What kind of wild guess was this? Twenty years was a long time. Who knew if they were even still—

Oraya's breath stuttered, slowed, and my panic overwhelmed me.

"*Tell me,*" I ground out, taking a step closer. The woman nearly threw herself into the fountain trying to get away from me, the man grabbing her arm and sliding fully in front of her.

They were terrified. And I couldn't even blame them for that. Or at least I wouldn't have, if I could even think, could even breathe, could even consider anything but—

"I'm Alya."

A voice came from behind me. I whirled around to see a middle-aged woman standing in a townhouse doorway, eyeing me warily. She had waist-length black, gray-streaked hair, and a serious, lined face.

I drew in a shaky breath and let it out. "I need—I'm—"

"I know who you are." Her gaze fell to Oraya, and her face softened. "I know who she is, too."

My exhale of relief was almost a sob.

"Can you—"

"Come in," she said, stepping aside. "Quick. And stop yelling before you alert half the district."

PART SIX

FULL MOON

INTERLUDE

It's not that hard to topple a kingdom.

It is already poised to collapse. And a slave is the perfect person to knock out those final remaining supports—privy to the most intimate parts of the castle and yet utterly invisible. The slave marvels at the fact that it had never even occurred to him to do this sooner. It's so easy. So well deserved. So much more elegant than the blade driven through his master's chest that he always had dreamed of.

He passes information to that promising Hiaj contestant throughout all four months of the Kejari. He feeds him guard schedules, castle layouts, fortification weak points. He watches the measures that his king takes to protect himself as the days pass and his paranoia grows stronger, and he feeds those along to the Hiaj contestant, too.

He is careful. He never reveals his face. He never reveals his name. He never whispers a word of it to anyone, not even the queen in their secret daylight meetings. The knife he drives into his captor's back is so slow and silent, he doesn't even feel it at all.

Weeks pass, months. The Hiaj contestant, as everyone knew he would be, is victorious again and again. The king grows more cruel, vicious in his fear. The slave's hatred becomes a quiet obsession.

And then, at last, the night has come.

The final night of the Kejari. The night the future king and the slave alike will offer up their final, devastating blows. The Hiaj contestant's will come in the form of a blood-soaked victory and a wish from a goddess. The slave's will come in the form of a letter overflowing with secrets, passed off in exchange for the guaranteed safety of those closest to him.

It is eerily quiet in the moments before the world changes. The sunset is still and stagnant. The slave has made his final move. Now all that is left to do is wait.

And in those quiet moments, he finally tells the queen. They had spent the evening hours together, her head against his chest, his hand rubbing her shoulder as he stared sleeplessly at the ceiling, thinking of all the ways everything will soon change.

He wakes her gently as the sun slips below the horizon, only an hour remaining until the kingdom collapses.

The words pour from his lips. He feels like he is offering her a precious gift that he has been saving for a very long time. And then, finally, he intertwines her fingers with his.

"We'll need to leave tonight," he tells her. "Right after the Kejari ends. He'll be distracted, if he's even still alive by then. We can get out of Sivrinaj before the worst begins."

He expects joy. Instead, she is horrified. She shakes her head.

"You have to undo it," she says. "This can't happen."

He doesn't know what to say for several long seconds.

"It's already done," he tells her. "It's already over."

Her face crumples, like she knew he would say this, but the truth still hurts just as much.

"I can't," she says. "I can't go with you. I need to stay here."

His heart sinks.

He spends those final minutes of their old life begging her — begging her *— to leave with him.*

And right up until the end, right up until she is prying her hands out of his, she refuses.

They have no more time. The final trial is about to begin. And at last, she grabs his face and kisses him fiercely.

"You go," she whispers. "But I cannot leave him. Not now."

For centuries, the slave would think about this moment. Why? Why would she choose to die in her cage rather than find freedom?

Everything within him rebels against the thought of leaving her. But he has worked for this for too long. As he sits behind his master in the colosseum stands for that final trial, he stares at the back of the queen's head and imagines carrying her out over his shoulder when he goes.

He is not watching the battle. But he knows when it is over by the scream of the spectators, deafening, bloodthirsty. The sky shifts, fragments of unnatural light circling above. The air holds its breath, anticipating the impending arrival of a goddess.

The king rises, his eyes locked to the sky.

But while everyone else is staring to the heavens, the queen simply looks over her shoulder at the slave. Her lips form a single, silent word: Go.

And he does.

He TRAVELS ON FOOT FIRST, *favoring stealth over speed. He has no possessions, and very little money. He has nowhere to go, other than "anywhere but here."*

He hears it echo through the air when the Hiaj victor takes his prize. The screams and cheers pierce the night, as if the House of Night is a single dying beast letting out a final roar.

Don't look back, *he tells himself.* It doesn't matter.

Yet for some reason, he still does.

He's at the outskirts of the city by then, wings outstretched, ready to take to the sky to make his final escape. The urge is sudden and overpowering — like a set of ghostly hands pulling him back.

He turns.

The colosseum is alight, bright and throbbing like an infected wound, ready to burst.

His gaze lingers there, but then rises — rises to the stars, where the strange shimmering light of the gods still hovers—and he suddenly cannot move.

Nyaxia is far away, floating up in the heavens as if observing the amusing consequences of her latest gift.

But one can always feel a god's eyes. And Nyaxia looks directly at him that night. He can feel her stare like a blessing, a curse, an iron stake nailing him to a destiny he does not want.

And she smiles—a cruel, beautiful, devastating sight.

He tries to tell himself that he does not sense what changes in this moment. He tries to tell himself that he imagines the dizzying, disorienting burst of power through his veins. He tries to tell himself that the sudden shock of pain up his spine is a figment of his anxiety.

But the truth is the truth.

This is the moment when the slave becomes a king.

He turns away from the Goddess, flying off into the night. Later, safely holed up in a little village where no one would ever think to look for him, he will stare in shock at the red ink on his back. He will pay some starving beggar without a tongue all the money he has to help burn his back, burn it so brutally he nearly kills himself, until the scars are so bad, they swallow the Mark.

He is no king, he tells himself. He is no Heir. He is just a free man, for the first time in nearly a century.

But just because one tells themselves something, understand, that does not make it true.

This is only the first night of thousands the Turned king will spend lying to himself.

It will be two hundred years before he would accept the truth.

61

ORAYA

I opened my eyes.

Some innate part of me expected to see the cerulean of my chamber's ceiling at the castle. Smell the familiar scent of rose and incense.

But no. The ceiling was old, haphazard wooden boards. The room smelled like lavender and the burnt wood of a fireplace.

So unfamiliar, and yet... so recognizable, in a way I couldn't place. Like the scent called to a version of myself I'd long ago forgotten.

I turned my head and was greeted with a wave of truly agonizing pain.

But—I was alive.

I was actually *alive*.

As pieces of the battle came back to me—Simon's monstrous face leaning over me—that seemed like a fucking miracle.

My eyes focused. I was in a tiny bedroom, lying in an old, beaten-down bed, covered with a quilt that was obviously home-made. Before me was a closed, slightly crooked wooden door, with a little wooden chair sitting beside it.

And in that chair—that tiny, rickety chair, comically over-flowing it—was Raihn.

He snored slightly, his head tipped back against the wall, skewed at a painful-looking angle. His arms were crossed over his chest. He wore plain cotton clothes that looked within one sneeze of bursting open at the seams. Dark, dried bloodstains marred the cream fabric, and his forearms were wound in tight bandages.

My eyes prickled. I stared at him, the image growing slowly blurry. My chest was so tight. I didn't think it had anything to do with my injuries.

I sniffed, and Raihn had been sleeping so lightly that that sound was enough to send him jerking awake with comical verve, nearly throwing himself off the chair as he reached for the sword that wasn't there.

I couldn't help it. I laughed. The sound was horrible—a gasping rasp.

Raihn barely managed to right himself. Then his gaze fell to me.

He went utterly still.

And then, with a single swift movement, he was on his knees beside my bed, hands cradling my face like he wanted to make sure I was real.

You're alive, I wanted to say, but all I could choke out was, "Did I scare you?"

I was smiling, laughing a little, though the sound was almost a sob. And soon Raihn was laughing too, and he kissed my face—my forehead, my brows, my nose, and finally, my mouth, leaving the taste of tears on my lips.

"Don't you ever do that to me again," he said. "Never fucking again."

The door opened.

A woman stood in the frame, holding a mortar and pestle in one hand, like she'd rushed over so fast she hadn't even had the time to put down what she was doing.

"I heard—"

But then her eyes found mine, and the words died.

I couldn't speak either. Nor could I look away. Because Goddess, she looked so *familiar*—so familiar that everything else fell away. Those green eyes reminded me so much of someone I used to know.

She let out a long breath.

"You're awake," she said, at the same time that I said, "I know you."

Those eyes crinkled with a sad smile.

"I didn't think you would remember me."

I didn't know if I did *remember* her, exactly. It was more like... recognizing an innate familiarity.

"I... you're..."

My words trailed off. I wasn't sure what I was trying to say, or how to name what I was feeling.

She stepped into the room and closed the door behind her.

"I'm Alya," she said. "I'm your aunt."

ALYA, brusque and businesslike, insisted upon examining me before we talked about anything more. So while she checked my pulse and re-dressed my bandages, Raihn answered all the questions he already knew I would ask.

We hadn't been here long, he told me, only a day. The others had retreated to the rendezvous point outside of Sivrinaj, in one of the cities that the Hiaj had managed to maintain control of, but it was just a matter of time until Simon would go after them there. They were licking their wounds, too, and would fall back farther to the cliffs when given the command.

The battle, in short, had been a fucking disaster.

Yes, we'd managed to destroy most of the defensive measures around Sivrinaj, and if nothing else, we'd managed to kill a large number of Simon's forces. But he'd killed plenty of ours, too.

And what Septimus had done to Simon… the pendant, the *teeth*…

Mother, had I imagined that? It felt like a dream. A Goddess-damned nightmare.

Where the hell did we go from here?

"We have to go back," I said.

"Not until you can travel," he said.

"I feel —"

Fine.

Shockingly enough, I actually *did* feel fine. Dizzy, yes. Weak. But… miraculously healed, all things considered. Alya was behind me, administering medicine to a wound on my back. It hurt, making me draw in a hiss through my teeth.

But pain was manageable.

Pain wasn't death.

I looked down at my arms, where I knew I'd been wounded badly. Only faint red marks remained, scabbing over with dark red.

Raihn followed my gaze, a faint smile twisting his lips. "It turns out your aunt is a hell of a healer."

"We had some help," she added. "From his blood."

Everyone was speaking as if this was all very normal. But the normalcy of it was the most confusing of all.

Aunt. Goddess help me. I didn't even know where to start.

"How did you know to bring me here?" I asked Raihn.

His smile faded — like he was slipping back into that memory.

"Honestly?" he said. "I don't have a damned clue. I knew the name from your mother's letters, and the city. I knew whoever had written them was a healer. And I was — I was desperate. I didn't know where to go. Not sure why I ended up here."

Behind me, Alya let out a low laugh. "Fate," she said. "It's beyond mortal understanding."

I wasn't sure if she was joking or not. She had a flat affectation that sounded like it could be either blunt seriousness or dry humor. Still… either way, I couldn't help but agree with her.

She lifted my left arm, checking a bandage around my shoulder. "You're lucky he thought to bring you here," she said. "Nyaxia's magic wouldn't have been able to help you nearly as well."

"What magic is this?" I asked.

"Acaeja's. Vampire magic alone wouldn't have been able to save you."

Alya let my arm fall and stood, repositioning herself at the foot of the bed so I could see her. She had a steady, piercing gaze. I didn't like it. It felt like she could see far too much of me.

That stare slid away, like it made her uncomfortable, too. "Never thought some twenty-five-year-old letters from my sister would lead us here. I'll tell you that much."

Vincent's lies had shattered my belief in fate. But the fact that Raihn had found those letters, this name, this place—the fact that he'd thought to bring me here, of all places, when in his panic—

It felt something like it.

Raihn looked a little pale. I wondered if he was having the same thoughts, about luck and all the ways ours could have been different. I touched his hand without thinking, sliding over his rough skin. He flipped his palm up, fingers closing loosely around mine.

My eyes fell to the bedspread, and Alya's weathered, bony hands sitting atop it. The sight struck me with another dizzying wave of familiarity.

Those hands.

I remembered holding those hands, long ago.

Yours are so much more wrinkly than mama's.

That's not very polite, Oraya.

"I lived with you," I blurted out.

Alya's brow twitched. Only the faintest hint of surprise. "I didn't think you would remember that. You were very, very young." She looked around the little bedroom. "You were born here, actually. In this room. That... that was a hard day. Wasn't sure if either of you would make it. I was doing everything I could to heal you both, but..."

She blinked, as if clearing away the past. "I haven't felt that way in a long, long time. Not until he showed up yesterday. Brings back... a lot of memories."

Goddess, I never thought I would ever have someone look at me the way she was now. With the nostalgic affection of a shared past.

I had so many questions. "How did—why—" And then, finally, "My mother..."

My voice trailed off. I didn't even know what I wanted to know first.

Everything. Anything.

A smile softened the hard lines of Alya's mouth. "She was wonderful. And she was obnoxious."

"She was an acolyte of Acaeja, too."

I didn't know why I was so eager to say that—to demonstrate that I knew something about her.

"Yes. It was her idea, actually. We were both young, growing up here, in the human districts of Vartana. And this life is a hard one, for humans in Obitraes. Vartana isn't as bad as Sivrinaj or Salinae, but there are limits to what a human can do with their lives in this kingdom. Alana never accepted that, though. She was ambitious. A dangerous quality for someone in her position. She was blessed with a touch for magic, and rather than pursuing the arts of Nyaxia, knowing she could never be more than passable at it, she decided to go in a different direction."

"Acaeja," I said, and Alya nodded.

"Yes. The only other god that would allow their gifts to be used by someone in Obitraes, even a human. But it was about more than that for Alana. She liked that Acaeja was the Goddess of Lost Things. She felt like we were all lost. Needed someone to guide us back. Eventually, I came to believe it, too, and studied alongside her."

Without meaning to, I'd started leaning across the bed, as if to get close enough to absorb the words into my skin. With each one, I painted color into that old ink portrait of my mother.

"So my mother was... a healer?" I asked.

"No, I was always the better healer. She didn't have the patience for it. Besides, I think it was too small for her. She wanted something big. Something *grand*. She experimented with sorcery, with seering." Alya laughed a little. "I always used to be after her for choosing the most useless skills to focus on. She told me they'd be useful one day, just wait."

Then the smile went cold. "I suppose that turned out to be true. When word got around that Vincent was looking for seers."

She said Vincent's name like a curse, something dirty to be expelled.

My eagerness snuffed out like a candle, leaving behind only dread.

So many things I needed to know.

So many things I did not want to hear.

"No one could stop her," Alya went on. "She wanted something more than this place, this life. So she went to Sivrinaj and offered herself up to him. She told us this was her chance at becoming something important. Money. Safety. Not just for her, she said, but for all of us." She shook her head. "I begged her not to go," she murmured. "But there was no reasoning with her."

I clasped my hands together, knuckles white. My body had gone rigid, like I was bracing for a blow. Maybe Raihn sensed this, because he put his hand on my back, and Mother, I was so grateful for that single steadying touch.

I had cursed Vincent in my own head countless times. Screamed into my pillow in rage and hurt over the things he had done to me, the lies he had told me.

And yet, he was still my father. I loved him. I missed him. I treasured what little pieces of goodness I had left in my memories of him. I didn't want to sacrifice them to what Alya was about to tell me.

But I wanted the truth more.

"What happened?" I whispered.

Alya laughed softly. "What happened? She fell in love. That's what happened. She was a pretty young woman with big dreams who had grown up in poverty. He was a handsome vampire king who made her feel—" She hesitated here, looking for the right word. "He gave her something she'd never had before. He gave her a *purpose*. Of course she fell in love with him. How could she not?"

I let out a shaky breath.

"What did he want her for?" I asked. "What were they working on together?"

"I didn't know at the time. I only got pieces, sometimes, when she would write to me for advice. I gathered she was trying to restore something that had been lost, or perhaps create something new. Something very powerful. But she was extremely secretive." Alya's eyes flicked to Raihn. "But now, after hearing about Vincent's supposed experimentations... I suspect she was helping him harness this god blood."

I blinked in surprise, then glanced at Raihn, who shrugged.

"We got to talking," he said. "While you were out."

"I didn't pry too much about it at the time," Alya said. "I didn't care about the machinations of a vampire king. I cared about my sister. She lived with him for years. And at first... she seemed happy. That was all that mattered to me. She came here with him, once."

My brows leapt.

Now that—*that* was beyond the wildest bounds of my imagination. Vincent, *here?* In a shack in the human district of a little town that barely made it onto maps?

Alya laughed bitterly. "I made that face, too, when he showed up at our door. And it was—Weaver, it was a *strange* visit."

"What was he like, back then?"

I couldn't help but ask. Couldn't stop myself.

She thought for a moment before answering. "I had suspected for a long time what was happening between them. But that night was when I was certain. She looked at him like he was the sun. And he looked at her like she was the moon."

My heart clenched at this—at the thought that maybe they had actually loved each other.

Why did it make me so happy, to believe that?

But Alya's face darkened. "But he looked at *us* like we were nothing. He looked at our life like it was repulsive. And that's when I knew. Maybe he loved her in a way. But he could never love her for what she really was. Loving everything in her but her humanity wasn't loving her at all. Even if he wished it was. Even if he wanted it with all his being."

My heart clenched. Her words slid straight through the weakest spots of the armor that I'd been nursing for months — hell, years.

Alya saw the pain on my face.

"Vincent was a complicated man," she murmured. "He was lonely. I think perhaps a part of him genuinely wanted to love her. But he had been alive for a very long time in a very cruel world. He had turned himself into something incapable of such a love in order to survive it."

"So what changed?" I choked out. "How did she leave?"

"She left," Alya said softly, "because of you."

A suspicion that hurt to hear confirmed.

"We had been hearing from her less and less over those last couple of years. I thought she was just preoccupied with her new, exciting life. But then, one day, she turned up at my doorstep and told me she was pregnant. She told me she left Vincent, and she wasn't going back."

Alya let out a shaky breath. "I was terrified. I thought, 'Weaver help us, she's about to lead an enraged vampire king to our doorstep, and he's going to kill us all.' But she said he wouldn't come after her, and... he didn't."

My brow furrowed. "He didn't?"

Even in my best possible memories of my father, he was never good at letting go of what he considered his.

"Months passed. And then years. And he never came."

This baffled me. "Why?"

"That, I can't answer. Like I said, maybe he wanted to love her. Maybe he was trying his best. For a while."

For a while.

Those words hung in the air for several long seconds. Alya's gaze lingered at the wall behind me, as if this next part was too painful to let me see in her eyes.

"When she met Alcolm, and they got married... That's when she started to get scared. For us. For you. For Alcolm. He had family in Salinae. She thought it would be safer there, in Rishan territory. Farther from Vincent's reach and eyes."

Alcolm. I remembered that name too, faintly—remembered it called affectionately between rooms in a too-small cottage. I remembered big, rough hands and an embrace that smelled like fresh chopped wood.

"I thought he was my father," I said.

"You thought he was your father because he became your father. He treated you just as he treated Jona and Leesan. You were all his children." A sad smile found her lips. "He was a good man."

Was.

Because all these people were dead now. Murdered, in an explosion that ripped our house apart.

"When I received that letter," Alya whispered, "it was the worst night of my life."

I remembered the wings blotting out the sky.

I remembered my mother trying to get me away from the windows—

I had thought it was the night I was saved. The night fate, and only fate, had brought me into Vincent's arms.

"Did he go there for me?" I asked.

I didn't want to know the answer.

Alya was silent for a long moment. "I can only speculate. I think he went to Salinae to destroy his enemies. But I think he went to that house, that night, for you. Maybe he tried for a long time to let her go. But when the wars started, and his enemies were at his throat, his true nature returned. He couldn't bring himself to leave his back exposed."

I couldn't breathe.

Did you kill them for me, Vincent?

Vincent, of course, was silent. He could never answer the hard questions.

"Why did he let me live?" I whispered.

I didn't even mean to say it aloud. But the question was always there, nagging at my soul like a piece of loose thread.

If he came there that night for me, why wouldn't he kill me?

That would be the logical choice. I was a danger to be mitigated. A wound to be cauterized. He had enemies. He had power to protect—power threatened by no one so much as it was threatened by me.

Did he go there that night intending to identify a body, or make sure he left one behind if I was still alive?

If so... why did he change his mind?

"I can't answer that, Oraya," Alya said softly. "I'm afraid no one will ever be able to."

The truth. But such an agonizing one.

"I thought you were dead," she went on, "for a long time. He kept you very quiet for the first few years. But then when you got a little older, people began to talk about you. The king's human daughter. I knew it had to be you. Ever since then, I've been following you. During the Kejari I had friends in Sivrinaj send me updates every trial. And then these last few months..."

She let out a long, slow breath. Her hand fell over mine. "I never thought I would see you again," she choked out, the emotion in that one sentence overwhelming, like it all poured forth at once.

Me neither, I wanted to say, but I couldn't even make myself form words.

"Your mother loved you," she said. "I hope you never doubted that, no matter what he might have told you. And so did the rest of us. Your siblings. Your stepfather. You were—are—so fiercely, fiercely loved. I always hoped that you felt that wherever you were, even if we couldn't tell you it directly."

And this—this was the thing that infuriated me the most. Because I *didn't* know. I knew that I was loved by Vincent, and

Vincent alone. But he'd erased everyone else. Let me believe that I was alone in this world.

He never deprived me of food or shelter or safety. But he deprived me of that, and it felt almost as horrific.

We sat there in silence for too long, and then Alya rose, that momentary wave of emotion replaced with stoic calm. She went to the dresser, opening the top drawer and rummaging through it. Then she turned back to me, hands cupped.

"She would want you to have this." She dropped a little glittering coil into my outstretched palm—a chain of silver, small black stones interspersed down its length.

"I noticed the ring," she added, nodding to my little finger. "I'd never seen the necklace before, though. I didn't know it was a full set."

It was, indeed, a full set—my necklace, my ring, and now, the bracelet, the onyx stones perfect mates to each other.

My eyes burned. I closed my hand, tight, relishing the press of the stones against my palm, as if I could still feel my mother's touch on them if I tried hard enough.

"Thank you," I murmured.

Alya nodded, hands clasped before her, looking a little awkward. She struck me as someone who was uncomfortable with emotion—maybe a family trait, because I was oddly relieved when she said, "I should check on dinner," and left us alone.

Raihn didn't say anything, and I was grateful for it, because I wasn't ready to speak. Instead, he silently sat at the edge of my bed, arm folding around me, offering me an embrace if I wanted it.

And Mother, I wanted it. I let myself slide into his arms with so little hesitation, I would have been ashamed of myself a month ago. But Goddess, how nice that touch felt, stable and secure and solid. Safety, even when nothing about this world—past or future—was safe right now.

I let my head fall against his shoulder. Let my eyelashes

flutter closed, as I breathed in his scent deep. Sweat and the sky and the desert.

The former maybe a bit stronger than the latter.

I said against his skin, "You haven't bathed since you've gotten here, have you?"

He let out a snort. "Ix's tits, princess. What a charmer you are."

"I'm in your armpit. I can't *not* notice."

"I had more important things to worry about than bathing. Besides, I hear some women find a natural musk attractive. Try to have that attitude."

I wasn't about to confirm it, but I did find it a little attractive. Or at least, strangely comforting.

He asked softly, "You alright?"

Alright. What did that word even mean? By any definition, I thought the answer must be no. I'd almost died. I'd led the people who followed me into a bloodbath. I'd lost my kingdom for the second time.

I pulled away just enough to give Raihn a hard look that said, *What the fuck kind of a question is that?*

He sighed. "Fine. I earned that."

I laid my head against his shoulder again. "You've talked to the others."

"A few letters to Vale. Not much. But the mirror survived the attack, so "

So I could talk to Jesmine. Thank the Goddess for that. I was glad I'd kept it on me.

Except, that wave of relief was followed by one of nausea.

What was I even going to tell her? They needed orders. They were waiting at the rendezvous point, counting the minutes until Simon went after them.

"How many did we lose?" I asked.

Raihn's slight hesitation told me more than his answer. "They were still counting, the last I heard from them."

A lot.

Fuck.

He went on, "We could consider a surrender, but—"

Surrender? To a Rishan noble prick and a Bloodborn snake? No. Never.

I scoffed. "Fuck, no. I'd rather die fighting."

No, I was sick of this. I'd spent a lifetime bowing before my supposed status as a weak human. Fuck if I'd die that way, too.

Raihn chuckled softly. "Glad you see it that way, too."

"We need to go back."

Back to Jesmine and Vale. Back to the armies relying on us, and quickly.

His thumb swept over my shoulder. "I'd tell you to rest longer, but I know better."

"Would you sit around if *you* were the one stuck here? This is my fight too."

"It is," he said, and I wondered if I imagined that he sounded a little proud.

"Besides," I said, "I don't know how much more time we have before Simon and Septimus go after them to finish the job. We need to do something before that."

The mention of Simon's name conjured a viscerally vivid image—his monstrous form looming over Raihn, looming over me, that mangled collection of steel and teeth nailed into his chest.

Mother, the look in his eyes—

I knew better than anyone that vampires could be monstrous creatures. I'd witnessed the worst of bloodlust, which reduced them to little more than animals. But whatever Simon had become was a far cry from typical vampire brutality. He had turned himself into something that should not exist at all.

Or more accurately, I suspected, Septimus had turned him into such a thing.

And I had the terrible feeling that what Raihn and I had witnessed—power that put both of our Heir magics to shame—was only a fraction of what it was capable of.

I knew that Raihn and I were having these same thoughts, in the silence that followed.

Finally, he said, "Here. Let me put that on for you."

He took the bracelet from my still-open palm and gently fastened it around my right wrist—the same hand that bore my mother's old ring. I flipped my palm over when he was done, looking at the two of them together.

"Perfect match," Raihn said. "You've completed the set."

They did look nice together. But more than that, it felt good to have one more connection to the past that had been taken from me.

"Thank—"

A sudden shock jolted through me. I gasped, lurching upright, pressing my hand to my chest.

My hand—My chest—

"What?" Raihn was already half-standing, one hand on my arm, ready to call for Alya. "What is it?"

I didn't even know how to answer that question. I felt... *strange*. The last time I'd felt this way, it was when I'd looked down to see the Heir Mark tattooed over my chest. My breath came in rapid gasps. My hand, my throat—"burning" wasn't quite the right word, but they—

I forced my hand away from my throat, splaying it out flat, doing my best to hold it steady through the tremors.

Raihn and I stared down at it.

"Well, fuck," he whispered.

Fuck, indeed.

Inked over the back of my hand, in a triangle formed between the ring and the bracelet, was a map.

62

ORAYA

All this time, I had been trying so desperately to decode my father's past, my father's secrets, to find the power I needed to reclaim my kingdom.

How fitting that in the end, it was my mother who gave me the answer.

Raihn and I hastily set up the mirror, dripping my blood into it and summoning an extremely relieved Jesmine. Vale, Mische, and Ketura joined her, and we called Alya into the room too, showing her the map on my skin.

Once the initial shock wore off, Alya seemed equal parts proud and sad when she pieced together what she was looking at. It was a spell, she explained, forged into the metalwork of the jewelry, only to be activated once all three were worn together by its intended bearer.

"My sister's magic," she said softly. "I'd recognize it anywhere."

She touched the bracelet—an affectionate caress.

"Too smart for her own good, that one," she muttered. "Always was."

"Wouldn't Vincent have known if the ring was enchanted?" I asked. "He was a powerful magic user, too."

"Of Nyaxia's magic, yes. But he wouldn't have had enough experience with Acaeja's to know what to look for."

A lump rose in my throat, my thumb sweeping over the little black ring. The one token he'd allowed me to have from my former life. Little did he know.

The map on the back of my hand depicted the House of Night, or at least a small part of it—Vartana in the bottom left corner, Sivrinaj in the upper right, and a little star marked at the top center, right over my knuckle. No town or city existed there. It was right in the middle of the desert, nothing but ruins.

Ruins that still managed to be uncomfortably, dangerously close to Sivrinaj.

"Do you have any idea what this could be?" I asked Alya.

I knew what I *hoped* it could be. I didn't want to dream. It seemed like too much to possibly wish for.

Alya tilted her head, thoughtful.

"In the end, she was scared," she said. "Scared of whatever she was helping him do. I remember that. She never would tell me the details, but I know my sister. I think—I think she was growing afraid of what that kind of power could do in the hands of someone so distrustful, especially if he was the only one who had access to it. Perhaps, she may have given you a path to that power too, just in case, knowing that your blood may allow you to wield it." A barely-there smile—a little sad, a little proud. "I can't say for sure. But I can imagine that."

I let out a shuddering exhale of relief, and with it, a flood of affection for the mother I barely remembered.

She saved us. Goddess, she *saved* us.

"That's if Septimus hasn't already gotten to whatever this is," Jesmine pointed out. "Whatever power he'd given Simon wasn't of this world. I'm certain of that."

But Alya shook her head firmly. "Based on what they described, what you saw wasn't any creation of my sister's. It sounds like cobbled-together magic. An activator hacked apart to force it to work with something it wasn't intended to."

"An activator," Raihn repeated. "The pendant."

Mische looked proud of herself—because this had always been her suspicion.

"From what you've described, it sounds like it," Alya said. "I'd assume that Vincent would have created multiple activators with Alana's help. And any of them, used with the right magic, could be twisted and modified to work with a power similar enough to their intended target. But it would be ugly, and it would be dangerous. Probably deadly to whoever used it, eventually."

I remembered Simon's glazed-over, bloodshot eyes and shuddered.

Yes, that was certainly ugly. He'd looked like he was already mostly dead.

"So Septimus only got a piece of what he wanted," Raihn said, "in the form of the pendant. It worked enough, for now. But it means it's unlikely he has what he really came here for."

"Meaning that the god blood, if it exists," I added, "is probably still out there."

I curled my fingers and gazed down at my hand, shifting it beneath the firelight. The strokes of red shivered slightly, like moonlight through rippling leaves.

"This all sounds," Vale said, "like a lot of conjecture."

"It is," Raihn replied. "But it's also all we have."

"I accept that sometimes we need to act based on what we don't know," Vale said. "But what I *do* know is that Simon and his armies will be coming for us at any moment, and if they meet us now, they will win. I know that they're searching for you both, and this map takes you right by Sivrinaj. I know that if you go there, they'll know, and they will come after you with far more power than you two could possibly fight off alone. So if we choose to make this our gamble, then it will need to be a big one."

494

A wry smile tugged at the corner of Raihn's mouth. "How big, exactly?"

Vale was silent. I could practically see him questioning all the life decisions that led him to this moment.

"We all converge there," he said at last. "Whatever men we have left, ready to meet them one more time. We hold them off while Oraya... does whatever she needs to do. And we pray to the Mother that whatever she finds there is powerful enough to buy us a victory."

I felt a little nauseous.

Raihn threw back his head and laughed.

"Oh," he said. "Is that all?"

"I told you it was a big gamble," Vale said, annoyed.

"What else can we do?" Mische asked, grabbing the mirror and tipping it toward her. "If Raihn and Oraya go by themselves, they get killed. If we wait for Simon to come for us, we get killed. If we attack Sivrinaj again, we get killed." She threw her hands up. "It sounds like this is the only option that gives us a *tiny little chance* of *maybe* not getting killed."

"Other than surrender," Jesmine pointed out, which earned a face of disgust from every single person in the conversation.

"If we surrender," I said, "they kill us all, anyway. And that's not how I want to go."

At least this way, I'll die *doing* something.

No one disagreed.

We were all silent for a long, long moment.

It was outlandish. It was dangerous. It was downright foolish in its riskiness.

It was also all we had.

My eyes slipped to Raihn—and he was already looking at me, resolve firm in his gaze. I knew that look. Same one we would give each other before yet another impossible Kejari trial.

"So it's decided," he said. "We go down fighting in the name of blind fucking hope."

None of us could argue with that.

At least if we were idiots, we were all idiots together. That counted for something, I supposed.

THE GEARS WERE, once again, set in motion. Alya left not long after, citing errands, leaving Raihn and I alone at her worn kitchen table. We spent the rest of the day there, strategizing with frequent correspondence with Jesmine and Vale. The hours blurred together.

When Alya returned, some time later, she was not alone.

I was so focused—and so exhausted—that I didn't even hear the door open, until I glanced up from my maps to see Raihn sitting rod-straight, looking at the door like he wasn't sure whether to run or attack.

Alya closed the door behind her and her two companions: a mustached man with cropped, peppered hair, and a woman, a fair bit younger, with curly dark hair bound tight at the back of her head. Both prominently bore weapons hanging at their hips —the woman a sword, and the man an axe.

I stiffened. For a second, the prospect of Alya's betrayal nearly shattered me.

"They're friends," Alya said quickly at our reaction, raising her palms. "Oraya, Raihn, this is my husband, Jace. And my friend, Tamyra."

Raihn didn't relax, and neither did I. I didn't quite like the way either of them were sizing us up—especially the woman, Tamyra, who seemed like she hadn't quite decided that she wasn't going to kill us yet.

Alya glanced between all of us and heaved a long-suffering sigh. "Mother help us, no one has time for this. That's not necessary, Tamyra."

The man approached first, each step slow, his eyes locked onto me. I rose, just because it seemed like I should. It wasn't

until he was just a pace away that I saw the gleam in his eyes—
the shine of almost-tears.

"You look just the same," he said, deep voice rough. "Never
thought we'd see you again, Alya and I, we —"

He snapped his jaw shut, as if abandoning words.

And then he lowered to his knees.

It took everything in me not to jump—because I found the
gesture that startling. And it was even more startling when,
behind him, Tamyra approached and lowered into a kneel as
well, bowing her head before me.

"Highness," she said. "It's an honor to meet you."

Mother, this was bizarre.

I cleared my throat. "You may... rise."

My voice sounded much weaker than Vincent's ever had
when issuing that command.

Jace and Tamyra stood, and Tamyra stepped forward. With
the lantern light falling across her face, I could see that she was
heavily scarred—an angry pink slash across one cheek, and even
what looked like fang marks on her throat, barely visible beneath
the grease-stained fabric of her collar.

"I know you're very busy, so I don't ask for much of your
time." Her voice was low and brusque—the kind of voice that
was impossible not to listen to. "My king, my queen, I consider
myself a protector of this city. For nearly twenty years, my
soldiers and I have looked after the safety of the people who live
in these districts. I'm sure you know that in the House of Night,
that's often not an easy task." Her gaze lingered on mine. "I hear
rumors that you've acted in a role much like mine for some years
now."

Once, not long ago, I would have been embarrassed to have
my nighttime activities so blatantly named. Not anymore. I
wasn't ashamed of what I'd done.

"There aren't too many of us, but we have enough," she went
on. "We network across cities throughout the House of Night.
Don't have a presence everywhere, yet, but we're expanding
every day. Organizing. Teaching humans how to protect them-

selves. The thing is, our work has gotten a lot easier these last few months."

Her eyes slipped to Raihn, full of reluctant admiration, though clearly much warier of him than she was of me.

"I've come to thank you," she said, "for prioritizing the safety of your human citizens."

Raihn kept his face neutral. But maybe I was the only one who saw his tell—the little bob of his throat.

"I was human once," he said. "A part of me always will be. Just seemed like the fair thing to do."

"Past kings didn't agree."

"I don't agree with much about past kings."

A ghost of a smile, like Tamyra liked hearing this. She turned back to me.

"I've come to make an offer to you, King Raihn, Queen Oraya, from one human to another."

Queen Oraya. Two words that left me slightly dizzy.

I didn't show it.

"If you can guarantee that you will continue to protect the safety of your human population during your reigns," she said, "then I can guarantee we'll offer whatever forces we have into helping you keep that reign."

My brows lurched before I could stop them.

"Like I said, we don't have many," she went on, "A few hundred, among the cities close enough to offer up troops in time for your march. My soldiers probably aren't as strong as the vampire warriors you're accustomed to. But we're well trained, and we're loyal as hell, and we know how to fight. You'll be glad you have us."

And then she just stared at us, expectant.

I could feel Raihn's eyes on me too, as if to say, *Go on, princess. This one's yours.*

"Thank you," I said. "We would be honored to have your men fighting beside us."

No flowery words. No performances. Just the truth.

I extended my hand.

Tamyra stared at it for a moment, blinking in confusion—which made me realize that probably, most queens didn't go around accepting oaths of loyalty with a handshake.

But then she grasped my hand firmly, a slow smile spreading over her lips.

"Then I won't waste time," she said. "I'll gather my soldiers and send word to the others. We move at your command."

I released her hand, she bowed once more, and left. Once she was gone, Jace approached, carrying a canvas sack.

"You'll need a weapon, I figured," he said. "But I can't salvage this, I'm afraid."

He dumped the bag out on the table with a clatter, and my chest clenched.

The Taker of Hearts.

It was in pieces. My father's sword had been decimated, reduced to nothing but faintly glowing, red shards. Even the hand guard was hopelessly warped.

"Jace and I can make magic-touched weapons together," Alya said, joining us beside the table. "We might have been able to repair this one, if more of it was intact. But..."

She didn't have to say anything more. If the debris on the table was all that remained of it, then more than half the blade was missing.

I picked up one of the shards, pressing it to my palm. The magic thrummed against my skin, calling to my blood—Vincent's presence near, as if his ghost loomed over the corpse of his prized weapon.

Another piece of him gone.

I had so wanted to preserve this weapon—to be worthy of wielding it. When I'd finally managed it, I felt like I'd achieved something he'd always held just out of my grasp, even if I had to do it in his death.

Yes, the sword was powerful. But was that really why it had meant so much to me?

Or was it just another way of chasing the approval of a dead man who couldn't give it to me?

I didn't even like wielding rapiers. Never had.

"The magic in it is strong," Alya said. "It would be a shame to waste it. I couldn't recreate it from scratch, but we may be able to use the pieces—"

"Could you forge them into something else?" I asked.

They exchanged a glance. "It'd be tough," Jace said. "But I've done harder."

I opened my palm and let the shard fall to the table with a metallic *plink*. Vincent's ghost stepped back into the shadows.

"Could you make them," I asked, "into dual blades?"

I glanced back at Raihn, and the pride in his face caught me off-guard. His eyes crinkled with a barely-there, knowing smirk.

And Goddess damn him, I could practically hear him saying it:

There she is.

63

ORAYA

aihn and I left the next day.

The orders had been given. The armies had been rallied. The contingencies had been accounted for. It seemed ridiculous to think there was little more we could do to prepare, but the truth was that time was more precious than planning for outcomes we couldn't guarantee.

Raihn and I flew off on our own. We'd set up rendezvous points with the other armies, which would be marching out not long after we left. We'd get a small head start, which, we all prayed, would allow us to slip by unnoticed while Simon and Septimus were distracted by the movement of our forces. Having everyone move individually would hopefully mean a much smaller chance of being intercepted.

We left with only sparse supplies, the new blades that Jace and Alya had forged for me at my hips. When they'd presented them to me before we left, I was speechless, cradling the weapons for so long that they exchanged an awkward glance.

"If they won't work for you—" Alya had started.

"No. No, they're beautiful."

Beautiful was a pitiful word, actually, for what these were.

Once I'd thought that the Nightborn craftsmanship of the blades Vincent had given me was the epitome of deadly elegance. But these — I'd never seen anything like them before. A mix of vampire and human artistry, the blades seamlessly melded between fresh polished steel and the red shards of what had once been the Taker of Hearts. I'd sketched my previous swords for Jace, and he'd achieved an incredible recreation, tailoring them to my preference in style and weight — the blades slightly curved, and incredibly light.

When my hands folded around those hilts, it felt like coming home. I could still feel the echo of Vincent's presence when I touched them, but it was only an echo — a part, not the whole.

These felt like *mine*.

Raihn and I flew for a long time without talking much, keeping an eye out for Rishan spies patrolling the air. I was glad we were leaving Alya's quickly, because Jesmine and Vale both suspected that Simon either knew where we were or would very soon, given how many resources he and Septimus would be pouring into finding us. Several times, we had to carefully reroute to avoid guards in the skies, hiding ourselves in the clouds.

We weren't far from our destination. The map on my hand moved with us, shifting in scale and angle to show us our position relative to our target. It was only a day's travel, even with the convoluted detours.

When dawn approached, we stopped in the desert and pitched a tent, hidden in a rocky area of stone and brush that would hide our location from above. We'd pushed our timing as far as we could on such a cloudless day — the sun was already peeking over the horizon by the time we crawled inside. The shelter was barely big enough for both of us, designed to be temporary and portable.

Raihn let out a grunt as he flopped down on the rough, uneven ground. We hadn't bothered packing bedrolls — we could sleep anywhere, we figured, for a single day. Better to save the weight.

"Now *this*," he said, "is what I expected when I became a king."

"I'm sure you'll miss it tomorrow."

"You're probably right."

He was still smiling, but the joke seemed a little less light-hearted.

I lay down beside him, hands folded over my stomach, staring up at the canvas. The fabric was so lightweight that while it kept out the worst of the sun, I could make out the outline of it through the cream fabric, like an all-seeing eye.

I thought about the hundreds of vampire soldiers sleeping today in tents just like this one, staring up at this sky, wondering if they were going to die tonight.

"They must be on their way," I murmured.

They. The Rishan. The Hiaj. The humans. Simon and Septimus. Everyone.

"Mm. Probably."

Raihn rolled over. I did the same, so we lay face to face. We were so close that I could see every strand of color in his eyes, faintly illuminated by the light through the canvas. So many disparate strands—brown and purple and blue and red and near-black. I wondered if they'd looked like that when he was human.

I found myself trying to commit them to memory, those eyes. Like coins I wanted to slip into my pocket.

In his presence, I felt safer than I did anywhere else. And yet, sometimes when I looked at him, paralyzing fear seized me, so much sharper than the fear I felt for myself.

In these moments, I thought of what Raihn's dead body had looked like in the colosseum sands, and I couldn't breathe.

A wrinkle formed between his brows. His thumb brushed my cheek, then the corner of my mouth.

"What's that face for, princess?"

I didn't know how to answer that question. "I'm scared" didn't say enough and said too much.

Instead of answering, I leaned forward and pressed my mouth against his.

503

The kiss was more than I had intended it to be. Deeper, softer, slower. He met it with equal fervor, lips melting against mine, tongue caressing me with gentle strokes. So easily, my hands found his face, pulling him closer as his touch fell to my sides. He lowered me to the ground, his body moving over mine, natural as the movement of the ocean over the shore, our kisses never parting.

We'd never been quite like this. I wanted to feel him from every angle before I died.

My fingertips ran down over his bare torso, tracing the lines and valleys of his muscles and scars with something akin to reverence. His played at the hem of my undershirt, and I whimpered my approval against his lips. Heat built between us, in the small sliver of flesh where my stomach met his. But it wasn't the raging, out-of-control fire of our previous encounters. It was the heat of a fireplace in a comfortable home, warm and familiar.

And yet, dangerous. Dangerous in its safety.

I shifted further beneath his body, my thighs opening around his hips, so his erection pressed against my core.

He pulled away just enough to break our kiss, his nose still brushing mine. His hair dangled around his face, tickling my cheeks. Those magnificent eyes searched mine. They seemed pained and full—full of words that matched the ones I couldn't bring myself to say.

"Oraya," he murmured.

"Sh," I whispered. "We don't have to."

And I kissed him again.

Again.

I felt his entire body melt with his acquiescence. His weight settled over me. I yanked at my camisole and he reached down to loosen my trousers. We shimmied out of our remaining clothing, shedding it between kisses, before his weight settled over me again, skin against skin.

I'd never had him like this before.

Never had anyone like this, since the night I lost my virginity and nearly lost my life for it. Even in fantasies, the idea of being so trapped had been inconceivable. And yet, now I craved so deeply the very thing that I'd found repulsive for so long—I wanted him to surround me. I wanted to feel his weight over me. I wanted as much of my skin against him as I could offer him.

Those kisses, soft and searching, never broke. I reached down and aligned him with my entrance.

One push, and he was everywhere.

I gasped against his mouth, capturing his groan. My legs folded around his waist, opening more to ease him deeper. His first stroke was slow and deep, as if he wanted to savor what it felt like, before he withdrew.

"Oraya," he murmured.

"Sh," I whispered against his mouth, and kissed him again, languidly, exploring every angle.

And that was the pace he kept, too, each thrust patient and deep and thorough, like he wanted to sear it all into memory— my skin, my body, and what it felt like to be inside me.

How did I know that was what he was doing?

Maybe it was because I was doing the same. Committing him to memory. Making sure that every movement, every breath, every sound he made was marked onto my soul. I wanted to capture him like rainwater. I wanted to savor him like blood. I wanted him to open me and touch everything within me that I'd hidden away from the world. How could there be so much pleasure in vulnerability? How could there be so much pleasure in fear?

My hips rolled with him, wringing that slow pleasure from every stroke of his cock, drowning in the way his breath hitched against our kisses with each movement, each contraction of my muscles.

The slow fire was building, building, into something overwhelming, consuming us both. But never out of control. Never terrifying.

My exhales became moans, matched by his, swallowed in each other's breaths. I wouldn't let him go, even when our pace quickened, even when breathing through our kisses grew clumsy and desperate.

I wanted to feel it through my entire body when he came, feel the way his muscles strained, hold him against me in those final moments.

He pushed deep into me now, hard. Goddess, I wanted more. Needed more. And yet, I never wanted this moment to end.

The need to tell him something, everything—Mother, I didn't even know what, only that it was so big, so important, so overwhelming—rose in my throat.

But I couldn't wrangle whatever I was feeling into words.

So I choked out, "Raihn," against his lips, a question, an answer, a plea.

Because that name was all those things, wasn't it? Raihn. My downfall and my most valuable supporter. My weakness and my strength. My worst enemy and the greatest love I had ever known.

All of that in one name. One person. One soul I knew as well as my own, just as confusing, just as flawed.

Pleasure built, spiked, in the place where we were connected.

I wanted to feel him everywhere. Give him everything.

"Raihn," I whimpered again, not even knowing what I was asking.

"I know, princess," he whispered. "I know."

And then, just as I knew we were both rushing to the precipice, he broke our kiss and pulled away.

I let out a small sound of protest, starting to move after him, needing to taste him in that moment of climax.

"Let me watch you," he murmured, voice rough. "Please. One last time."

And Mother, the way he said it. Like it was the only thing he wanted out of his life before he let it go.

I couldn't deny him even if I'd wanted to, because then he reached down and guided my thighs wider, opening me more for one final push, touching the deepest parts of me.

My back arched, pushing myself against his chest. I didn't

mean to cry out, but the sound escaped me anyway, uncontrollable. My fingernails dug into his shoulder, clutching him through the wave of pleasure—clutching him so I could feel him straining too, riding with me into the end.

But even as we lost ourselves, neither of us closed our eyes. We watched each other, gazes locked, bare and exposed through the most vulnerable parts of our pleasure.

He was so beautiful. Lips parted, eyes sharp, his focus fixed entirely on me. Every angle of his face, every scar, every flaw.

Perfect.

The wave melted away, and with it, so did the tension of our muscles. Raihn rolled off me, and I settled easily into the crook of his arm, surrounded by the cadence of his breathing.

We didn't speak. There was nothing more to say. I kissed the scar on his brow, and the upside-down V on his cheek, and finally, his lips, and then I settled back into his embrace, welcoming our final oblivion.

64

RAIHN

Oraya and I lay together for a long time, eyes closed, but neither of us slept. I wondered if she knew that I always knew it when she was awake—I knew it when she was a room away from me, and I certainly knew it now, with her bare body against mine and my arms around her, feeling the cadence of her breathing against my chest.

Maybe some might've thought it was a waste to just lie there like that, in the hours before our potential death. Hell, the last time I'd faced death with Oraya, I'd wanted to spend every sleepless moment of that day inside her, working my way through a list of pleasures.

But this... this was different.

I didn't need to collect more carnal moans. I wanted the rest of it. The way she breathed. The way she smelled. The exact arrangement of her dark lashes over her cheeks.

What it felt like, just to be next to her.

Maybe that was why, despite all we had to face come night-fall, I was glad I never fell asleep, not even when Oraya finally—finally—slipped off into a light, fitful rest.

Instead, I watched her.

Before the end of the Kejari, two hundred years ago, I had lain beside Nessanyn on a sleepless day not unlike this one. It was hours before Vincent would win the final trial, kill Neculai, and throw my life and the House of Night into chaos. Hours before I would beg Nessanyn to run away with me, and she would refuse.

That day, I'd watched her sleep, and I'd been so certain that I loved her. The fact that I loved her was, actually, the *only* thing I was certain of.

I was desperate to have something to love. Something to care about when I didn't give a damn about myself.

But so little of it had anything to do with her. It was never frightening to love Nessanyn. It was a survival mechanism.

Loving Oraya was terrifying.

It required me to see things I didn't want to see. Face things I didn't want to face. Allow another soul to witness parts of myself I didn't even want to acknowledge.

I now felt like such a fucking fool that I had never thought of it in that way, with that word, until this moment.

Of course it was love.

What else could it be, for someone to see that much of you? To see so much beauty in the parts of someone that they hate in themselves?

I almost wished I hadn't had the realization, because it made what loomed ahead that much more devastating. Easier to have nothing to lose.

I'd gotten us all into this mess. If I had to die to end it, so be it. But Oraya dying for my mistakes—

That would be a tragedy. The world would never recover.

I, I knew in this moment, would never recover.

But right now, she was safe. We had a few precious hours until everything changed, for good or for bad. I wouldn't waste a single one of them on sleep.

I spent them counting the freckles on her cheeks, memorizing the pattern of her breaths, watching the flutter of her eyelashes.

And when the sun went down, and Oraya stirred and blinked

blearily at me with those moon-bright eyes and asked, "Sleep well?"

I just kissed her forehead and said, "Perfect."

And I didn't have a single regret.

65

ORAYA

People don't really talk about how the days that make history, the days that change the course of entire civilizations, start in such mundane ways. Raihn and I got up and put on our leathers like it was any other night. We choked down a few bites of food, though my stomach was so nervous I could barely keep it down. We did a quick pass over our weapons. We broke down our tent.

All of it rote, unremarkable routine. We wasted no time. The sky was still stained purple with the remains of sunset. By the time it would turn pink with dawn, everything would be different.

Raihn and I didn't talk. After yesterday, I didn't have anything to say, or at least I told myself I didn't, when the reality was just that I didn't know how.

The map on my hand was now closer, the scale shifting and detail increasing as we ventured closer to our destination. We had only a short flight to the star, now at the center of the back of my hand, situated in the center of little illustrations of rocks and mountains that shifted with the angle of my hand when I tilted it.

We left the tent behind. No matter what happened, by dawn, we wouldn't need it anymore.

We rose into the sky, the remnants of it disappearing below us. It was a mostly clear night, the sky before us bright with velvet darkness and silver stars, some thickening clouds lingering to the west, obscuring the distant skyline of Sivrinaj.

We flew for several hours, the deserts beneath us morphing gradually into rocky foothills. The distant silhouette of Sivrinaj grew closer, though still little more than smears of light through the clusters of clouds. I hated how much those clouds obscured our visibility.

"Look," Raihn murmured, swooping close to me as we approached our target. He pointed out to the north, where some of the clouds had begun to part.

The smile broke out over my face before I could stop it—a big, stupid grin.

Because there in the sky was an unmistakable sight—a distant morass of wings, both featherless and feathered, blotting out the stars. They were far away, but if I squinted, I could make out the figures at their head: Jesmine, Vale, and Ketura, Mische in her arms.

And then, far below them, to the west, was another welcome sight: a wave of troops cresting the hills on foot, dressed in mismatched, makeshift armor and wielding scavenged weaponry, but bearing it all with their heads held high.

The humans.

We had a damned army. An unlikely, cobbled-together one, yes. But an army, nonetheless.

I let out a rough breath of relief, nearly a choked sob. I hadn't allowed myself to think too hard about all the endless possibilities of how tonight might go. And yet the fear had remained in the back of my head—that Simon could have destroyed the rest of our forces before they even had the chance to make it to us.

The hope that seized me at the sight of them made the dark night a little bit brighter.

We gave them a wave of greeting they were probably too far to see, then soared down and landed among the foothills.

From above, this area had looked like nothing more than rocky desert, hidden in shadows and mottled moonlight. But from the ground, the scale of it all was staggering. Jagged stones loomed over us. What from above had appeared to merely be textures of the earth were revealed to be pieces of old buildings —stone beams and broken columns protruding from the sands, long-buried glimpses of some version of this society that had fallen long ago, worn down by time.

My skin burned where the necklace, ring, and bracelet touched it, the triangle of flesh that displayed the map tingling. A sudden sharp pain had me hissing an inhale when we landed.

Raihn shot me a questioning, concerned glance, and I shook my head.

"It's fine," I said. I cradled my hand and squinted down at the map. We were so close now that the lines reoriented with every step.

Glancing between the two, I stepped gingerly through the rocks, winding a convoluted path through the ruins. As the target grew closer, I got impatient, stumbling into a near run over the uneven debris.

I stepped beneath a half-buried stone arch, then tripped, barely catching myself before I went to my knees.

"Woah." Raihn grabbed my arm. "Easy. What was that?"

Mother, my hand hurt. My head spun. The ground felt as if it was, very literally, tilting, to the point where I wanted to turn to him and say, *Really? You don't feel that?*

I glanced down at my hand.

The black stones in my ring, and my bracelet, now glowed— an uncanny black light, wisps of shadow that brightened to rings of moonlight. But whatever I was feeling drew from deeper than the jewelry that sat at the surface of my skin. Like my blood itself was calling to...

To...

Raihn called after me as I pulled away from his grasp and stumbled down the path.

My eyes fell to a single fixed point ahead.

The door blended in so thoroughly with everything around it, partially submerged in the sand, hidden in the shadows of the tipped-over columns and shattered rocks. In any other circumstances, I probably would have passed right by it, oblivious to what was right under my feet.

Now, my entire being pulled me to that spot, even though every step hurt—like some invisible power was ripping me apart to get at whatever lurked under my skin.

"It's here," I said.

Raihn stopped beside me. He didn't question me. He touched the stone, then yanked his fingers away.

"Ix's fucking tits," he hissed, cradling his hand—bubbling burns now marking his fingertips.

I unsheathed one of my blades and opened a shallow cut across my palm, then reached for the door.

"Wait—" he said.

But I didn't hesitate.

I gasped when my skin touched the slab. For a moment, I lost my grip on the world.

I am the King of the Nightborn, in possession of something that no living being should ever possess. I thought that holding such a thing would make me feel powerful, but instead I feel smaller than ever.

Beside me, she leans close. Her eyes are white and milky, her goddess's magic coursing through her. She looks otherworldly when she does this— beautiful in a way that frightens me.

She touches the door—

I pulled my palm away.

When I opened my eyes, the stone door was gone. In its place was a tunnel of darkness. Goosebumps rose over my skin, already reacting to the magic of whatever lurked within.

"Every shred of my being is screaming not to let you go down there," Raihn said.

Every shred of mine was beckoning me closer.

"This is it," I said.

I'd doubted the existence of Septimus's god blood before. And maybe whatever my parents had hidden in this cave might not be blood, but I now found it hard to believe it was anything but touched by the gods. No one who felt this could deny it.

This wasn't of this world.

Raihn reached for the door, but I slapped his hand away.

"Don't be a fucking idiot," I snapped. "You can't go in there."

He grimaced, glancing at his burnt fingertips, recognizing the truth even if he didn't like it.

"So what? You go down alone?"

"We always knew that would be a possibility."

I stared into the abyss. A slow, cold fear wrapped around my heart.

Fear is a collection of physical responses, I told myself.

Even though the darkness before me was frightening in a way that seemed so much bigger than a few fangs.

For a moment, it boggled me that those were my biggest problems, a year ago.

Raihn was getting ready to argue with me. I knew what that looked like by now. But just as he opened his mouth, his eyes flicked up to the sky.

"Fuck," he murmured.

Something about his face told me exactly what I was going to see when I turned around. And yet, when I did, the sight of the wave of Rishan and Bloodborn warriors, emerging from the clouds and over the terrain in a seemingly-endless tide, still made me stop breathing.

There were just so *many* of them.

The army I had just been so relieved to see now seemed so pathetically small. We had been so worn down, fighting with the loyal fragments of forces cobbled together into something that had to be—Goddess, *needed* to be—enough.

I needed to believe it would be enough.

I whirled back to Raihn. His jaw was set, brow low over his eyes, the shadows making them seem redder than ever.

515

I knew what he was going to say before he opened his mouth.

"You go," he said. "I'll hold them off with the others."

Now I understood how he must have felt when I told him I'd go into this tunnel alone, because every part of me screamed in protest at that sentence. The impulse to stop him, to beg him not to go up against the man who had almost killed him, was briefly overwhelming.

I didn't.

Raihn could not come with me where I was going, either, and I knew he wanted to stop me just as much.

Neither of us gave in.

I had no choice but to walk through that door, and no choice but to do it alone. Raihn had no choice but to lead the people who had followed him into the shadow of death, and no choice but to be the only one who might—might—be able to hold off Simon long enough for me to secure this weapon.

Neither of us had chosen our roles. But they were a part of us anyway, seared onto our souls as clearly as the Marks on our skin.

It's hard to describe the sound of thousands of wings. A low, ominous, rolling roar, like thunder rising in a slow build. I was a child the last time I'd heard it, peering out the window to see the wings blotting out the moon.

I'd lost everyone that day.

They were approaching fast. When I spoke again, I had to raise my voice over the din.

"Give them fucking hell," I said. "Alright? Don't you dare let him win."

The corner of his mouth quirked. "I don't plan on it."

I started to turn away, because the pressure in my chest was too much, the words I couldn't say too heavy. But he grabbed my wrist and pulled me back, holding me close in a brief, fierce embrace.

"I love you," he said, in a single, urgent breath. "I just—I need you to know that. I love you, Oraya."

And then he kissed me once, roughly, messily, and he was gone before I had the chance to say anything else.

Just leaving me standing there, swaying, with those three words.

I love you.

They lingered too long. I wasn't sure if it was them or the magic that made me so dizzy, unsteady on my feet, chest tight, eyes burning.

I watched Raihn's silhouette rise into the air, soaring toward that wall of darkness.

A single speck, against a wave.

Suddenly, I felt so incredibly small. Like the human Vincent had always told me I was, helpless and weak, in a world that would always despise me. How did I get here, standing at the foot of my father's legacy, fighting to rule the kingdom he told me I couldn't even exist in?

I turned around and faced the doorway.

The darkness was unnatural, all-consuming.

You don't want to see what's inside there, Vincent whispered in my ear. He sounded oddly sad. Ashamed.

No, I thought. *You don't want me to see those things.*

For nearly twenty years, I had seen only what Vincent had wanted me to see. I had become only what he wanted me to be. I had forged myself by his hand, by the bounds of the mold he'd poured me into, and never further.

It had been comfortable.

But now, too damned much was relying on me to not venture beyond those walls.

I stepped into the darkness.

66

RAIHN

One would think that after almost three hundred years as a vampire, I'd stop feeling like a human. One would think that after two hundred years of freedom, I'd stop believing the things that Neculai had once told me.

The divide was always so clear—us versus them. The Turned would always bear some mark of our human weakness, human flaws. I'd spent so fucking long sawing away all evidence of those weaknesses in myself. I was physically stronger than I'd ever been. Stronger, maybe, than even Neculai had been.

But when I flew up into the night sky—a sky that was an unnatural, ungodly black with the wings of Rishan warriors—I was fucking terrified.

As a young man, I used to think that bravery was the absence of fear. No. I'd learned since then that the absence of fear was only stupidity.

I let myself feel it for thirty seconds, as my eyes took in that wave of warriors that just kept going and going and going, and then I stuffed it down my throat.

I veered left, soaring toward Vale. The army had split now,

Ketura's troops sweeping to the ground in a wave of fluttering feathers, like rain falling down over the desert, to join the human soldiers to face the Bloodborn.

Everyone was moving fast. Too fast. Minutes, and these unstoppable forces would collide.

I still wasn't quite used to seeing Vale look relieved to see me.

"Highness," he said, raising his voice over the wind and the steady drumbeat rhythm of wings.

"Don't let them get beyond the ruins," I commanded.

He looked down to the rocks below. I saw him put the pieces together—what must be down there.

"Understood." His eyes flicked to me, the question in them obvious. "Did you—"

"Oraya is searching."

That answer made it sound so mundane. Not like I'd just left her to wander off into an ominous magical pit.

I veered closer, as close as we could get without colliding.

"Hold that line, Vale. No matter what. Understood?"

Understanding flickered in his face. He knew the frantic edge to my voice wasn't just about the artifact, no matter how powerful it was.

"We'll hold it," he said, voice firm. "I swear it."

I lifted my head to face the onslaught of warriors ahead, speeding toward us in a steady, unrelenting wall. Vale drew his sword, face stone, jaw set.

"Weapons up!" he roared, voice booming through the air, the echo rolling through the armies as his captains passed the order along.

Simon's army was now close enough that I could see their faces.

And clearer than any of them, I saw Simon's—blood-streaked, rage-drenched. He practically reeked of otherworldly power, a faint, crimson-tinted smoke collecting around his wings, the glow at his chest simmering like hot coals in the night.

One look at him, and I knew he'd rip through whatever poor

bastards threw themselves at him. Heir power might be enough to hold him off. Maybe.

"Stay away from him," I said to Vale. "He's mine."

The truth was, it wasn't all that selfless. I was ready for a rematch.

I drew my sword.

67

ORAYA

I couldn't see a damned thing. I cursed my human eyes as I staggered through the darkness—darkness so all-encompassing that within just a few steps, it swallowed up even the distant remnants of the moonlight through the open door. One hand blindly felt my way forward as I ventured into the dense shadows, the other holding up an orb of Nightfire that didn't even begin to penetrate the black.

What was I even looking for?

A safe? A chest? Where would Vincent have hidden something so powerful? Would he have made it into a weapon? Should I be groping around these walls for—what, another magical sword ready for the taking? Or—

My next step did not find ground where I expected it.

My backside hit the floor hard, sliding down a set of stairs. My hands clawed at the walls to slow myself, Nightfire sputtering out.

With a clumsy *THUMP*, I slid to a stop.

"Fuck," I hissed.

My tailbone ached. I'd lost count of how many steps I'd struck on the way down.

But nothing, thankfully, seemed broken. It would be awfully pathetic if, after everything I'd been through, a fall down a flight of Goddess-damned stairs was the thing to take me now.

I pushed myself back to my feet, wincing as my bruised muscles whined in protest. I conjured Nightfire in my palm again, holding it out before me.

The unnatural stubbornness of the darkness had, apparently, broken, because now the cold light bloomed through the shadows.

I let out a shaky exhale at the sight before me.

I was in a circular room crafted entirely of stone. I stood in an arched doorway. At the center of the room rose a massive column, stretching floor to ceiling. Two circular barriers surrounded it, as tall as my waist, expanding from the center and each bigger than the last. The stone was black and polished, clearly the work of fine craftsmanship. Unlit lanterns lined the walls, six around the outskirts of the circle.

Every inch of this place—the walls, the barriers, the obelisk itself—was covered in carvings. I'd never seen anything quite like them. They didn't seem to be a language, exactly—they weren't arranged in the linear, neat lines of writing. Most of the symbols formed circles, though some floated off on their own or were wedged between other sets of carvings.

Glyphs, maybe? Sigils?

Wielders of Nyaxia's magic used them rarely, aside from summoning, but I'd heard that some sorcerers who drew from gods of the White Pantheon did. A few of the marks, upon closer inspection, reminded me of some of the symbols I'd seen in my mother's notes.

I gingerly stepped from the last stair—cringing slightly, half expecting that the floor would fall out beneath me or burst into flames. When no such thing happened, I let out a sigh of relief and walked around the perimeter of the room, lighting each lantern with Nightfire.

Something was off about this place. My skin felt itchy, the air too thick, like the atmosphere itself was heavy with magic. It was an unpleasant sensation. It reminded me of how I'd felt when I'd wielded the Taker of Hearts for the first time, but much, much stronger.

The magic in this room, I knew, wasn't meant for me. My blood was close enough to let me in, but it was wary about me. Goddess knew what kind of horrible death I'd meet if it decided to expel me, like an unwelcome virus.

With the lanterns lit, the room didn't look any less eerie. If anything, the flickering blue light made this place seem more unsettling. I took another walk around the circle, fingertips trailing over the half-wall before me—feeling for something, anything, that might guide me.

My gaze fell to the center of the room. The column. Now that looked important. It *felt* important, like it was calling to me.

I attempted to hoist myself over the first wall, only to immediately find myself knocked back to the ground, as if I'd just thrown myself against an invisible barrier.

Goddess damn it.

My ears were ringing now, though I wasn't sure if it was from the impact or the magic, which suddenly seemed overwhelmingly thick.

I pushed myself up. My knees shook slightly. I didn't think it had anything to do with the fall.

Alright, then. No climbing.

My teeth ground as my impatience rose. It was unnaturally silent down here. I couldn't hear even the faintest echo of the world above. But I knew that Simon and Septimus's armies must have been upon us by now.

Raihn was probably locked in battle with the man who had come so damned close to killing him.

I didn't have time for this.

Fucking think.

I pressed my hands to the dividing wall, hard enough that the carvings dug into my skin. I closed my eyes. I let myself feel the sensations that I'd been trying to avoid—the magic that burrowed into all of my most shameful vulnerabilities.

Magic this powerful required an offering from those who used it. And Vincent had wanted to protect this place from any other soul but him. Anything of his that I'd used—the mirror, the pendant, even this door—I'd had to offer it something in return.

The one thing that had always been my greatest weakness.

I withdrew my blade and opened a wider cut across my palm, a fresh river of crimson flowing across pale, fragile skin.

Then I pressed my hand to the stone.

Red flowed through the carvings in the smooth black, filling the sigils. I drew in a gasp as they drank it down eagerly, like a vampire in bloodlust.

And the gasp became a strangled cry as the magic swelled in a sudden rush, sweeping me away.

68

RAIHN

S imon was looking right at those ruins.

It was like he knew. How? Maybe melding pieces of a god's corpse into your flesh gave you some inexplicable awareness of other terrible magic. Maybe what Simon had made a part of himself now called wordlessly to its mate.

I couldn't explain it, and I wouldn't try. But when I got close enough to see that—the little turn of his head, the greedy glint of interest in his eyes—everything else fell away.

It was just like the wedding, when I'd seen Simon talking to Oraya and suddenly not a single other thing in the world mattered. My singular purpose became getting between him and that door.

I dove for him, and didn't slow as we careened into each other like stars colliding in the night sky.

My sword was out, my hold on my magic loose, ready to unleash everything I had. And when Simon turned to me in that final moment, his blade lifting to meet mine, his own magic swelling, we were nearly evenly matched.

The burst of power—light and darkness, red and black, stars and night—obliterated us.

My ears popped. Every sound grew muffled and distant, as if underwater. My eyes, wide open through the whole thing, railed against the intensity of it, leaving the world in spotted outlines as the magic faded.

The two of us hurtled through the air, our courses thrown by the staggering force we'd just unleashed. In the background, several warriors plummeted to the ground, limp and broken-winged, unlucky enough to be caught in the indirect impact of our blows.

I didn't have time to count how many were mine, and how many were his.

Didn't have time to think about anything but Simon.

When he smiled at me through the onslaught of steel and magic, he looked just like Neculai. Just like the version of him that I'd seen in the Halfmoon trial, in the darkness before the battle began. The same version I saw in my nightmares, still, all these Goddess-damned years later.

Never again.

I moved on instinct now, meeting every blow, every dodge, relishing every time my blade struck flesh. I'd learned to communicate with my fighting strategies over the years, make each match a performance. Not tonight.

Tonight, I just fought to kill.

I twisted my body as Simon evaded one of my lunges, using his follow-through against him, spearing one of his wings.

It wasn't the first time I'd hit him. But it was the first time I'd surprised him.

He lurched, and I smiled at the way he blinked in shock, like he didn't fully believe I'd gotten him until he was dipping sideways in the air.

I didn't waste the moment.

My next strike went to his side, exposed as he fought to right himself, arm lifted to reveal the weakest point of his armor—right beneath his armpit.

The sensation of the blade piercing his flesh was the most

satisfying thing I'd experienced all night—second, maybe, only to the snarl of pain he let out next.

It was totally worth what came after.

He grabbed me as I yanked my sword free, spraying black blood over my face, holding me by the neck of my armor with an iron grip. The world rushed around us, the sky behind him a smear of bloody bodies and distant blurred stars.

He wrenched me close, so close spittle sprayed my face when he spoke.

"This kingdom was never made for people like you," he growled. "Who do you think you are? You think you can become him? *You?*"

Fucking incredible, how it all just snapped together in such perfect clarity.

My worst fear for so damned long. Neculai looking into my eyes and telling me that my crown cursed me to become just like him, or that I would lose it because I couldn't be.

Simon was right. He was everything Neculai's successor should have been.

And that would be exactly what would destroy him.

I smiled at him. I leaned closer, gripping his shoulder, forcing my head to his ear. The man even *smelled* like Neculai, that sickening mix of blood and withered roses that followed me on my darkest nights.

"You're right," I said. "I'm just a Turned slave. All I'll ever be."

And just as Simon turned his face to me, confused, I slipped my free hand through the opening in his armor, grabbed the twisted, ragged edge of the metal forged into his skin, and pulled.

He unleashed a roar of agony.

The world went white.

Everything disappeared for a few horrible seconds. I lost my grip on my senses.

When I regained them again, Simon and I were rushing toward the ground.

6 9

ORAYA

The moment my blood touched the stone, I wasn't here anymore. I wasn't Oraya anymore. I was somewhere long in the past, pulled into the soul of another.

I recognized him immediately, just as I had the night I yanked the pendant from his father's wings. I would recognize him anywhere, even from within his own memories.

Vincent.

I WATCH her as she observes this place. She looks at it with such amazement, even though it's little more than a cave. She has always been good at seeing the potential in things. Perhaps this is what drew me to her a year ago. Perhaps she reminds me that I used to be a dreamer once, too.

Yet, I can't deny I feel some of it, too. It has taken us so long, so many sleepless nights and days, to get here. She has taken the unrefined artifacts I uncovered long ago and turned them into something incredible. And now, here, this place, serves as a physical monument to all that we have accomplished together.

The first layer of our lock has been constructed, the stone smooth and polished beneath my palms. Her cheeks are dusted with black soot from the hours she has spent carving into it, perfect interlocking circles of spellwork.

"You need to give it something of yourself," she tells me. Her hands caress the stone like a lover. I watch her delicate fingers move back and forth, back and forth, across the smooth onyx.

"Blood," I say, blandly.

"It will take more than blood. Just like that took more than your blood." She nodded to my hip—to the sword hanging there. "You gave that thing a piece of your soul, and this will guard a much more powerful weapon."

"Soul, then." I deliberately sound bored, partly because I know it will make her scowl. Sure enough, it does, the wrinkle on her upturned nose scrunching the black marks.

"Belittle it all you want, my king. Just think of something powerful when you spill your blood over this. The stronger the emotion, the better. You can't choose what this magic will take from you. But you can offer it strong options to choose from." Her big, dark eyes flick back to me, and she smirks. "Think about, I don't know, your ravenous desire for power and whatnot. Maybe the last enemy you killed. That kind of thing."

I scoffed. "Is that who you think I am?"

Her smirk becomes a smile. I watch it bloom across her lips, and the distraction frustrates me.

"Isn't that who you want to be? Isn't that why we're doing this?"

She's right. Yet, the conclusion is even more aggravating than that nuisance of a smile. I take her dagger and draw it across my hand, then press my palm to the stone, letting my blood pool in the carvings she spent so long on.

I try to think about power and greatness. I try to think about the way my blade felt piercing the heart of Neculai Vasarus. I try to think about the weight of this crown upon my head for the first time. I try to think about the dead body of the father I hated, and my satisfaction when I spat *on his grave. Something powerful, she said. These are my most powerful moments.*

But I cannot tear my gaze away from her mouth, or the speckles of dust across her nose, or the little scar on one of her eyebrows.

"Come here," I say, before I can stop myself.

No one disobeys me when I make a command. Not even her. The smile fades. Brief uncertainty glints in her eyes.

She steps closer.

She smells so wonderfully human. Sweet and savory and complex. Flowers and the earth and cinnamon. She tilts her head back slightly.

"Yes?" she murmurs.

Her heartbeat has quickened.

Strange, that mine has, too.

It is exhausting to desire. I can no longer remember when this set in, how many days passed with her in my presence before it became maddening. I despise it. I cannot think when she's near me.

It makes me feel powerless.

My right hand is still pressed to the stone, my blood now dripping over the edge of the wall. But my left comes to her face, wiping away that smudge of black with my thumb, leaving a smear in its wake.

Her skin is so unbelievably warm.

Her mouth is warmer.

I STAGGERED BACK, clutching my hand, which was now covered in blood. Vincent's memories and my own tangled. The image of my mother's face—Goddess, my *mother*—was seared so clearly into my mind, I could still see its outline when I closed my eyes.

I was so disoriented that I didn't even feel the ground trembling until I heard the grinding of stone. I blinked away the remnants of Vincent's memory to see the wall before me lowering, inch by inch, until it was flat against the ground. The carvings on the stone beneath my feet and that of the wall's lip matched up seamlessly, all pulsing with faint red light, still stained with the remnants of my blood.

The realization of the vision settled into me.

This was a *lock*.

Each wall was a layer, a phase, like the pins within a padlock. And the column in the center was the final piece—the turn of the key.

I drew in a shaky breath and let it out. I took several careful steps to the second ring of stone. The magic in this room seemed to grow thicker, more noxious, than it was minutes ago. My head pounded. My stomach threatened to empty. My limbs shook.

But far more pressing than any of that was the thought of Raihn, fighting for his life above.

I didn't have time for this shit.

I pushed myself through it, half-stumbling to the next wall.

This time, I didn't hesitate. I opened the wound in my hand again, urging forth a streak of fresh blood, and pressed it to the stone.

My hand is already bleeding.

Rage. Utter rage. It's raining outside, one of those rare, powerful monsoons that occasionally roars over the deserts. My hair drips rainwater onto the carvings. She had finished these not long ago, the dust still settled into the rivulets, collecting with my blood into a black sludge as it pours into the divots.

I hate them.

I hate her.

I shouldn't have come here in this state. This is not the mark I want to leave on something so important. This was supposed to be a thing to make me powerful—instead, it is becoming a monument to my weaknesses. But I needed to come here tonight. Needed to know that she had not betrayed me with her final slight—needed to know that I had enough power to finish what we had started together.

Did she really think that it could end here?

Did she really think that it would stop me if she left?

She called me power-hungry. I called her weak. What right did she have to speak to me that way? She came from nothing. I gave her everything.

I was ready to give her eternity.

I was ready to give her all of it, and she looked into my eyes and spat in my face.

Did she know how many women would have died for such an opportunity? How many humans would kill to be made into vampire royalty?

Did she think I wouldn't smell my own child on her?

With that thought, fear spears my chest. It is difficult to breathe.

My child.

A threat. Not just a threat, but the greatest threat. How many kings die at the hands of their children?

If she had stayed—if she had listened—

We could have dealt with that.

But now, she is gone, and I will have a child out there in the world, and I am—I am—

I sink to my knees, my forehead pressing to the sharp edge of the wall. My chest hurts fiercely. I stand on a blade's edge between two emotions, neither of them pleasant, and I hate her for making me feel this way.

I'm ashamed of myself.

I think of every word I said to her. Every flinch of pain across her face.

I never asked for any of this. She was the one who came to my door. She was the one who kept finding ways to stay.

The thought of an empty bedchamber in an empty castle hits me, and it's more painful than any battle wound I've ever endured.

I should go after her. I should hunt her down. I should snip the loose thread in my tapestry, mend this chink in my armor. It's what my father would have done. It's what all the prior Nightborn kings would have done.

But she had looked into my eyes and asked me if she would be safe if she left. If years of love and companionship had earned her that right.

I said, "You're welcome to leave whenever you want. Arrogant of you to assume I'd care enough to go after you."

Much of that conversation has become a blur, cruelties blending into cruelties. But I remember every word of that answer.

Here, in the face of the magic she created for me, I cannot lie anymore. And it was, indeed, a lie. A childish one.

Here, I cannot lie to myself.

She's gone. She is not coming back.

And even if I found her, I wouldn't be able to kill her.

The weakness in this confession to myself astounds me. Embarrasses me. I hate myself for it.

And yet, I know I would hate myself more, standing over her dead body. I think of another dark-eyed woman, a former queen who had been kind to me when I hadn't deserved it, who I had not spared, and feel a little pang of regret.

What I felt for Alana was — is — so much greater than what I once felt for a kind enemy I barely knew. My body physically recoils at the thought of what the wound of her death might feel like.

I force myself back to my feet. My hands are so badly cut that the blood overflows the carvings. I got some of it on my face, stinging my eye.

I raise my gaze to the thing of beauty before me. This fortress, designed to hold a greater power than any king, Nightborn or otherwise, had ever wielded before me.

And yet I concern myself with some human woman?

I force my shame and my hurt away to a dark place in the corner of my mind, never to be acknowledged again.

Let her go, I tell myself.

She isn't worth anything, I tell myself.

I pull my hand away.

I FELT SICK. I didn't even come back to awareness this time until the wall was already down, and I had fallen to the floor with it. I was on my hands and knees on the stone, retching. I'd eaten very little today. Nothing had come up but a few spatters of putrid liquid.

I wiped my mouth with the back of my hand and raised my head.

Now the only thing that stood before me was the column. Column—no, that wasn't a strong enough word for it. An obelisk. The carvings on this one were, I could see now, a little different than those in the rest of the cave, even if I couldn't fully articulate how—the strokes a little messier, the circles a little more crooked. The Nightfire had dimmed—or did I imagine that the room was darker now? The angry red glow of the carvings seemed more aggressive with each of my heartbeats, matching them in cadence.

My father's memories—hurt, anger, fear—burned in my veins. The terrifying dual-blade of his love and his disgust for my mother. I hated feeling it.

I hated *him* for feeling it.

I stared at that obelisk. I blinked and a tear rolled down my cheek.

I didn't want to.

The memories, the emotions, had only grown more intense as I moved to the center of the room. I was losing my grip on myself. This, I feared, might break me. Worse, it might break whatever fragile image I still had of the father that I'd loved—the father that had loved me.

What a fucking coward it made me, to still treasure that, after everything.

But I came here for a reason. There was only one place to go next. One remaining piece of the lock.

I stood, swaying on my feet. Stepped into the final circle.

I didn't need to open the gash again. My hand was already covered in blood.

I laid it against the stone.

7 0

RAIHN

My wings wouldn't work. I couldn't slow myself, stop myself, before the ground rose up to hit me.

Pain. I tried to move. Something cracked.

I couldn't make my eyes open. When I tried, a face I hadn't seen in a very, very long time leaned over me.

My brow furrowed.

Nessanyn?

She looked just as she had two hundred years ago, curly dark hair falling around her face as she leaned down next to me. Her eyes, chestnut-dark and a million miles deep, stared hard into me, wet with tears.

Who wins? she asked, voice cracking. *Who wins, if you fight him?*

She'd said it to me so many times, back then. Countless times, dragging me back from the line every time I thought I would cross it.

I'd always thought that Nessanyn was so much stronger than I was.

But now, in this version of her, it seemed so obvious that she was just terrified. She was a lonely and abused woman who was a prisoner in her own marriage.

535

She didn't fight because she was too afraid. Because it took a stupid kind of courage to keep fighting even when you knew every odd was stacked against you.

I reached out and touched her chin. She grabbed my hand and held it there, a tear rolling down her cheek.

Who wins? she said again.

Maybe not me, I replied. *But worth a try, right?*

She tried to hold onto my hand, but I pulled it away.

I opened my eyes.

Above me, carnage unfolded in the skies. Spatters of blood from warriors locked in battle hundreds of feet above dripped onto the rocks like black rain. A drop of it struck my cheek.

It was a nightmare. The kind of sight that, I knew in this moment, would wake me in a cold sweat ten years from now. If I was lucky enough to make it that far.

I tried to push myself up. A spasm of agony took my breath away.

Ix's fucking tits. My body was broken. Absolutely broken. I'd pushed it too far these last few weeks. Whatever Simon had just done to me had nudged it over the edge.

I'd died before. I knew what it felt like to stand on the precipice of the end.

Not yet.

I lifted my head. Another drop of blood from above struck my forehead, rolling down into my right eye, tinting the world black-red. Through it, I took in the ruins around me. I'd landed on a rock, smashing up my right side. My wings were still out, though I could tell right away that the right one was now useless. That arm, too, refused to cooperate when I reached for my sword. I grabbed the hilt with the left one instead, every muscle protesting the weight.

I lifted my head.

There, through the ruins, Simon staggered to his feet. The front of his leathers was smeared with blood. One of his wings was askew in all the wrong places, sticky black blood matting the feathers. The—thing on his chest pulsed brighter now, bright enough that it surged through the night and illuminated the harsh panes of his face from below.

He swayed back and forth, clutching his head, letting out a chilling roar that sounded like it belonged to an animal.

Then he straightened, and his eyes fell on me.

I dug my sword into the ground and used it to force myself upright.

Sun fucking take me.

My knees almost buckled. Almost.

I didn't show it. I just smiled. Didn't realize how much blood was in my mouth until the expression made it dribble down my chin.

I was eternally conscious of the door behind me—the door that Simon's gaze fixed on, before returning to me.

No, he wasn't getting past me.

I'd spent long enough letting him into my thoughts, my fears. I'd given him too damned much already.

This was where it ended. Whatever it cost.

I lifted my sword, forced my violently trembling right arm to join my left.

Come on, I told my body, when it nearly wept in protest. *One last fight. You've got it in you, old man.*

Amazing what a mindset could do.

Because when Simon lunged at me, lips twisted into a snarl, unnatural magic flaring around him like fire around a match, I was ready.

71

ORAYA

My father stood before me.

The room had grown dim and hazy, as if coated in a thick fog. Nothing felt real except for the foggy, gray nothingness.

Foggy, gray nothingness, and *him*.

I had dreamt of Vincent countless times. But this version of him felt so much more real than even the most vivid of them. The fine details of his face struck me like a knife to the chest—all the things I didn't realize I'd forgotten, like the slight crookedness to his nose or the way his hair favored the left side over the right. The version of him in my mind was generic, sanded down by months of absence, even as my grief clung to him.

I said, mostly because I needed to remind myself, "You're not real."

None of this was real.

Vincent smiled sadly at me.

"Aren't I?"

Mother. His *voice*.

"I'm real in every way that matters," he said.

"You're a dream. A hallucination. I've lost a lot of blood and —"

"I left so much of myself here, in this room." Vincent's eyes lifted, as if taking in this place beyond what was shrouded in darkness. "More than I ever had intended to give it. And all of that still remains, even if I do not. Isn't that real, little serpent?"

It seemed so, so real.

"I'm inventing you," I whispered. "Because you're what I want to see."

He lifted one shoulder in a delicate half-shrug. It was such a familiar movement, it made my breath stutter. "Perhaps," he said. "Does it matter?"

In this moment, it felt like it didn't.

He stepped closer, and I took a step back. He froze, momentary pain crossing his face.

"The things you've seen here have so tainted your image of me? I meant to give this place all my greatest achievements, my greatest ambitions. Instead, it became a monument to all my greatest mistakes."

So many mistakes in the end. Never you.

Vincent's final words flitted through my mind. He flinched, as if he heard them too.

"So many mistakes in the end," he murmured. "I never wanted you to see this version of me."

"I never wanted to see you this way."

And Goddess, I meant it. Sometimes I envied myself from a year ago, who'd known, beyond any doubt, that her father loved her. Yes, it was the only thing she could believe in, but that, at least, was solid, immovable.

Losing my trust in Vincent was more than losing trust in a single person. It had broken something within me, destroyed my ability to put that trust into anyone else.

Pain flashed over his face, there and gone again so quickly, I thought it might be a trick of the light. The idea that this version of him could be a figment of my own mind slipped further away.

If it was a hallucination, it was such a perfect one that it might as well be real.

And with him standing right in front of me, the anger that I'd been suppressing for months bubbled up to the surface.

"You lied to me," I ground out. "My entire life, you told me the world was a cage. But it was you that put me there. You manipulated me from the time I was—"

"I saved you," he snapped, lurching closer.

Then he winced, as if he had to clamp down on his anger, force it back.

"You *kidnapped* me," I choked out. "You killed my mother and you—"

"I did not kill her."

"Yes you did!" My voice boomed through the room, echoing off the stone ceilings. "You went to Salinae that night knowing she lived there. You *destroyed* it knowing—"

"I—"

No. I'd had enough of this. "*No more lies.* I've had almost twenty years worth of them. I'm done. *Done.*"

Vincent snapped his jaw shut. A muscle twitched in his cheek, as if flexing with the force of withheld words.

The room seemed to grow a little more solid, the fog thinning. He turned to the column, laying his hand against it. He drew in a breath and let it out slowly, his shoulders lowering.

"This magic," he said, more calmly, "is a living thing. And this, the center, is the most demanding piece of all. I've had to come back over the years, feed it more of myself to keep the spells strong. It's the most important one, and yet the weakest, because I had to get a different sorcerer to help me finish it. After—"

After she left. He didn't say it. Didn't need to.

His gaze slipped over his shoulder. The anger was gone. Only sadness remained. Suddenly, my father looked so breathtakingly old. Not the old of wrinkled skin or graying hair, but the old of sheer exhaustion, right from the soul.

"Do you want to see, little serpent," he murmured, "what memory it took from me?"

No, I almost said.

I didn't want to see it.

But I'd come too far to turn back now. Swallowed too many lies to turn away the truth.

Slowly, I joined him at the obelisk. I lifted my hand, and laid it over his.

THE NIGHT IS COLD, the only heat from raging fires that burn the city of Salinae.

I do not feel either. As I fly over the city, a shell of what it once was, I feel nothing but satisfaction. It has been a hard year. I've worn this crown for close to two centuries. Few Nightborn kings—few Obitraen kings, in general—manage to cling to power for so long. I have known this for a long time. But lately, my enemies have been stirring in the shadows. I feel them surrounding me at every party, every meeting. I feel their eyes on me when I am alone in my bedchamber and when I stand before my people.

Power is a bloody, bloody business.

I have gotten soft these last few years.

But the time for softness is over. I need to carve away my weaknesses like rotting flesh. And there is one particular necrosis that I've allowed to plague me for too long, because I've been weak. Too weak to give up my little fantasies about a woman—a human woman—who scorned me, and the bizarre comfort I got from the idea that she was still alive somewhere, and my shameful commitment to a promise I once made to her.

Lately, I've been having dreams. Dreams of her. Dreams of myself, driving my sword through my father's chest. Dreams of a silver-eyed little boy thrusting a blade through my heart.

I didn't come to Salinae to kill her.

I tell myself this, though I don't know why. No previous Nightborn king would hesitate to kill such an obvious liability.

You're too soft, *my own father whispers to me, and I know he's right.*

I don't need to kill her, I tell myself. I only need to kill the child. The child is the danger. She is inconsequential.

But when I fly over the Salinae human districts, burning and burning with Nightfire, and I land before the pile of ruin that used to be a house, I'm not expecting the intensity of emotion that spears me.

I stare at the house—what once was a house—for a long moment.

I smell no life. I hear no heartbeat. Once, I could sense her from across the room—across the castle—like her body itself called to me, making its presence constantly known.

Her absence now is even more overpowering. A great hole that has opened up in my soul.

Regret, fierce and unrelenting, tears me up.

Three of my soldiers surround the remains of the house, but they haven't yet seen me. I consider flying away. Every part of me wants to turn away from this wreckage and lock it somewhere I don't have to think about it.

But the absence of the heartbeat I was looking for made me miss the one that remained. The three Hiaj below were circling something, their interest piqued with hunger.

I can, at least, finish what I came here for.

I land. One of the soldiers is cursing and rubbing his bloody hand.

"A lamb?" he mutters. "More like a viper."

Then the warriors notice me and hurry to bow. I don't pay attention to them.

Because by then, I have seen you.

You are a lone flicker of light in an expanse of death. The only living thing in this pile of rubble.

In my dreams, my child is a mirror of myself. It is my own face I see when I think of dying by my Heir's hand.

But you, little serpent, look so much like your mother.

I kneel before you. You are so very small. Surely small for your age, though I'm not sure exactly how old that is. Time can be strange for vampires. Your mother has lingered with me for so long that sometimes, I can't remember how long it has been since she left.

You have long, slick black hair that covers your face, and freckles over your nose that blend with the smears of blood and soot, wrinkling as you sneer at me. They make me think of another time, long ago.

But those eyes.

You have my eyes. Silver as the moon, round and full of steel rage. The rage is mine, too. The fearlessness.

I reach for you, and though I can hear in your heartbeat that you're afraid, you don't hesitate to snap at me, sinking your little teeth deep into my finger.

I will not lie to you, little serpent.

I was expecting to kill you that night.

But what I was not expecting was to love you so devastatingly much.

It hits me so suddenly, so overwhelmingly, that I don't even have time to brace myself against it.

You glare at me, like you're ready to go down fighting even against one of the most powerful men in the world, and I smile a little, despite myself.

It takes me a minute to recognize the sensation in my chest. Pride.

I think of my own father and the way he spent my entire life crippling me out of fear of what I would become. Think of the night he casually threw my newborn baby brother out the window to the demons.

It is incomprehensible to me that my father ever felt for me the way I feel in this moment.

Surely no one ever has.

I cannot describe the depth of that emotion, nor the intensity of the terror that comes with it, bound together so inextricably. I came here to excise my greatest weaknesses, and instead, I now offer up my heart to it.

From that moment, little serpent, I could not entertain the possibility of killing you.

I'll do the next best thing, I tell myself. I will raise you. I will protect myself from you by protecting you from a world that would teach you how to kill me.

It can be different, I tell myself, than how it was with my father and me.

It can be different than how it was with her.

I pick you up. You're so tiny and fragile in my arms. Even though you're terrified of me, you cling to my neck, like some part of you knows exactly who I am.

I'm already more afraid than I ever have been.

Afraid of you and what you could do to me. Afraid of the world that could kill you so easily. Afraid of myself, gifted with another fragile heart that I know I cannot keep.

But, my little serpent, it is the most wonderful fear.

Every minute with you is, even if I already regret all the mistakes I know I will make.

I DREW IN A GASP. My chest hurt. The air burned.

I was on my knees now.

I forced my eyes open through the noxious smoke. No—not smoke. Magic of some kind, thick and red, shimmering in a million colors at once.

Maybe that was why tears streaked down my cheeks.

Maybe not.

Vincent was kneeling beside me. His hand was on my shoulder, but I couldn't feel his touch, and for a moment that devastated me.

No matter how real he felt, no matter how real he looked, he was gone.

He smiled sadly at me.

"I tried, Oraya," he murmured. "I tried."

I understood the depth of what he was admitting in those two words. Centuries worth of brutality ingrained into him, revered above all else. Millennia worth of generations of bloody ends and bloody beginnings.

I had never seen Vincent admit weakness before. And those words were a concession of so many failures.

And yet, I was still so angry at him.

"It wasn't enough," I choked out, fractured with an

almost-sob.

His throat bobbed. "I know, little serpent," he murmured. "I know."

He tried to stroke my hair, but I felt nothing.

Because Vincent was dead.

All of it was true at once. That he had saved me. That he had crippled me. His selfishness and his selflessness.

That he had tried.

That he had failed.

And that he had loved me, anyway.

And I would carry all of that forever, for the rest of my life.

And he would still be dead.

I forced myself to my feet. I turned to Vincent. His image, once so sharp, was starting to fade.

He looked to the obelisk.

"I think," he said, "this is what you came here for."

I followed his gaze. The pillar had opened, revealing a cavity full of rippling crimson light.

And there, at its center, was a little vial, floating, self-contained, in the air. The liquid within contained impossible multitudes of color, shifting and changing with every passing second. Purple and blue and red and gold and green, all at once, like the range of shades in a galaxy.

"The blood of Alarus," I whispered.

"Your mother and I gave up so much to distill this." His gaze found mine again. "But we gained so much, too."

"What do I do with it? Do I drink it or—or wield it—"

"You can drink it. Only a little bit. Or you can put it in your blades. It will find a way to give you its power, however you wield it. Your blood is the catalyst."

"What will it do to me?"

I thought of Simon, and his bloodshot, empty eyes. Those teeth that had taken more from him than they had given.

"It will make you powerful," Vincent said.

"What else?"

"I cannot say."

There was a reason, I knew, why he had never used the blood. It was a power so great it could only be an absolute last resort.

I reached into the compartment and closed my hand around the vial.

It took a moment to realize the scream that sliced the air was mine. Everything disappeared but the pain for several long seconds. I was dripping with sweat when, inch by inch, I withdrew it from the obelisk.

Vincent's form now flickered. The light that imbued the carvings shuddered and skipped.

"Go," he said. "You don't have much time."

His voice sounded so far away.

He gave me a gentle smile. "Don't forget those teeth of yours, little serpent."

And Goddess, despite everything, I hesitated. Despite everything, I was not ready to let him go.

I would never be ready to let him go.

"I love you," I said.

Because it was still true. After everything, it was still true.

I didn't wait for him to say it back to me. I wiped the tears from my cheeks and turned away.

The image of Vincent withered away into darkness.

I didn't look back.

72

RAIHN

S imon didn't let up. And I matched him.

The two of us locked ourselves in nonstop combat, swords and magic clashing in a blurred cacophonous melody. The blood from the battle in the skies above now rained down over us in a steady rhythm, drenching us in black — covering us in so much blood it was impossible to tell how much of it was our own. I no longer felt the blows. The pain was so constant that I just let it fall into the background, another distraction to be ignored.

I wasn't sure how I wasn't dead yet. Felt like I should be. My body threatened to give out with every movement.

I just kept telling myself, *One more swing.*

One more.

I didn't expect to come out of this alive. But I sure as fuck wasn't about to let Simon live, either.

Whenever I could steal precious seconds, I glanced over my shoulder, to the distant doorway in the ruins — an abyss of black, with no sign of Oraya.

With every passing minute, my heart crawled up my throat.

Come on, princess. Where are you?

I was grateful that holding off Simon took all my focus. Otherwise, I'd linger too long on the millions of horrifying scenarios that danced in the back of my head—Oraya's body broken by traps or crushed by stone or burned up by magic she couldn't control.

SMACK.

An especially devastating strike from Simon slammed me against a sheet of rock. I felt the impact in my bones. My head lolled. My vision dipped into fuzzy white.

When I forced myself back to consciousness, mere seconds later, the first thing I saw was Simon's snarling face rushing toward me.

I barely managed to roll out of the way.

Countered, clumsily.

Warmth dotted my face in a fresh spray of blood. I hit something. Wasn't sure what. Couldn't count how many blows I'd gotten in by now.

He roared and returned my strike.

Another spatter of red-black over his cheek, now. Another distant throb of pain. Another wound.

Couldn't count those, either.

I tried to swing my sword and realized my left arm had now completely given up on working. *Fuck.* I switched hands quickly, drawing back—

Too slow.

I slammed against another column, the broken edge jamming into my spine at just the right angle to knock the breath from my lungs. My body slumped against it and wanted desperately to stay that way.

Don't you dare, I told it. *Get the fuck up.*

Simon stalked toward me. He was a pathetic sight, too, limping, blood smearing down his face. One eye was now missing, or at least seemed like it was, beneath the mess of tattered flesh.

Still, that damned magic pulsed at his chest, stubbornly clinging on despite every blow I levied to it. Keeping him going long after any mortal body would give out. Making him stronger than I ever could be.

"You," he growled, "should not be so much trouble."

Movement out of the corner of my eye.

I made the mistake of looking.

Oraya.

For a moment, I thought maybe I was hallucinating. She staggered from the darkness. Blood drenched her hands and smeared her face. She was running, though half-stumbling, looking around wildly.

And she was surrounded by magic.

I'd seen her wielding her Nightfire before, but this—it was fucking magnificent. It embraced her now, licks of stunning white-blue cutting through the night, fanning out around her like the wings of the gods themselves.

Yet the magic that pulsed around her left hand, which was closed tight, was different than the Nightfire. I could sense it even from here—*feel* it, in the air. The clusters of smoke around that clenched fist were red and dark, and otherworldly in a way that made my skin crawl, even from all the way over here. It clung to her like it was made for her, wisps lingering at her skin and the blades at her hips.

I had no doubts of what I was seeing.

She had it. She fucking did it.

For a few endless seconds, my relief and pride battled each other for dominance, neither winning.

But then I saw Simon's head turn. His bloodthirsty fury melted away, replaced by something even more terrifying: lustful desire.

He knew. He felt it too.

He dropped me and started to turn.

Oraya's gaze met mine across the ruins. A second of eye contact that seemed to last an eternity, holding a million unspoken words, teetering on the edge of the end.

I wished I could use this moment to say all that I wanted to. So many things I wished I'd said.

I hoped she knew it all, anyway.

Because I didn't even have to think before I charged.

It was like my body knew what was happening, and deemed it a worthy cause for one last push beyond the edges of my capability. Every shred of my remaining strength—physical and magical—united in this single lunge. Asteris roared to the surface of my skin, clinging to my blade, my hands. My arms managed to lift the weight of my sword one last time.

I leapt at Simon, wings spreading to propel me through this final strike, and I buried my sword into his back, pouring every scrap of magic I had into that blow, ripping him apart from the inside out.

Black light overtook my vision.

Simon let out an animalistic bellow and whirled around. The only piece of the world I managed to cling to was the hilt of my sword. Everything else withered.

I'd just unleashed something in Simon, his strikes now nothing but feral rage. Gone were the final vestiges of the calculated warrior. He was practically coming at me with teeth and fingernails.

He hurled me against the wall. His hand slammed against my throat, pinning it to stone.

I couldn't see. Couldn't feel anything but my grip around that hilt.

That was all I needed, anyway.

Because as his fingers tightened around my throat, as his blade drove into my flesh over and over again, I clutched that hilt with everything I had and *pushed*.

And pushed. And pushed.

The blade parted leather, muscle, organs.

He was so far gone that it took what felt like an eternity for the wound to catch up to him. Slowly, his eyes, bloodshot and frenzied, went distant.

At least, I thought to myself, I got to see what that looked like.

His arm faltered mid-swing. My strength gave out. My hand,

blood-slicked, slipped from my sword, which was now lodged firmly into his torso.

I couldn't reach for it again.

A sudden release of pressure, as someone grabbed Simon and yanked him off me.

The blurry image of Simon's slackening face was replaced with Oraya's.

Now that was a welcome trade. I tried to tell her so, but I couldn't speak.

Her eyes were so wide and bright, like two silver coins. She said something I couldn't hear over the rush of blood in my ears. She was shaking.

You don't have to look so scared, princess, I tried to tell her. But when I attempted to straighten, I only fell to my knees.

And everything was dark.

73

ORAYA

"R aihn!"

I didn't mean to scream his name. It ripped itself from my throat when he fell. I barely heard it so much as I *felt* it, a distillation of emotion too powerful to remain inside me.

I had run from those tunnels into the bowels of fucking hell.

The sight of it had shocked me, horrified me. The sky was dark with warriors tangled in combat, and the sandy ground of the ruins drenched with flower-bloom spatters of blood that rained from the bodies above. In the distance, beyond the rocks, our ground forces were locked in combat with the Blood-born—human, Hiaj, Rishan, Bloodborn, all tearing each other apart.

No horror story could top this. No nightmare. Not even the prison of the gods could be worse than this.

And yet, none of it was as horrifying as seeing Raihn like this, a collection of broken tissue and tattered flesh, lying on the ground.

Suddenly I was on the grounds of the colosseum in the final trial. Suddenly I was losing him all over again.

"Raihn." I grabbed him by the shredded leather of his armor and shook him, hard. "Get up. Get the fuck up."

His head lolled. I expected a bleary blink, a half smile, a *fuck you, too, princess.*

What I got was nothing.

I pressed my hand to his chest. Or at least, I tried to, even though it required me to do the impossible—find an expanse of skin that wasn't an open wound.

It rose and fell. So, so weakly.

He was alive. But I knew that wouldn't last. I'd spent so much of my life sensing death looming over me. I knew what it felt like when it was near.

Out of the corner of my eye, I saw Simon stir. He was a monster at this point, a grotesque puppet of twisted flesh and gore. But that magic, that noxious, terrible magic, would keep him going.

I shook Raihn again. "*Raihn.* I forbid you to die on me. Do you understand? Get the fuck up. You swore to me—you swore—"

Never again, he'd promised me, in the springs. He swore to me that he would never betray me again.

And this—losing him—felt like the greatest betrayal.

No. No, I refused to let it happen.

I grabbed my blade and sliced my hand open again, squeezing the blood into Raihn's parted lips. It pooled and dribbled out pathetically from the corner of his mouth, useless.

And still, he did not move.

Everything else in my mind simply shut down. Grief cracked open inside me, drowning me, uncontrollable.

Behind me, Simon twitched again, gurgling groans rising from his decimated body.

Above me, blood rained down from the heavens.

Around me, my people fell to the blades of my enemies.

Before me, my husband died.

And in my hand, clutched against burnt flesh, was a power strong enough to end it all.

All my life, I had wanted to be something to fear. It was my father's dream, shouldered from the moment I could understand how to build the strength he expected of me and excise the weaknesses he disapproved of.

If I used the blood of a god, I would certainly become something to fear. I would be more terrifying than Simon was. I could destroy him. Septimus. The Bloodborn. I could kill every enemy and make sure no one ever would question or threaten me or my people ever again.

They would write legends about me.

But that would be the power of destruction.

I would not be able to save Raihn.

I opened my palm. The skin cracked and bled, charred by the power of the vial I clutched against it. Yet that ugliness only highlighted the incandescence of what sat within it, the blood a galaxy of colors against the darkest shadows of night.

It was so incredibly beautiful.

I blinked and a tear rolled down my cheek.

I wouldn't lose one more thing. One more person. I couldn't.

This blood could be used as a tool of destruction, yes. But how else could it be used?

Once I had cherished my dead father's dirty wine glasses. I'd wrapped myself in his discarded clothing. If someone had offered me a piece of his hair, I'd have wept for it.

This blood was more than a weapon. It was a piece of someone who had once been loved. It was a bargaining chip, priceless to the one being who I knew would treasure it above all.

As Simon grunted and pushed himself to his hands and knees, I lifted my eyes to the sky. Beyond the winged bodies above, storm clouds swirled in unnatural wisps—like fish circling a pond, fragments of suspended lightning dancing between them.

I'd only seen the sky like that once before. When we had the attention of the gods.

I raised the vial above my head, as if offering it to the heavens.

"My Mother of the Ravenous Dark," I screamed. "I call upon you, Goddess of Night, of Blood, of Shadow. I offer you the blood of your husband, Alarus. Hear me, my Goddess, Nyaxia."

74

ORAYA

For a few long, terrible seconds, nothing happened.

The battle continued. Simon kept slowly pushing himself to his knees. Raihn kept dying.

More tears welled up in my eyes.

No. This had to work. It had to.

My arm shook as I held that vial to the sky, held it as high as I could, my eyes staring unblinking into the god-touched night above.

Please, I pleaded, silently. *Please, Nyaxia. I know I've never been yours. Not really. But I'm begging you to hear me.*

And then, as if she heard my silent prayer, there she was.

Time seemed to slow, the figures above moving in slow motion. The breeze through my hair grew cold, the strands suspended in midair. My skin pebbled, as if in the moments preceding a strike of lightning.

Just like last time, I felt her before I saw her. A staggering sensation of overwhelming adoration, and overwhelming smallness.

"What," a low, melodic voice said, deadly as a drawn blade, "is happening here?"

There was only one thing, I realized in this moment, more terrifying than the presence of a god.

And that was the rage of one.

I slowly lowered my eyes.

Nyaxia floated before me.

She was just as beautiful, just as terrible, as I remembered her. Hers was the kind of beauty that made you want to prostrate yourself before her. Her hair floated in tendrils of ink-black night. Her bare feet hovered, delicately pointed, just above the ground. Her body, dipped in silver, gleamed and shone like moonlight in the darkness. Those eyes, revealing every shade of the night sky, were dark and stormy with utter fury.

The world itself felt that fury. Ceded to it. As if the air was desperate to please her, the stars moving to soothe her, the moon ready to bow to her.

Perhaps the fighting stopped, when Nyaxia appeared, soldiers on all sides shocked by what they were in the presence of. Or perhaps it just seemed that way, because everything else ceased to exist when she arrived.

Her shoulders rose and fell with heavy breaths. Her bloody lips contorted into a snarl.

"What," she ground out, "is this *atrocity?*"

She spat the word, and with it, a burst of power shook the earth. I cringed, my body folding over Raihn's as rocks and sand cascaded from the ruins. Wisps of stormy shadow surrounded her, leeching out into the air with the ominous darkness of tragedy.

Simon had managed to get himself up to his knees. He turned to her, bowing, blood spilling from his mouth as he spoke. "My Goddess —"

I didn't even see Nyaxia move. One moment, she was before me, and the next, she was at Simon, hoisting him up with a single hand and ripping the pendant from his chest with the other.

It was so sudden, so brutal, that I let out a little gasp, my own body bracing tighter over Raihn's.

Nyaxia let Simon's corpse, limp and bleeding, fall to the ground without so much as a second glance.

Instead, she cradled the twisted creation of steel and teeth in her hands, staring down at it.

Her face was blank. But the sky grew darker, the air colder. I was shaking—whether with shivers or fear, or maybe both, I wasn't sure. I still leaned over Raihn, and I couldn't bring myself to stop, even though I knew it was pointless.

I couldn't protect him from the wrath of a goddess.

Her fingertips traced the pendant—the broken teeth welded into it. "Who did this?"

I wasn't expecting that. For her to sound so... broken.

"My love," she murmured. "Look at what you've become."

The pain in her voice was so naked. So familiar.

No, grief never really left us. Not even for the gods. Two thousand years, and Nyaxia's was still tender as ever.

Then, in an eerily sudden movement, her head snapped up.

Her eyes landed on me.

My head emptied of thought. The full force of Nyaxia's attention was devastating.

The pendant in her hands disappeared, and suddenly, she was before me.

"How did this happen?" she snarled. "My own children, using the body parts of my husband's corpse for their own pathetic gains? What incredible disrespect."

Talk, Oraya, an urgent voice reminded me. *Explain. Say something.*

I had to force the words out.

"I agree," I said. "I'm returning what is rightfully yours. Your husband's blood, my Mother."

I opened my fingers, offering her the vial in my shaking palm.

Her face softened. A glimmer of grief. A glimmer of sadness.

She reached for it, but I moved it away—a stupid move, I recognized right after I'd done it, when her sadness was replaced by anger.

"I ask for a deal," I said quickly. "One favor, and it's yours."

Her face darkened. "It is already mine."

That was a fair point. I was gambling with something that was not mine to trade, with leverage that was laughable against a goddess. I was so afraid. I was grateful I was kneeling, because otherwise, I was sure my knees would have buckled.

I tethered myself to the sensation of Raihn's fading heartbeat beneath my palm, and my own heightening desperation.

"I appeal to your heart, my Mother," I choked out. "As a lover who knows grief. Please. You're right, your husband's blood is yours. I know I cannot, and would not, keep it from you. But I—I ask you for a favor in return."

I swallowed thickly, my next words heavy on my tongue. If I wasn't so distracted, maybe this would have been funny. My entire life, I'd dreamed of asking Nyaxia for this very gift—but never did I think it would be under these circumstances.

I said, "My Mother, I ask you for a Coriatis bond. Please."

My voice cracked over my plea.

A Coriatis bond. The god-given gift I'd once thought would give me the power I needed to be Vincent's true daughter. Now, I was giving up my father's greatest weapon to bind myself to the man I'd once thought was my greatest enemy. To save his life.

Love, over power.

Nyaxia's gaze flicked down. She seemed to notice Raihn for the first time since she'd arrived, with only passing interest.

"Ah," she said. "I see. Much has changed, I suppose, since the last time you begged me for his life."

Before, Nyaxia had laughed when I'd asked her to save Raihn's life, amused by the antics of her mortal followers. But there was no amusement in her eyes, now. I wished I could read her face.

I wished I had better words for her.

"Please," I choked out, again. Another tear slid down my cheek.

She leaned down. Her fingertips caressed my face, tipping my chin toward her. She was so close that she could've kissed me, close enough that I could count the stars and galaxies in her eyes.

"I told you once, little human," she murmured. "A dead lover can never break your heart. You did not listen to me then."

And Raihn had broken my heart that night. I couldn't deny that.

"You should have let the flower of your love remain forever frozen as it was," she said. "So beautiful at its peak. So much less painful."

But there was no such thing as love without fear. Love without vulnerability. Love without risk.

"Not as beautiful as one that lives," I whispered.

A flicker of something I couldn't decipher passed over Nyaxia's face. She reached for the vial in my palm, and this time, I let her. Her fingers touched it tenderly, like the caress of a lover.

She let out a soft, bitter laugh.

"Spoken by someone too young to see the ugliness of its decay."

Was this what she told herself? Was this how she stifled her grief over her husband's death? Did she convince herself it was better this way?

The last time I'd met Nyaxia, she had seemed a force greater than any mortal could comprehend.

Now, she seemed... so tragically imperfect. Fallible in all the same ways as us.

"It would have bloomed," I said softly. "If he had lived. You and Alarus. Your love wouldn't have withered."

Nyaxia's eyes snapped to me, like I'd startled her by speaking —like she'd gone somewhere far away, forgetting I was here at all.

For a moment, grief collapsed in her beautiful face.

Then she shuttered it behind an ice wall, pristine features going still. She snatched the vial from my hand and drew herself back up to her full height.

"I feel your pain, my child," she said. "But I cannot grant you a Coriatis bond."

The words obliterated me.

My skin went numb. My ears rang. I could not hear anything over the sound of my heart shattering at my goddess's feet.

"*Please*—" I begged.

"I am a romantic," she said. "It brings me no pleasure to deny you. But you and him—you were created, thousands of years ago, as enemies. Those roles are marked onto your skin. Hiaj. Rishan."

My chest burned, my Heir Mark pulsing, as if awoken by her mention of it.

"Roles given by *you*," I said, even though I knew it was stupid to argue with her—

"Roles given by your forefathers," she corrected. "Do you know why I created the Hiaj and Rishan lines? Because even before Obitraes was the land of vampires, your peoples fought. A perpetual power struggle that would never end. It is what you are meant to be. If I grant you a Coriatis bond, your hearts would become one, your lines intertwined. It would erase the Hiaj and Rishan legacy forever."

"It would eliminate two thousand years of unrest."

And it wasn't until Nyaxia nodded slowly, giving me a long, hard stare, that I realized:

We were saying the same thing.

Nyaxia had no interest in ending two thousand years of unrest.

Nyaxia liked her children squabbling, constantly vying over each other for her affections and favor.

Nyaxia would not grant me a Coriatis bond with Raihn, would not allow me to save his life, out of nothing but petty stubbornness.

I opened my mouth, but nothing came out. My anger swallowed all words.

Nyaxia sensed it anyway, though, a flash of disapproval over her features. She leaned close again. "I'm handing you victory for the second time, my child. Perhaps you should simply take it. Don't all little girls dream of being queens?"

Did you? I wanted to ask her. *Did you dream of becoming this?*

Instead, I rasped, "Then tell me how to save him."

Her perfect lips thinned, another drop of blood rolling down her chin with the shift of her muscles. Her lashes lowered as she took in Raihn's mangled body.

"He is practically already dead," she said.

"There has to be something."

Another indecipherable emotion over her face. Perhaps genuine pity.

She flicked a tear from my cheek.

"A Coriatis bond would save him," she said. "But I cannot be the one to give it to you."

She rose and turned away. I didn't look up from Raihn's battered features, which blurred with my unshed tears.

"Oraya of the Nightborn."

I lifted my head.

Nyaxia stood at Simon's broken body, nudging it with her toe.

"Treasure that flower," she said. "No one will ever be able to hurt you again."

And then she was gone.

No one will ever be able to hurt you again.

Her words echoed in my head as I let out the sob I'd been choking back. I leaned over Raihn, pressing my forehead to his.

His breath, ever-fading, was so weak against my lips.

I did not care that Simon was dead.

I did not care that the Rishan were retreating.

I did not care if I had won my war.

Raihn was dying in my arms.

Slow rage built in my chest.

Treasure that flower.

Perhaps you should just take it.

Spoken by someone too young to see the ugliness of its decay.

With every memory of Nyaxia's voice, it grew hotter.

No.

No, I refused to accept it. I had come this fucking far. I had sacrificed so much. I refused to sacrifice this, too.

I refused to sacrifice *him*.

A Coriatis bond, Nyaxia had said. *But I cannot be the one to give it to you.*

The answer was right there.

A Coriatis bond could only be forged by a god. And yes, Nyaxia had denied me. But Nyaxia wasn't the only goddess my blood called to. She was my father's goddess.

My mother's was just as powerful.

Crazed hope seized me. I looked up to the sky—the sky still bright and swirling with the thinning barrier between this world and the next. And maybe I imagined it—maybe I was a naive fool for it—but I could have sworn I felt the eyes of the gods on me.

"My Goddess Acaeja," I cried out, my voice cracking. "I summon you in the name of my mother, your acolyte, Alana of Obitraes, in my greatest time of need. Hear me, Acaeja, I beg you."

And perhaps I wasn't insane after all.

Because when I called, a goddess answered.

75

ORAYA

caeja's beauty was not the beauty of Nyaxia. Nyaxia was
beautiful the way many women hoped to be, albeit a
million times over, a force greater than a mortal mind
could even comprehend.

Acaeja's beauty, though, was terrifying.

When she landed before me, I started shaking.

She was tall, even taller than Nyaxia was, with a regal, strong
face. But more imposing than her stature were the wings—six of
them layered over each other, three to each side. Each one acted
as a window to a different world, a different fate—a field of blossoms beneath a cloudless summer sky, a bustling human city
beneath a lightning storm, a forest raging with fire. She wore
long white robes that pooled around her bare feet. Strings of
light—the threads of fate—dangled from her ten-fingered hands.

Her face tilted toward me, cloudy white eyes meeting mine.

I gasped and tore my gaze away.

A second of that stare, and I saw my past, my present, my
future, blurring by too fast to comprehend. Fitting, that was
what one would see, looking into the eyes of the Weaver of
Fates.

"Do not be afraid, my daughter."

Her voice was the amalgamation of so many different tones—child, maiden, elder.

Fear is just a collection of physical responses, I told myself, and I forced myself to meet Acaeja's gaze again.

She knelt before me—observing Raihn, and then me, with detached interest.

"You called," she said simply.

You answered, I almost replied, because I was still in shock that she actually *had.*

I groped for words and came up empty-handed. But she grabbed my chin, gently but firmly, and looked into my eyes like she was reading the pages of a book. Her gaze flicked back to Raihn.

"Ah," she said. "I see."

"A Coriatis bond," I managed. "I ask you, Great Goddess, for a Coriatis bond. My mother devoted her life to you, and I—I'll offer you anything if—"

Acaeja raised a single hand.

"Hush, child. I understand what you seek. Your mother was indeed a devoted follower of mine. I am quite protective of those who walk the unknown beside me." She scanned the carnage that surrounded us, lips thinning with a brief wave of disapproval. "Even if they walk it, at times, to questionable ends, tampering with forces that should not be disturbed."

I bit back a wave of shame on my mother's behalf.

"Please," I whispered. "If you grant us a Coriatis bond, if you help me save him, I swear to you—"

Again, Acaeja raised her palm.

"Do you understand the gravity of what you ask of me?"

This, I knew, was not a rhetorical question.

"Yes," I said. "I do."

"Do you understand that you are asking me for something I have never once granted before?"

My eyes prickled. Another tear rolled down my cheek. "Yes."

Only Nyaxia had ever granted a Coriatis bond. Never a single god of the White Pantheon.

But I was willing to try anything. Anything.

"Countless times, my followers have begged me to save their loved ones from death. Death is not the enemy. Death is a natural continuation of life. An intrinsic part of fate." The visions in her wings shifted, as if to demonstrate—revealing glimpses of dark skies and bones and flowers growing from rotting flesh. "What makes you different?"

Nothing, I thought, at first. I was just another grieving lover, standing on the precipice of one more loss she couldn't bear.

But I rasped out, "Because he could do such great things for this kingdom. We could, together. We could make things so much better for the people who live here. People—" My voice grew stronger. "People like my mother, who devoted her life to you, even when trying to survive so many hardships here."

Acaeja tilted her head, as if she found this answer interesting. Compared to Nyaxia's blatant emotionality, she was distant, calculated. I couldn't read her.

I knew Nyaxia, despite her cruel dismissal, felt my pain. Acaeja, I feared, was only analyzing it.

"My cousin spoke the truth to you," she said. "Granting a Coriatis bond between two Heirs would alter the course of the House of Night forever."

"It would end millennia of warfare."

"Yes. But it would come with many challenges, as well."

My hand closed around Raihn's limp, bloody fingers. "I know. We would face them."

It almost surprised me, how easily this answer came to me. It wasn't a platitude, wasn't a performance. It was the truth.

Acaeja stared at me for a long moment. A shiver ran up my spine—the uncomfortable feeling that my past and future were being rifled through like pages in a record log.

Then she let out a soft chuckle. "Humans," she said softly. "Such hope."

I waited, not breathing.

At last, she said, "If I grant this request, do you swear that to me? That you both will use the power I am granting you to fight for what is Right in this world and the next, even against great opposition?"

My heart leapt.

"Yes," I said. "Yes. I do."

"You will be under my protection as an offspring of my acolyte, and that protection will extend to him, as your heart-bonded. But understand that my cousin will not be happy about this development. She will not act against you. Not today. Not tomorrow. But someday soon, Oraya of the Nightborn, there will come a day when Nyaxia brings a great reckoning. And when that day comes, you must be prepared to face her displeasure."

Goddess fucking help us.

And maybe I was a fool for it, but I still didn't hesitate.

"Yes," I said. "I understand."

"I see your truth. I see the possibility in both your futures. I see that there is still much to come. And for that reason, I will grant you a Coriatis bond."

The words were so unbelievable. At first, I couldn't even grasp them.

"Thank you," I tried to say, but it drowned in a sob.

"Quickly," Acaeja said. "He fades."

My eyes fell to Raihn's face—motionless, battered, covered in blood, features broken beyond recognition. And yet, for some reason, the image of that same face on our wedding night came to my mind. The night he had promised himself to me, and I couldn't offer him the same.

"This will be painful," Acaeja warned.

She touched my chest, right over my heart.

"Painful" was not the right word for it. I gasped at the bolt of agony—like someone was spearing me straight through, hooking my heart and dragging it through my ribcage.

Still, I didn't flinch, didn't close my eyes. I looked only at Raihn's face. Through the haze of pain, I heard our wedding vows:

I give you my body.

I give you my blood.

I give you my soul.

Acaeja drew her hand from my chest, slowly, as if pulling a great weight, and then pressed it to Raihn's. A blinding white light engulfed us.

The pain intensified.

From this night until the end of nights.

I doubled over, my forehead leaning against Raihn's.

From daybreak until our days are broken.

Acaeja drew her hands back, a thread of light between them.

"I bind these hearts together." Her voice rippled through the air like water. "Their souls are one. Their power is one. From this moment, until their threads cross this mortal plane."

Her hands splayed, twenty long fingers weaving together our fates—and then, in one abrupt movement, drawing the threads taut.

I doubled over, unable to move, to breathe. My eyes squeezed shut. My head emptied of everything except for five words:

I give you my heart.

The words I wouldn't—couldn't—say to Raihn that night. The vow I could not make.

Now I whispered those words over and over again, clinging to them, as my soul itself shattered and reformed.

"I give you my heart," I murmured against his skin. "I give you my heart. I give you my heart."

The light faded. The pain ebbed.

Acaeja sounded very far away, her voice like a wave rolling from the shore, as she said, "It is done."

The words faded off into oblivion.

And so did I.

PART SEVEN

DAWN

76

ORAYA

I did not dream of Vincent.
I dreamt of nothing at all.

I OPENED my eyes to a blue cerulean ceiling. It was the same ceiling that I had awoken to every day for nearly twenty years. But this time, from that first moment, everything felt different. As if my innermost self had been rearranged.

I felt... stronger. Like my blood thrummed through my veins with greater force.

And...

I laid my hand over my chest. Over my heart.

And... weaker.

Like a piece of my soul, the most vulnerable part of me, was now outside my body.

My mind pieced together the events of the battle, not quite in order, and then I shot bolt upright.

Every thought disintegrated except for his name.

Raihn.

My room was empty. An unoccupied chair sat beside my bed, and a few empty cups and plates on my nightstand, like someone had been here but had just left.

Raihn.

I threw back the covers and stood, only to immediately topple back to the bed with a dizzy spell that had my stomach lurching. An odd tug on my awareness disoriented me, like I was seeing something out of the corner of my eye that wasn't there, or witnessing this room from another angle.

Mother. I must've really hit my head.

I got to my feet again and went out into my living room, then threw open my apartment door.

Raihn.

I wasn't sure how I knew exactly where he was. Only that, without thinking, I was walking over to his chambers and —

The door swung open just as my fingertips brushed the knob.

He was alive.

He was alive.

I didn't take in anything else about him, only that he was here and alive and standing right before me and alive and smiling and *alive.*

And then his arms were around me, and mine around him, and the two of us held each other for a minute and an eternity, like two halves reunited. I buried my face against the bare skin of his chest and squeezed my eyes shut against the tears.

For a long time, we stayed like that.

And then eventually, he murmured against my hair, "So you missed me."

Arrogant prick, I thought.

But aloud I said, "I love you."

I felt his shock at those words — actually *felt* it, like it was my own. And then, the wave of contentment that followed, like the sun falling over my face.

His arms tightened. "Good. Because now you're really stuck with me."

I scoffed, but the sound was muffled against his skin, and it sounded much weaker than I'd intended.

His lips pressed to the top of my head.

And he whispered, "I love you too, Oraya. Goddess fucking help me, I do."

HE PULLED me into his apartment, though it was more of a stumble, the two of us not wanting to let go of each other long enough to properly close the door, let alone walk. The need to be physically close to him was disorienting—like our very essences had been united, leaving us with an innate need to get our flesh as close as possible. It wasn't sexual—or at least, it wasn't sexual *right now*. It went deeper than that. More intimate.

I realized, after a few moments, that our heartbeats had aligned—his quickening slightly, mine slowing. And I knew this because I could *feel* his, the same way I could feel my own.

He noticed it the same time as I did.

"Strange," he murmured. "Isn't it?"

Strange was an understatement. And yet it also seemed like... too negative of a word. It didn't feel wrong. It didn't feel unnatural. It didn't even feel frightening, which shocked me, because I would have thought that having my soul linked to another person's would be utterly terrifying.

Linked. Bonded.

Goddess, we had actually *done* that. We had a Coriatis bond.

The realization hit me so hard that I pulled away from Raihn abruptly, nearly sending myself toppling over until he caught me.

"Easy."

I stopped short. My brow furrowed.

I grabbed his shoulders, not to steady myself, but to hold him straight.

I'd been so relieved to see him that I hadn't even stopped to really look at him. He was shirtless, wearing a pair of low-slung cotton trousers, his torso covered with the fading remnants of his injuries and the bandages that had treated them.

But my eyes fell to his chest—his throat.

And the Heir Mark that now covered it.

"Ix's tits," I whispered.

He frowned, looking down at himself, but I dragged him to the mirror instead.

When he saw himself, his eyes bulged.

"Ix's tits," he agreed.

The Mark was nearly identical to mine, albeit slightly modified to match the shape of his body. I was wearing a loose camisole that exposed my neck and shoulders, leaving our two Marks visible side-by-side. The resemblance was uncanny. He had the same layered phases of the moon over his throat, and the smoky rendering of wings over his clavicle and shoulders— except his were the feathered wings of the Rishan.

We stared at each other in the mirror, and then had the same idea at the same time. Raihn turned me around, sliding the straps of my camisole off my shoulders, letting the garment pool around my waist and leaving my torso exposed.

He positioned me, my back was to the mirror, and I peered over my shoulder into it.

Sun fucking take me.

Beside me, Raihn turned around and matched my pose.

The Heir Mark on his back was nearly identical to the one I now bore on mine. The phases of the moon spread across the top of my back, spears of smoke running down my spine.

We looked at each other. The reality of what we'd done—of what had changed—settled over us both.

Nyaxia and Acaeja had both warned us that a Coriatis bond would mean the end of the Rishan and Hiaj Heir lines, combining them into one.

We'd altered the course of the House of Night forever.

I felt a little dizzy, and not from my injuries.

A wrinkle formed between Raihn's brows. The corner of his mouth twitched in an uncertain almost-smirk. "Regrets, princess?"

Regrets?

The answer was easy and immediate. "Fuck, no."

The smirk became a full-on smile, and if I'd had any regrets, that smile would have erased them, anyway.

"Good," he said. "It looks better on you than it does on me, anyway."

I glanced at Raihn's muscled back and wasn't sure that I agreed.

I jumped a little as the door burst open.

"Gods!"

I looked up to see Mische whirling around, nearly dropping the tray in her hands in her hasty effort to cover her eyes.

"I leave you two alone, *unconscious*, for *five minutes* and you're already in here tearing each other's clothes off? At least lock the damned door!"

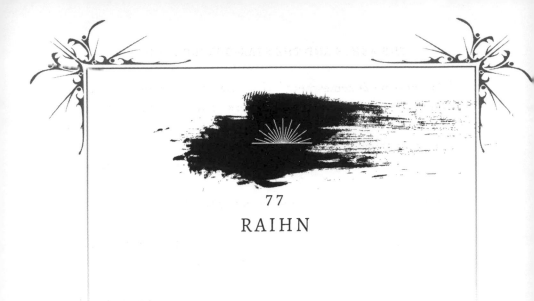

77

RAIHN

I thought it would be more of an adjustment than it was. The Coriatis bond, it turned out, was the easy part. Yes, it was a little odd to get used to. It wasn't as if I could read Oraya's mind, or communicate without speaking, or feel everything she felt—and hell, what fun would that be, anyway, to take all the mystery out of things? It was more that I was now constantly, innately *aware* of her. A biological attunement to her presence, her state, her emotions.

Right now, though, I didn't need any kind of magical goddess-gifted heart bond to know that Oraya was pissed.

She was wearing that *a-cat-is-pissing-on-my-leg-and-you're-the-cat* face. My favorite of the diverse library of Oraya faces. Her arms were crossed over her chest, her foot tapping impatiently. We were in the meeting room, me leaning back in my chair, Oraya bolt upright in hers. Ketura, Vale, Lilith, Jesmine, and Mische sat scattered around the table. Mische was half-slumped across the desk, Lilith was eternally thoughtful, Ketura and Vale were both visibly annoyed, and Jesmine was, of course, ever the ice queen.

"He has to be somewhere," Oraya said.

"I'm sure he *is* somewhere," Jesmine said, pursing her lips. "Snake that he is. But that somewhere is not in the House of Night."

"Did you check —"

"We checked everywhere," Ketura said, throwing her notes down. "Everywhere."

Ketura's frustration, I knew, wasn't with Oraya. It was with herself. She hated losing.

"He must have retreated with the rest of the Bloodborn," Jesmine said. "Was quick about it, apparently."

None of this surprised me.

I wanted Septimus in captivity as much as anyone else. But I was under no illusions that he was about to let himself be caught easily. He was far too smart for that, as much as I hated to give him the credit.

These last few weeks had been a blur, establishing the fragile legs of our new kingdom and eliminating the final parasites of the old one. The Bloodborn, at least, had been easy to get rid of—the minute the goddesses showed up, they apparently knew nothing good was happening and began their retreat. By the time the fighting had stopped and Jesmine and Vale had retrieved Oraya and I, most of the Bloodborn troops were already on their way out of the kingdom.

No one objected to letting them go. Good riddance.

The only one we wanted was Septimus.

But he, it seemed, had been the first to leave. Though Jesmine and Vale both gave orders to have him detained immediately, before Oraya and I had even awoken, he had simply disappeared. And these last few weeks had been no more fruitful, not even as our guards tore through all potential strongholds and searched fleets of departing Bloodborn soldiers.

Septimus was long, long gone.

Vale let out a sigh and rubbed his temples. "Let him slink away with his tail between his legs. If that's how he needs to deal with his defeat, so be it. We have plenty of other traitors to prosecute, and at least those won't start a war."

He tapped the parchment in front of him, black with dozens —hundreds—of names.

"*Another* war," Jesmine corrected, and Vale sighed again.

"Yes. Let's avoid another war. Especially one with another House."

Mische shifted uncomfortably in her seat. I knew she was thinking about the House of Shadow.

We'd been lucky so far. Not a word from them about their prince. If that changed, our strategy was to pin it on Simon, let them believe that justice had already been served.

Risky. But it was the best we had.

Mische, I knew, thought about this possibility more than she let on.

"We did find someone else," Ketura said, jerking my attention back to the meeting. "In the latest set of raids."

I blinked, turning to her. "Someone important?"

Her face hardened, like she'd just smelled something very unpleasant.

"Someone I think you might want to talk to."

CAIRIS LOOKED HORRIBLE. Then again, it would be a little disappointing if he didn't, after hours of questioning by Ketura and Vale's men.

He looked up through the bars, a ray of moonlight falling over his face as he squinted up at me through a swollen eye.

"Oh." His mouth twisted into a wry smirk, a pathetic recreation of his typical smile. "Hello. Sorry I won't be very useful. I already told them everything."

"I figured as much."

I sat down in the chair before the bars, elbows on my knees. Behind me, Oraya slipped into the room too, lingering in the shadows against the wall.

I found it satisfying the way his face dropped with actual fear when he saw her. She found it satisfying, too—I sensed it alongside my own.

"So what, then?" he said. "You've come here to execute me yourself?"

He stood up, as if to prepare himself to meet death standing.

"No," I said. "My time's too valuable for that."

Confusion flitted over Cairis's face. "Then what?"

"Ketura and Vale wanted to execute you." I nodded back toward Oraya. "Your *queen* wanted to execute you."

Bloodthirsty little thing that she was.

"But," I said, "I managed to convince them otherwise."

His brow furrowed. "You—"

"I wanted to make sure I saw your face when the man you betrayed saved your life," I said. "And I also wanted to make sure you knew it was no mercy. Actually, the queen that wanted to kill you was probably the merciful one."

I stood, my silhouette casting a shadow over Cairis's form. I towered over him. He wasn't a small man, either—but he seemed it, now.

I supposed he always had been.

But how could he be anything but?

He'd spent his entire life in fear. He'd learned to survive by bending his spine to fit into his cages. For a while, he'd been able to make himself into something more.

For a while.

But as soon as he found himself staring down the possibility of being a slave again, he just couldn't go back. No values were strong enough to supplant that fear.

I wasn't sure if it made it better or worse that I understood it.

He lowered his eyes. There was shame—real shame—in them.

"I deserve to be executed," he said.

"You do. That's why you won't be. That, and..." I cocked my head and smiled at him, wide enough to reveal my fangs. "I think you might be useful, one day. So you'll be locked up in Tazrak.

Spend a decade or four there, until I decide if I need you for something. People who have something to prove are the most useful kind."

His eyes rose to meet mine again, round. His mouth opened, but nothing came out.

"If you're considering whether or not to thank me," I said. "I think the answer is probably no."

He shut his mouth. But he still said, a moment later, "Thank you."

I chuckled. I started to turn away, but he said, "Do you really think you're going to be able to make this work?"

I stopped. Oraya and I exchanged a glance.

I turned around. "This?" I questioned.

I saw it on Cairis's face, the moment he saw Oraya's back — the Heir Mark, visible above the low back of her blouse, before she, too, turned back to him.

His eyes widened.

I laughed softly and pulled open the top two buttons of my jacket — revealing my Mark, too.

"They're new," I said. "Like them?"

"You did it," he breathed.

The shock on his face was so satisfyingly genuine. Either he'd been living in true isolation wherever he'd been hiding out, or he'd heard the rumors and thought we were lying. Either option amused me.

"We did," Oraya said.

He paled.

"What?" I said. "Realizing now you picked the wrong side?"

I was only half joking, because Cairis really *did* look like he was questioning everything he'd held as truth. He had played by the rules of Neculai's game, right up to the end, thinking it was the only strategy that could ever win.

And here we were, crowns on our heads, having blown the entire board to bits.

He said softly, "Yes. I am."

"You're lucky for it," I said. "Simon would've had you skinned by now."

I started to turn away, but he again called out, "Wait."

Now I was getting impatient.

I turned back, brows raised expectantly.

"Septimus isn't done," he said, then raised his hands, as if in preemptive defense. "I've told Ketura everything I know. I don't have any more facts. I just... It's a feeling. I know it. He's doing something big, Raihn. I don't know what it is. But don't let your guard down."

My smirk faded. Oraya and I exchanged another glance. She raised her brows in a way that said, *See? Didn't I tell you?*

I gave her a flat stare that said, *Yes. You told me.*

"Well," I said to Cairis. "We'll be ready for him. Whenever he decides to show up."

The truth. What else could we offer?

I closed the door behind us as we left, leaving Cairis alone in the dark.

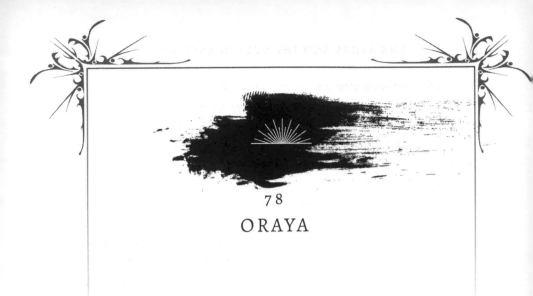

78

ORAYA

I was nervous.

I stood in front of the mirror for a borderline embarrassing amount of time.

I could admit that I looked good. A small army of servants had seen to that, painting my face, smoothing my hair, pinching and prodding my body so that every swell swelled and every dip dipped in all the right places in this dress. Though, I definitely couldn't take credit for making this thing look good. It was nothing short of a work of art. Even more magnificent, somehow, than the one I'd worn at Vale and Lilith's wedding.

It was dark purple, nearly black, and tailored close to my body. It was scandalously revealing—cut low enough to reveal the dimples at the base of my spine, and plunging in the front, the bodice dipping between my breasts. It was designed to frame both my Marks, and it did that very well, the shape complementing every curve and point of the tattoos. The bodice was boned with deep red that echoed the color of the Marks, and those bones, at my hips, gave way to dots of scattered silver that resembled stars, growing thicker as they reached the skirt.

It rivaled the craftsmanship of every weapon I'd ever held.

And I did look every bit a queen. As I should.

The first few weeks of our joint reign had been tense, uncertain. But over the last month, Raihn and I had worked hard to cement our rule over the House of Night. The traitors had been sentenced. The Bloodborn had been expelled. Rebellious nobles had been deposed.

No one had come for our heads.

Yet.

But tonight was the first major festival to take place since the end of the war. Raihn and I would appear before the most respected of vampire society, and we'd make our offering to Nyaxia for the new lunar year. We'd need to be...

Royal.

Fucking *royal*, when one year ago, I'd spent this holiday barred up in my room, forbidden by Vincent to come to the festivities. It had been just a few short weeks before the start of the Kejari.

Little did I know, then, how close I was to everything changing.

I knew Raihn was approaching before I heard his footsteps. I often did, now.

He appeared behind me in the mirror, peering through the open doorway. He let out a low whistle.

"Really?" I said, turning around and examining the dress from the back. "You think so?"

"What the hell else would I think?"

He approached, and I watched him through the mirror. Goddess, the tailors were damned artists. His outfit complemented mine, cut from the same shade of deep purple cloth, the cuffs and the collar adorned with the same star accents.

It was also incredibly flattering. The jacket was shaped impeccably to his body. The buttons started low, leaving the top open to reveal deliberate glimpses of his Mark. Along with a decidedly noticeable expanse of muscled flesh.

"You know," Raihn said, "it's very easy for me to tell now when you're doing that."

"Doing what?" I said innocently.

He was one to talk. As if I didn't also feel his eyes on my chest.

I turned around to face him. My fingertips ran down his throat, tracing the lines of his Mark all the way down to the soft hair of his chest. I thought of the night of the Halfmoon ball, when he'd opened his jacket for me and practically offered up his heart.

Are you going to kill me, princess?

Turned out that answer was yes.

He tipped my chin up. "You look too good to be this nervous."

"It seems like whenever I look this good, something terrible happens."

He choked a laugh. "You may have a point there. I've survived a few coups now and you looking good was a factor in at least two of them."

Bloodshed and ballgowns. They really went together.

But I wasn't ready to joke about it. The memory of the wedding was still too fresh. That, too, had been a grand gesture to show off the power of a new regime to its most important subjects.

And look at how that had ended.

Raihn swept his thumb over the wrinkle on my brow. "What's that face for?"

I stared at him, deadpan, because he knew what that face was for.

"Nothing to be nervous about," he said.

My eyebrows lowered, because fuck that bullshit, I knew he was nervous too.

He sighed. "Fine. You have me. But I'm feeling better already, because if you walk in there wearing that face, it'll put any doubts about our brutal, terrifying power to rest."

I couldn't help it. I laughed.

"There we go."

He smiled. Even though I could still feel the unease beneath it, the expression tugged deep in my chest. There was genuine happiness in that smile. Something a little looser, that hadn't existed when we'd first met.

I remembered the first time I'd heard Raihn laugh, and it had struck me because I didn't know it was possible for anyone to laugh like that—so freely. He smiled like that too. Totally un-vampiric.

I couldn't help but return it.

A knock rang out at the door. Ketura poked her head in.

"The moon is rising," she said. "Everyone's ready for you."

Raihn glanced at me and raised his brows, as if to say, *Well, this is it.*

I took his arm and very subtly wiped the sweat from my palms on his sleeve.

"Nice," he muttered into my ear, as we followed Ketura out the door.

RAIHN and I were led to the balcony of the castle. Not long ago, Raihn had been strung up here to die. Now, we would stand here to address our people.

This feast was always one of Sivrinaj's grandest, and this year's was especially grand besides. In light of our current unique circumstances, we'd decided to open it up more than usual, allowing citizens of Sivrinaj into the outer reaches of the palace grounds. Within the innermost walls, the nobles and officials gathered—all those, of course, who had sworn loyalty to the new king and queen. A crowd of Hiaj, Rishan, and human, alike.

A year ago—hell, *months* ago—such a thing would have been incomprehensible.

A year ago, the thought of even being among all these people, with my throat exposed, would have been paralyzing.

A wave of that terror passed over me as Raihn and I

approached the doorway and I saw the sea of faces beneath—hundreds, maybe thousands. I paused at the silver arch, dizzy. Raihn's hand found the small of my back, his thumb swirling a single comforting circle on bare skin.

He leaned close to me, his lips brushing my ear.

"You're safe," he murmured.

Seemed like some kind of magic, that he always made me believe him.

I straightened my back, wound my fingers through his, and strode out to greet my people alongside him.

Somewhere below, voices rang out in perfect unison:

"Announcing, on this blessed eve, the arrival of the King and Queen of the House of Night!"

The words shivered through the air, hanging there like smoke. They slithered over my skin. I felt Raihn flinch at them, too, like the reality of them struck him in a way he wasn't expecting.

A ripple of movement, as all those countless eyes turned to us.

I stopped breathing.

And I still didn't breathe—couldn't—as all those people, Rishan, Hiaj, and human, lowered into bows, like a wave rolling across the sea.

Goddess help me.

What a sight it was.

I let out a shaky exhale. I was grateful for Raihn's hand, clutching mine so hard it trembled.

He glanced at me through the corner of his eye, crinkled slightly with a smile of relief.

I muttered, quietly enough for only him to hear, "And you didn't even have to rip off anyone's head."

Raihn stifled his chuckle.

THE CEREMONY ITSELF WAS BRIEF—NO vampire wanted to spend more time watching a bunch of religious ritual more than they wanted to spend it eating and drinking and fucking. The feast was to commemorate the end of one lunar year and the beginning of a new one. I'd seen Vincent perform this rite only once before, and I'd had to sneak out to do it, watching from the rooftop of a nearby building and quietly creeping away before anyone could smell me.

It was, needless to say, very different when you were at the center of it.

Raihn and I had to give Nyaxia three offerings.

First, wine—to thank her for the abundance of the year and ask for abundance in the next. We held the glass goblet up together, raising it to the sky, our magic urging the liquid from the glass in an eel-like swirl of deep red and sending it to the stars above.

Then, the bone of an enemy—in appreciation for her protection, and in request for continued strength. We had more than enough to pick from this year, but it seemed particularly appropriate to offer her one of Simon's—a finger bone. We held the polished piece of ivory up to the sky, and with a flash of black light, Raihn's Asteris reduced it to dust, swept away in the wind.

And finally, we would offer her our blood. This was the most important of the three offerings, the one that signaled our eternal loyalty and devotion. She had made our blood what it was, the scriptures said, and thus we would offer it back to her as a sign of our fealty.

Tonight, this seemed a little redundant, given just how much of it we'd spilled for her over the last few months, but neither of us was going to complain about a little more.

Raihn and I made this offering together, our blood shared. We used my blade—because of course, I still carried them everywhere—to open cuts across our palms. Then we pressed our hands together and cupped them. When we lifted them to the night sky, we offered Nyaxia a pool of mingling crimson and black.

Traditionally, Nyaxia would take this offering herself, calling the blood up to the stars.

But now, nothing happened.

Long seconds passed. Raihn and I both grew silently more tense.

If Nyaxia didn't accept the offering, it would make a terrible impression on such an important night. I was prepared to fake it if I had to. It was all a show, after all. Our magic was more than capable of convincingly swirling some blood around in the air.

But finally—after what felt like an eternity, but was only seconds—the blood rose. It danced against the velvet-black like an unfurling wisp of liquid smoke, before being consumed by the darkness.

Raihn and I let out simultaneous exhales of relief.

The spectators, oblivious, broke into applause, mostly cheering that they were now free to go feast and drink. We turned to address them, raising our hands in celebration and thanks, and we looked every bit the picture of the royalty we were supposed to be.

But my eyes drifted up to the night sky, where swirls of odd, gleaming clouds lingered, like clustered fragments of moonlight.

And for some reason, Acaeja's warning rang out in my mind:

There will come a day when Nyaxia will bring a reckoning.

Not today. Not tomorrow.

But it will come.

Then I blinked, and the strange clouds disappeared—like they'd never existed at all, just another figment of my imagination.

79

RAIHN

The feast was one for the record books. Historians would, one day, write about this party, though they'd have to make some things up, because if they were there, they were probably too drunk to remember it firsthand. It was almost a shame that Cairis wasn't around to appreciate it. He'd have been impressed.

After the ceremony, Oraya and I were thrown into engagement after engagement, shuffled around by Vale and Lilith from one set of nobles to another, making deadly-polite conversation and making sure all the right people knew just how frightening and powerful we were.

I preferred the Kejari. I was much more comfortable fighting with swords than words. Still, Oraya and I both turned out to be better at this than we thought. The hours wore on, and the event was, by all accounts, a success.

It was the small hours of the morning by the time I finally managed to slip away from my obligations. Oraya and I had gotten separated some time ago—Vale dragging me one way and Jesmine dragging her another—but one of the many benefits of the Coriatis bond was that I now always knew when Oraya was safe and when she wasn't. I sensed no hint of distress, so instead of fighting through the crowd to look for her and risking getting pulled aside by yet another Rishan noble, I decided to find someone I actually wanted to talk to.

It was never that hard to find Mische at these types of events. She was always either near the food or the flowers. This time, I found her near the flowers. She'd wandered away from the main party, walking through the garden's blooming shrubberies. When I came across her, she was staring into a wall of blossoms, silhouetted against them.

I'd paused for a moment, my smile fading.

Something about the image was so... sad.

"Careful where you wander unannounced out here," I said, approaching her. "There are at least a dozen couples fucking somewhere in this maze."

She laughed a little as she turned to me. A bit of my concern eased when I saw the overflowing plate of food in her hand. If she'd been empty-handed, I'd know we were really in trouble.

"Surprised you're not one of them," she said.

"Yet."

That thought distracted me briefly. I was joking, but also, it wasn't a bad idea.

She scoffed, then took a bite of a pastry. "That went well," she said, through a mouthful. "The ceremony. The party, too. I haven't seen anyone die yet."

I wasn't sure if that was the measure of a successful royal vampire party or an unsuccessful one.

But that thought faded away as I watched her. She was now carefully avoiding eye contact, looking very interested in the flowers.

"Thought you were done keeping secrets from me, Mish," I said.

She stopped mid-chew. Then turned to me, wide-eyed, dismayed.

"She *said* she wouldn't tell you!"

She?

My eyes narrowed. "*She?*"

Mische's eyes widened more. "Fuck," she hissed.

"Right. Fuck. Who's she? Oraya?"

"I've got to go look at the—"

She started to turn away, but I grabbed her elbow.

"Mische. What the hell is wrong?"

She let out a long sigh, then turned back to me. "I just—I didn't want to do this here."

"Do what?"

I hated when suspicions were confirmed. Mische hadn't been herself the last few weeks. She hadn't been the same since the prince. Or—who was I kidding? She hadn't been the same since the Moon Palace. My gaze fell to her arms, and the long gloves covering the burn scars she didn't let anyone see —even me.

"What, Mische?" I asked, more gently.

She nudged food around her plate with her fork. "I'm... I decided I'm going to go away for a while."

My heart sank.

"Away? Where?"

She shrugged. "I don't know. Everywhere. Anywhere."

"We already did that. You and I. We saw everything worth seeing."

"We never made it to the Lotus Islands."

"I have. They're not that great."

She still wouldn't look at me.

"Mische, if this is because of the House of Shadow—" I started.

"It's not," she said, too quickly. "It's—argh." She winced, squeezing her eyes shut, then set her plate down on a stone wall.

"Whatever the House of Shadow does, we will deal with it," I said, voice low. And fuck, I meant that. "We'll protect you. I'd never, *never*, let them—"

"I know," she said. "Trust me, I know. It's not about that."

"I don't believe you."

"Well—" She shrugged, opening her hands. "You have to. I

was never meant for staying still, Raihn. You know that. Not even — *before*."

Funny how hundreds of years later, she still stumbled over it every time she referenced her Turning.

But she was right. I did know that. That's why Mische and I had made such good companions for so long. We were running from a lot together. Content to spend eternity letting the wind take us where it would.

"I thought that, too," I said. "But..."

My voice trailed off. Because I hadn't really thought about it this way before — that I actually felt like I had a home now, beside Oraya. I didn't have to run from anything anymore.

For all the times I'd reassured Oraya about her safety, I'd never felt safe myself. Not until, I realized, now.

"This can be good, Mische," I said. "You have a home here."

She smiled weakly. "*You* have a home here. This isn't my home."

But, I wanted to say, *I thought your home was always with me.*

But none of this was about me.

For a long time, Mische had been my little sister. I'd treated her as something to be protected. But she wasn't a child. She was an adult, and a damned capable one.

"When?" I said.

"Not for a while still. I told Oraya maybe a few weeks —"

Oraya. Oh, I'd almost forgotten about *that* interesting little bit.

"Speaking of Oraya," I said, "why do I have to start talking to my wife to find out what's going on in your head?"

Mische shrugged and said casually, "Maybe I just like her better than you."

I touched my chest and made an exaggerated expression of pain. Such a casual, fatal shot.

She laughed, and I was so grateful for the sound I didn't even care about the insult. Hell, I was glad she felt comfortable talking to Oraya, if she wasn't going to be comfortable talking to me.

But her laughter faded. "It was just... easier," she admitted. "It's just... It's you and me, you know?"

I did know. I understood exactly. Sometimes she and I were so close we couldn't really see or understand each other.

"And," she added, "I just didn't want to see you make that face. That sad face."

The sad face?

"Did I make it?" I asked.

"Yes. It was heartbreaking."

I wasn't sure how to feel about that.

"Listen, Mische... I will always support you going where you want to go and doing what you want to do with your life. And yes, I'll miss the hell out of you."

Ix's tits, I really would miss her.

"But if this is what you really want, then who am I to question that? You said this place isn't your home. But it can be. A home is somewhere you come back to. And if you really feel like you need to leave, that's fine. But this place—us—we will always be here for you to come back to."

Her eyes, big and round, gleamed in the moonlight. Her lip wobbled slightly.

The sad face. Goddess damn it.

"None of that bullshit," I grumbled. "You said a few more weeks. We can do this then."

But before the words were out of my mouth, she threw herself against me in a hug. I grumbled, but folded my arms around her anyway, squeezing her tight.

A few weeks, I reminded myself.

Hell if I wasn't grateful for them.

Saying goodbye to Mische would be like saying goodbye to an entire version of myself. Wasn't sure I was ready to do it tonight.

"Thanks," she murmured.

For everything.

I knew exactly what she meant.

I knew it, because I felt it, too.

"It's nothing," I said. Even though we both knew it wasn't true.

THAT WAS ENOUGH UNCOMFORTABLY blatant emotion for Mische and me. We'd said all there was to say, and Mische wandered off, significantly lighter, to go find more food, leaving me alone to wander the gardens. I took a few minutes of solitude, collecting myself.

I hadn't had much quiet time, lately. It was actually nice. Even if it was occasionally punctuated by the vocal moans of one couple or another from the shrubs.

Eventually, I decided to go find Oraya. I wondered if she was still trapped in conversations with nobles, or if she'd finally managed to extract herself, too.

Just as this thought crossed my mind, I turned a corner to see her standing at one of the garden walls, looking out over the festivities below.

I stopped short.

I couldn't help it. I needed to just take a minute to look at her. Her wings were out now, the red shockingly vibrant even under the moonlight. Her gown glittered like the night sky itself. And her posture—she held herself like such a queen.

Sometimes, I found it impossible to imagine how Oraya had ever thought of herself as helpless. She was the most powerful person I'd ever met.

I approached her. She turned before I made it to her side, and the little smile she gave me eased the remaining lingering tension in my chest.

"You escaped," I said.

"So did you."

"In a way. I found Mische instead."

Maybe it was the bond that told Oraya what that meant, or

594

maybe it was my face, or maybe both, because she cringed slightly.

"Oh."

"Mhm."

"Are you alright?"

I shrugged. "She's her own person. If that's what she needs to do, that's what she needs to do."

Oraya stared hard at me in a way that told me she knew I wasn't feeling quite so nonchalant about the whole thing. I sighed.

"A few weeks is a few weeks. We'll deal with it then."

I took a drink of my wine, and then frowned down at it, wishing it was something more satisfying.

Oraya followed my gaze.

"I think this party is hosting itself at this point," she remarked, looking out over the crowd. Then she met my eye with a playful, knowing glint. "Do you want to go somewhere more fun?"

No hesitation.

"Fuck, yes."

8 0

ORAYA

I'd admit it. I now thoroughly enjoyed the taste of piss beer. Raihn and I sat on a rooftop in the human districts, trailing our fine clothing all over the dirty clay roof, and watched the sky over the blocky buildings, the party reduced to a sparkling smear of light in the distance.

Raihn took an enthusiastic swig of beer.

"This," he said, "is much better."

I agreed.

It was even worth the mild commotion that we'd caused getting the beer—crowns and all. At least the public reaction out here was more "dumbstruck awe" than "pant-pissing terror" these days. We'd been able to escape quickly afterwards, slipping off onto a quiet, shadowy rooftop in a near-abandoned block.

I took a gulp of my own. It burned a little going down. Probably doing some kind of lasting damage.

"I have to say," I said, "it's grown on me."

"It's the Coriatis bond. It gives you good taste."

I chuckled. I watched him take another sip, transfixed by the wave of utter contentment that fell over his face.

Mother, I just—I loved watching him.

The last time he and I had come up here in our fineries, escaping a stuffy party to go drink on a slum rooftop, I'd had every intention of killing him. The moment I had realized I couldn't was one of the most frightening of my life.

And this moment now—as it hit me, all at once, just how staggeringly much he meant to me—came in close second.

His eyes slipped to me. "What's that face for, princess?"

I stared down into my beer, watching the reflection of the stars in the foamy darkness.

I didn't answer right away.

"Do you ever feel afraid?"

It went against decades of training for me to even ask that question, and reveal the weakness that lay beneath it. Even now. Even with Raihn, my husband, my bonded, whose heart was literally linked to mine.

What was wrong with me?

I wouldn't have blamed Raihn if he'd laughed at me. But he didn't. His face was steady and serious. "Everyone feels afraid."

"It feels..." I struggled to find the right word.

I had lost everyone I had ever loved. And even those loves had been laced with so much pain, so much complication. My love for Vincent, tangled up in his lies and controlling disapproval. My love for Ilana, hidden in shadows and sharp words. My love for my mother, stolen from me entirely.

The love I felt now, for Raihn, was... terrifying in its ease.

I was afraid that something would come to rip it away from me.

I was afraid that I would destroy it myself, by not knowing how to feel something so right.

"It feels like a trap," I whispered. "The..."

"Happiness," he finished.

I didn't confirm it, even though he was right. It felt like a ridiculous thing to admit.

"You've been fighting your entire life, Oraya," he murmured. "It makes sense. I feel it too."

My gaze snapped up. "You do?"

He scoffed. "You think I'm not terrified every time I look at you?" He touched my face—tracing the curve of my cheek, down to the point of my chin, his smile softening. "Fuck, of course I am. You have my *heart*."

You have my heart.

Those words struck me hard—so true, on so many different levels. Raihn had my heart, no matter how long I had denied that. He'd had it in every sense of the word, long before I asked a goddess to bind it to him. And the Coriatis bond, powerful as it was, was still no less frightening than the love I felt for him. Hell, maybe the love scared me even more.

To give someone that much of yourself. To give someone the power to destroy you.

I could understand it—why Vincent never learned how to do it. I could understand how it would be easier to never feel that kind of vulnerability.

And yet.

I pressed Raihn's palm to my face, leaning into his touch.

And yet. There was such safety in that vulnerability, too. The ultimate paradox.

But that made sense for us, didn't it? Raihn and I were paradoxes. Human and Rishan and Hiaj. Slaves and royalty.

"I know we'll still have to fight," he said. "But we'll never have to do it alone again. That counts for something."

It counted for everything.

I smiled against his hand. "You're an alright ally."

He laughed, full and bright and alive, and Mother, I would never in my life hear anything else so beautiful.

I pulled away and turned back to the horizon. The sky was starting to turn pink.

"Sunrise soon," I said. "We should be getting inside."

But Raihn shook his head. "Not yet."

I gave him a skeptical stare, and he shrugged. "It's not going to kill me. I promise. Besides." He pointed up, to the crooked metal awning above him, and made a point of scooting back flush against the wall. "Look. I'm in the shade."

I wasn't convinced. "That's a stupid idea."

"Please, princess. Just a few minutes. You go out there and feel the sunrise. Maybe I'll feel it too. Bond and all that. I'll stay in the shade and then we can go a block away to the apartment and I can make passionate love to you for the next seven hours."

My eyes narrowed. He smirked.

"It's appealing to you," he said. "I can tell."

Goddess damn him.

Then his face lit up. "Look."

I turned to see the sun scorching the horizon. The sky became a blazing fire of reds and pinks and purples as the orb of brilliant light rose above the sands of the dunes.

My heart caught in my throat.

I rose and stepped from beneath the awning, into the red-orange light of the infant sun. The warmth suffused my skin, bathing me in it.

I'd never much enjoyed the sunlight. For most of my life, I'd avoided it. Just another reminder of how I was different—inferior—to the beings that surrounded me.

Now, that seemed outrageous.

I spread my arms out and closed my eyes, soaking it into my skin.

"It's something," I said. "Isn't it?"

"Yes," Raihn said softly. "It's really something."

But when I glanced over my shoulder back at him, he wasn't looking at the sun at all.

My chest tightened, overflowing.

"So?" I said. "Do you feel it?"

"I'm not sure." He held out a hand. "Come here."

I obeyed, crawling back under the awning. And as soon as I was in arm's reach, his hands were all over me, his lips on my shoulder, my arms, my throat, my chest.

"Yes," he murmured. "I think I feel it now."

I let my eyelids flutter closed. Let myself be surrounded by him, as he kissed the dawn off my skin. My husband. My ally. My lover.

Facing a new day beside me.

And as that golden sun crested the horizon, as a new year broke, as his lips found mine, my answer rose to the surface of my skin like the moon rising in the night sky.

And not a single part of me doubted it as I whispered into his kiss, "I feel it, too."

THE END

AUTHOR'S NOTE

Thank you so much for reading The Ashes and the Star-Cursed King! This was a very challenging book to write, mostly because I really wanted to bring Oraya and Raihn's (main) story to a satisfying and emotional close. I truly hope, from the bottom of my soul, that you loved it just as much as I loved writing it. I connected so deeply with their story, and I hope you did too.

Though the Nightborn Duet, which primarily follows Oraya and Raihn, is now complete, the core Crowns of Nyaxia series is 6 books total. There is a lot to come! Book 3 will take us to the House of Shadow... and you may already be a fan of our next primary FMC, a bright and cheerful magic wielder who's masking some serious shadows of her own...

Book 3 will be coming in spring/summer 2024!

If you enjoyed this book, I would truly appreciate if you'd consider leaving a review on Amazon or GoodReads. I can't overstate how important reviews are to authors!

And if you'd like to be the first to know about new releases, new art, new swag, and all kinds of other fun stuff, consider signing up for my newsletter at carissabroadbentbooks.com, hanging out in my Facebook group (Carissa Broadbent's Lost Hearts), or joining my Discord server (invite at linktr.ee/caris sanasyra!).

I would love to keep in touch!

READY FOR MORE OF THE CROWNS OF NYAXIA WORLD?

If you enjoyed The Serpent and the Wings of Night and The Ashes and the Star-Cursed King and are looking for more in the Crowns of Nyaxia world, you're in luck!

Book 3, The Songbird and the Heart of Stone, will be coming in spring/summer 2024.

But, if that sounds so far away, you may want to check out…

-

Slaying the Vampire Conqueror

Coming April 27

A standalone , full-length novel in the Crowns of Nyaxia world.

She was commanded to kill him with a single strike to the heart. She didn't expect her own to betray her.

Sylina has sacrificed everything for her goddess–her soul, her freedom, her eyes. Life in service to the Arachessen, a cult of the Goddess of Fate, has turned Sylina from orphaned street-rat to disciplined killer, determined to overthrow Glaea's tyrannical king.

But when a brutal vampire conqueror arrives on their shores, Sylina faces an even deadlier adversary. She's tasked with a crucial mission: infiltrate his army, earn his trust… and kill him.

Atrius is a terrifying warrior carving an unstoppable path through Glaea. Yet when Sylina becomes his seer, she glimpses a dark and shocking past–and a side of him that reminds her far too much of parts of herself she'd rather forget.

Sylina's orders are clear. The conqueror cannot live. But as the blood spilled by Glaea's tyrant king runs thicker, her connection with Atrius only grows stronger. A connection forbidden by her vows. A connection that could cost her everything.

Slaying the Vampire Conqueror *is a standalone fantasy romance set in the* Crowns of Nyaxia *world, full of heart-wrenching forbidden romance, dark curses, and epic battles – perfect for fans of* The Bridge Kingdom *and the* From Blood and Ash *series. It is an installment of the heart-pounding fantasy romance series,* Mortal Enemies to Monster Lovers. *If you like forbidden romance, dark curses, bad*ss heroines, and morally-gray heroes, you'll devour this sexy, addictive series.*

Available for Preorder Now!

SIX SCORCHED ROSES

A standalone novella in the Crowns of Nyaxia world

Six roses. Six vials of blood. Six visits to a vampire who could be her salvation… or her damnation.

Lilith has been dying since the day she was born. But while she long ago came to terms with her own imminent death, the deaths of everyone she loves is an entirely different matter. As her town slowly withers in the clutches of a mysterious god-cursed illness, she takes matters into her own hands.

Desperate to find a cure, Lilith strikes a bargain with the only thing the gods hate even more than her village: a vampire, Vale. She offers him six roses in exchange for six vials of vampire blood—the one hope for her town's salvation.

But when what begins as a simple transaction gradually becomes something more, Lilith is faced with a terrifying realization: It's dangerous to wander into the clutches of a vampire… and in a place already suffering a god's wrath, more dangerous still to fall in love with one.

Six Scorched Roses is a standalone fantasy romance novella set in the world of the Crowns of Nyaxia series, perfect for those who love dark, romantic tales with bite and fans of Sarah J. Maas or Jennifer L. Armentrout.

Available Now!

ALSO BY CARISSA BROADBENT

If you like the Crowns of Nyaxia series, check out The War of Lost Hearts series, an epic romantasy trilogy full of romance, revenge, and redemption — and best of all, it's *complete and ready to binge.*

Book 1: Daughter of No Worlds

Book 2: Children of Fallen Gods

Book 3: Mother of Death and Dawn

Available on Amazon and free to read in Kindle Unlimited.

GLOSSARY OF TERMS

ACAEJA - The goddess of fate, spellcasting, mystery, and lost things. Member of the White Pantheon. Only god to be on somewhat civil terms with Nyaxia, though that seems to have been changing lately...

ALARUS - The god of death and husband of Nyaxia. Exiled by the White Pantheon as punishment for his forbidden relationship with Nyaxia. Considered to be deceased.

ASTERIS - A form of magical energy wielded by Nightborn vampires, derived from the stars. Rare and difficult to use, requiring significant skill and energy.

ATROXUS - The god of the sun and leader of the White Pantheon.

BLOODBORN - Vampires of the House of Blood.

BORN - A term used to describe vampires who are born via

biological procreation. This is the most common way that vampires are created.

CELEBA - A continent in the human lands to the east of Obitraes.

CORIATIS BOND - A rare and powerful bond that can be forged only by a god, in which two people share all aspects of their power, linking their lives and souls. Nyaxia is the only god known to grant Coriatis bonds, though any god is capable of doing so. Those who are bound are referred to as each other's CORIATAE. Coriatae share all aspects of each other's power, typically making both stronger. Coriatae cannot act against each other and cannot live without each other.

DEMONS - A term used to describe a broad variety of beasts common in Obitraes. Some demons are naturally born and free-running in Obitraes. Other demons are more rare and are summoned by magic wielders, usually to be used as weapons in warfare. There are many different types of demons, ranging from common to extremely rare, and they vary tremendously in appearance, behavior, intelligence, etc.

DHAIVINTH - A poison that temporarily paralyzes.

DHERA - A nation in the human lands. Vale is currently living there.

EXTRYN - The prison of the gods of the White Pantheon.

OBITRAES - The land of Nyaxia, consisting of three kingdoms: The House of Night, The House of Shadow, and the House of Blood.

HEIR MARK - A permanent mark that appears on the Heir of the Hiaj and Rishan clans when the previous Heir dies, marking their position and power.

HIAJ - One of the two clans of Nightborn vampires. They have featherless wings that resemble those of bats.

THE HOUSE OF BLOOD - One of the three vampire kingdoms of Obitraes. Two thousand years ago, when Nyaxia created vampires, the House of Blood was her favorite House. She thought long and hard about which gift to give them, while the Bloodborn watched their brothers to the west and north flaunt their powers. Eventually, the Bloodborn turned on Nyaxia, certain that she had abandoned them. In punishment, Nyaxia cursed them. The House of Blood is now looked down upon by the other two houses. People from the House of Blood are called BLOODBORN.

THE HOUSE OF NIGHT - One of the three vampire kingdoms of Obitraes. Known for their skill in battle and for their vicious natures, and wielders of magic derived from the night sky. There are two clans of Nightborn vampires, HIAJ and RISHAN, who have fought for thousands of years over rule. Those of the House of Night are called NIGHTBORN.

THE HOUSE OF SHADOW - One of the three vampire kingdoms of Obitraes. Known for their commitment to knowledge; wielders of mind magic, shadow magic, and necromancy. Those of the House of Shadow are called SHADOWBORN.

IX - Goddess of sex, fertility, childbirth, and procreation. Member of the White Pantheon.

KAJMAR - God of art, seduction, beauty, and deceit. Member of the White Pantheon.

THE KEJARI - A legendary, once-per-century tournament to the death held in Nyaxia's honor. The winner receives a gift from Nyaxia herself. The Kejari is open to all in Obitraes, but is hosted by the House of Night, as the Nightborn hold the greatest domain over the art of battle out the three vampire kingdoms.

LAHOR - A city on the eastern tip of Obitraes, once great but now little more than ruins. Vincent's homeland.

LITURO RIVER - A river that runs through the center of Sivrinaj.

MOON PALACE - A palace in Sivrinaj, the capital of the House of Night, specifically there to house contestants of the once-in-a-century Kejari tournament held in Nyaxia's honor. Said to be enchanted and to exert the will of Nyaxia herself.

NECULAI VASARUS - The former Rishan king of the House of Night. Turned and subsequently enslaved Raihn. Usurped and killed by Vincent 200 years prior to the events of this book.

NIGHTBORN - Vampires of the House of Night.

NIGHTFIRE - Like Asteris, another form of star-derived magic wielded by the vampires of the House of Night. While Asteris is dark and cold, Nightfire is bright and hot. Nightfire is commonly used in the House of Night but very difficult to wield masterfully.

NYAXIA - Exiled goddess, mother of vampires, and widow of the god of death. Nyaxia lords over the domain of night, shadow, and blood, and as well as the inherited domain of death from her deceased husband. Formerly a lesser goddess, she fell in love with Alarus and married him despite the forbidden nature of their relationship. When Alarus was murdered by the White Pantheon as punishment for his marriage to her, Nyaxia broke free from the White Pantheon in a fit of rage, and offered her supporters the gift of immortality in the form of vampirism— founding Obitraes and the vampire kingdoms. *(Also referred to as:*

the Mother; the Goddess; Mother of the Ravenous Dark; Mother of Night, Shadow, and Blood.)

PACHNAI - A human nation to the east of Obitraes.

RISHAN - One of the two clans of Nightborn vampires. Have feathered wings. Usurped by the Hiaj 200 years ago.

SALINAE - A major city in the House of Night. Located in Rishan territory. When the Rishan were in power, Salinae was a thriving hub, functioning as a second capital. Oraya spent the first years of her life, before Vincent found her, in Salinae.

SHADOWBORN - Vampires of the House of Shadow.

SIVRINAJ - The capital of the House of Night. Home to the Nightborn castle, the Moon Palace, and host to the Kejari once every 100 years.

TAKER OF HEARTS - Vincent's legendary sword, a rapier that was soul-bonded to him.

TAZRAK - A notorious prison in the House of Night.

TURNING - A process to make a human into a vampire, requiring a vampire to drink from a human and offer their blood to the human in return. Vampires who underwent this process are referred to as TURNED. Vampires who are Turned take on the House of the vampire who Turned them. For example, a vampire Turned by a Shadowborn vampire will be Shadowborn themselves, etc.

WHITE PANTHEON - The twelve gods of the core cannon, including Alarus, who is presumed deceased. The White Pantheon is worshipped by all humans, with certain regions potentially having favor towards specific gods within the

Pantheon. Nyaxia is not a member of the White Pantheon and is actively hostile to them. The White Pantheon imprisoned and later executed Alarus, the God of Death, as punishment for his unlawful marriage with Nyaxia, then a lesser goddess.

ZARUX - The god of the sea, rain, weather, storms, and water. Member of the White Pantheon.

ACKNOWLEDGMENTS

I say it every time, but I'll say it again now: I can't believe I'm writing these yet again! Right now I'm typing this while seven months pregnant, and at the end of a multi-month-long crunch zone while I prepared *three books* for publication barely over a month away from each other. I am barely human anymore, and I have so many people to thank for helping me make it here alive and for helping to make this book the best it can possibly be.

Nathan, you will always come first in these acknowledgments. Thank you for being the best partner in the world and for being the north-star of every well-adjusted love story I've ever written. Thanks for being my best friend, my brainstorming buddy, my art director, my hype-man, and so much more. I love you!

Clare, thank you so much for being such an amazing friend, support system, and author "co-worker." I would never survive this wild author ride without you! Thanks for keeping me sane during the production of this book and for all your constant support, brainstorming, troubleshooting, and general shooting-the-shit.

KD Ritchie at Storywrappers Design, thank you for being an incredible cover designer and such an amazing supportive force in general! I love working together.

Noah, thank you for the incredible editing and for putting up with literal months for my bizarro delivery schedules. You make every book I write so much better, in every phase of its creation. Thank you!

Rachel and Anthony, thank you for being fabulous proofreaders and typo-catchers. Rachel, thank you even more for all of the wonderful reader reaction notes, I love them!

Ariella, thank you for the beta reading and for generally keeping me sane and making sure I stay on track while finishing and launching this book. You are awesome!

Deanna, Alex, Gabriella, thank you for your invaluable feedback and support and for being the best beta readers ever. You're the best!

Thank you to my agent, Bibi, for generally being awesome and also for providing invaluable career advice and for helping the Nyaxia series reach heights and distances that I honestly never ever could have dreamed about a year ago.

Thank you to my Swords & Corsets crew, JD Evans, Krystle Matar, and Angela Boord, for keeping me sane and listening to me bitch all the time. Special shout-out to Krystle for being my sprinting buddy through the entire creation and editing process of this book!

And finally, the biggest thanks of all goes to *you*. These last few months have been absolutely surreal and I know as soon as I launch this book, it's going to hit me like a truck. I am not exaggerating when I say I literally could not have imagined any of this a year or even six months ago. Thank you for your fan art, your messages, your emails, your aesthetic boards, your reviews, your TikTok and Instagram and Goodreads posts, and in general, the immense support and enthusiasm you've given these characters. I am gobsmacked every day! I hope you love what comes next!

ABOUT THE AUTHOR

Carissa Broadbent has been concerning teachers and parents with mercilessly grim tales since she was roughly nine years old. Since then, her stories have gotten (slightly) less depressing and (hopefully a lot?) more readable. Today she writes fantasy novels with a heaping dose of badass ladies and a big pinch of romance. She lives with her husband, one very well behaved rabbit, one very poorly behaved rabbit, and one perpetually skeptical cat in Rhode Island.

instagram.com/carissabroadbentbooks

tiktok.com/carissabroadbent

facebook.com/carissabroadbentbooks

twitter.com/carissanasyra